Praise for the novels of *USA TODAY* bestselling author Delores Fossen

"The plot delivers just the right amount of emotional punch and happily ever after."
—*Publishers Weekly* on *Lone Star Christmas*

"Clear off space on your keeper shelf, Fossen has arrived."
—*New York Times* bestselling author Lori Wilde

"This book is a great start to the series. Looks like there's plenty of good reading ahead."
—*Harlequin Junkie* on *Tangled Up in Texas*

"Delores Fossen takes you on a wild Texas ride with a hot cowboy."
—*New York Times* bestselling author B.J. Daniels

"An amazing, breathtaking and vastly entertaining family saga, filled with twists and unexpected turns. Cowboy fiction at its best."
—*Books & Spoons* on *The Last Rodeo*

"I love the storyline here. The plot is fast-paced and the characters well-developed."
—*Harlequin Junkie* on *Settling an Old Score*

"Fossen certainly knows how to write a hot cowboy, and when she turns her focus to Dylan Granger…crank up the air conditioning!"
—*RT Book Reviews* on *Lone Star Blues*

**Also available from Delores Fossen
and HQN**

Lone Star Ridge

Coldwater Texas

Wrangler's Creek

To see the complete list of titles available from
Delores Fossen, please visit www.deloresfossen.com.

DELORES FOSSEN

TEMPTING IN
Texas

HQN

Recycling programs
for this product may
not exist in your area.

ISBN-13: 978-1-335-41996-5

Tempting in Texas
Copyright © 2021 by Delores Fossen

Whatever Happens in Texas
Copyright © 2021 by Delores Fossen

This edition published by arrangement with Harlequin Books S.A.

For questions and comments about the quality of this book,
please contact us at CustomerService@Harlequin.com.

HQN
22 Adelaide St. West, 40th Floor
Toronto, Ontario M5H 4E3, Canada
www.Harlequin.com

Printed in Spain

CONTENTS

TEMPTING IN TEXAS

CHAPTER ONE

CAIT JAMESON FIGURED it was stating the obvious, but getting stabbed hurt—even when it was just a little stab wound.

Sitting on the examination table in the ER, she scowled over both the pain and the now-missing sleeve of what had been her favorite shirt. Even if the overly eager EMT, Ty Copperfield, hadn't literally ripped the sleeve from its seams, the shirt that Cait had nicknamed Old Betsy would have been a loss anyway. She didn't know how to get out regular stains from her clothes, much less her own blood.

Plus, there was that whole ick factor of actually touching a bloody garment.

She might have been a cop in her hometown of Lone Star Ridge, Texas, for six years now, but that didn't make her immune to stuff like puke and blood. Just looking down at her wound made her feel light-headed and queasy. If she puked, she would be a goner, and that couldn't happen.

Not in front of her three brothers.

She'd never hear the end of the teasing, and the babying, and it would be a decade or more before they stopped looking at her as if she couldn't take care of herself. Then teasing her about not being able to take care of herself.

Cait could thank the idiot Ty for calling all three of her brothers and probably half the town to let them know about the *altercation* that'd taken place at the old Crockett ranch. Everyone would also know that *altercation* was just a polite word for the fight between Wilma Crockett and Harvey, her husband of seventy-plus years. A fight that usually resulted in the pair shouting, along with throwing and thrusting things at each other. Because they were elderly and their eyesight was as bad as their aim, they usually missed.

Not tonight, though.

Tonight, the sharp end of the meat thermometer had gouged Cait's arm.

In a twist of fate that often befell kid sisters and other unlucky people, all three of her brothers had arrived around the same time she had. At least she hadn't arrived in an ambulance with the siren blaring as Ty had insisted. Cait had nixed his insistence, the sirens and instead driven herself.

Of course, now she would have to clean up blood from the seat of her SUV, but she'd saved a little of her dignity by walking into the ER on her own two feet.

"You couldn't dodge a meat thermometer from a ninety-year-old woman?" her oldest brother, Shaw, grumbled.

Okay, that cost her some dignity points, but the truth was the truth. "Wilma Crockett's a lot more spry than she looks," Cait pointed out. "And besides, it was an accident. She wasn't exactly aiming for me."

Harvey had been his *beloved*'s intended target, but the man had not only ducked behind Cait, he'd also pushed her forward, practically right into the Weber Instant-Read Thermometer that Wilma was in the process of thrusting at him like a mini makeshift sword.

Cait handed the now-bagged *weapon* to Leyton, her brother who was standing in the middle of the staring trio. Leyton, as in *Sheriff* Leyton Jameson, her boss. That meant he had more potential than the others for thinking she couldn't take care of herself. But, hey, it was just a little stab wound, for Pete's sake.

One that hurt like the devil.

She tried not to wince when the nurse, Mandy Culpepper, dabbed at the wound to clean it. Mandy must have been using extra-strength acid, though, because it stung worse than the cut itself, so Cait ended up wincing anyway. That caused all three brothers to huff and roll their eyes.

"She'll probably need a tetanus shot," her third brother, Austin, piped in, speaking to the nurse.

Cait aimed narrowed eyes at him. Austin was usually the brother who gave her the least amount of grief, maybe because they were so close in age. Only a year apart. Maybe, too, because he was a widower and had gone through the stage where his family had coddled and babied him more than he wanted. But the shot reminder definitely fell into the "high amount of grief" zone. Along with being icked out at the sight of blood, Cait had this "needle phobia" thing.

Austin might have added more, perhaps suggesting an entire battery of booster shots and blood work, but his phone rang, giving Cait a reprieve.

"It's Mom," Austin said after he glanced at the screen.

Crap. There went her reprieve. Obviously, someone had called their mother, Lenore, and told her that her daughter was in the ER. She loved her mom, and the woman had done an amazing job raising four kids practically alone, but the coddling would be taken to a whole different and much higher level if her mom showed up tonight.

"I'll babysit for you for a month if you tell her I'm fine and that she shouldn't come," Cait bargained with Austin.

It was a solid offer since Austin had three-year-old twin girls, Avery and Gracie. Yeah, Cait loved them, too, all the way down to their often grubby little toes, but they could be a handful.

"You'll babysit for a year," Austin countered while his finger hovered over the answer button.

Because she'd figured this was coming, Cait was ready for it. "Four months and that's my final offer. If you don't agree, I'll tell Mom that you want her to make the food for the wedding reception."

Austin might have been a tough thirty-three-year-old cowboy and well seasoned by fatherhood, but he went a little pale. Shaw and Leyton had similar reactions because the upcoming weddings and reception were for all three of them. In a twist that would create a next generation of double first cousins and pay a weird homage to *Seven Brides for Seven Brothers*, her three brothers were marrying triplet sisters. Since everyone in town knew both the brides and grooms, there would be lots of people attending.

And lots of food.

Their mom had a kind soul but the absolute worst culinary skills in the tristate area. Lenore could ruin the reception, and her brothers knew it. That's why Shaw and Leyton tossed "don't screw this up" scowls at Austin.

Austin nodded, hit the answer button and greeted their mom with, "Cait's fine. It's just a scratch." He stepped aside to finish the conversation that would hopefully reassure their mother that there was no reason to come to check on her thirty-two-year-old *little girl*.

Leyton tipped his head to the bagged thermometer he was holding. "I'll go out to the Crockett place and arrest them both. Even if it's a stupid way to do bodily harm, I can't let them get away with assaulting a police officer," Leyton added when Cait opened her mouth to disagree with him.

She argued anyway. "I'm sure they're sorry about what happened. Wilma even offered to drive me to the hospital." An offer Cait had declined with lightning speed because

Wilma hadn't been able to pass a driver's test in two decades and therefore didn't have a valid license. "And Harvey called the ambulance."

Of course, Harvey hadn't done Cait any favors by doing that, but with surprising speed, he'd made the 911 call before she could stop him. He apparently dialed as fast as he ducked and dodged his wife's attempts to maim him.

"It won't do any good to put people that old in jail," Cait pointed out.

"That's where you're wrong," Leyton insisted. "If they're finally punished for the crap they've been getting away with for years, then maybe they'll finally stop."

Cait knew this wouldn't stop them, and neither had the counseling they'd been forced to get over the years. In fact, she suspected the couple enjoyed fighting. And in all the decades they'd been doing it, this was the first time anyone had actually gotten hurt. Leave it to her to break some kind of long-standing record like that.

"I'm arresting them," Leyton grumbled as his parting shot before he took the evidence bag and walked out of the ER.

Shaw only shrugged when Cait turned to him to plead her case. Then she nixed the pleading notion because Mandy doused her arm with cleaning acid again. Cait used up every molecule of her available breath on huffing and muttering some profanity before Mandy finally numbed the area with some kind of gunk and then did a couple of quick stitches.

"Austin's right," Mandy told Cait as she slid back the privacy curtain, the only thing that divided this particular examining area from the rest of the ER. "You need a tetanus shot. There's no telling where that thermometer was before you got stabbed with it. I'll be right back with what I need to fix you right up."

The nurse was way too cheery about the *fixing up*, and it occurred to Cait that Mandy was going to have a firsthand account of this incident to blabber about. Lone Star Ridge wasn't exactly a hotbed of important news, so people had to take their gossip where they could find it.

By tomorrow, the thermometer wound would be seriously embellished, and that in turn could lead to many "get well soon" calls, along with some dropped-off meals to help Cait through her *infirmity*. That last part was the only silver lining in this. She was hoping for a batch or two of snickerdoodles. Everyone knew they were her favorite, and there were plenty of good bakers in town.

"I talked Mom into staying home," Austin said, stepping back toward them. "Four months of babysitting," he reminded Cait. In true Austin fashion, though, he only gloated about that for a couple of seconds. "You want me to wait around and drive you to your place?"

"No. I can do it." Her house was less than a mile away. "You should get back to your girls. They've got pre-K in the morning, and McCall might need help getting them into bed."

Though that last part was a stretch. Austin's fiancée, McCall Dalton, was a counselor and had a way of getting the twins to cooperate. Still, Cait didn't want Austin hanging around with her when he could be home with his kids and fiancée.

Austin finally nodded, not a convincing one, though, and he looked at Shaw. "You'll wait here with her and make sure she doesn't fight Mandy on the shot she needs?"

"Oh, for Pete's sake," Cait protested. "I'm not six years old."

She wouldn't fight. Not physically, anyway. But she was so going to snatch one of those cherry suckers from the reception desk to help soothe the childhood trauma memories of the times when she had fought like a wildcat during immunizations.

"I'll stay," Shaw assured his brother just as Cait said, "You should both go home."

"I'll stay," Shaw repeated, and that was enough assurance for Austin. He gave Cait a noogie on the top of her head, followed by a quick kiss on the same spot—gestures that were textbook "big brother" stuff—and he headed out.

Two brothers down. One to go.

"You really should go home, too," Cait added to Shaw once Austin was out of earshot. "You should be with Sunny."

Because gossips might be within hearing range, Cait refrained from adding anything about Sunny being pregnant, but she was. Pregnant, puking and extremely happy. Happy about the baby, not the puking, that is. There was no reason for Sunny not to have her soon-to-be husband with her, especially since he was in no way needed here at the hospital.

She saw the debate about leaving her go through Shaw's smoky gray eyes that were a genetic copy of her own. Debate and then concern about Sunny. Cait was pretty sure she had just about convinced him to go so she could wince in peace, but the commotion at the ER doors stopped him.

Mandy, the nurse, made an un-nurse-like shrieking sound, and her sensible-soled white shoes slapped against the aged linoleum as she hurried to those doors. So did Anita Parker, the retired high school history teacher, who was no doubt in the ER because she was coughing enough to bring up internal organs.

And speaking of internal organs, the man who came through the ER doors might have lost some of his for real.

Cait's stomach lurched when she saw the blood. It was on his head, his face, his arm and pretty much the rest of him, including on the motorcycle helmet he had dangling from his hand—which was also bloody.

Forgetting all about her own injury and the fact that she might puke from the sight of the blood, Cait bolted off the examining table and ran toward him. Shaw was right on her heels. Thanks to Cait's head start, she got there ahead of her brother, and she slid her arm around the injured man's waist. Mandy did the same thing on the other side of him, and they began leading him toward the examining table that Cait had just left.

"Don't put him there yet," Mandy insisted.

Mandy let go of the man so she could rip off the paper lining on the table and replace it with a fresh one. She managed to do that in just a couple of seconds, and then the three of them helped the bloody guy onto the table.

"Hey, Cait," he said.

The almost lazy greeting had Cait doing a double take, which involved looking again at the man's blood-streaked face. Because she was having to bargain with her suddenly queasy stomach to set up a no-puking rule, it took her a moment to look past the blood, then past the scrapes and bruises so she could see his actual features. Dark brown hair, blue eyes, strong jaw and a mouth…that she had no trouble recognizing.

Because Cait had fantasized about that mouth since she'd first sprouted breasts.

"Hayes Dalton," she said.

Or as she often thought of him—Heartthrob Hayes.

Cait could say without a doubt that Hayes was the absolute last person she had expected to come into the ER tonight. He didn't even live in Lone Star Ridge. Hadn't in, oh, sixteen years and eight months. Hayes had left less than a minute after he'd graduated from high school, moved to

Hollywood and eventually become the star of a TV show about a motorcycle gang. Thanks to *Outlaw Rebels*, Cait got a weekly visual dose of Hayes.

At least.

She'd watched some episodes many, many times. But the watching had turned out to be useful. She had seen Hayes so much that he was the human equivalent of white noise, and she no longer felt that kick of heat when she looked at him. It was now more like a lukewarm nudge. And it would stay that way unless he said his signature demand that he often did to his many love interests on the show.

Climb on, bitch, and kiss me.

It wasn't just the irreverent demand but the way he drawled that invitation for a biker bitch to climb on his Harley and, well, tongue kiss him. Hayes combined the demand with the slight hitch of a smile on his pretty mouth. A mouth surrounded by all the sexy dark stubble. Oh, and he paired that smile with the scorcher look in his eyes. It was the whole heartthrob package in a hot package of snug jeans, boots and a black tee.

Identical to the clothes he was wearing now.

"Hayes?" Shaw questioned, also moving in closer for a look. "Hell," he added when he verified that was actually his soon-to-be brother-in-law. "What happened to you?"

"An accident of sorts," he said while Mandy started in on that acid cleaning. Hayes did some wincing, too. "Say, don't tell Sunny and my other sisters about this. I don't want Sunny upset."

Since he'd named that specific sister, it meant that Hayes knew Sunny was pregnant. No surprise there. Even though Hayes rarely saw his sisters, their granny Em kept the family filled in on the news. Cait knew this because she was close friends with all of Hayes's triplet sisters. That meant she also knew that Sunny was trying to keep her pregnancy hush-hush until after the wedding.

"There's no reason for my sisters to come running here to the hospital," Hayes added.

"I can relate," Cait muttered, giving Shaw a glance. "But trust me, they'll find out if they haven't already. In between hacking up a lung, Anita Parker is sitting over there and texting as fast as her bony fingers can poke at letters."

She tipped her head to the woman who was likely sending out some kind of global information beam to announce that Heartthrob Hayes was back in town and that he was banged up to heck and back.

"I won't call Sunny or your sisters, yet," Shaw assured him. "But Cait's right. They'll find out. What do you mean you were in an accident *of sorts*?" Shaw tacked onto that without pausing.

Cait had been about to ask him that very question, along with others that she might need to include in a police report. She'd planned on waiting on that, though, until they had at least found out if he was all right.

"I was on my motorcycle and someone ran me off the road," Hayes said in that same lazy drawl that he'd used to greet her.

Of course, Hayes had a habit of drawling that made the words seem like testosterone-drenched foreplay. She wasn't alone in thinking this, either, and she'd read plenty of the social media posts from other women to prove it.

"Someone ran you off the road?" Cait repeated. No drawl for her. Her cop's voice kicked in.

He attempted a shrug and ended up wincing instead. "More or less. Less," he amended when his bloody forehead bunched up in thought. "I was on that curvy stretch of road just about a mile outside of town, and a car going way too fast came up behind me. It was going to hit me, so I tried to get off the road, but I ended up in the ditch."

Cait's mouth dropped open. "And the driver just left you there, wounded and bleeding?"

"I'm not sure he or she actually saw me," Hayes answered.

Cait and Shaw both muttered some profanity. "How'd you get to the hospital?" Shaw asked.

"I dragged my motorcycle out of the ditch and rode it here."

That earned him stares from Shaw, Cait and Mandy. But Shaw stopped his staring long enough to give her a "big brother" glance to remind her that she'd done something similar by driving herself to the hospital. The difference was her injuries were minor compared to Hayes's.

"The front end of my motorcycle's messed up," Hayes added, shaking his head. "I'll need to have it fixed."

"Your body needs repairs, too," Mandy pointed out.

Mandy was in nurse mode, but Cait also saw something else. The fawning. A flushed face, some lip nibbling, eyelash fluttering and the potential for drooling. It was something that happened a lot whenever Hayes was around. Not just in Lone Star Ridge, either. Cait had seen tabloid photos of fawning fans.

"Uh, how long are you going to be back in town?" Mandy asked, eyelashes still fluttering, and since Cait didn't think the woman was fending off gnats or gummed-up mascara, the fawning had moved to flirting. That question sounded like the start of *Hey, maybe we can go for a drink or something?* Emphasis on the *or something.*

Cait narrowed her own unfluttering eyes to let the nurse know she wasn't acting very professional.

"I'm not sure how long I'll be here," Hayes answered almost idly. He was flexing his hand and had therefore missed the visual cues of Mandy's attempted come-on.

Mandy cleared her throat. "Uh, I'll get you set up with X-rays," she said, and abracadabra, she became the nurse again. "And I'll call the doctor—"

The loud wail stopped the reformed Mandy from continuing and had all four of them turning toward the ER doors. A tall blonde in a very short blue dress came rushing in. Cait was reasonably sure she'd never seen her before. She certainly wasn't from around Lone Star Ridge, but judging from the tabloid pictures Cait had seen of Hayes, the woman was very much his type. Boobs galore, mile-long legs and the kind of face that you could only get from many hours of cosmetic surgery followed by more hours of pampering.

Cait hated her on sight.

And she hated that she hated her. Crap. She clearly had to work on more white noising when it came to Hayes.

"Is he dead?" the blonde howled. "Oh, God. I saw his wrecked motorcycle outside. Is he dead?"

Hayes groaned, shook his head. "Shit."

The woman's gaze zoomed right in on Hayes, and she sprinted toward them. "Oh, thank the sweet baby Moses in a basket. You're alive."

"I take it you know her?" Cait asked him.

"Of course Hayes knows me," the blonde answered before Hayes could speak. She hurried to him and threw her arms around him. "I'm Shayla Weston, the love of his life."

CHAPTER TWO

HAYES COULD THINK of many things to describe Shayla Weston. But *love of his life* sure as hell wasn't one of them.

He didn't like putting labels on people, but if he had to come up with one for Shayla, then *dingbat stalker* was a pretty close fit. Unfortunately, this particular dingbat had way too much time and money on her hands. A bad combination when she had her attention homed in on him.

"Uh?" Cait said, and it seemed to Hayes that it'd taken some mustering for her to come up with just that one questioning sound.

Hayes first peeled Shayla off him, and despite the jabs of pain it caused him physically, it was worth it to move her back so that she was no longer plastered against him. He cut off what would have no doubt been a loud sob and another dive toward him by shaking his head and holding out his hand in a stop gesture. The fact that his hand was coated with blood hopefully added a sinister element to it.

"Shayla mistakenly believes we're soul mates," Hayes explained to Cait, knowing his truthful remark would elicit a whine of protest from Shayla.

It did.

"Hayes *is* my soul mate," she insisted. "I've had more than a dozen psychics and even a monk tell me that."

Hayes figured the monk was a dingbat, too, and the psychics, well, they had told Shayla what she'd paid them to tell her.

"But I knew we were soul mates before that," Shayla went on. "I knew from the first time I watched you on TV, and you said *Climb on, bitch, and kiss me*." She sighed and pressed her hand to her heart as if to steady it.

"Shayla, I didn't say those words to you," Hayes grumbled, trying to keep his voice level. That was always hard to do with her. "They're written in a script, and I say them because that's what I'm paid to do." And he was wasting his breath again. So he narrowed in on the gist of the matter. "Remember, I have a restraining order against you, so you shouldn't be here."

"But I have to be here," Shayla protested. "I might have nearly killed you."

Well, that last part was news to Hayes, but when he gave it some thought, things got a whole lot clearer. "You were in the car that caused me to run off the road?" he asked.

Shayla's eyes widened and filled with tears. Hell, not tears. It was hard to stop her once she got started. "I didn't know," she insisted. "I mean, I was driving on the road that leads to Lone Star Ridge."

"A white car?" he pressed.

Shayla nodded, cried. "When I was on one of the curves, I thought maybe I heard something like a thud, but I had the volume on the music turned up high, so I figured it was part of the song. But then I spotted your banged-up motorcycle in the parking lot of the hospital, and I came in to check if you were here." She motioned toward his bloody face, and, yeah, the tears started dripping down her cheeks. "Am I responsible for this?"

Hayes didn't have positive proof that she'd been the one behind the wheel, but right now Shayla was the most likely candidate. Apparently, Cait thought so, too, because the look she gave Shayla was all cop.

"I'm Deputy Cait Jameson. You didn't see Hayes on his motorcycle when you were driving?" Cait asked, and she tapped the badge that she had clipped to her belt.

The badge tap only caused Shayla to wail louder, cry harder and start shaking her head. "I was freshening up my makeup. I wanted to look nice when I saw Hayes, so I might not have been paying enough attention to the road."

Clearly, Shayla had missed some steps here. Not with the makeup. That was applied with abundance as usual. But Shayla had whizzed over the fact that she shouldn't have been anywhere near him.

Hayes didn't want to know how she'd found out his location, either, but it was possible she had hacked into his computer again. Also possible that she had just followed him to the airport where he'd boarded a friend's private plane with his motorcycle. From there, she could have bribed someone in the airport and then followed him in her own private plane. Or rather the one that belonged to her mother. It was that whole "too much time and too much money" thing that'd brought her here.

"There's really a restraining order?" Cait asked him. She sounded like a cop, too. A pissed-off one. But that was the norm. Cait was usually riled or a smart-ass whenever she was around him.

"There's a restraining order," Hayes verified just as Shayla insisted, "It was all a misunderstanding." She would have tried to sidle up to him again if Cait hadn't interceded.

"Don't touch him," Cait warned the woman, and she took hold of Shayla's arm.

Hayes didn't miss the grimace of pain that Cait made, and he spotted the fresh stitches on her arm. And her ripped-off shirtsleeve. Obviously, he wasn't the only one who'd had a run-in with things that could gouge the skin and tear the clothes. Other than that, though, Cait looked pretty much the same as the last time he'd seen her about eleven years ago.

When she'd turned him down after he had asked her on a date.

Yep. Turned him down without so much as blinking an eye.

Hayes wanted to believe that he hadn't been trying hard to convince her to have dinner with him. Dinner that he'd thought might lead to sex. But he had indeed been trying. Heck, he had doled out a couple of gallons of charm, and it hadn't affected her one little bit. He was still trying to figure out (a) why she'd done that and (b) why it still mattered to him.

Tonight, her long dark brown hair was pulled up into a ponytail, and she had on only a light smattering of makeup. The jeans and plain blue shirt she was wearing seemed more suited for doing ranch work than cop stuff. Over the years, he'd heard some say she was on the plain side, but there was no way she could ever be plain. Not with that interesting face.

"I'll walk your *friend* here up the street to the police station," Cait said to Hayes. "I'll hold her on a possible violation of a restraining order and reckless driving. Depending on your statement, there could be other charges."

"The police station?" Shayla howled. "You're arresting me for trying to be with the man I love?"

"You bet your Sunday britches I am," Cait said without hesitation. "I'm not being overly judgy when I say that love doesn't give you the right to violate a restraining order and break the law."

"But I had to come," Shayla insisted. "Hayes is grieving, and he needs me."

He was indeed grieving, but in no way could Shayla help with that. And just by bringing it up, she was actu-

ally making things worse. Hayes didn't want Cait or anyone else asking him about that.

"Is she talking about your girlfriend?" the nurse asked.
"The one who died a couple of months ago?" Apparently,
the nurse Mandy Culpepper read the tabloids.

"His ex-girlfriend," Shayla promptly provided, and, yeah,
she added some territorial snark to it through her continued sobs. "Hayes hadn't been with Ivy Malloy in years."

Hayes tried to let the conversation pass right over him.
Tried not to think about it at all. He needed some steel to
deal with the memories of Ivy, and the pain from his injuries wasn't going to let him pull up much steel right now.

When Shayla tried to latch on to Hayes again, Cait huffed
and led her away from the examining table and a few yards
farther into the ER waiting room.

"Sit," Cait ordered, putting Shayla in a chair, "and if you
try to resist or run, I'll restrain you."

Shayla's chin came up. "You don't have handcuffs," she
pointed out in a whiny protest. "Or a gun. Are you even a real
cop? Where did you get that badge? It could be fake. It looks
fake," she amended, her questions and comments spewing
together in a babble fest.

Again, no hesitation from Cait. "Yes, I'm a real cop, and
I got the badge from the badge store. I have a gun secured in
the locked glove compartment of my SUV, but I don't need it
right now because I have three older brothers who taught me
how to kick butt. As for restraints, I'm sure I can find some
duct tape around here that I can use to keep you in that chair.
Stay put," Cait added as a last warning before she made her
way back to Hayes.

Shaw took up guard duty, moving closer to Shayla, but
Cait continued to make glances back at her soon-to-be pris-

oner. The nurse stepped aside, too, and he heard her contacting the doctor on call.

"Is that woman anywhere near the ballpark of being sane?" Cait asked Hayes as she tipped her head to Shayla.

"No." But that was a knee-jerk reaction. Legally, Shayla was sane. She probably was, anyway. "She really does believe in psychics and such and is convinced we're soul mates and should be together. That happens sometimes, but Shayla's taken that to a whole new level."

"That happens sometimes?" Cait repeated. "You get a lot of women who think you're their soul mate?"

If he answered honestly and said yes, it would make him sound cocky. Or a magnet for weirdos. Which he often was. Still, if he complained, it made him sound like a spoiled Hollywood dick who didn't appreciate that he got paid obscene amounts of money for pretending to be someone he wasn't.

So, yes, women wanted him, and men—well, some men, anyway—wanted to be a motorcycle-riding ballbuster like the one he played in *Outlaw Rebels*. All that adoration and shit came with a price tag, and sometimes it caused situations like Shayla.

"*Fan* is sometimes short for *fanatic*," Hayes settled for saying. "Usually, though, those fanatics don't follow me over a thousand miles and cause me to wreck my Harley."

Hayes went to reach in his pocket, but the pain stopped him cold. Hell, his shoulder throbbed like a bad tooth, and the pain radiated all the way down to his fingertips.

"I have the contact info for her mother on my phone," Hayes explained to Cait. He kept his voice low so that Shayla and anyone else in the waiting area wouldn't be able to hear. "If you call her, she'll make arrangements to come and get her. Her mom will put her back in therapy."

Hayes angled his hip toward Cait. Again, more pain, and he was betting most of his right thigh and ass cheek were one giant bruise. He motioned for her to take out his phone.

Cait reached right in. Then she froze. Probably because her seeking hand came very close to his crotch. He was pretty sure she gave his dick an unintentional finger graze.

One that his dick definitely noticed.

He might have been all beat to hell and back, but he apparently wasn't hurting enough to stop lust from kicking in. Lust that he should in no way be feeling for Cait Jameson, who didn't want him anywhere on or near her radar.

Cait whipped out his phone from his pocket and handed it to him so he could pull up Shayla's mom's number. "Frances Weston. She's sane, mostly. And if she gives you any lip about her daughter, just tell her that you think Shayla and I are hooking up. That'll get Frances running here to stop it. She definitely doesn't want her little girl with the likes of me."

"The likes of you," Cait muttered.

Hayes wasn't sure if that was a question or not, but he gave Cait an answer anyway. "An actor with nudity credits. Of course, if the nudity had been in an art film, that'd be okay with her. And that's a long-winded way of saying she's a snob who wants only snob-approved men who keep their asses covered."

Crap, could he possibly break Shayla's babbling record? Apparently so. But he was nervous, and that didn't happen to him very often. There was just something about Cait that made him want to try.

Cait tore her gaze from him, perhaps because she realized he'd finally finished, and used the camera on her phone to take a picture of the woman's contact info. "I'll need you to come to the police station when you can," Cait instructed before she handed him back his phone.

She turned to Mandy, who'd finished her call to the doctor and was now assembling some supplies. Hayes recognized the tools of the trade for cleaning and giving stitches. Apparently, he was in for another round of pain.

"Any idea just how bad Hayes is hurt?" Cait asked the nurse.

Mandy shook her head. "Sorry, but I can't get into patient stuff."

Cait rolled her eyes. "This isn't gossip. His condition plays into what kind of initial charges I dole out to his *soul mate*." She gave said *soul mate* a quick glance to make sure she was staying put. She was.

Mandy sighed as if it would be a severe strain on her professionalism to reveal what would no doubt be general info or an outright guess to someone who had a genuine need to know.

"Well, Hayes is obviously banged up and could have internal injuries," Mandy finally answered. "The doctor might admit him to the hospital."

"No. The doctor won't," Hayes argued. He needed to take care of some family business and then be on his way. Exactly where *on his way* was, he didn't know yet, but it wasn't here in Lone Star Ridge.

Cait made a "we'll see about that" sound to his insistence that he wouldn't be admitted to the hospital. "Call me when you know his condition," Cait added to the nurse. "I'll get our reckless-driving suspect to the police station."

"Hold your horses," Mandy snapped. "You didn't get your tetanus shot, and I have it ready." She turned to wash her hands in a small sink.

"I can get that some other time," Cait said, but her cop's voice was gone. She looked a little panicked.

Hayes mimicked Cait's "we'll see about that" sound,

causing her to toss him a glare. Mandy was fast, though. By the time Cait had finished the glare, the nurse had swabbed her arm and poked Cait with the syringe.

Cait closed her eyes, and he was pretty sure she was fighting to stay calm. Clearly, she had some kind of shot phobia, but Hayes had to hand it to her. She quickly braced herself and mumbled something about getting two red suckers.

"Say, why were you in the ER, anyway?" Hayes asked, glancing at Cait.

"Long story," Cait said just as Mandy volunteered, "Cait had a run-in with a meat thermometer."

Hayes stared at Cait, waiting for her to explain, but she merely grumbled "Long story" again before she turned and marched away. She snagged Shayla by the arm before heading to the ER doors.

"Should you go with Cait to help her?" Hayes asked Shaw when the man made his way back to the examining area.

"I could if I wanted Cait to get pissed off at me. She can handle herself," Shaw added in a mumble, but he cast a glance back over his shoulder as if checking on his little sister.

Hayes was a big brother, too, so he understood some of the dynamics going on and that Cait likely didn't want her siblings interfering. From what Hayes had heard, though, the Jamesons were more or less a tight family, with the exception of their patriarch, Marty Jameson.

Marty was basically a screwup.

The man had fathered many kids without actually *fathering* any of them. Over the years, some of Marty's offspring had shown up in Lone Star Ridge, and Cait and her other siblings—their mom, too—had done their best to do right by them. The Jamesons didn't shirk responsibility and were the backbone of Lone Star Ridge. Hayes wasn't sure how his family, the Daltons, fit in, but he seriously doubted anyone had ever thought of them as backbones.

More like bohemians, misfits.

Possibly even degenerates.

Part of that was his fault. He wasn't exactly the darlin' of the town and had caused, and finished, his own share of troubles. But the *bohemians* label had started before that, when he was just a kid. That's when his triplet sisters had become the stars of the reality TV show *Little Cowgirls*. It'd stayed on the air for over a decade and had been filmed right here in Lone Star Ridge.

The show had managed to capture way too many miserable and embarrassing moments in his sisters' lives before *Little Cowgirls* had been canceled when the triplets were fifteen.

Hayes had escaped some of that misery and embarrassment just by being antisocial and leaving when he turned eighteen, but his sisters were still paying for their fame with plenty of emotional baggage. Bad memories could be a bitch, and he was certain Sunny, McCall and Hadley felt that particular bitch breathing down their backs way too often.

That reminder led Hayes to another one. Sunny was pregnant, and Shaw should be with her.

"You should go home to Sunny," Hayes told Shaw. "Let her know I'm okay."

Shaw's eyebrow lifted. "Uh, are you okay?"

"Okay enough." And that was possibly the truth. "After the doctor examines me, I'll get cleaned up and…" He checked the time and frowned. It was nearly 10:00 p.m. He'd been about to say that he would go see Sunny and the others, but it'd likely be late by the time he finished up here.

"Tell Sunny I'll see her tomorrow," Hayes amended. He was about to add that he'd get a room at the inn rather than disturb anyone in his family for a place to crash, but Hayes saw the derailment of that idea come walking through the ER doors.

Granny Em.

Hayes could count on one hand the number of people he loved, and his grandmother was one of them, so it was hard not to smile when he saw her. Of course, the smiling caused his jaw to hurt like hell, but it was worth it because his smile caused her face to light up like Christmas morning.

Em definitely didn't move like a woman in her seventies. Or dress like one. She was wearing a pair of rhinestone jeans and a red top that she'd tied at the waist. Her long gray hair fell loose and a little wild on her shoulders. What was out of the ordinary for her was the ruby-and-diamond ring that Hayes spotted even from a distance.

An engagement ring.

Yep, at an age where most folks' lives were winding down, Em had agreed to marry her childhood sweetheart, Tony Corbin. Hayes had yet to meet the man and he'd heard good things about Tony from his sisters, but Hayes doubted Tony was good enough for his grandmother. Of course, no man ever would be.

"Told you Hayes was here," the coughing woman in the waiting area muttered to Em.

Hayes remembered that the woman's name was Anita Parker. Remembered, too, that she was one of the unofficial town criers who kept everyone informed whether they wanted to be or not.

Well, that explained how his grandmother had found out, and if Em knew, then maybe his sisters did, too. He'd really hoped not to have a family reunion tonight, but perhaps Anita didn't have his sisters' phone numbers.

Em gave Hayes the once-over as she went to him, and

studying his face, she finally brushed a kiss on his right cheekbone. Maybe because it was one of the few bruise-free spots.

"Got banged up, I see," she said. She smelled like vanilla and strong coffee. "You won't get any free passes from the ladies with the way you look right now."

He knew what passes she was referring to. Even though he'd had nothing to do with the DNA stew that had created his looks, those looks had earned him plenty of attention, aka free passes. It had also gotten him a stalker or two, aka Shayla.

"Are you hurt bad?" Em asked. As if he were five again, she eased his hair away from his face.

"No. I'm fine, really."

"That's to be determined," Mandy argued, glancing at Shaw and Em. "The doctor will be here in a few minutes, and y'all will have to step out while he does the exam."

"I should be going anyway," Shaw said. He reached out as if to give Hayes a pat on the back but then pulled back his hand when he no doubt remembered the injuries. "I'll see if I can talk Sunny and her sisters into staying put."

Hayes thanked him, but Em didn't say anything until Shaw and Mandy had stepped away. "You gonna tell me why you're home?" Em asked. "Are you here for the wedding, or is something else going on?"

Home. That wasn't the right label for Lone Star Ridge. It'd been the place where he was raised. The place he'd left. But then so had his sisters, and one by one they had all come back. He wouldn't do that.

Or rather he couldn't.

"I needed to talk to you," Hayes said. He didn't want to get into all of this here, but the clock was ticking, and he didn't want Em to be blindsided by this.

"All right," Em said, and judging from her tone, she already knew something was wrong. Of course, his being here had already confirmed that.

Hayes gathered his breath. "If it hasn't hit the tabloids already, it will soon. There'll be stories that say I got fired from *Outlaw Rebels*. I wasn't, but I am taking a break from the show."

It cut that the break hadn't been his decision. Though Hayes couldn't help but think that the cut should have felt much deeper and that he shouldn't be feeling any relief.

But he did.

He just didn't have the juice to pour himself into make-believe right now. Even if that make-believe was his life.

Hayes had to do another round of breath gathering to say the rest of what he had to tell Em. "There's more," he went on. "And it's not good. Some of those tabloid stories will say I tried to kill myself."

He saw the shock on Em's face, followed by exactly what he knew would be in her eyes. The worry that only a grandmother could have for a child she loved. With some wincing and with his eyes watering from the pain, Hayes managed to stand so he could pull her into his arms and give her all the reassurance he could.

Which might not be much.

But he didn't manage even a smidge of reassurance because the room started to spin. Not a little spin, either. This was an F5-tornado kind of whirl. Worse, the bones in his legs dissolved.

The last thing Hayes saw before he lost consciousness was the hard linoleum floor that he was about to hit.

CHAPTER THREE

THERE WERE TIMES Cait loved her job and thought there was nothing else in the solar system that she'd rather do. Tonight wasn't one of those times.

She wanted to throttle several people, and at the top of that throttling list was Shayla, who hadn't stopped crying or whining since Cait had brought her to the police station and booked her. However, Wilma and Harvey Crockett weren't far behind the whimpering soul-mate wannabe in Cait's strong throttling urge. The couple had continued their argument and sniping at each other even after Leyton had put them behind bars.

Unfortunately, the feuding husband and wife were behind those bars together.

The police station only had one holding cell, and months would go by without a need for it to be used. Cait couldn't recall another time when she'd wished they had more places to lock people up, but tonight she also wished she could shut each of their three prisoners up and put them far, far away from her where she was trying to do reports. Because of the lack of cell space, though, Shayla had been relegated to sitting in the chair next to Cait's desk.

"You're so ugly you have to slap your feet to get them to go to bed with you," Wilma spit out. The insult, as all her others had been tonight, was aimed at her husband, and it appeared to have been taken from the pages of a very corny joke book.

Harvey came back with his own unique insult by imitating a loud braying donkey. The sound before that had been a crowing rooster, so obviously the man had a repertoire of farm-animal noises that he considered good retorts for Wilma's corny scorn.

Cait could only hope that laryngitis or exhaustion would soon set in because those would probably be the only things that would shut them up. In Shayla's case, dehydration might do the trick to get her to stop crying.

At least there was a silver lining as far as Shayla was concerned. Cait had gotten through to her mother. Frances Weston did indeed have that snobby vibe that Hayes had warned Cait about, but she'd also had what appeared to be genuine concern for her daughter.

That concern had climbed several rungs on the motherly ladder when Cait had mentioned that Hayes and Shayla might be renewing *things*. She'd purposely made *things* sound vague but also lascivious. It was more than enough to spur Frances and her snobbery to action. The woman was sending an attorney from San Antonio who would do whatever legal wrangling was necessary to get Shayla back to California and into treatment ASAP for her mental health issues.

Cait couldn't see the charges being dropped, considering Shayla could have killed Hayes, but Cait intended to cooperate with any lawyer who could spare her the sound of more wailing and whining.

It was too bad there were no such silver linings for the Crocketts. Even though they had apologized to her for the meat-thermometer incident, both had refused to call a lawyer and had insisted they wait in jail—together—until there could be a bond hearing. Cait was sure Leyton was working hard to arrange that, but ASAP wouldn't be nearly soon enough. Heck, the next fifteen seconds wouldn't be soon enough.

At least Cait hadn't had to sit through all of this in what was left of her favorite shirt. She'd thankfully had a change of clothes in her locker and made use of them. Made use, too, of some over-the-counter pain meds that she'd snagged from Leyton's desk. The stitches on her arm were now causing a constant dull throb. Ditto for her headache. And she was counting the minutes before she could down another dose.

"I need to see Hayes," Shayla said to absolutely no one, but she continued to prattle out such things while sopping at snot and tears. The woman had already gone through all the tissues that Cait had been able to round up and was now on her second roll of toilet paper.

Cait glanced through the open door of her brother's office and saw that Leyton was diligently working on paperwork. Unlike her, he seemed so focused, and it took her a moment to spot the earplugs he was using. Wise choice for maintaining sanity, but then he missed Wilma's "clever" next round.

"If all your brains were dynamite, you still wouldn't be able to blow your own nose."

The woman sure managed to come up with some gems worthy of needlepoint pillows. Harvey responded with a sound that a constipated mule might make.

Since there was no telling how long it would take for Shayla's lawyer to arrive, Cait decided to throw in the towel. She'd been on shift for going on fifteen hours now, and she could call in the night deputy, Willy Jenkinson. Maybe then Leyton would leave, too, because he'd put in as many hours as she had.

They didn't always have the office manned this late but instead had the calls filtered through a dispatch operator.

But with both Shayla and the Crocketts in custody, some-one would need to be in the building.

Cait's phone rang, cutting through the sobs and animal sounds, and she went a little stiff when she saw Sunny's name on the screen. It was late, nearly midnight, and Cait seriously doubted this was a social call from her soon-to-be sister-in-law.

"Sunny," Cait answered, getting up from her desk. Even though it wouldn't give her much privacy from Shayla, she went to the other side of the room. "Is everything okay?"

"No. But it's not the baby," Sunny quickly added. "It's Hayes. He passed out, hit his head and had to be admitted to the hospital."

Well, crap. "How bad is it?"

"I'm not sure. Hayes says he's fine, and he's clamoring to be released. He also asked to speak to you."

"Me?" Cait questioned, but then she realized that Hayes probably wanted an update on Shayla. He clearly had enough worries without wondering if a stalker was going to show up in his hospital room.

"I just left the hospital and am heading home," Sunny went on. "Em's with Hayes, but I told him I'd call and find out if you could go see him. He said to tell you that he's in room 102."

Cait glanced around just as Shayla made another snotty plea to see Hayes and the Crocketts went another round. "Sure. I can walk down there now. I need to get Hayes's statement anyway."

Though Cait was pretty sure his statement could wait until morning, it would still get her out of the police station. But maybe this was a case of frying pan/fire. After all, she had felt that old nudge of heat when she'd seen

Hayes earlier. Heat despite them both being injured and him looking like hell.

However, beneath the hellish look, he was still Heart-throb Hayes.

A heartthrob who thankfully didn't want to use and discard her as he had so many other women. That was the good news that might keep her out of the fire below the frying pan. The only thing she had to do was what she had always done—keep her tingly parts in check whenever she was around him.

She called Willy and got his assurance that he'd come right in, so Cait stepped into the doorway of Leyton's office. She motioned for him to take out his earphones.

"Sunny called and said Hayes passed out and had to be admitted to the hospital," she relayed in a soft enough voice that Shayla hopefully wouldn't hear. Cait didn't want the woman trying to tag along with her when she left.

Leyton nodded. "Yeah, Hadley texted me."

Hadley, his fiancée and one of Hayes's triplet sisters. "She's at the hospital, too?"

"Was," Leyton corrected. "So was McCall." The other sister. So, Hayes had had all of his siblings there with him. "Hayes ordered them all to go home."

Cait was betting some fast-talking had gone into convincing them to leave. Or maybe he'd just played the Em card and reminded his sisters that their grandmother would go if they did.

"Hayes wants to see me," Cait went on. "I think he wants to tell me about the accident. Willy will be here in a few minutes."

Leyton looked at her, then at Shayla, then rolled his eyes when he heard the next round from the Crocketts. Apparently, Wilma had run out of the longer insults and was now just repeating "Your mama." Harvey oinked, but it was softer than some of his other comebacks. So maybe that meant things were winding down and they would soon fall asleep.

"Go on home after you're finished at the hospital," Leyton finally said. "I'll keep an eye on our stalker until Willy gets here. Once her lawyer shows up, I'll see what I can work out with him."

Cait glanced back at Shayla. The woman appeared to be winding down, as well. She'd put her head on Cait's desk and was using the roll of toilet paper as a makeshift pillow.

"Don't stay here all night," Cait told her brother. And because she suspected that's exactly what he would do, she added, "Hadley might be upset about her brother and probably wants you home with her."

That seemed to do the trick, proving that Hayes wasn't the only one who could do some fast-talking. Leyton nodded and motioned for her to go.

Since Shayla seemed to be falling asleep, Cait tiptoed back to her desk to get her purse, and then she stepped outside into the night air. It might be September and officially fall, but it was still hotter than Hades. Even the night breeze felt as if Mother Nature was blowing air out through a raging furnace.

Cait walked down the block, entering the hospital through the ER doors since those were the only ones that would be unlocked at this time of night. As expected, no one was in the waiting area or at the reception desk. Along with not being a hotbed of crime, there weren't a lot of emergencies in Lone Star Ridge. Having two in one night—Hayes's and her own—had been a big anomaly that she was betting no one wanted to repeat anytime soon.

Cait snagged another red sucker from the reception desk, backtracked a step and took a second one for Hayes before she headed toward his room, which should be just up the hall. However, she stopped when she heard Mandy talking.

"He could have wrecked the motorcycle himself," the nurse said. "That's a hard way to put an end to things, but it could have happened just that way."

Cait only heard the murmur of a response to Mandy's comment, but Mandy had to be talking about Hayes. She scowled, wondering why in the name of heaven Mandy would believe something like that.

"It goes back to that woman," Mandy went on. "The one who killed herself a couple of months ago. It was all over the tabloids. Hayes and she were tight, and I guess it messed him up when she died. One suicide can trigger someone else to do the same, you know."

Cait's scowl turned to some serious concern. Maybe Mandy was way off base here, but just to be sure, Cait stepped into the ladies' room and used her phone to do a quick search for any recent news about Hayes.

Heck. She got thousands of hits.

So she narrowed it down, using the word *suicide*, and she soon saw the string of articles on the death of a woman named Ivy Malloy. A suicide. She'd been a child actress but had become a makeup artist. There were photos of Hayes and her at various fancy events. Some candid casual ones, too, of them holding hands and gazing at each other—while obviously unaware of the photographer.

Still scanning the articles, Cait saw plenty of speculation about Ivy's depression. And a possible rift with Hayes. Of course, some of the stories took out the "possible" part and added what were no doubt some embellishments about the woman dying from a broken heart—one that Hayes had given her.

Well, crap. Had Ivy been in love with him? Judging from

the pictures, she didn't appear to be a Shayla-like stalker. Not with the way Hayes was holding her hand and looking at her. But things could have changed. If the relationship had gone south, then maybe Hayes had indeed broken up with her.

And now blamed himself for her death.

Cait still thought the motorcycle accident was just that. An accident. But there were other reports that Hayes had indeed tried to kill himself after he'd been fired from *Outlaw Rebels*.

It was hard for her to wrap her mind around the possibility of Hayes doing something like that, but it might explain why he had come home. *Might explain.* And all of the stories could be malarkey, as tabloid accounts so often were.

Cait was ready to put away her phone and ask the source about those stories, but another one caught her eye. Because this one had her name in it.

The title of the story was "Not Lonely for Long in Lone Star Ridge." It'd been published in one of the tabloids, *The Tattler*, and was about the *Little Cowgirls* all marrying brothers from their hometown. The article said the only hookup left was between Hayes and the brothers' kid sister, Cait, and that rumors claimed the hookup was imminent.

Imminent?

It wasn't even on the radar.

The anger swarmed through her like really-pissed-off bees, but it didn't take long for the feeling of violation to set in. Her personal life, even total fibs about it, wasn't up for speculation.

Both the anger and violation continued when Cait saw that this wasn't the only article about Hayes and her. Nope. There were three others. In those, Hayes and she were practically footnotes to the meat of the article about the *Little Cowgirls* finding their "Big Cowboys."

Cait wanted to gush out some of those bullshit animal sounds like the ones Harvey Crockett had made, but she forced herself to put all of this in perspective. Hayes and the triplets had to deal with this sort of lying publicity stuff all the time, and it wasn't as if anyone she knew had actually read the stories about Hayes and her. Cait knew this because if someone local had indeed seen it, she would have already heard about it.

She finally tamped down enough of her anger to get moving. The candy sucker helped with that. A slow sugar high from the repeated licks gave her the boost she needed to shove her phone in her pocket and go to Hayes's room.

"It's me, Cait," she said, lightly tapping on the door. If he didn't answer right away, she would come back tomorrow morning when her mood was better. But he answered before she'd even finished the tap.

"Come in." His voice had an edge to it. Definitely not his usual smoky drawl. And Cait soon saw the reason for it. Along with the scrapes and bruises, there was something on his face that she recognized.

Pain.

He had a lot more injuries than she did, and he didn't seem very happy about being in the hospital. It was hard to keep up her snark barrier when he looked as if he'd been ridden hard and put up wet. And not in a good sexual way, either.

"The taste is just one notch above cough syrup," she said, handing him the second sucker. "But it's probably better than anything else you'll get to eat around here. It's your reward for surviving the ER and bashing your head on the floor when you passed out."

The corner of his mouth lifted into an almost smile. "And what's yours a reward for? Before you answer, I should tell you that I saw you get a sucker when you left earlier with Shayla."

Cait didn't hesitate. "It's a second reward for putting up with Shayla. The woman's batshit."

"Yeah, she is." He shook his head, opened the sucker and popped it into his mouth.

It was such a simple gesture. But heck in a handbasket, it gave her the tingles. Maybe because those idiot parts of her tingling wondered if that mouth was made for as much sin as it appeared.

Cait was betting the answer to that was a big-assed yes.

"Speaking of which, how is Shayla?" he asked.

Cait picked through the last two hours and tried to come up with the best memory for him. One that wouldn't add to the pain and troubles he was no doubt already feeling.

"She was asleep when I left the police station." And that was as good as it could possibly get when it came to the woman. "Her mother hired a lawyer who's on his way. We'll go from there, but I think Leyton's leaning toward doing whatever it takes to get her out of Texas."

"A wise decision," he agreed, moving the sucker around in his mouth. Wincing a little, too.

His wince gave no part of her body a tingle. But it did give her a slathering of sympathy, and it tugged at her. The tugging merged with what she'd just read in those articles, and some genuine worry set in. Worry that she preferred him not to see. When it came to Hayes, it was best for her own self-preservation if she kept up the ploy of the white noise. Thankfully, it was hard to look overly concerned with a sucker poking out of her mouth.

"So, you passed out?" Cait said in the most conversational tone she could manage. "Not very *Outlaw Rebels* of you."

"Probably not." He smiled. Winced. And gave her another tug of worry. "The doc thinks my blood pressure dropped too fast when I stood up."

Cait considered that a moment. "Does that mean your injuries aren't that bad?"

"Only a cracked rib or two," he said.

Which, of course, didn't fall into the "aren't that bad" category. Especially since she was about 100 percent sure that Hayes would downplay any injuries. Cait made a mental note to try to get the truth from one of his sisters. And to keep the worry off her face when she did it. She didn't want the triplets believing she had a thing for their brother.

Since she didn't want to sit on the edge of his bed—too intimate and too close to that sinful mouth of his—Cait took the chair. "Will a cracked rib or two affect you filming *Outlaw Rebels*?" she asked.

He started to speak but shifted the sucker again, and he closed his mouth as if rethinking what he'd been about to say. Then he did something bad. Really, really bad. He looked at her with those bedroom eyes so blue that Cait was certain they alone had seduced too many women to count. Apparently, his sinful mouth had some competition in that area of seduction.

"Can you keep a secret?" he asked.

Well, that was a question that hadn't been on her question radar, and Cait thought she might not want to hear the rest of what went along with it.

"No," she said.

"Liar," he said just as fast. "I told you a secret years ago and you didn't spill to anyone."

Cait had to take a trip down memory lane, and after a couple of long moments, it finally occurred to her what he was talking about. When he was twelve and she was nine, Hayes had told her that he had a crush on her then-babysitter, Lizzie Chaplain.

"Because it was a lame secret and not worthy of blabbing," she explained. "Every boy in town had a crush on Lizzie. In part because of her double Ds and heart-shaped butt."

"Still, you kept it a secret," he concluded. Then he paused, made that tingle-inducing eye contact with her again. "The producers of *Outlaw Rebels* told me to take a break from the show. They'll excuse my absence by having a rival gang kidnap my character and hold me where no one can find me."

"Slade," she quietly supplied and was glad she hadn't also supplied the entire character name. Slade Axel Mc-Clendon. Cait was also glad that she hadn't blurted out that she knew each scene where he'd bared his butt for a steamy love scene. But there was something else she was going to delve into only so she could be sure that it hadn't played into the motorcycle accident.

"Does this have something to do with you losing your... friend?" she settled for saying.

Because Cait was looking straight into his eyes, she didn't see any surprise that she knew about Ivy. But there was sadness and maybe resignation.

"Some," he admitted, and she thought that was in the same understated, underreported category of a cracked rib or two. "I need a break from the show."

Now she was the one who opened her mouth, closed it and rethought what she'd been about to say. She wanted to ask if he had actually tried to kill himself. And if that in part was what had happened tonight, but Hayes spoke before she could find her words.

"My sisters are getting married in a month," he continued a moment later. "I'd like to stay here in Lone Star

Ridge until the wedding. I need that time to fix some things in my head."

So, the articles had been true. Well, true-ish, anyway. There was something that Hayes needed to deal with, and at least some part of it had to do with his friend's suicide.

"But the fixing won't be easy if I have the press hounding me about my mental state," he added.

No way could she argue with that. Cait remembered the way the reporters had hounded and pestered the triplets when *Little Cowgirls* had been abruptly canceled after Hadley had been arrested for joyriding in a stolen car. *Outlaw Rebels* was a popular show, so the hounding and pestering might be even worse.

"There are a lot of stories floating around out there about me," he went on. "Most are bullshit, but there's bits of truth in them."

She wondered if one of those bits that was true or even true-ish was about him trying to kill himself.

"How can I help?" she asked because it was obvious he wanted something from her. After all, he'd asked her to come here.

He stayed quiet a few more seconds. "Some of those stories are about you and me. Plenty of tabloid reporters think you and I will get together because our siblings are getting married."

Cait pooh-poohed that with the wave of her hand and a laughing snort. "As if."

Hayes leaned closer and made more of that tingling eye contact. "I'd like for you to tell everyone that the stories about us are true."

CHAPTER FOUR

CLEARLY, HAYES HAD some convincing to do, because Cait looked at him as if he'd just suggested they take a quick trip to Pluto.

"You'd like for me to lie and say the fake stories about us aren't actual lies?" she asked.

Yep, that was it in a nutshell, but Hayes wasn't sure if Cait had any such skills to bend the truth. Or in this case, break the truth to bits. That's why he had to pull out a big gun of persuasion, and this time his trademark looks weren't going to give him any leverage.

"Sunny," he said, drawing that big gun. "She was in earlier, and she looked exhausted."

Cait lifted her shoulder, the one with the stitches, and she winced. "The pregnancy. Shaw said she's been tired a lot."

"It's more than just the fatigue," Hayes went on. He took a lick of the sucker and learned Cait was wrong. The flavor wasn't a step above cough syrup. It tasted exactly like the medicine. "It's the added stress of being worried because I'm hurt and because of all the stories about me in the tabloids."

He fanned his hand over his bruises and cuts, causing his own wincing. Hayes made a mental note to do less gesturing. Maybe he could cut back on the breathing, too, because his ribs were throbbing.

"You want me to lie so that Sunny won't be stressed

about your injuries and tabloid gossip," Cait paraphrased, along with giving him a look as flat as a pancake.

"Not just Sunny but Em and my other sisters." He paused and figured out how to tap-dance around this. "The rumors in the tabloids could give them more reason to worry. Worry that I'd prefer they not have about me. Especially about me," he emphasized. "I'd rather my family focus on the baby, the weddings and Em's engagement."

That last one was something he needed to give a little more focus, too. He had already had a background check run on Tony Corbin, but Hayes wanted to dig a little deeper there. Em was too important to him to get involved with someone who could give her trouble. Over the years, Em had had enough of that, what with her own daughter, Hayes's mother. Heck, Hayes's father, too. Em had stepped up to the plate to raise Hayes and his sisters when their parents had basically abandoned their kids.

"I don't want to have a worry-fest discussion with my family where they grill me about the reasons I've come back," Hayes continued. "I'd rather them believe I'm here because of you."

Cait kept that flat gaze on him. "What exactly are the reasons you've come back?"

Of course, she would ask that, and Hayes went with a variation of what he'd already told her. "I need some time to get my head back on straight and deal with what happened to my friend."

There was more, but it might not even be a "big gun" to Cait.

Because he was watching her so closely, Hayes thought that maybe he'd put a dent in her resistance, but the dent vanished and the moment was lost when her phone rang.

"Leyton," she muttered, glancing at the screen. "I need to take this."

Cait took a couple of steps away from him, but Hayes still managed to hear her brother say Shayla's name. Hell. He hoped the woman wasn't giving them any more trouble, but Hayes couldn't get a lot about the conversation just by listening to Cait. She answered in sounds of approval, one of disapproval and a couple of long pauses.

While she listened to whatever her brother was saying, she paced, though she couldn't go far in the small room. Still, it was enough space for her to do complete turn-arounds and give him a glimpse of her jeans-clad ass. It was a superior ass, and seeing it caused his breathing to kick up a notch. That in turn notched up the pain. Despite that, he still felt the spark of heat in his body.

Hayes looked away from Cait because he figured a hard-on right now would be excruciating, and he didn't want to disgrace himself by whimpering. That would hardly go with the tough-guy Slade McClendon image that he'd carved out for himself.

"I'll let Hayes know," Cait said right before she ended the call. With her back, and therefore her butt, still toward him, she took another moment before she finally turned around to face him.

"Good or bad news?" Hayes asked.

"A little bit of both." And she launched into an account of what she'd just learned. "Shayla's lawyer finally showed up. He wants to try to cut her a deal, but Leyton isn't going to back off on the charges that caused you to wreck. That means he'll let Shayla go. For now. But she'll have to come back to appear in front of a judge to answer those charges. Depending on how that goes, she could get some jail time."

Hayes wasn't sure if that last part fell into the good or

bad category. He didn't especially want to see Shayla behind bars, but nothing else he'd done had worked to get
the woman to back off. Of course, what she really needed
was some psychiatric help, and maybe if she got that, then
the judge would go easy on her. Even if he didn't, Hayes
couldn't take this on. He already had way too much guilt
on his shoulders.

"There's more," Cait went on a moment later. "Some reporter checked into the inn about an hour ago. A guy named
Jenner Franklin. Leyton figures he's here because of you."

Hayes didn't have to *figure* it. He knew Franklin, had
had his share of run-ins with the reporter's "no boundaries"
approach to journalism. It sure hadn't taken him long to
sniff out where Hayes had gone. And to follow him. Franklin was indeed in Lone Star Ridge to try to get a story on
why Hayes had come home.

"He works for *The Tattler*," Hayes explained. It was one
of the tabloids that often dished dirt on him and his family.

Cait nodded. "Leyton will warn the guy not to bother
you here at the hospital, but once you're discharged, he'll
probably try to see you."

Oh, yeah. He would, and he wouldn't stop there. Franklin
would dig for anything he could find on the triplets' weddings, too. Even though *Little Cowgirls* had been off the air
for years, news about his sisters could still sell newspapers.
It would especially generate sales if the stories had a "soul-
sucking, complete violation of privacy" angle to them.

"I'll give Em and the others a heads-up about this reporter," Cait went on. "And I can ask folks not to stir up
any gossip with him."

Hayes muttered a thanks, a heartfelt one. However, he
could hear the *but* in her tone. "But?" he spelled out for her.

Sighing, she shook her head. "About that fake story you

want me to do… I'm sorry, but I just don't think I can pull it off."

"Kiss me and find out," Hayes challenged before his mind caught up with his mouth.

It was a totally dumbass thing to say, and worse, he'd done it in Slade's voice. With Slade's cocky "you're sure you don't want to tap this?" smile.

Cait blinked, clearly surprised. Or something. Hayes couldn't quite figure out her expression or why she swallowed hard. It wasn't as if she wanted to "tap this."

Was it?

He was usually pretty good at picking up on cues like that, but the pain meds were clearly dulling his brain. No. Cait had zero tapping ideas when it came to Slade or him. Especially him.

"Everything will be fine without the lies," Cait said with no confidence whatsoever, and with that, she turned and walked out.

Hayes was about to curse, but he heard a single word come from the other side of the door. A single word from Cait that gave him hope that maybe she was battling the tap after all.

"Shit."

"I wanta play cops and bobbers," Avery Jameson announced the moment Cait had her strapped into her car seat. Cait's three-year-old niece proceeded to make loud farting noises to imitate the sound of running footsteps.

"No. Let's play fairy princess," her twin sister, Gracie, suggested. No farting sounds for her, but she did start waving her invisible fairy wand around and nearly bopped Cait in the eye.

Cait dodged more eye bops, got Gracie secured in her

car seat and climbed behind the wheel of her SUV so she could deal with the second round of family stuff. Her half sister, Kinsley, was riding shotgun with a nearly naked picture of Hayes on her lap. Not a little picture, either.

No siree, Bob.

This was a glossy eight by ten, and the shot had obviously been taken from one of the sets of *Outlaw Rebels*. Hayes was in a bedroom, his back to the camera, and he was wearing boxers that revealed every curve, dip and nuance of his superior butt. Cait had never thought of butts having nuances, but Hayes's sure did.

Incredible well-shaped nuances.

"Cops and bobbers," Avery repeated, more insistent now, as Cait drove away from Austin and McCall's house.

It was her nieces' favorite game, a variation of cops and robbers that didn't include any hints of violence. Mainly it consisted of those farting sounds, a few arm pumps to imitate running and Avery doling out an occasional "Book 'em, Danno." That was something Avery had gotten from Cait, who loved watching reruns of the old TV show *Hawaii Five-0*.

Gracie, who had a much quieter nature than her former womb buddy, merely kept twirling the magic fairy wand while Cait started the drive to their preschool. It was something she did as often as possible to give her brother Austin and his fiancée, McCall, a little time to themselves. Ditto for Cait dropping off Kinsley at the high school so that Shaw wouldn't have to interrupt his busy day to drive her. Since he ran the family's sprawling ranch, pretty much any time of day interrupted something he had to do.

Normally, though, Cait didn't have to do the drop-offs while her brain was only partly engaged and while functioning on just a couple of hours of sleep. It'd been two in the morning before she had finally gotten to bed, and heaven knew what time it was before she'd actually managed to sleep. She could blame Hayes and his nuanced butt for that.

Imagine him wanting her to pretend to be his love interest.

But Cait could indeed imagine it. Worse, she could feel it, and even the discomfort from her stitched arm hadn't been able to tamp down the tingles. Or the ridiculous fantasies of what it would be like to have her hands on that incredible butt of his.

"Well?" Kinsley prompted, drawing Cait's attention back to her.

Usually her often sullen sister was half-asleep and only communicated with grunts and eye rolls at this early hour. But apparently Kinsley had plenty of verbal stuff to say today. It'd started the moment Cait had picked her up from the ranch where Kinsley had been living since her mother abandoned her. Her father, too, but then Marty Jameson made a habit of abandoning kids. Of course, when it happened as often as it did with Marty, it was more of a way of life than a mere habit.

"Can you please get Hayes to autograph it for me?" Kinsley asked. *"Please."*

Her request wasn't a newsflash since the girl had already repeated it three times. As she'd already done three times, Cait turned the photo facedown. Avery and Gracie likely wouldn't be able to see it from the back seat, but it was best not to give their nieces that kind of eye candy.

"He's straight fire," Kinsley added in a sigh-y voice as she peeked at the picture again.

"Straight fire?" Though Cait had a fairly good idea what

Kinsley meant. It was probably on par with Heartthrob Hayes.

"Smokin'," Kinsley verified. "And it doesn't matter that he's like old or anything. He's still straight fire."

Thirty-five was indeed old in a teenager's mind. Once you hit the big 3-0 mark, the younger generations started counting age like dog years. One equaled seven. However, Cait suspected that Hayes was one of those guys who'd keep his smokin' good looks until he went to the grave.

A thought that gave her more of a mental jolt than it should have.

She remembered the tabloid stories about Hayes maybe trying to off himself. Remembered, too, what Hayes had said about them. *There are a lot of stories floating around out there about me. Most are bullshit, but there's bits of truth in them.* If the truth had to do with the grave and Hayes wanting to speed up his trip to that particular destination, then she should do something to try to help him.

But what?

And how could she help without risking a whole bunch of things? Like making it worse. Or the heart ding that Hayes could almost certainly give her.

"Wouldn't you just gobble him up if you could?" Kinsley went on, going in for another peek of the photo.

That turned Cait's attention back to her sister and the picture. Cait had no intention of telling the girl that Hayes had already offered her a gobbling opportunity. Well, not an actual one but rather the chance to spend time with him as his pretend girlfriend. A pretense where she would have to be around him and get multiple looks at his face and perhaps even his butt—while covered with his jeans, that is. The pretense would be easy for him. He was an actor, after all. But she didn't want anything getting past the immune barrier she'd set up for men like Hayes.

Men like her father.

There were a lot of differences between Marty and Hayes. For one thing, Hayes actually had some redeeming qualities, like caring about his family. But there was that pesky similarity of both of them leaving and staying gone. Yes, they both made visits, but this place was no longer home to either of them.

"So, will you get him to autograph the picture?" Kinsley tried again as Cait pulled to a stop in front of the preschool.

"Hayes is kind of messed up right now, what with his injuries. When I saw him in the hospital last night, he looked pretty bad."

"But maybe he can still sign his name," Kinsley begged. "Just see if he'll sign it and maybe write *Climb on, babe, and kiss me* on it."

Well, at least Kinsley had suggested *babe* instead of *bitch*. So had the network execs, and Cait remembered that in certain TV markets, Hayes had been forced to pull back a notch on the *B* word and use *babe*. That tamed down the saying, *some*, but Cait knew the climbing-on part wasn't solely an invitation to get on his motorcycle.

"I'll take some of your babysitting hours," Kinsley bargained.

Cait certainly hadn't forgotten about the deal she'd struck with Austin and the twins. Babysitting in exchange for him not worrying their mother with the fact that she was in the ER. That was sort of like what Hayes had done by asking her to tell everyone that he had come back home for her.

Sort of.

Obviously, she'd had a better bargaining chip than Hayes had. Childcare was a premium, especially for the twins, but Cait wasn't going to cave and press Hayes for a favor. Not when she'd turned down the favor he had asked of her.

"Give Hayes a few days to recover, and we'll see about getting an autograph," Cait muttered.

She put a pause on the conversation to take the twins out of her SUV and walk them to the door of the preschool. Avery was still making farting noises, and Gracie was doing more wand waving, but Cait worked in some hugs and kisses.

"Don't get married today or make any weapons of mass destruction during activity centers," Cait joked. The girls giggled like loons, though they didn't have a clue what that last one meant. However, it did earn Cait some hairy eyeball from the teacher's assistant, Fredricka Myers.

"It helps their vocabularies," Cait reasoned.

"There are better words, better vocabularies," Fredricka scolded. Her voice dropped some judgmental octaves to include, "Better choices."

Cait was reasonably sure the woman had doled out the exact same words of wisdom and identical hairy eyeball when Cait had been in preschool. It wouldn't make Cait mend her ways, not when she could give the twins a giggling start to their school day.

"So, you'll ask Hayes to sign the picture tomorrow?" Kinsley asked the moment Cait was back in her SUV.

Cait sighed. Apparently, there would be no giggle start for her. "In a day or two, and I said we'll see."

Of course, Kinsley had heard her just fine before, but the girl would probably continue to push this. And Cait would likely end up doing more sighing. Then caving. She just wanted the sting of turning him down to fade a little first before she went to see him and beg him for an autograph. Also, Cait would try to find a different picture, one where

Hayes was fully clothed. That way, it wouldn't earn her any hairy eyeball from Kinsley's teachers since her sister would very likely take it to school to show it off.

The high school wasn't far, less than a quarter of a mile from the twins' preschool, so it didn't take Cait long to drive there. During the entire ride, though, Kinsley continued to ogle Hayes. Continued to mutter, too, about his extreme hotness.

"Thanks," Kinsley said when she got out.

"You forgot your picture of Hayes," Cait pointed out when the girl left it on the seat.

"Oh, I have others. Remember to have him write *Kiss me, babe* when he signs it." Kinsley smiled, patted her backpack and headed off toward her friends—who were also gawking at pictures.

Cait was reasonably sure that the photos were also of Hayes. Reasonably sure that the girls were imagining that Hayes would indeed say to them, *Climb on*—insert the *B* word of their choice—*and kiss me*. If she did ask Hayes to do the autograph for Kinsley, she wouldn't have him include the kiss part, and the *B* word would definitely be *babe*. It felt creepy to have her teenage sister lusting over the same guy who was tweaking her own hormones.

With her aunt and sister duties done for the day, Cait headed for work. She wasn't on the schedule, but there would be paperwork to do. Always was. Plus, she wanted an update on the Crocketts and Shayla. However, she was just pulling into the police station parking lot when her phone rang, and she saw Shaw's name on the screen. Her first thought was that her brother wanted to discuss the Hayes photo that Kinsley had, but after hearing her brother's voice, Cait knew this was much more serious than that.

"Cait," Shaw said. "Sunny's spotting, and I just brought her to the ER."

Cait's stomach twisted and then sank. No. No. No. Not a miscarriage. Sunny had waited years to get pregnant with this baby, and it would break her heart to lose it. Shaw's, too.

"I'll head down there now," Cait said, getting out of her SUV so she could start walking. Or rather running. "What do you need me to do?"

"Em's here, as well. She was at the house when Sunny told me she was spotting. Em will need some, uh, soothing."

It sounded as if Shaw also needed some of that *soothing*, but Cait figured that wouldn't be in the cards for him. "I'll be there in a minute."

Cait texted Leyton while she ran. If the rest of the family didn't already know about Sunny, then he could take care of that. She hit the send button on the text just as she bolted through the ER doors. She didn't see Shaw, but she immediately spotted Em.

Oh, yes, the woman needed someone to help with settling her down. Em was standing in the center of the waiting room, looking lost and very, very worried.

Em turned, her attention landing on Cait, and while the loss and worry stayed in place, there was also some relief. Cait hadn't needed a reason to be glad she came, but Em had just given her one.

"Sunny and Shaw are with the doctor now. McCall and Hadley are on the way," Em said when Cait went to her. There were tears in her eyes. Actual tears. Seeing them was a first for Cait because, unlike the wailing Shayla, Em definitely wasn't a crier.

Cait looped her arm around Em and had the woman sit. The hard plastic chairs weren't especially comfortable, but it would get Em off her feet, which were looking as shaky as the rest of her. Thankfully, the waiting room was empty except for them. Cait didn't want the family to have to deal with gossips on top of the fear they had to be feeling.

"Sunny's scared," Em muttered. "Shaw, too. I blame myself for this," the woman added before Cait could say anything. "I was going over the wedding plans with Sunny, and it's too much."

The wedding plans were indeed unwieldy, but Sunny was smart enough not to let something like that get to the "too much" stage. She loved Shaw and wanted to marry him, but Cait had no doubts that both Sunny and Shaw had put this baby, their child, first.

"I'm sure Sunny will be okay," Cait said, hoping it would soothe.

It didn't. Em just continued her mutterings while adding some actual hand wringing to her self-battering. "I should have done more of the planning myself. And I shouldn't have talked to her about Hayes. I know that upset her."

"Hayes?" Cait questioned.

Em nodded, sped up the hand wringing. "He downplayed his injuries, but I've heard talk that it's much worse than he's saying."

Maybe. Probably, Cait silently amended. She was betting he had more than a *cracked rib or two*. Since agreeing with Em on this would definitely take a bite out of any possible comfort, Cait kept it to herself.

"But did I keep my mouth shut about Hayes?" Em asked, and then she answered her own question. "No, I did not. I hung my wash on somebody else's line, and now I feel as low as a fat penguin's butt."

Sometimes, it took Cait a while to make sense of some of

Em's sayings, but she got these right away. Em hadn't kept her worry about Hayes to herself. She'd spilled to Sunny.

"Look, I'm not an expert on pregnancy and such," Cait said, "but I don't think worry can bring on this sort of thing."

Em turned to her, their gazes connecting, and it seemed as if Em were searching for some kind of hope that she could latch on to. But after a moment, there was no latching. Em patted Cait's hand.

"You're a good girl," Em declared. "Thoughtful and kind."

Uncomfortable with the compliments, Cait added, "Smart-mouthed."

Em smiled a little. "That, too. Always did appreciate that about you, and I figure it's why Hayes is smitten with you."

Smitten?

Smitten!

Cait was too stunned to actually get out the protest, but Em just kept on talking. "I need to tell Hayes about Sunny. But I have to get my head straight first. I don't want him to see me like this."

"I agree," Cait said hastily but still didn't have time to broach that *smitten* issue before Em started again.

"It wouldn't be good for Hayes to see his grandmother so distraught and muddled," Em said. "But I can't dawdle on this. I figure I've got an hour, maybe less, before somebody tells him that his sister's in the ER."

"It's definitely less," Cait assured the woman when she saw Hayes come walking up the hall.

He was wearing a green hospital gown, was barefooted and was making a wobbly beeline toward them. The nurse, Sharon Kay Garcia, was right behind him, clearly trying to get him to stop, but he just waved her off.

And he winced.

It was the pained expression of a man with a cracked rib or two. And maybe a lot more injuries than that.

"Where's Sunny?" Hayes demanded.

Since she doubted the petite Sharon Kay would succeed in stopping Hayes, Cait hurried to him and gently slid her arm around his waist. She didn't want to take the chance of him falling again.

"The doctor's with your sister now. Throttle back a notch," Cait added in a whisper. "Em's ready to lose it."

Of course, Hayes looked ready to lose it, too.

"He should be back in his room," Sharon Kay insisted. She also lowered her voice. "He's not wearing underwear, and the back of the gown is open."

Judging from the way Hayes scowled at the nurse, he wasn't going to add that to his worry plate.

"His butt's not much of a mystery," Cait reminded Sharon Kay. "Anyone who watches *Outlaw Rebels* on a regular basis has seen it multiple times." Still, Cait reached behind him and pinched the gown closed.

Hayes didn't scowl at her, but Cait thought he was attempting a frown. It came out as a grimace. One that vanished the moment Em joined them. Now he tried to give his grandmother some facial reassurance, but he failed big-time.

"You need to get back in bed," Em insisted. "We're already worried enough about you."

And there it was. The words that no doubt any member of Hayes's family could have said to him. *Already worried enough about you.* Words that would hopefully give him enough of a guilt trip to make him get off his feet and not risk another head-bashing concussion.

But Hayes stayed put.

No budging, not an inch.

Maybe it was the avalanche of emotions whirling in the room or that devastated look on Em's face. Heck, maybe it had something to do with the fact that Cait had her hand on Hayes's butt cheek while she stopped him from providing a derriere peep show to anyone who walked by. Whatever the reason, Cait heard herself say something she hadn't planned to say.

A lie.

"There's no need for any of you to worry about Hayes," Cait assured Em, and she just kept on lying. "He's really not hurt that bad."

Em shook her head and whispered, "But those stories in the tabloids—"

"Are not true," Cait interrupted. She didn't even pause to draw in what would be her next lying breath before she continued, "Hayes didn't come to Lone Star Ridge because he was having trouble. He came here to assure you that he was okay and so he could see his family. And me."

It seemed as if everything suddenly got very quiet. Maybe time even stopped, and Cait braced herself for a lightning bolt to strike her and set her lying pants on fire.

However, she got a bolt of a different kind.

"Yes, that's exactly why I came back," Hayes said, and then he added with a wink, "Climb on, babe, and kiss me."

CHAPTER FIVE

HAYES WASN'T SURE he'd ever seen someone's lips go so stiff while still managing to gape. But that was exactly the right description for Cait's mouth. Stiff, unyielding and gaping, probably because there was a boatload of surprise playing into this. She clearly hadn't expected him to hit her with his trademark come-on.

Then again, he hadn't expected to say it, either.

Once he'd realized that Cait was offering him a lifeline to ease his grandmother's worrying quota, he had thought maybe to give her a knowing wink, something that would clue Em into the fact that he was flirting with his love interest. However, the kiss demand was overkill. Especially adding that *babe* to it.

Shit on a stick, he hated that line, hated that the writers tried to work it into as many episodes as possible. And here he'd used it on Cait, the woman who was doing him a big-assed favor. Not just by covering said ass—literally—but by helping him out with his family.

Since he'd already committed himself, Hayes leaned in and dropped a kiss on her still-gaping mouth. It barely qualified as a kiss, but Hayes then had to pretend to himself that it didn't pack a wallop.

He wasn't in the wallop market right now.

All he wanted was his family to stop worrying about him and for Sunny to be okay. He couldn't do much about the

latter, but being with Cait would fix the worry. Well, hopefully it would. Hopefully, the walloping would stop, too,
so that he could do this facade without risking a hard-on.

He pulled back from the kiss, expecting to see shock
and maybe some anger in Cait's mist-gray eyes. Nope. Neither of those things. Instead, she looked a little unsteady.

Aroused, maybe?

But he had to be wrong about that. Yeah, she'd agreed to
this ruse, but that didn't mean she was going to sink into a
heat pit from their kisses. Especially one that started with
a lame line like *kiss me, babe.*

Em cleared her throat, and while he was pleased that his
grandmother no longer seemed concerned to the bone, Em
also didn't look convinced that the kiss had been the real
deal. Not yet, anyway. Hayes had faith in his acting skills
and believed that he would soon have Em taking him off
her "people to worry about" list.

The doors to the ER opened, and he saw McCall, Austin, Hadley and Leyton come rushing in. The troops had
arrived, and Em went to them, no doubt to fill them in on
what was happening. That gave Hayes a moment alone with
Cait. Well, kind of alone. The nurse was still hovering behind him, where he hoped she would stay put instead of
trying to get him back to his room.

"Thank you for doing that," Hayes whispered to Cait.

She blinked hard a couple of times, maybe in an attempt
to focus. "Sure." She opened her mouth as if she might say
more, possibly to take back her offer, but Cait just repeated
her "Sure" and looked away when his sisters and their
fiancés came toward them.

He got hugs from McCall and Hadley—gentle ones,
thank God—and Hadley gave him a little smirk when she
glanced behind and saw that Cait was holding his gown. If

this situation hadn't been so damn scary, with Sunny in distress, she likely would have made a joke, something along the lines of him showing his ass again. But there were no jokes today. However, both his sisters and Cait's brothers did notice that Cait and he were standing hip to hip and that Cait had her arm around him.

And that brought Hayes to a part of the plan he hadn't considered.

His sisters would be fully on board with him making a play for Cait, but her brothers might not approve. Like most good brothers, they wanted their sister to be happy. That translated to Cait not getting involved with the likes of him. The Jameson men especially wouldn't approve once Hayes got his act together and left town again. But that was a dragon he'd have to wait to slay another time because the door to the examining room opened.

Dr. Mendoza, who'd been in Lone Star Ridge for as long as Hayes could remember, approached the family and eyed the large gathering not with surprise but resignation.

"Sunny gave me permission to tell you that she should be fine," the doctor explained right off.

No one made any sighs of relief. Hayes especially didn't. That's because it was possible that Sunny had told Dr. Mendoza to say that to tone down the family worrying. Of course, maybe Hayes thought that because it was exactly what he was doing.

"And what about the baby?" McCall asked.

"He or she should be fine, too," Dr. Mendoza assured her. "Sunny's not having contractions, and light spotting often happens in the first trimester."

"So, it's not a miscarriage," Hadley murmured, and now there were some relief-generated sighs.

The doctor shook his head. "For now, she's okay, and I

want to keep it that way. She'll be on bed rest for a couple of days."

Since Hayes made a living at bullshitting people, he watched the doctor carefully to see if there were any telltale BS signs that he was sugarcoating any of this. He wasn't. And Hayes finally released the breath that had been backed up in his lungs.

"The best thing y'all can do for Sunny is go home and maybe fix some meals so she won't have to worry about that," the doctor added a moment later. "Keep the visits to a minimum, though, because she really does need plenty of rest."

"So, we can take Sunny home?" Em asked.

The doctor nodded. "But if she starts cramping, Shaw has instructions to bring her back ASAP." He started to leave, but he stopped when he spotted Hayes. "You should be in bed."

"That's what I told him." Sharon Kay spoke up.

"Listen to the nurse," Dr. Mendoza warned him and walked away.

Sharon Kay tried to take hold of Hayes again, but Cait stepped in and moved closer to him. "I'll make sure he gets back to his room," she tried to convince the nurse.

There must have been something in Cait's maneuver that garnered the attention of not only his siblings but also Sharon Kay. Many eyebrows lifted. Many puzzled looks and unspoken questions followed. She suspected her brothers did some unspoken questioning of her sanity, as well.

"Hayes came back to town to court Cait," Em volunteered, raising her own eyebrow.

Clearly, that was a surprise to, oh, everyone. Even Sharon Kay. Hayes got the feeling that there would have been some laughter over the absurdity of it had the surprise not turned to shock.

"Yes, that's why I came back," Hayes confirmed because the situation seemed to call for him saying something. Of course, that something should have been a whole lot better and without a hint of *Climb on, babe.*

"You should probably know, though," Cait said, sliding glances at both Em and him, "that Hayes and I won't be getting together. I mean, he did come back to see if there could ever be something between us, but I'm not interested in Hayes that way. Actually, I don't think he's truly interested in me, either, but I'm sort of the one who got away." She lifted her chin. "I'll have no trouble resisting him."

That was a good spin on things. One that he wished he'd thought of. It would cut down on the lies that Cait would have to tell. He could make advances, along with stupid requests for her to kiss him and such, and she could continue to look at him as if he were a severe case of jock itch. That wouldn't be a warm fuzzy stroke to his ego, but his ego was plenty big enough to come out unscathed.

He hoped.

The bottom line was this would be a much smoother way to go about this. Smooth and as slick as spit.

"Not getting together," Leyton repeated, staring at his sister.

"Not interested in Hayes that way," Austin piped in, giving Cait a hard stare, too.

"I'll have no trouble resisting him." Em, that time. "We'll be real careful of the piles of malarkey you're splatting around."

Well, hell.

Maybe this wasn't going to be slick as spit after all.

THE MOMENT CAIT got into her SUV she spotted the gun. Not a real one that most cops carried. This one was neon yellow plastic and fired out sponge darts. Obviously, this was some kind of joke that'd stemmed from her not being armed during the altercation with the Crocketts.

She glanced around and spotted Willy and the other deputy, Clara Rodriguez, peering out the window of the police station. Since they were giggling like toddlers on a sugar high, Cait surmised they were the culprits. It was indeed a fine joke—by their toddler-ish standards, anyway—but the joke was on them since Cait would fire it at them first chance she got. Which wouldn't happen for an hour or two because she had a two-prong chore to do.

Picking up Hayes from the hospital and, now that he was being released, driving him to Em's.

Hayes didn't know she would be doing this particular chauffeur duty. Not yet. Cait had only found out a few minutes earlier herself. It'd been a series of events that led her to be chosen as the main candidate for this, but Cait suspected there was more to the "series of events" than met the eye. There was perhaps some matchmaking going on. Hopefully, not any from the fates or destiny, though. Cait didn't want any cosmic crap interfering and pushing her toward Hayes.

That's why she'd avoided him for the past two days.

Of course, it was easy to avoid a man who was hospitalized, but she hadn't been able to escape the chatter about him going on in town. The chatter about her, too. And she especially hadn't dodged the yakking about Hayes trying to hook up with her. Cait wasn't sure who the source of that information had been, but she suspected it was the nurse, Sharon Kay. The woman probably hadn't revealed anything covered by privacy laws, but she'd likely blabbed about the personal stuff. Hayes's declaration, aka the lie, of returning to town to be with her was definitely blabber-worthy.

Cait tossed the dart gun onto the passenger seat and drove up the street to the hospital. She parked and was walking toward the main doors when she saw Hayes coming out. He was in a wheelchair, a nurse right behind him. Hospital rules, no doubt, but the rules apparently ended the moment he was outside. Gripping a little white bag, he immediately got out of the chair and glanced around the parking lot, probably looking for Hadley, who was supposed to be picking him up.

His gaze landed on Cait.

His face was more yellowy green today than the purplish red that it'd been when she'd seen him two nights ago. He was healing and had obviously mended enough to warrant his release. But there was none of his usual swagger or spring in his step when he made his way to her SUV. It was sort of a slow limping lumber, and he was obviously still in some pain. Cursing softly, Cait hurried to him.

"You volunteered to pick me up?" he asked.

"Sort of." She slipped her arm around his waist, taking some of his weight. "The twins have fevers, so Austin and McCall are taking them to their pediatrician. Shaw's with Sunny, making sure she stays in bed. And Hadley and Em got delayed in San Antonio with some wedding stuff, so Em called and asked me to come."

"Thanks," he muttered, "but if it's any trouble, I could get one of the nurses to drive me."

There would have certainly been volunteers coming out of the woodwork, but Cait suspected asking for favors like that came with a price tag. Those volunteers would then want to spend some time with him. And that was "time" with a side order of sex. A mere look from a hot guy like Hayes could be taken as an invitation for a whole lot more.

"It's no trouble," she assured him.

Well, not the kind of trouble he meant. This was her short shift at work, so even though it was noon, she was already done for the day. But there was the possibility for trouble of a different sort. After all, she had her arm around him again and was hip to hip with him. And, yes, the blasted tingles started.

"By the way, I'm to tell you that Leyton arranged to have someone take your motorcycle to Em's, but it'll need fixing. If you're interested, Barney Darnell has a repair shop at the end of Main Street."

"Thanks. I'll give him a call."

"The other thing I'm to tell you," she went on, "is that Shayla's mom talked to Leyton. She said that Shayla's back in a mental health facility in California." Cait hoped the woman got the help she needed and stayed out of Texas.

Because of Hayes's obvious aches and pains, Cait couldn't actually hurry the walk to her SUV, but she got him there as fast as their turtle-speed pace allowed. She opened the passenger door and froze. There was an assortment of things on the seat that she wished she'd taken the time to put away. Plastic handcuffs for the cops-and-bobbers game she played with Avery and Gracie. A sparkly fairy wand—also for games with them. On top of those was the sponge-dart gun. But the most visible thing by far on the seat was the photo.

The one of Hayes.

"Uh, my sister left that with me," Cait quickly explained, scooping it up and putting it and the other things on the dash. She made sure the photo went facedown and that the other stuff got piled on top of it. "She wanted me to get you to sign it."

The corner of his mouth lifted in that "panty melting" smile that was just as much of a trademark as the line that Kinsley had wanted in the autograph. Of course, all this body-to-body contact was trademark, too, and Cait got a multiple dose of it when she helped him into the seat. His arm grazed her breasts, and mercy, did her nipples notice it.

And they responded.

The little traitors puckered and tightened with arousal, which sent a stupid signal to the rest of her that it was a really good idea for Hayes to be touching her like this. It wasn't. No good could come from aroused nipples and the needy warmth that spread through her.

She could have sworn that Hayes noticed the whole arousal thing, too, because he flashed another of those smiles, followed by the heavily-lidded eye contact when he finally got in the seat and his gaze connected with hers.

"Why don't you like me?" he asked. He took the photo of himself that she'd tried to bury on the dash, fished around in her glove compartment and came up with a pen that he used to sign the picture before he slid it back where it had been.

The autograph didn't surprise her. He was probably used to doing things like that, but the direct question wasn't something she'd expected. Especially considering that his gaze then dropped to the front of her shirt, where he could see all that ridiculous nipple puckering going on. She looked like she was prepping to win a wet T-shirt contest.

"You mean, why don't I fawn over you like other women?" she grumbled. Cait shut the door, not as hard as she wanted, though, and she walked away to get back behind the wheel.

"Fawn over?" he questioned. "What the heck does that mean?"

When he winced as he was putting on his seat belt, she sighed and helped him with that, too. She wasn't trying to get back at him—probably not, anyway—but her forearm slid across the front of his jeans. And, yeah, she got a little satisfaction at feeling some nudges and twinges in that area.

"Fawn over," she repeated. Best to get her mind back on the conversation rather than the very vivid images she was getting of what had nudged and twinged. "It means getting all tongue-tied and eye fluttery. It's the same reaction that many women have for my dad."

Cait really hadn't intended to tack on that last bit. It'd just come sliding right out of her mouth, complete with the venomous tone she usually had whenever she mentioned her father.

"Ah, that explains a lot," Hayes said as she drove out of the parking lot.

Cait wasn't sure exactly what her remark had explained, but maybe Hayes thought she was comparing him to Marty Jameson. Which she was doing. Heck, what she'd already done only a couple of days ago.

"Both Marty and you are celebrities," she explained. "Both have the looks to draw in all the female attention you want."

And the biggie—both could and would crush a woman's heart in the blink of an eye.

"I haven't fathered a slew of kids like Marty," Hayes said, pointing out the big difference between her dad and him. "In fact, I haven't fathered any kids."

That was good, considering his often wonky Hollywood lifestyle. But there was another difference between Hayes and her dad. A massive one. Over the years, Hayes had actually been there for his sisters and Em. He'd stepped up time after time to help them, even if that help often came from a distance. Cait had no doubts that he would give up a kidney for any one of the triplets. Marty wouldn't bother even if there was nothing more than a fingernail donation involved.

"Still, I guess there are enough similarities to put you off making a play for me," Hayes added a moment later.

Well, there was that whole crushed-heart outcome. She could make that play for him and haul him into her bed, but then he'd leave and she would have to live with that broken heart. Worse, she'd have to live with the sympathy it would cause and do that in a town, and a family, where everyone would know just how hurt she was. Her brothers would use that to try to shelter her for years to come.

Considering all of that, and some other things as well, Cait started the drive to Em's. "I believe the only reason you want me to be interested in you is because I rejected you." When he gave her a blank look, she added, "Eleven years ago when you'd come home for a visit. We ran into each other at the Watering Hole, where I was celebrating my twenty-first birthday."

The Watering Hole was the town's only bar, and she gave Hayes a moment to recall the incident. She suspected he had many memories of bars. And of hooking up with women in them. But Cait finally saw the light in his eyes when it clicked.

"Yeah," he said, and judging from his change in tone, he was making a quick trip to the past. Or rather trying to do that. Cait suspected he didn't remember much about that night.

But she was wrong.

"Red dress," he went on. "That's what you were wear-

ing, and it was short. About yea high." He motioned to a
spot about midthigh. "You were wearing sandals. Silver
strappy ones that sparkled."

That was true. The sandals had been a new purchase,
to show off the pedi that Sunny had talked her into getting. In those days, Sunny hadn't made it back to town that
often, but she'd made a point of coming in for Cait's birthday. Cait had welcomed it even if Sunny usually treated
her like a kid sister.

"You had your hair down that night," he went on, and
he was obviously giving her a dose of that honeyed voice.
"And it was a little wispy with sweat because the AC was
barely sputtering out cool air."

"Wispy?" she questioned.

It was a bad question because it caused him to touch her
cheek. Well, actually, he skimmed his finger over her skin.
Damn tingles.

"Wispy," he verified, doing another finger skim before
finally drawing back his hand. "As in clinging to your face.
It made you look as if you'd just gotten out of bed after
having great sex."

Of course, he would equate a sweaty face with bed/sex.
Then again, she'd sort of thought the same thing about him
that night. He'd been wearing his usual jeans and tee, but
he'd been "wispy" faced, too. Mostly from the heat, but
perhaps the birthday tequila shots had added to it.

"Red dress, yes," she verified. "Strappy sandals, yes.
And yes, to me rejecting you."

Now he frowned, and his forehead bunched up. "We
were both a little drunk," he admitted. "Would you really
call that a rejection?"

Cait gave him a flat look. "You were more than a little
drunk, and you asked me to go to Prego Trail with you."

Prego Trail was the local make-out spot, and it hadn't been named for the spaghetti sauce but because more than one girl had gotten knocked up there. Despite the dubious reputations of both Hayes and the trail, Cait had been flattered.

And very tempted.

But she'd also had her three brothers nearby. If she had gone staggering out with Hayes, one of them would have tried to stop her. Or at least one would have attempted to talk some sense into her. It turned out, though, that her temptation was short-lived because Hayes had gotten a call. He'd stepped out to answer it and hadn't come back into the Watering Hole.

So, maybe the whole incident hadn't actually been an all-out rejection. But she had managed to give Hayes a scowl when he'd made the sloppy no-finesse pass at her, and she'd told him she wasn't interested.

Thankfully, Cait didn't have to dwell on it anymore or keep talking about it because they reached their destination. Cait pulled to a stop in front of the two-story yellow Victorian. Em's house. It was practically a landmark since all twelve seasons of *Little Cowgirls* had been filmed right here.

Hayes looked around as if trying to take it all in. There were plenty of good memories here. At least she thought there were. But Cait was also well aware of the bad ones, too. Hayes's folks had basically treated him like dung to be mucked out of the horse barn. He'd never been given a big part in *Little Cowgirls* but instead had been pushed to the shadows. Almost like a footnote. He'd been the triplets' surly brother who had turned from the cameras and spent most of those years behind the locked door of his bedroom.

Considering that he'd become such a big name in Hollywood, it was ironic that back then neither his parents nor the show's producers had seen the "star" potential in him. That was probably a good thing, though, because of his moneygrubbing mother, Sunshine. If Sunshine could have figured out a way to use Hayes and make money off him, she would have done it.

Cait got out, and she played another round of human crutch to get Hayes from the SUV. This time, the touching went up significantly when he slid off the seat—and against her. Crud. Her nipples reacted again. Her breath hitched. She probably went a little dewy looking.

Just like before, Hayes noticed, too. "You really want to keep pretending you're not interested in me?"

Cait had an easy answer for that. "Yes."

He chuckled, a husky, manly sound doused with so much testosterone that her body whined for an orgasm. Thankfully, there was no chance of that happening, and her body cooled when she spotted the woman in the doorway.

Bernice Biggs.

She was Em's part-time housekeeper, and like the twins' assistant preschool teacher, Fredricka Myers, Bernice brought crotchety to a whole new level. Cait had never seen the woman smile, and it quickly became clear that she wasn't going to see such a cheery expression today. Bernice scowled and then scowled harder when her attention landed on Hayes.

Despite the woman's obvious disapproval, Hayes doled out one of his grins to her. "As beautiful as ever," he told Bernice. He dropped a kiss on her cheek when Cait led him past her.

Bernice swiped away the kiss as if he'd left a slathering of Ebola-laced spittle on her. "You're not taking him upstairs to have sexual relations with him, are you?" she snarled at Cait.

"Absolutely," Cait said.

She considered making sure that Bernice realized that what she'd said was a snarky comeback and not the truth. Just so the woman wouldn't spill the gossip about it as gospel. But then Cait remembered Bernice didn't like anyone enough to shoot the breeze with them.

Cait led Hayes through the foyer and stopped at the bottom of the stairs. "Can you do this or should you just stay in one of the downstairs rooms?"

"I can do it," he assured her. "What's a little pain when possible *relations* is the reward?"

Cait appreciated his attempt to keep this light, but about halfway up, she realized this just wasn't a good idea. Hayes's breathing became labored, he had a white-knuckle grip on the stair rail and some sweat popped out on his face. It definitely didn't give him a wispy romantic look. Just the opposite. She thought he might keel over.

She stopped, giving him a minute to compose himself. "Just take a breath. We're in no hurry."

He looked at her. Gave her a little glimmer of a smile. And she thought he might do or say something to cover up the pain that he didn't want her to see. He didn't.

"Thanks for helping me," he murmured. There was no testosterone overload now, just the pain coating his voice. "I couldn't have done this without you."

"Sure you could have. You would have done it one step at a time. But you don't have to do it alone. I'm pretty good at lending a shoulder when needed."

"Yes, you are." His gaze stayed locked with hers. "Thank you for helping me," he repeated.

Okay, this chat had just moved below the surface. She saw the whirl of emotions there in his eyes. Like the pain, it was the very emotions he was trying to cover up with everyone else.

Apparently, not with her, though. Because they were right there for her to see. Maybe this was because she'd rejected him, but it was also possible that she was just Switzerland to him. Not a family member. Not a lover, current or ex. Not someone who planned on being his lover, current or ex. Just…neutral.

"FYI," Cait offered. "You don't have to pretend you're okay when you're around me."

He nodded and continued to stare at her for several long moments. "Why?"

Cait tested out that question a couple of different ways before responding, but she wasn't sure what he meant. "Why what?" she challenged.

Hayes started to say something. Then he stopped. He shook his head. "I was going to ask why you're being nice to me, but that sounds way too dick-ish and needy. Like fishing for you to say things other women say to me without fishing. Instead, I'll just say another thank-you. First for the help and second for giving that help in your own unique Cait way."

Now it was Cait who started to say something and then stopped. She hadn't considered his question dick-ish at all, but she could see the change in his eyes. It was almost a plea for her not to push this, that he'd already been pushed to his limits today. She got that. And she backed off.

Not literally.

Hayes would have fallen on his superior butt if she'd let go of him, but she wouldn't keep up this little chat about feelings and other things. For now, they were back to surface stuff.

"Why am I being nice to you?" Cait repeated, and she went with light. "Well, I have to take my relations whatever way I can get them."

He chuckled, winced and squeezed his eyes shut a moment. Steeling himself up. And it must have worked because when he opened his eyes, the other emotions were gone, and they got moving. They started up the steps again. It took them a while. Slow, easy movements. One at a time. Then an equally slow one-step-at-a-time walk down the upstairs hall to his room.

"You remembered which room was mine," he mumbled.

Oh, yeah. No way could she put that out of her memory. She'd visited his sisters here often enough, and once when Hayes had been about seventeen and she fourteen, she had gotten an eyeful when he'd come out of his room in just his boxers. It didn't matter that he had done that to yell at them for making so much noise. Nope. A memory like that stayed with a teenage girl.

Apparently, it stayed with a grown woman, too.

Cait had to do some maneuvering to get them both through the doorway of his bedroom. More touching. More grimaces and grunts of pain from Hayes. But she finally got him to his bed. She nearly tumbled down on it with him, but she anchored her feet to the floor just in time.

"Meds." He thrust the little white bag he'd been carrying at her. "I'd appreciate it if you opened the bottle and got me a couple of pills."

Cait did open the bottle, dropped two capsules into his somewhat shaky palm and then went into the adjoining bathroom to get him some water. By the time she made it back into the room, he'd already taken the pills and was trying to get his boots off.

"Drink," she insisted, helping him with that and then tackling the boots.

She considered he might want her to help him strip down, but he dashed that notion when he lay back, his head sinking into the pillow, and he pulled the side of the covers over him. His eyelids drifted down.

Cait didn't mean to stare, but like her nipples, her eyes also had minds of their own when it came to Hayes. Good grief. Even banged up like this, he was, well, straight fire, and just looking at him put a serious dent in her willpower. Thankfully, though, she wouldn't have to worry about that for long.

"Do you have your phone charged in case you need to call someone?" Cait whispered.

He nodded, and with his eyes still closed, he patted his pocket.

When he didn't add anything else, Cait took that as her signal to leave. She turned to tiptoe out, but the sound of his voice stopped her.

"I need to ask you for one more favor," he said. "A big one."

"No, I'm not going to have relations with you," she joked.

Even though he smiled a little, Cait could tell that whatever he was about to ask would indeed be big.

"Maybe in a day or two, then." His smile faded, and he opened his eyes, his gaze zeroing in on her. "I have an appointment in San Antonio next week, and I was wondering if you could take me if I'm not in any shape to drive yet. I don't want my family to know, so that's why I can't ask one of them," Hayes added.

She nodded, cautiously. "I can take you. Are you sure you're up to a ride like that?"

"I have to be." He stared at her. "Since I know you can keep secrets, I'll tell you that it's an appointment with a psychiatrist."

Well, that got her attention, and Cait thought of all those tabloid rumors about Hayes maybe trying to kill himself.

"Okay," she said, waiting for him to tell her more.

But he didn't follow through on her suspected *more*. Hayes just muttered a thank-you and closed his eyes again.

Cait stood there several more moments. Still nothing from him. But she saw the rhythmic rise and fall of his chest that let her know he'd gone to sleep. Or else he was pretending to sleep so she would just leave. So that's what she did. Cait turned and left, understanding that he was putting a lot of faith in her. Then again, she was indeed good at keeping secrets.

After all, Hayes had no idea just how much she cared about him.

And if she had any say in the matter, he never would.

CHAPTER SIX

HAYES DIDN'T MAKE a habit of studying himself in the mirror, but he did plenty of that today. He didn't especially want to walk into a shrink's office while looking as if he'd had the ever-livin' crap beat out of him. He already had enough to talk about without adding that to the appointment. Plus, if anyone recognized him in San Antonio and snapped his picture, which would almost certainly happen, a bruised face would pump up the gossip and speculation.

He'd filled his speculation quota for a while, and the gossip bucket had long since overflowed.

The bruises were almost all gone, thank God, and he no longer had a sore ass. A week could do that, but those seven days hadn't totally repaired his ribs. He could feel the dull ache in his right side. Still, it was better, and most of the time he could cover the grimace he made whenever any sudden movement caused the pain to spike.

He was feeling well enough that he had texted Cait to let her off the hook about driving him to his appointment with the shrink. He'd told her that he could arrange for a rental car to be brought to him. But Cait had nixed that and had merely texted back, asking what time she should pick him up.

Maybe Cait's feelings toward him were softening. More likely, though, she just felt sorry for him and doubted he was telling the truth when he said he could drive himself.

She was a cop, after all, and it could be she thought his cracked ribs might cause him to wreck. So, it was maybe some civic duty thrown in with the pity.

His phone dinged with a text from Abe Simon, his agent, and in Abe's usual chatty manner, the entire message was a single question mark. Hayes figured Abe was asking plenty, though. Since Hayes had told him about the motorcycle wreck, Abe likely wanted to know if he was recovering and maybe even when he would be back in California. Not that there was a pressing demand for Hayes's return, but Abe might be having to make reports to the studio.

Following Abe's "chatty" way, Hayes texted him back a thumbs-up emoji.

Unless something big broke with the studio, that would probably be the only conversation Abe and he would have during these next weeks before Hayes had to go back.

Since it was only about fifteen minutes before Cait was due to arrive, Hayes made his way down the stairs. Quietly. He'd told Em the night before that he would be going out with Cait today, but he didn't want her to quiz him about it. Especially since Em clearly wasn't buying his lie that he'd come back to town to test the waters with Cait and assure Em that he was truly okay. However, it wasn't Em he saw in the foyer.

It was Hadley.

Out of all his sisters, she was the best one for him to run into. Hadley was the least likely to quiz him on the whole "Cait" lie. He didn't play favorites with the triplets, but Hadley and he had more in common than he did with the others.

They were the biggest misfits in their misfit family.

Added to that, Hadley had lived in LA for years, where she'd had a costume-design business, so he saw her more often than Sunny or McCall. That would change, though, now that Hadley had moved back to Lone Star Ridge to marry Leyton.

Hayes approved of the marriage and thought that Leyton and his sister would smooth out each other's rough edges. That, and they were crazy in love. Plus, Hadley could continue to do her costume designs from here, so it would give her a way to carry on her career while actually having a life.

"Leaving for your *date* with Cait?" Hadley asked. Oh, yeah. She knew about his lie, and while this wasn't exactly a quiz, she was letting him know she wasn't buying his BS.

"Soon." He brushed a kiss on her cheek. And promptly switched the subject. "What are you doing here?"

"Helping Em with a few chores and working on the wedding dresses. Say, are you up to feeding a duck before you leave?"

"A duck?" Hayes frowned. "Is that some kind of euphemism or code?"

Hadley shook her head. "Nope. It's a real duck named Slackers. Are your ribs healed enough to feed it?"

He gave her a flat look. "I'm fine. Plenty healed enough to handle a duck."

"Maybe not this one. It belongs to Sunny, and he's meaner than a barrel of pissed-off snakes."

"Why the heck would anyone own a mean duck?"

Hadley shrugged. "It was a gift. A connection to the books that Sunny illustrates."

Slackers Quackers. Hayes knew about those. Hadn't known about the real-life duck.

"Anyway," Hadley went on, "Em had Slackers brought over here so that Sunny wouldn't try to take care of it herself, but Em's busy with some beading on the dresses and asked me to do it. I would, but the last time I tried, Slackers pecked the crap out of me."

"And you don't think it'll try to peck me?" he asked.

"No, I'm sure he will," Hadley readily admitted, smiling. "Slackers is an equal opportunity pecker, but I thought I could spread the fowl assaults around. I'll ask McCall to take duck duties tomorrow. Then I'll be back on board for Wednesday. By then, my current welts should have healed, and I'll be able to handle the new ones."

Ah, family. Sometimes sharing involved pecks, welts and other pitfalls, and if it was his turn in the feeding barrel, he would manage. After all, a mean duck was still just a duck.

"I'll take care of it," Hayes assured her.

"Good. The feed's in the barn in a bin by the first stall. Just remember to close the barn door after you feed him, or he'll get out. Don't want Sunny freaking out if we have to tell her we lost her brat of a duck." Hadley was about to walk away, probably to join Em in the sewing room, but Hayes stopped her with a question.

"Any updates about Sunny?" he asked.

"She's fine. No more spotting. We're still holding her off, though, on doing too much for the weddings."

Hayes was betting it wasn't easy to keep her on light duty. The weddings were only three weeks away, and Sunny would want her hand in that.

Hadley turned back to face him. Then hesitated. "I'm going to tell you something, but you should try to stay calm."

Hayes figured there was little else she could have said that would have made him feel the opposite of staying calm. "I'm not Sunny," he reminded her. "Spill it."

His sister gave an "all right" nod. And then dropped a bomb. "Sunshine called Sunny last night."

"Shit." Their mother was definitely a pitfall and far worse than any demon duck could ever be, and Hayes lost any shred of calm. Just the thought of Sunshine could make his blood boil. "What the hell did she want?"

"An invitation to the wedding. Apparently, she gave Sunny a sob story about wanting to see us all find our happily-ever-afters."

"Right," he grumbled. "She's up to something."

Hadley didn't hesitate with the sound of agreement she made. "Shaw's on it and will take any other call from her. He doesn't want our Satan's spawn of a mother upsetting Sunny."

Good. Shaw could handle that, but Hayes could work it from his angle, too. Basically, that would mean calling Sunshine and telling her to back the fuck off. He couldn't be even marginally polite with the woman because she would take it as an opening to try to do whatever she had up her sleeve.

"She probably thinks she can record the ceremony and get a crap-load of money for it when she sells it to the tabloids," Hadley suggested.

Yeah, and that meant he definitely needed to have that talk with her and lay down the law. He didn't want Sunshine anywhere near his sisters. "Isn't there still a restraining order against Sunshine?" he asked.

Hadley nodded. "It was part of a deal she worked out with Em. But Sunshine wants that order to be lifted long enough for her to come to the wedding. That's not going to happen."

No, it wouldn't, and Hayes was trying to figure out how best to keep Sunshine at bay as he started toward the door. But Hadley stopped him again.

"Do I need to thank you for the two new contracts I got

to do some costumes for a TV pilot and a music video?" she asked.

"No." He could answer that truthfully. No thanks was needed.

She rolled her eyes, kissed his cheek. "Thanks. I know you had a hand in it, maybe more than a hand," she amended, "and I appreciate it."

He shrugged, not comfortable with the praise. He was just doing what any brother should do.

"You're a great designer," he told her. "Those people are lucky to get you."

Apparently, Hadley wasn't comfortable with praise, either, because she did some shrugging, too.

After kissing her cheek, he made his way out of the house and toward the barn. It wasn't far, but the porch steps caused him a few winces. Maybe the duck wouldn't add to those aches. Even if it did, he didn't intend to complain to anyone about it. He didn't mind scuffing up his tough-guy image, but he didn't want it torn to shreds.

Hayes had just reached the barn door when Cait's SUV pulled into the driveway in front of the house. She was early, which was fine. This way they could take their time getting to San Antonio.

She spotted him, waved and then started toward him. Hayes forgot all about winces and possible image-ruining pecks as he watched her.

Oh, man.

Cait certainly had a way of capturing his complete attention, and she did it with seemingly no effort whatsoever. Today, though, he thought she might have indeed made an effort.

She was wearing a denim skirt instead of her usual jeans and sandals and a top that was the color of ripe peaches.

Her hair was down, and it spilled over her shoulders in a way that reminded him of the night of her twenty-first birthday. No wispiness, though. Nor was there any sweat. Not yet, anyway. But it was Texas hot today, so there was still a chance of that.

Her stride was as no-nonsense as the rest of her. She didn't swagger or move her hips the way some women did. It was just the steady, brisk pace of long, shapely female legs that brought her closer to him.

When she stopped next to him, Hayes caught her scent— where there might be some "nonsense" after all. She smelled like a meadow of softly scented flowers. And sin. Heavy on the sin. And he didn't think he was projecting.

"I have to feed the duck," he told her.

She blinked, and what he thought might be some mild horror crept into her eyes. "Slackers is in there?" she asked, tipping her head to the barn.

It might not have been a very manly reaction, but her obvious fear tightened his gut a little. "You know about Slackers?"

"Everybody knows about that feathered he-witch." Her answer was fast. Her expression as serious as if they'd been talking about Jack the Ripper. "The only ones who can feed that little turd without getting welts are Sunny and Em. Why did Em want you to do this?"

"Not Em. Hadley. And I more or less accepted the challenge because I thought she was BS-ing me about how mean Slackers is."

She looked at him with what could have been sympathy. Not the sympathy she'd doled out to him over his pain. No, this was more for his gullibility in letting Hadley talk him into taking on this chore.

"There's no BS exaggeration when it comes to Slackers,"

she declared, and Cait took the wooden rake that was propped against the side of the barn. "Let me help you get him into his pen. If you try to feed him while he's loose, he'll come at you."

"Crap," Hayes grumbled. "If this duck is so bad, why isn't he kept in the pen all the time?"

"Em thinks he needs exercise." Cait rolled her eyes at that. "He'll get it, too, when he comes flying at us. I'll go in ahead of you. Grab a broom or whatever else you can find once you're in there, and then bat it around until you can corral him into his pen."

"But we're not actually going to hit the duck, are we?" Hayes asked. He might have a tough-guy image on TV, but the idea of hitting a critter, even an ornery one, didn't hold any appeal to him.

"No hitting," Cait assured him. "Just protect yourself by swatting around whatever you find. Slackers is plenty fast enough to avoid a strike, but we can use his dodging to steer him in the direction we need him to go."

It sounded like a battle plan, and he glanced back at the house to make sure Hadley wasn't watching—and giggling—from the window. But nothing. If his sister had any watching or giggling plans, she was staying out of sight.

Since she was "armed" with the rake, he did let Cait go in first, and Hayes snagged a broom that was by one of the stalls. They stepped in, closing the door, and he used his elbow to turn on the switch for the stingy overhead light. It was just one dangling exposed bulb of seriously low wattage. With the door closed, there were plenty of dark corners and spaces for an ornery duck to hide.

"I don't see him," Cait whispered.

Just as all hell broke loose.

The sound was something Hayes thought he might hear

again in nightmares for years to come. It was sort of a screaming squawk, accompanied by wing flaps so loud that they could have come from a condor. This was no condor, though. It was a white duck—yeah, and he was seriously pissed off—and he swooped seemingly out of nowhere, dive-bombing right at them.

Cait used the rake to deflect him, and with what had to be record-breaking agility for a duck, Slackers dodged Cait and came at Hayes. He held up the broom like a shield. Good thing, too, because Slackers tried to peck the crap out of it.

Hayes had to keep dodging, deflecting, because Slackers just continued on swooping, trying to peck and maim. Cait used Hayes's maneuverings to hurry to the pen and yanked open the mesh wire door. She also scooped up some feed and threw it inside the pen.

He wasn't sure if ducks had actual nostrils, but Slackers had no trouble smelling his lunch, and he must have been hungry. Well, hungry-ish. The damn critter got in a few more peck attempts before it lit down onto the ground and waddled into the pen. Hayes thought it looked like a victory waddle, too, coupled with a smirk that Slackers gave when he shot a look back at them.

The moment the duck was inside the pen, Cait slammed the door shut and threw down the latch. Good grief, both Cait and he were breathing hard, and her hair that'd looked so sexy and flowing just minutes earlier was now mussed. Hayes figured he was plenty mussed, too, and he probably had bits of pecked-off broom straw all over him.

"Why isn't his feed in the pen?" Hayes asked in the midst of all that heavy breathing. "Then he might never come out."

"Again, that's Em's doing. She's delusional about Slackers and thinks he can be treated like a normal farm animal and fed like other ducks. He's not normal. He's batshit." Her head whipped up, and her gaze snapped to his. "Sorry about that."

It took him a moment to realize why she might be apologizing. "You think you offended me because I might be batshit, too?"

She shook her head. "No, it's, uh, just an insensitive thing to say, considering we're about to leave for your appointment."

Hayes listened for any hints of judgment about that from her, but there weren't any. Just the embarrassment because she'd inadvertently made a reference that might or might not have applied to his current mental state.

"It's a bad cliché, I know," he said. "An actor in therapy."

"Maybe it's a cliché for a reason," she muttered. "As in maybe it's needed for someone in a profession where make-believe can be just as real as reality."

"Maybe," he repeated. "But I know what people say. What the hell do I have to be depressed about? I'm rich and successful. Hell, women throw panties at me."

"I'll bet some do that while they're still wearing them." Her lips bent a little with a dry smile.

It was the perfect thing to say, and despite the battle with Slackers that they'd just had, the moment seemed sort of perfect, too. Not for what he wanted to do—which was kiss her—but the perfect time to get something off his chest.

"I've been on antidepressants for a while now," he confessed. "That's why I need this appointment, so I can get a refill. I also need to get what I call a tune-up. I just have to talk a few things out with someone who knows how to handle the mess going on in my head."

Again, he watched for any signs that Cait would indeed think he was batshit. Or too self-absorbed Hollywood.

Or the worst—that he was someone to be pitied.

He could handle the first two but not the third. Pity was what people had doled out to him when his sisters were in the spotlight during the *Little Cowgirls* years. Pity was what made you feel like nothing.

But again, Cait didn't appear to do any judging or pity-ing. "You lost a dear friend in one of the worst kind of ways. That sucks, and if the meds and tune-ups get you through that, then that's what you should do. The mistake would be not getting the help you need."

Like her panty remark, it was the right thing to say. Still, it was damn hard for him to dump all of this on Cait. Hard, sometimes, for him to dump it on himself. Hard to accept that he had some broken pieces inside him that might never be all put back together again.

There was shame over not being able to handle the de-pression. Shame at not being able to fix himself. He was a man, after all. The big brother. The one who should be able to mend himself and everything around him. Because of the therapy he'd had, Hayes had figured out that the feel-ing of shame went back to his childhood. The roots were there—of Sunshine creating the havoc and then insisting they all deal with it.

On their own.

No way in hell would she have wanted it to get out that one of her kids was in therapy. Then the press might get wind of it and speculate that she wasn't the perfect mother that she pretended to be in front of the camera.

He hated Sunshine for that. But sometimes he hated himself even more for not being able to take that power away from her and make himself whole again. His imper-fect mother didn't deserve to have the right to mess with his mind like this.

"I'll bet you've never seen a shrink or been on anti-depressants," Hayes threw out there.

"No," she agreed, but then she paused. In the quiet, Hayes could hear Slackers pecking at his food. "But I'll bet you've never had cramps from hell and needed double doses of extra-strength Midol."

Whatever he'd been expecting her to say, that hadn't been it. And it worked. It pushed away those lingering bad thoughts of Sunshine and turned his attention back to Cait. "Uh, that's true."

She made a sound as if she'd just proved her point and turned back toward the duck. "And I'm kind of sorry I just told you that. I should have come up with a different comparison."

"Like maybe pimple cream or wart-remover drops?" he tried, hoping to steer this back in a lighter direction.

It worked. She made a snarky little chuckle that sounded like music to his ears. "Yeah, but you're never going to forget the 'cramps from hell' confession. You'll never be able to see another bottle of Midol without thinking of me."

That was possibly true. Then again, there were a lot of things that would make him think of Cait. Including the image of her standing there with that rake still in her hand. It was a good image. Because her face was glowing a little, maybe from perspiration, but she was definitely in the wispy realm right now. And she looked good enough to eat. Or kiss.

Kissing her was probably the better option.

But not a wise one. Still, he'd done plenty of other un-wise things that hadn't given him as much of a kick of plea-sure as kissing Cait would. However, before he could jump into that unwiseness, his phone rang.

The sound cut through the barn and sent the duck squawking and flapping its wings. It didn't have a much better effect on Hayes when he saw Frances Weston's name on the screen. Hell. He hoped Shayla's mom wasn't calling to tell him that her daughter had skipped out of the treatment facility and was up to her old stalking tricks.

"I should take this," he said, showing Cait the screen before he put the call on speaker.

There was nothing Frances could say about Shayla that Hayes didn't want Cait to hear. After all, this might turn into a police matter if Shayla was on her way back to Lone Star Ridge to violate that restraining order he still had on her.

"Don't hang up," the caller said the moment she was on the line. Not Frances but rather Shayla. "Please. Don't hang up. I just need to talk to you for a minute. It's part of my therapy."

Hayes huffed. "Did you steal your mom's phone, or is she in on this?"

"I, uh, borrowed it. But that's not important."

Yeah, it was, because it meant Frances probably didn't have a clue that her daughter had lifted her phone to make a call she shouldn't be making. It also likely meant this wasn't actually any part of therapy.

"I need to apologize to you," Shayla went on. "I'm so sorry about everything I did, but I'm especially sorry about the accident. You know the last thing I'd want to do is hurt you."

Hayes wasn't sure of that at all. Maybe Shayla wouldn't intentionally run him off the road, but her "fervor" made her a very loose cannon.

"Shayla, I don't want you to call me again," he said and was about to hit the end-call button when Shayla blurted out something.

"It's because of that cop, right?" Shayla said, and Hayes heard the sob at the end of that question. "You're seeing that cop now, and you don't want anything to do with me."

Hayes nearly did some blurting of his own so he could tell Shayla that he'd never wanted anything to do with her, that she'd been a pain in his ass. But there was no need to slop out intentional hurt when there was a better way to go here.

"Shayla, you're violating the restraining order by calling me," Hayes reminded her.

"I know, but I had to talk to you." More sobs followed by more fast-talking. "I had to find out if you're really with that cop like the tabloids are saying."

So Shayla had read those. Hopefully, Sunny had gotten wind of them, too, so she'd quit worrying about him. "Yes, I'm with the cop," Hayes lied.

Except it wasn't technically a lie. He was indeed with Cait, and there was that whole thing about him wanting to kiss her.

"I don't know why you'd want to be with her," Shayla continued. Her voice had some whine in it now. "She's not even that pretty."

He winced and rethought his stupid idea to have this call on speaker. "Cait's a knockout," he disagreed. "She also wouldn't violate a restraining order or run me off the road. If she had a mental health problem, say like a pattern of stalking, she'd get help for it. And she's a pro at feeding ornery ducks."

That last part had just tumbled from his mouth, but he was glad it had when Cait snickered. He enjoyed seeing her happy. Enjoyed feeling that way himself, and that's why Hayes ended the call. He pressed the button without so much as a goodbye, and then he blocked Frances's number.

"A knockout," Cait repeated, snickering again. "You shoveled out some deep BS when you told her that one."

He turned to her, snared her gaze. "No, I didn't."

Hayes figured that Cait had picked up on the change in his tone. Definitely not snickering material. He was serious, and she must have seen that change on his face because she took a step back.

Cait shook her head. "I don't want to become just another seat warmer on your Harley."

"Yeah, I got that. But you're more than a seat warmer." Whatever the heck that meant. Hayes thought maybe it was like bedpost notches, but whatever it was, it notched up that need again to kiss her.

So that's what he did.

He didn't go with a "testing the waters" approach. He'd been testing Cait for years and didn't want to give her the chance to move another step back before he'd gotten a good taste of her. Hayes hooked his arm around her waist, ignoring the twinges he got from that moving around. Twinges be damned, he put his mouth on hers.

Oh, she was good and tasty, all right, and her mouth was a whole lot softer than he'd thought it would be. Soft and very welcoming. As was the soft sigh she made. He took in that sigh, letting it slide right into his own mouth as he deepened the kiss.

And he realized this was a big-assed mistake.

He got her taste, all right. Got the feel of her, too, in his arms. Ditto on receiving the maximum amount of pleasure you could get from a kiss. But pleasure that intense didn't stay in the mouth region. Nope. It zip-lined straight to his groin, causing his dick to get very interested in what might happen next. In fact, his dick, which was often delusional with stupid plans, thought this was a really good start to barn sex.

Cait might have been on the same barn-sex wavelength with him, too. That was a shocker. But Hayes got a strong impression of exactly that when she looked up at him. Her eyes had a dreamy look in them. *Wispy*, even. And her warm breath hit like kisses against his mouth. He didn't see a single sign that she was going to stop, so he figured she was about to go back in for kissing, round two. Followed by barn sex, round one.

Or not.

Shaking off that dreamy, wispy look as if it were a piece of broom straw, she started walking toward the door. Even though he'd been wrong about her wanting more kisses and barn sex, Hayes figured she would say something to acknowledge what'd just happened. Maybe even issue some kind of declaration that they should never share another lip-lock again. And she spoke, all right, without even looking back at him.

"We need to leave now," she said, as if discussing the weather. "Don't want you to be late for your appointment."

CHAPTER SEVEN

WITH THE FAMILIAR female chatter going on around her, Cait used the hot glue gun to put a seed pearl on the garter that one of the triplets would be wearing for the wedding. Across from her at the massive dining room table that they were using for the crafts, Sunny and McCall were tackling the little satin bags that would hold party favors for the guests while Em and Hadley were hand stitching lace on the dresses.

They'd moved these particular preparations to the Jameson ranch—Cait's childhood home and where her mother, Lenore, lived—where Sunny and Shaw lived now, temporarily, so there'd be room for Kinsley and the baby.

Kinsley had really gotten into the spirit of things and was painting the sign that would be at the entry of the reception. *This way to love, laughter and happily-ever-after.* Or rather *afters*, since there'd be three sets of "I do"s. Lenore was creating dried flower centerpieces that would go on one of the reception tables.

Cait didn't mind helping, but the decorating gene apparently hadn't dropped into her DNA pool. The mindless gluing of the seed pearls was one of the few such duties she could manage because, plain and simple, she sucked at the other stuff. But Cait plugged away at it, trying not to think that she still had about eight million pearls to go. Trying also not to think of Hayes.

Trying not to think that she was so screwed.

Cait had become acutely aware of that when Hayes *screwed* her with that barn kiss. In that scalding-hot span of thirty seconds or so, she'd realized she was going to lose this battle she was having with herself over guarding her heart or having great kisses and sex with Hayes. The great kisses and sex were winning out.

She'd spent three days trying to rid herself of these feelings. Sort of like one of those detox diets, but instead of kale smoothies and lemon water, she'd thrown herself into work. Cait had volunteered to do all of Leyton's reports along with her own. She'd done patrol duty—hardly a necessity in Lone Star Ridge—and she'd binge-watched everything in her Netflix queue.

It hadn't fixed diddly-squat.

Her body still wanted more kisses and the sex. And she hadn't been able to convince herself that Hayes's screwing her over wouldn't continue until he grew tired of said screwing and moved on.

According to tabloid stories she'd browsed over the years about Hayes's relationships, she estimated she had about a two-week shelf life. In other words, the eggs she'd bought today would still be fresh after Hayes had had his way with her and then dumped her. That wasn't much time in the grand scheme of things, but she was betting whatever he did with her, and to her, it would be far more memorable than an egg.

When Cait heard someone clear their throat, she looked up to see that every eye in the room was on her. Considering the set of their expressions, they'd been staring at her for quite a while.

"What?" Cait protested, automatically wiping her face with her glue-dotted hand.

"Uh, you muttered Hayes's name," Kinsley explained.

"And something about kale smoothies," McCall added.

"Eggs, too." That came from Sunny.

"*Sex* was the only word I caught," Hadley supplied.

Good grief. Now she'd taken to random mumbling? She couldn't even keep her private thoughts to herself? Apparently not. She'd just blabbered enough of her mental conversation aloud. Now everyone was waiting for an explanation.

"I'm not hooking up with Hayes," Cait said, hoping that would clarify things and silence any questions. She glanced around the room and thought she had allies here. "I mean, none of you can possibly believe Hayes would be the right choice for me."

Her mother smiled and winked at her. "Depends on what you're thinking about doing with him."

Cait frowned because she was sure that was a sexual comment. From her own mother, no less. Which made it worthy of a gazillion frowns along with some ick.

"Well, Hayes isn't exactly the 'white picket fence' type," Hadley tossed in, speaking to Cait around the pins she had in her mouth. Some of her words came out a little garbled, but Cait got the gist and was about to agree with her when Hadley added, "But then neither are you."

"Am, too," Cait protested and frowned again because she sounded whiny. And she was lying. The only fence she wanted was the one around the small pasture where she kept her horses. Not a picket one, either, but one strong enough so that the horses couldn't break through it.

She sighed, regrouped and tried again. "Hayes wants to see if he can try to make things work between him and me, but the chances of that happening, even temporarily, are nil. He'll leave after the wedding."

Cait was 100 percent sure that no one in the room could

dispute that last part. However, the *temporarily* was definitely on the dispute table. Thankfully, Hadley helped nix any discussion about that.

"I need to fit the bodice on you," Hadley told Sunny. "Your boobs are growing like fertilized weeds, and I want to make sure it isn't too tight."

Sunny stood, and with some help from Em, Hadley slipped the bodice over Sunny's shirt. Hadley gave it a few tugs, frowned, tugged some more. During the whole adjustment, she continued to glance at Cait as if prompting her to continue. Em, Sunny and McCall were doing the same thing.

Cait pretended she didn't notice.

There was silence, for a long time, and McCall was the one to break it. "Can you tell us where you took Hayes three days ago?"

Oh, that. Cait hadn't expected the quick shift in conversation, but she should have. This was Hayes's family, after all, and they'd want to know. She considered giving something about Hayes and her simply wanting to spend time together, but since she'd sucked at the other lies, she went with a dodge.

"Not really," Cait answered. "Anything about that should come from him, not me."

More silence, accompanied by lots of staring. Again, McCall spoke. "Do we need to be worried about him?"

"No," Cait said as fast as she could.

Of course, that was a partial lie, but she had to choose her battles here. She really didn't want Sunny upset, so it was a lie for the good of her future sister-in-law and future nephew or niece. And that gave Cait a reason to shift the conversation again.

"Do we need to be worried about you?" Cait asked Sunny.

"Yes, good question," McCall agreed. "Do we?" With the pins still in her mouth, Hadley muttered something similar.

"I'm fine. Really," Sunny added when she continued to get concerned stares. "The spotting has stopped. I also had the appointment with my OB, and he did an ultrasound. All is well."

The words were right, but Cait heard something she couldn't quite put her finger on. Apparently, the others heard it, too. Well, her mother didn't. Lenore kept her usual la-di-da expression—which was probably the way she avoided a lot of stress—but everyone else just kept staring at Sunny.

Finally, Sunny huffed. "I was going to wait and do a big reveal after the wedding, but I guess I can tell all of you now." She smiled, and as if a fairy princess had doused her with magic glow powder, Sunny's face lit up, and she slid her hand over her belly. "I'm pregnant with twins."

The surprised silence lasted a few more seconds before everyone dropped what they were doing and went to her. Sunny got a boatload of hugs, some of them transferring glitter, seed pearls and even some paint to her clothes and hair. But she didn't seem to mind. Her amazing smile only brightened even more, and it pleased Cait all the way down to the soles of her feet.

Out of all the triplets, Sunny was the one who'd most wanted to be a mom. Ironic since she would technically be the last to accomplish that particular goal. McCall had Austin's twins, whom she was planning on adopting, and in somewhat of a bombshell, Hadley had been a surrogate for a friend. The child she'd carried, Bailey, was now a big part of Hadley's life and had already spent some time with Leyton and her. Times were definitely changing for the former *Little Cowgirls*.

Cait was mega happy for them. She truly was. Equally happy for her own brothers, too, but for the first time in her life, she was starting to wonder if one day she, too, would want more. Frowning at that thought and mildly pissed off because her body was giving her nudges for Hayes to be considered in that "more" future, she pushed all of that aside.

"Hayes," Kinsley said.

Cait practically snapped to attention. Good grief, had she done more of that mindless mumbling and said his name? But when she glanced up, she realized Kinsley's attention wasn't on her. The girl was looking out the window.

"It's Shaw," Kinsley added, "and he has Hayes with him."

"Shaw shouldn't see the dresses," Em quickly pointed out. Or at least that's possibly what she said. She had pins in her mouth again and mumbled some syllables that didn't exist in the English language.

Sunny shook her head and got a scolding from Hadley, who told her not to move. "Someone should go to the door and warn him." She glanced around the room, and at that exact moment, the only one who didn't have some kind of wedding stuff in her hands, or her mouth, was Cait.

Cait suspected a tad of matchmaking might be going on, but she chose to take care of the duty herself when Kinsley volunteered. This was despite the fact the girl was holding a dripping-wet paintbrush and was far too eager to ogle a straight-fire man that Cait didn't want her ogling.

"I'll do it," Cait muttered, and she headed to the door, ignoring the giggly twitter of conversation that started the moment she stepped out of the room.

Yeah, this was matchmaking. More than a tad of it, too.

That should have riled her, and it might have, if Cait hadn't been just a teensy bit thrilled at seeing Hayes. Of course, she'd eat every bit of the wedding decorations, seed pearls and pins included, before admitting that.

She hurried to the door and opened it before Shaw and Hayes could just waltz in, but she quickly learned that Shaw had no such waltzing intentions anyway. He was already heading toward the barn. Hayes was in the front yard, glancing around, but he turned toward her the moment Cait stepped onto the porch.

He smiled.

And it was indeed that panty-melting smile.

"You can't come in," Cait warned him. "There's a rule that no one with a penis can see the wedding dresses. Or something like that," she added in a mutter.

The smile made it to his equally panty-melting eyes. "I think that only applies to the grooms, but don't worry—I won't be coming in. Shaw needed to get something to fix Slackers's pen, and I rode over with him so I could get out of the house. I suggested a moat and castle guards for the pen, but Shaw figured a sturdier latch would do the trick."

One could hope.

It occurred to her that Hayes might be getting cabin fever. After all, he had a very busy, very public life in California, and other than Em's truck, which his grandmother had driven here, he didn't have a vehicle. If the rumors she'd heard were right, it'd be another day or two before the parts came in for his motorcycle to be fixed. Even then, he might not be up to riding it for a while.

With that smile still in place, he stepped on the porch with her. He reached up, and her heart skipped a couple of beats when she thought he was going to touch her. And he did, sort of. Hayes plucked a seed pearl from her hair and held it up to examine it.

"Wedding decorations," she supplied, snatching the seed pearl and flicking it away.

Hayes removed another. Then another. And then several more from her cheeks. Of course, that meant he was now touching her in multiple places, and she wasn't backing away.

"I can't stop thinking about you," he said in that foreplay drawl.

"Really? I haven't given you any thought whatsoever."

Her comment would have been a whole lot more believable if she hadn't sighed a little at the end of it. But she couldn't help herself. Now that she knew what it was like to have his mouth on hers, Cait was having trouble not remembering, well, his mouth being on hers.

And wanting it there again.

"You should go on a date with me," Hayes added, and this time she didn't think his touch on her cheek was for seed-pearl removal. He lingered there a little too long before he slid his fingers down her chin.

"Your family doesn't believe the ruse that you came back here to be with me," she pointed out. And, crap, she sighed again. Apparently, touching was just as effective as full-out kissing. "So there's no reason for us to go on a date."

"Sure there is. We could have dinner, do some more kissing and see where that leads us."

Cait managed both a scowl and an eye roll. "We already know where kissing would lead us."

He smiled, leaned in.

Cait stopped him with her hand to his chest. "So help me, if you say *climb on, bitch, and kiss me*, I'm going to make sure you get duck-feeding duty for an entire week."

That didn't stop him, and before Cait could come up with a worse threat, Hayes managed to sneak in a kiss. It was just the slightest brush of his lips, but it rang her bell way too loud, and she might have reached out and hauled him to her for a real kiss, but another sound got her attention.

Shaw.

He cleared his throat, and when Cait managed to get her vision clear, she saw he was in the yard. He had a toolbox in one hand and was sporting an expression of brotherly disapproval. Of course, that only made her want to French Hayes just to show Shaw that he didn't have any say in her love life. Or rather her kissing life. But she wasn't stupid and didn't want to get scorched playing with the fire whose name was Hayes Dalton.

Hayes looked back at Shaw but didn't offer any kind of apology, either. "I was just asking Cait out on a date."

Shaw's eyebrow rose while his mouth bent into a deeper frown. "If I tell her that's a shitty idea, she'll do it to spite me."

Her brother clearly knew her well.

"So," Shaw went on, "it's a shitty idea."

The smile he added to that had her doing a mental double take. Was this some kind of reverse-reverse psychology, or did he actually want her to go on a date, one that was probably a shitty idea, with Hayes? She doubted it was the latter. After all, Shaw knew Hayes's reputation when it came to women, so it was obvious that her brother was trying to be sneaky.

"All right," Cait said, flashing her own smile. "Hayes, I'll go out with you."

She wasn't sure who was more surprised by her acceptance, Shaw or Hayes, but Hayes quickly recovered. "Friday night around six?" he asked, quickly nailing down the date and time.

"That works for me," she assured him, keeping her gloating gaze on Shaw.

However, Shaw was no longer looking at her. He had his attention on the white sedan that was turning into the driveway. It wasn't a vehicle that Cait recognized, but it could be someone who'd come for ranch business with Shaw. Or maybe even a "fan," since her brothers had been getting a lot of press because of the upcoming weddings.

The car pulled to a stop, and even though the driver turned off the engine, it took several long moments before she stepped out. Correction—before *they* stepped out. It was a silver-haired woman who appeared to be in her sixties and a lanky teenage boy with dark brown hair. They both took deep breaths before they started walking toward the house.

"Can I help you?" Shaw asked, but then she saw her brother freeze. It was almost comical the way his mouth dropped open.

Almost.

But Cait figured her own mouth had done some dropping open as well before the muttered cursing started. Not just from her but also from Shaw.

"What?" Hayes asked, following her gaze to the approaching visitors.

Cait hadn't thought Hayes would see the connection that Shaw and she had already made. After all, Cait and her brothers had had a lot of experience with this sort of thing. Still, Hayes worked it out, no doubt when he saw the strong family resemblance between the boy, Shaw and her.

She went down the porch steps, not hurrying—more like resigned—and she joined Shaw in the yard. Neither of them said anything. They just waited for this particular bowling ball to come rolling at them.

"I'm Debra Randall," the woman greeted them, her voice cracking. "You're Marty's children?"

"Yes," Cait verified. "This is my brother Shaw, and I'm Cait."

Like her voice, Debra's nod was plenty shaky. So was her hand that fluttered toward the boy. "This is Adam Wallis. He's, uh—"

"My father's son," Cait provided, and she bit back the litany of curse words she wanted to aim at Marty. Shit on a stick, would the man never learn to keep his jeans zipped?

Debra shook her head. "No."

Cait cut off the spate of mental profanity that was about to flow and did another double take of the boy. He was about thirteen or fourteen, she guessed, and he had the same color of hair as Shaw and her. Same gray eyes, too. He was also the spitting image of her dear ol' dad.

"Not Marty's son," Debra corrected. "This is his grandson."

"Oh," Cait muttered, and that was pretty much all she managed to get out.

"I'm afraid I'm going to need to ask a big favor," Debra continued. "I'm going to need Marty to take temporary custody of Adam."

CHAPTER EIGHT

FOR YEARS, HAYES had heard about the steady flow of Marty's offspring showing up in Lone Star Ridge, but apparently he was now a firsthand witness to it.

Or rather a witness to the next generation of the man's offspring.

Hayes was betting that Cait and her brother hadn't seen that one coming. But it made sense in a Marty sort of way. Marty was in his sixties, and since he'd been sleeping around for decades, it seemed inevitable that one of his "love" children would have a child of their own.

"You want Marty to take custody of him?" Cait repeated. "Of Adam?" she amended, staring at the boy.

Adam, however, didn't look at Cait or Shaw. He was doing some serious gaze dodging, along with looking as if he wanted to be anywhere but here.

Debra nodded. "I don't have any other options. Marty has to take Adam for a couple of months." She wasn't dodging anyone's gaze. In fact, she continued to shift direct eye contact between Cait and Shaw. "May we go inside and talk?"

Shaw didn't budge because he might be considering if this would upset his mother. Then again, this whole offspring showing up wouldn't be Lenore's first rodeo.

"Mom and the others are in the dining room," Hayes heard Cait tell Shaw. "Doing wedding stuff," she said to

Debra. "Shaw can't go in there because his fiancée doesn't want him to see the dress."

Shaw nodded, and he motioned for Debra and Adam to follow him. "We'll go in through the kitchen," Shaw suggested. Then he added to Cait, "Let the others know what's going on but tell them to stay put. I'll handle this."

After some hesitation of her own, Cait mumbled an agreement. "Go with Shaw," she whispered to Hayes. "I'll be there in a few minutes," she added and then went back into the house through the front door.

Hayes couldn't imagine why Cait would think he would be of any help when it came to something like this. But then maybe she just wanted Shaw to have some moral support while she dealt with her mother. With Kinsley, too. After all, Adam was the girl's nephew.

Debra fell in step with Shaw as he started toward the back of the sprawling house. Hayes trailed along with Adam. The boy glanced at Hayes, and when Adam did a quick double take, Hayes saw the recognition in his eyes.

"You're Slade McClendon," the boy said with a little awe in his voice. "I mean, that's who you play on *Outlaw Rebels*."

Since the kid looked as if he could use it, Hayes smiled and extended his hand in a friendly greeting. "I'm Hayes Dalton."

For the first time since Adam had stepped from the car, he seemed to relax a little. It didn't last. After the handshake, they walked into the Jameson kitchen, and Hayes could practically see the nerves jumping off the boy.

"Have a seat," Shaw offered, motioning for them to sit at the table that was just as sprawling as the rest of the house. "You want something to drink?"

Debra shook her head. Adam muttered something that sounded like a no. They sat, but Shaw poured himself a glass of ice water and was probably wishing it was a stiff shot of whiskey. Hayes helped himself to a Coke and got out two extras in case Adam and Debra changed their minds.

"This is my soon-to-be brother-in-law, Hayes Dalton," Shaw said, making introductions. He stayed standing.

Debra gave him a polite nod, and as Adam had done moments earlier, Hayes saw the recognition hit her. "Yes. I've read about you. I'm sorry about your friend dying. Ivy Malloy. The stories say you're having a hard time getting over her death."

Hayes hadn't expected Ivy's name to come up, so he hadn't steeled himself for it. As always, he felt the thick layer of grief wash over him. This wasn't about him, he reminded himself, but obviously the tabloids were still playing up the story. And as long as they did, there'd be people like Debra doling out sympathy. Most people meant well, but each reminder was like getting a sucker punch to his cracked ribs.

"Thank you," Hayes muttered to the woman, even though he certainly wasn't grateful to her for bringing up the subject.

Debra nodded again and turned her attention back to Shaw. She also dragged in a long breath. "Marty and I were together years ago. I read about his engagement to your mom the day I found out I was pregnant. I didn't want to disrupt his life, so I didn't tell him. My daughter, Renee, is Marty's daughter and Adam's mother."

Hayes didn't want to pass judgment on someone he'd just met, but he hoped like hell no woman ever did that to him. If he had a kid, he'd want to know about it. Then again, he wasn't Marty Jameson. Marty probably considered it a blessing that Debra had kept such monumental news to herself.

"I never got married," Debra went on. "Neither did Adam's

mother. Adam's father has never been in the picture, and I don't even know how to get in touch with him. I don't have anyone else to turn to." She paused, swallowed hard.

"My mom's in jail," Adam filled in for his grandmother just as Cait walked into the kitchen.

Hayes had to hand it to her. Cait didn't look shocked at the jail revelation. Then again, they'd dealt with a lot of fallout from Marty's crap over the years, so maybe this was a version of old news. Marty was the one person who could give his own mom a run for the "worst parent ever" title. At least, though, Marty hadn't robbed his kids the way Sunshine had, but then, to the best of his knowledge, Sunshine hadn't left a string of offspring.

"The others won't come in here," Cait relayed to her brother. She took Hayes's Coke, downed a long gulp the way one would take bad medicine and turned back to Adam. "Your mom's in jail?" she repeated, no doubt to prompt the boy to continue.

However, it was Debra who took up the explanation. "Renee and I had a little flower shop in San Antonio. We worked hard at it, built it from scratch, but we allowed the wrong person to help us run it."

"My mom's boyfriend, Eddie," Adam supplied, his voice a disapproving grumble.

Debra nodded. "Renee and I had Eddie manage our finances, and he used our business. Used us," she amended and then paused. "We were all convicted of money laundering."

Hayes held back a wince. It wasn't the most serious crime you could be arrested for, but it was still big.

"Eddie got the longest sentence, ten years," Debra continued. "Renee got six months and has already started serving her time. I have to surrender myself next week. I only got three months, and the court gave me some time to put our personal matters in order."

Hayes didn't have any trouble following the dots on this one. Neither did Cait. Adam was the personal matter, and that's why Debra had brought him here.

"And you thought Marty would take his grandson for those three months," Cait summarized.

Debra's next nod was even shakier, and she was blinking back tears. "Marty wouldn't have to do much, just give Adam a safe place to stay. I've already gotten permission from his school so he can take his courses online." Her words ran together with her rushed breathing. "I've been trying to find someone else to take Adam, but I don't have anyone. I asked the parents of all of Adam's friends, but—"

"I don't have friends anymore now that my mom's in jail," Adam interrupted.

Kids could be Satan's spawn when it came to things like this, but Hayes suspected those kids' parents wouldn't want to take in Adam when his mom and grandmother were criminals.

"Then I read in one of the tabloids that Marty was raising a child, a teenager, who he recently found out was his," Debra went on. "So I thought maybe he could take Adam for a little while, too."

Cait's face and entire body language was a scowl. "The tabloids got it wrong. Marty didn't take in a teenager. My mother, Shaw and his fiancée are raising my sister, Kinsley."

"Oh, I see." Debra's voice had gone even quieter, and she was losing the battle on blinking back those tears.

"Gram, they don't want me here," Adam said. No tears for him. No bitterness, either, though Hayes thought it wouldn't be an overreaction for the kid to feel some of that, what with his mom and grandmother headed off to jail.

"It's not that," Cait insisted. She stopped scowling when she turned to Adam. In fact, she seemed to turn a little sisterly. There was plenty of sympathy in the look she gave him. "It's just that Marty doesn't live here. He doesn't really live anywhere. He owns several houses, but he's rarely in any of them. He spends most of his time in his tour bus."

Debra nodded. "But one of the articles said he'd be back for his sons' weddings. Since that's only in a couple of weeks, I thought he might be around."

"He might come," Shaw said on a huff. "Or not. Marty's not reliable." He took out his phone. "But I'll try to call him."

"No, I'll do it," Cait insisted. She yanked her phone from her pocket and walked out.

If there were a picture of awkward silence, Hayes decided it would be what was going on in the kitchen right now. Debra was obviously humiliated and desperate. And Hayes had to feel for the boy, especially since he doubted Marty would just come rushing back to help.

Cait might have stepped out to have some privacy when she made the call, but she hadn't gone nearly far enough into the house. Her voice carried into the kitchen, and all of them heard her once the conversation got started. It was possible that people two counties away had heard it.

"Your grandson's here and he needs your help," Cait snapped, and then she paused, obviously listening to what her father had to say. "That's right, your grandson." Another pause. "Debra Randall." More pausing. "It doesn't matter if you don't remember her because this kid is your grandson. He's the spitting image of you."

He was. Hayes thought Marty wouldn't dispute that if he got one glimpse of Adam.

"You need to come back to the ranch and deal with this," Cait added to her father several seconds later. "Adam's grandmother and mother are in legal trouble, and they need a place for him to stay for a while." A very long pause followed. "No, *you* need to come back now. Not your agent. Not a friend. And that's *now* as in normal time, not Marty Jameson time of whenever it suits you."

Hayes didn't need to hear Marty's side of the conversation to know that the man was trying to put Cait off, and he wondered just how often they'd gone through similar conversations.

Shaw groaned when he heard Cait grumble some profanity, and on a heavy sigh, he excused himself and went in the direction of his sister's voice. Hayes considered starting some small talk with Debra and Adam, but he doubted it would help put them at ease. The boy's immediate future was on the line here, and Cait's call was the focus of their attention.

"I didn't have Marty's number," Debra said softly. "Do you think it would help if I tried to talk to him?"

Considering that Marty didn't seem to even remember the woman, the answer to that was no. "It's probably best to let Cait and Shaw handle this," Hayes settled for saying.

"No, you can't wait until the weddings to come," Cait told her father. Whatever Marty's response was, it caused both Shaw and her to groan. "For once in your life," Cait snapped, "man up and do the right thing by at least one person in your gene pool."

Debra and Adam probably thought Cait was being rude by speaking to Marty like that, but they didn't know the family history/gene pool that Marty had created.

"I didn't want to cause trouble for anyone," Adam murmured just as Shaw came back into the kitchen.

"You didn't," Shaw assured him. "None of this is your fault, and we'll work it out."

Hayes wondered how many times Shaw had said that, too. Plenty. And, yep, for the most part, he'd worked it out with the help of his siblings. Marty hadn't raised any of his own kids, but his kids had basically raised each other. Cait hadn't credited herself with that when she'd named who was taking care of Kinsley. Cait did plenty for her sister. Just as she'd likely do plenty for Adam.

Cait was a little flushed when she came back in and muttered, "Sorry about that. Marty says he'll try to clear his schedule so he can come home. He's supposed to call me back to let me know."

That was Hayes's cue to leave and let them finish sorting this out. He wanted to go to Cait and hug her. Wanted to try to cool down that anger he saw bubbling inside her, but she might not appreciate any PDA right now.

"I should be going," Hayes said, checking his watch for no particular reason. "I'll take Em's truck, and when she's finished with the sewing, I'll come back and get her." He snagged Cait's gaze. "If I can do anything to help, let me know."

He left them there and considered going in to tell Em about the truck, but he wasn't up to answering any questions about their visitor. That should come from Cait and Shaw once they'd decided how to deal with it. So Hayes left Em a note to let her know he had her truck.

As expected, he found the keys in the ignition, right where his grandmother always left them because there was no chance of anyone stealing the vehicle. He felt a twinge of pain in his ribs when he shifted the gears on the old manual transmission and started the drive back to Em's ranch. It was a reminder that he was healing but wasn't 100 percent. That in turn gave him another reminder of something that'd happened before Adam and his grandmother had shown up.

His date with Cait.

Since he wasn't an idiot, he knew the only reason she had agreed to go out with him was because Shaw had been giving a warning glower. So Hayes owed her "yes" to Cait's defiant streak, but maybe once he had wined and dined her...

He mentally stopped.

Then what? More kissing? Sex? Yeah, all of that was still on the proverbial table. Which might mean he was an idiot after all. He wanted to be with Cait. Wanted it more than he wished his ribs would stop aching. But there was that whole "big picture" thing. In three weeks, give or take a day or two, he'd be leaving, and he really didn't want to hurt her.

Hayes mentally stopped again.

There was no way Cait would just hand him her heart. Not when she thought of him as having the same morals as her father or the strayest of stray alley cats. Hayes didn't make it a habit of sleeping around, but Cait wouldn't believe it. That meant her attraction to him was just that.

An attraction.

It likely wouldn't go beyond kisses and then possible sex. They could spend a little time together having fun and burning off some of that heat they'd generated, and then...

He had to mentally stop yet again.

Shit.

Hayes was about to launch into an argument with himself about why flings could get messed up, but the moment he pulled to a stop in front of Em's, his phone rang. He saw a familiar name pop up on the screen. Kurt Benson. He played Hayes's father on *Outlaw Rebels*, and at seventy-four, Kurt was still as much of a womanizer as Marty. Kurt also wouldn't be calling to bust Hayes's chops about his forced hiatus from the show.

"Kurt," Hayes greeted him when he answered the call.

"Hello, Hayes," the woman responded.

Hayes responded, too, with another "Shit," but this one he said aloud. Not Kurt, but he instantly recognized the voice of the caller.

His mother, Sunshine.

"Don't hang up," Sunshine immediately said. "And don't blame Kurt for this. I sneaked his phone because I knew you wouldn't answer the call if you knew it was me."

"Damn straight I wouldn't have. Did you do something to Kurt?" Hayes snapped.

"No." She sounded damn right cheery. "I'm just spending some time with him these days."

In other words, Sunshine had probably slept with Kurt, maybe gotten him drunk—which wouldn't have been hard to do—and then she'd coaxed his phone password out of him.

"There's nothing you've got to say that I want to hear," Hayes told his mother.

"Yes, there is," she insisted. "I need to see you and your sisters, and trust me, this is a meeting you'll want to take."

Hayes was about to hit the end-call button when Sunshine said the one thing that could make him stop and listen.

"This is about Ivy."

CAIT WAS TRYING hard to rein in her temper because she didn't want Adam to think one drop of her anger was aimed at him. The boy was already in a bad place and didn't need her adding anything negative to it. Still, it was hard not to spew some venom about her father.

The very father who was supposed to call her right back.

Well, the *right back* was going on an hour now, and while that wasn't a huge amount of time for most things, it was when Adam and Debra were waiting to hear the outcome of their fate.

Shaw had updated Sunny and the others as to what was happening, and Em and the triplets had appeared in the kitchen only long enough for introductions before going back to the sewing and decorating. Cait considered that a wise thing to do since it might be even more hours before Marty called.

Or never.

However, Lenore and Kinsley had stayed in the kitchen, which made sense since this was, after all, a family crisis and they were family. Well, Kinsley was by DNA and Lenore was family in a big-picture kind of way because she had more than enough heart to accept any of Marty's offspring who showed up. She'd done that especially with Leyton and had ended up adopting him. Lenore likely would have done the same to Kinsley had Shaw and Sunny not stepped up to the plate.

Her mother was doing her usual "cheerful hostess" stuff and had made a fresh pot of coffee and arranged some apple muffins that she'd gotten from the diner onto a pretty plate. The fact Lenore hadn't baked them herself was the reason the muffins were actually getting eaten.

Kinsley added some teenage surliness to the mix—again aimed at Marty. Kinsley might only be fifteen, but she already knew the score when it came to their father. When she wasn't simmering in surliness, though, Kinsley had also managed to engage her nephew in some chatter about high school, favorite subjects.

And their shared interest in *Outlaw Rebels*.

That in turn led to chatter about Hayes. Apparently, the teens had some hero-worship thing going on, though Cait knew that Kinsley's interest was because Hayes was straight fire. Adam seemed to be a big fan of the show itself, and he liked the motorcycles.

"Would any of you like some of my special tuna surprise casserole?" Lenore asked.

Cait didn't gasp, but it was a close call. Eating anything that Lenore had prepared wouldn't help Adam's situation. He'd have digestion issues from Hades to go along with the wait to hear what was going to happen to him.

"No, thank you," Debra said, causing both Cait and Shaw to release the breaths they'd been holding. "You're being very kind to us, and I appreciate that." She gave her grandson's hand a gentle squeeze. "I just want you to know that I was with Marty before he married you. I don't want you to think he cheated on you with me."

Lenore dismissed that with a wave that halted in mid-wave when Cait's phone rang. The sound shot through the room, and everyone was clearly waiting for her to check her screen.

"It's Marty," Cait verified.

She debated putting the call on speaker, but since you never knew what would come out of Marty's mouth, she opted against it. No use hitting Adam with another hammer if Marty was about to refuse to help.

Cait pressed the answer button on her phone but didn't issue a greeting. Instead, she let Marty start the conversation, and if it wasn't what she wanted to hear, she'd take the call into another room and verbally kick his sorry butt into the middle of next week.

"Okay, I cleared a few things on my schedule," Marty said, "and I can be at the ranch in a day or two." Cait relaxed just a fraction until her father added, "A week or two at the latest."

Crap. That could turn into *a month or two at the latest*. Or years. There'd been a long stretch of five years once when Marty hadn't shown his face in Lone Star Ridge. During that time, he'd probably knocked up multiple women and turned his back on more of his own kids.

"Can you nail it down to a more specific day and time?" Cait snarled once she managed to unclench the muscles in her jaw. "Maybe like tomorrow at noon?"

"Sorry, but I can't do that. I've got gigs scheduled, and I can't just ditch them."

That was ironic since he had no trouble ditching daddy or granddaddy duty. She wanted to growl something snarky, but Adam was staring at her, not only listening to her every word but watching her body language.

"A day or two?" Cait repeated instead. "Get here then." And she made sure that didn't sound like a vague suggestion but the demand that it was.

"I'll sure try," Marty answered. Unfortunately, that did indeed sound vague to Cait. "In the meantime, see if your mom can take the boy until I can get there and work something out."

Cait opened her mouth to say that wasn't acceptable, that he wasn't going to dump this on his ex-wife, but she would have been talking to the air because her father had already ended the call. She took a moment to compose herself before she turned around to face Adam. He must have picked up on the gist of her conversation with Marty and was already getting to his feet.

"I can stay by myself," he said. "It's only a couple of months, and I've got a little money saved. I could probably find a place if the rent's cheap enough. I checked, and there's no law in Texas that says I can't stay alone."

Cait sighed. "You're how old, fourteen?" she asked.

Adam's head dipped a little. "Thirteen."

After another sigh, Cait was about to launch into an explanation of while him staying alone might be legal, it surely wasn't safe. But Lenore spoke before she could get started.

"Do you like snickerdoodles?" Lenore asked, smiling at Adam. "I have some I got from the diner, and I could get you a couple with a glass of milk." In the grand scheme of things, that offer just didn't seem relevant, but Lenore made it so by adding, "Then we can talk about you staying here with me."

Debra and Adam stared at her, probably because they didn't know that Lenore made a habit of doing this sort of thing.

"The house is big," Lenore went on. "We have seven bedrooms and only three are being used right now. Shaw and Kinsley are here. So is Shaw's fiancée, Sunny. You're welcome to stay until...Marty comes to get you."

Cait figured her mom had had to tamp down a little disgust when she said that last part. She'd tamped down her skepticism, too, because Lenore's bright expression made it seem as if everything would be just as sweet and fine as a snickerdoodle.

"Miss Lenore's nice," Kinsley offered when neither Debra nor Adam said anything. "Sunny, too. And Shaw's okay most of the time."

Kinsley and Shaw exchanged one of those big brother/ little sister glances. Glances like the ones Shaw and Cait shared. Yeah, he was nice most of the time, when he wasn't trying to be an overprotective oldest sibling and butting his nose into their private lives. Of course, nose-butting was fine until Kinsley reached her eighteenth birthday.

"You'd really be all right with Adam staying here?" Debra asked. The tears were in her eyes again, but Cait thought these were ones of relief.

"Of course," Lenore quickly assured her. "We'll be right

as rain, and I'll have someone new to test out all these recipes I've been wanting to cook."

Kinsley and Cait both tried to give Adam subtle head shakes to warn him off that last offer. Later, she'd pull him aside and explain that they basically cooked for themselves or brought in food from the town diner. Of course, it would only take a bite or two for the boy to learn to steer clear of Lenore's culinary attempts.

"We'll help you get your things here," Shaw offered, looking first at Adam but then shifting his attention to Debra. "We also need to stop by the lawyer's office and do some temporary guardianship papers."

"I've had those drawn up already and they're in the car," Debra said, standing. "They're for Marty's signature."

"We should have those redone with my name on them," Shaw countered. "Just in case Marty's delayed in getting here."

Debra nodded and made a sweeping glance at all of them. The relief and gratitude were obvious in every bit of her body language, but Cait suspected the sadness would soon set in. After all, she was basically handing over her grandson to strangers. Good strangers, but Debra didn't know that.

"Let me have a look at the guardianship papers." Shaw started toward the back door but stopped when Sunny came in.

One look at her face, and Cait knew something was wrong. Shaw knew, too, and he went straight to her.

"What happened?" Shaw asked.

"Hayes," Sunny said, her voice barely a whisper, but Cait was close enough for her to hear.

"Hayes?" Cait repeated. God, had something happened to him? Her body obviously thought so because it went into a weird overdrive, and she got a hard smack of adrenaline. "What's wrong with him?"

Sunny must have noticed how alarmed Cait was. No surprise there. She probably looked the picture of hyped-up gloom and doom. "He's okay. I mean, he wasn't hurt or anything."

The adrenaline eased up enough that Cait could level her breathing. But not her worries. Because something was clearly wrong.

"What happened?" Shaw asked Sunny.

"It's Mother. Sunshine," Sunny supplied. "Hayes is on his way over to tell us about the trouble she's causing. It's bad, Shaw," she added, stepping into her fiancé's arms. "It's bad."

CHAPTER NINE

HAYES CERTAINLY HADN'T expected to be making another trip this soon back to the Jameson ranch, but he needed a family meeting, and his sisters were already all there. Too bad he was going to have to add another layer of problems onto what was no doubt already going on.

Sunny was likely in the middle of the discussion about what was to be done with Marty's grandson. Along with the troubles she was having in her pregnancy, Hayes normally wouldn't want to put anything else on her. But this couldn't wait.

Cursing his mother under his breath, Hayes parked Em's truck in the very spot where he'd driven it away a little over an hour earlier. He hadn't headed to the Jameson ranch immediately after finishing the call with his mother, though. First, he'd had to rein in his temper and pretty much the rest of his emotions, too.

Even now, all these minutes later, he was still pissed off all the way to the marrow, but he didn't want his sisters to see that in him and feed into it. They had a right to their anger, of course, but wanting to throttle their mother wasn't going to fix what Sunshine was trying to set in motion. And it would only add to the stress Sunny was already dealing with.

Damn Sunshine for trying to use them this way. And he wished he could send her straight to the deepest pit in hell for threatening to use Ivy.

It was Cait who met Hayes at the door, and he was thankful for it. Even though he could see the worry in her eyes, that worry meant there were also concerns. And feelings. Hayes didn't know what the heck to do with those feelings she had for him, but it was nice to have someone in his corner. Of course, his family was in that corner. Probably the Jamesons, too. But it felt especially good to have Cait right here.

"Are you okay?" Cait asked, giving him a quick hug and then easing back to study his expression.

Yeah, it was nice.

"I've been better. How are things with Adam?" He tipped his head to the driveway. "His grandmother's car isn't here."

"No. Shaw, Mom, Adam and Debra left to go get some guardianship papers amended at the lawyer's office in town."

Hayes lifted an eyebrow. "Marty came through?"

"Not a chance." She took him by the arm, urging him into the foyer. "Mom and Shaw will take Adam while Debra's serving time in jail. We're not counting on Marty lending any help whatsoever."

That was wise considering the man's track record. But there was another track record, as well. Lenore might end up being the boy's legal guardian, but Cait and her brothers would step up to help.

"Your sisters are in the kitchen," Cait told him. "We talked Sunny into sitting down while McCall's fixing her something to eat. They're waiting for you."

He'd expected that. The waiting. The dread. Because when Sunshine poked her greedy talons at something, it was always something to be dreaded.

Hayes followed Cait a few steps, but then he stopped and moved in front of her. Before he could change his mind, he kissed her, and man, had he needed that, too. Even better, he needed that Cait didn't move away from him. She melted into the kiss right along with him.

Progress.

Well, it was if he were vying for the "most stupid of the year" award. He apparently was because he let the kiss go on way too long before he finally eased back from her.

"Don't read anything into that," she muttered in such a way that he was dead certain she'd read plenty into it.

"A pity kiss?" he asked, trying to keep the moment lighter than it ever could be.

"You bet. There's absolutely no other reason I'd kiss you."

Despite what he was about to face, he smiled and then realized that Cait was probably the only person who could have managed to get him to do that. Bolstered and a whole lot calmer than he had been when he'd stepped through the door, Hayes started toward the kitchen.

"I'll be in the dining room if you need me," Cait said. "Not that kind of need," she added when he gave her his best dirty-minded leer.

This wasn't the time for dirty minds or leers but, mercy, it felt good to be with Cait for just a moment longer. Hayes considered asking her to go with him. He might be able to use another dose of what she'd just doled out to him, but this discussion needed to at least start with just him, his grandmother and his sisters. Then he could fill in Cait later. Maybe by then he'd have an actual fix for the mess that Sunshine was trying to start.

Steeling himself up some more and trying to put on a calm face, Hayes went into the kitchen and found Em and his sisters exactly where Cait said they would be. Sunny was at the table, sipping some kind of flowery-smelling tea. Hadley was across from her, drinking a Coke. McCall and Em were at the counter, putting the finishing touches on some sandwiches.

They all looked up when he stepped in, but McCall went ahead and set the sandwich tray along with a bag of chips on the table. Em got him a beer from the fridge.

"How bad is it?" McCall asked just as Hadley said, "What'd that she-witch do now?"

"It's what she's trying to do," Hayes started. He sat and waited for the others to do the same before he continued. "First of all, Sunshine's not here in town. There's a restraining order against her."

"Damn straight there is," Em volunteered. "That's the deal Sunny and I struck with her earlier this year. Sunshine got some jewelry that belonged to Sunny and McCall, but for my greedy daughter to get her hands on it, she had to agree not to show her face around here again."

It was a relief to know that Sunshine wouldn't crash the wedding. Or maybe she wouldn't. Hayes doubted a restraining order would hold her back if there was money to be made.

"Sunshine wants to have reporters and photographers at your wedding," Hayes threw out there, and he got the responses he'd expected. Groans from Sunny and McCall. A "no way in hell" from Hadley. Em gave a sarcastic "Is that all?" followed by a humph.

"Of course, Sunshine intends to sell the coverage to the highest bidder and says she'll take one hundred percent of the money in exchange for giving us back the rights to *Little Cowgirls*."

Rights that Sunshine owned because of the way she'd originally set up the contracts for the show. Over the years, Sunshine had tried to shop the reruns around, but she hadn't gotten any takers for her asking price. Still, there was always the threat that someone would bite, and that's why Hayes had tried to buy them himself. His mother had refused. Maybe because she figured she could use them as a bargaining tool one day.

Like now.

His sisters exchanged glances, and Hayes could almost see thought bubbles over their heads. *Little Cowgirls* had basically played out the triplets' every embarrassing moment for the sake of TV ratings, and provided plenty of emotional baggage. They wouldn't want all that aired again, but they also didn't want to open up their wedding to Sunshine and reporters.

"If we're voting, I say no." Hadley spoke up.

McCall, Sunny and Em all echoed that no. Again, it was what he'd expected, but now he had to tell them the rest.

"I told Sunshine that none of us would go for tabloid wedding coverage," Hayes continued, "and that's when she brought up Ivy."

Silence. For a long time.

"What about Ivy?" Hadley finally asked.

She was the only one of his sisters who'd met Ivy, but apparently the name wasn't unfamiliar to the others. There was no huh or blank looks. That meant either Hadley had talked about her or they'd read the tabloid stories about her.

Since there was a lot of misinformation in those stories, Hayes started with, "Ivy was a friend. My best friend," he amended after he tamped down the damn lump in his throat. "Ivy suffered from depression, and she killed herself a couple of months ago."

All three of his sisters reached out to put their hands over his. Until they did that, Hayes thought he'd been doing a good job keeping the emotion out of his voice and off his expression. Apparently not.

"Somehow, Sunshine got access to some of Ivy's emails," Hayes went on. "Personal, private emails that I know Ivy wouldn't want published."

Hadley cursed. "But that's what the she-witch threatened to do."

That brought on a chorus of groans but not one bit of surprise. Just the opposite. This was the kind of shit that Sunshine loved to spread around.

Hayes nodded. "I suspect Sunshine used a hacker to get to the emails," he explained. "Ivy's family could try to get a court order to stop her from using them, but Sunshine claims that Ivy shared them with her."

"Bullshit," Hadley concluded.

"Very deep, smelly bullshit," he agreed. "Sunshine met Ivy. Or rather Sunshine arranged to run into Ivy, probably so our *beloved mother* could try to get some dirt that she could use to milk some money out of me."

"What's in the emails?" Sunny asked.

"I don't know for sure, but Sunshine read me a couple of excerpts. In one of them, Ivy talks about killing herself. That's true. Ivy sent me an email where she said that, and the moment I read it, I called Ivy and then went over to see her." He paused. "Still, Sunshine can use the emails to make it seem as if I didn't do anything to stop her from taking her own life."

He had done something. But it hadn't been nearly enough. Maybe one day he'd be able to look at himself in the mirror and not think of that. Maybe one day he'd forgive himself.

But it wouldn't be today.

"Despite the emails and some of the articles that were printed about Ivy, I didn't have anything to do with her death," he went on. "I didn't drive her to kill herself because I wouldn't marry her or do whatever the hell else the tabloids say she wanted from me."

"The story I saw said she killed herself because of her parents," Hadley commented. "True?"

"Partly," Hayes admitted. Hell, he was going to have to get into Ivy's big-assed dark past so they'd get the big picture of what Sunshine was trying to do here. "Ivy's parents got divorced when she was a kid, and one of her mother's boyfriends molested her. She told her mom, but she didn't believe her. Probably because at the time her mom was using drugs. Ivy ran away to her dad's, but he was newly married and didn't want her, so he sent her back."

Obviously, this wasn't painting her parents in a good light. And it shouldn't. They'd screwed up big-time, and Ivy had paid the price. She'd kept paying through a lifelong battle with depression that had eventually claimed her life.

"Her parents aren't the same people they were back then," Hayes went on. "They've both gotten treatment for their problems and tried to make amends with their daughter. It would crush them to know Ivy had maybe killed herself because of them."

They all stayed quiet a moment. "One of the stories I read said Ivy had a miscarriage and that's why she took her own life," Sunny added.

Hayes nodded. Yet another dark pit of memories. "She had a miscarriage, and, no, it wasn't my baby. She got pregnant by some loser who walked out when she told him she was carrying his child."

More silence, and Hayes could feel the question coming before McCall even asked it. "Did you try to kill yourself?"

"No," he answered as fast as he could. Though this was one of those gray areas of truth. "I didn't specifically set out to kill myself," he amended when they continued to stare at him.

He could almost feel Em and his sisters taking collective breaths. Well, everyone but McCall. She always could see right through him, and she had no doubt picked up on the wording. He hadn't set out to do it, but he'd come damn close.

"So, if we don't let the she-bitch trash our wedding, she'll publish these emails about Ivy," Hadley summarized. "It'll create a media firestorm about you and about her parents."

Hayes nodded. "Maybe about Cait, too, because a lot of the tabloids are now linking me with her. The trash reporters could say I'm using her to get over Ivy or that I dumped Ivy to be with her. They could end up blaming Cait for what happened to Ivy."

He didn't have a chance to add more because Em's and his sisters' attention shifted to the doorway. Where Cait was standing. Judging from her uncomfortable expression, she'd heard that last part.

Hell.

Cait held up a phone, her gaze going to McCall. "You left your phone in the dining room, and someone's called four times."

Since McCall was a counselor, those calls could be important, and that's why his sister quickly took her phone, muttering to herself when she checked the screen. "I need to take this," she said, stepping out.

Hayes stood when Cait started to leave as well, and he took hold of her hand. "I'm not using you," he said.

Then he frowned. Because that's exactly what he was doing. Or rather it's what he'd started out doing. He'd asked her to help lessen his family worries by pretending he'd come back to be with her.

But it wasn't like that now.

"I'm not using you," he repeated, some of his own frustration coming through in his voice.

She managed one of those wiseass Cait smiles. "All right, then I'll use you."

That got a cackle of laughter from Em, who was likely all for any *using* since it might lead to the real thing—him pairing up with Cait. Still, Hayes was beginning to think that a temporary pairing up was inevitable. Along with being plenty satisfying. That would have to go on the back burner, though, because he still had the Sunshine issue to deal with.

"My mother's up to her old tricks," he told Cait to bring her up to speed. "She's trying to blackmail me so that she can profit off the wedding."

"Sunshine's stinkier than a dead skunk," Em declared, and no one could argue with that.

He waited until McCall was back in the room before Hayes continued with what he had to say. He made eye contact with each of his sisters. "You are not having paparazzi or reporters at your wedding. That's not up for discussion. I've got the ball rolling with Ivy's parents so they can try to stop Sunshine from publishing those private emails. If it doesn't work, though, I just wanted all of you to be prepared for the fallout."

"I could maybe bargain with Sunshine," McCall offered. Obviously, she just wasn't going to buy into letting him handle this. "I've got stuff from the set of *Little Cowgirls* that I could offer to get her to back off."

"Same here," Sunny piped in. "I have photographs, some jewelry and clothes. Sunshine could sell it as a collection of memorabilia."

It twisted at his guts to hear how quickly his sisters were able to come up with possible solutions. They'd had to go through this "been there, done that" crap way too many times. Not in the same vein as what Marty was doing to his family, but it was still creating the havoc stream that never seemed to end.

"I could just kick her ass," Hadley grumbled, confirming the nickname of Badly Hadley that she'd gotten from the show.

"I could help you," Em said to Hadley, confirming his grandmother's disgust with her own daughter.

Hayes couldn't shake his head fast enough. "I don't want any of you confronting her. Don't take her calls or texts, either. Just give it a day or two and see if Ivy's folks can come through."

If not, then Hayes had his own backup plan. And, yeah, it would involve a bribe similar to the ones his sisters had just offered. Well, it would if he could pull it off. He didn't have the clout that he'd once had on the set of *Outlaw Rebels*, but if he jumped through enough hoops, he might be able to work it out so that Sunshine could get some exclusive interviews with the cast that she could in turn sell. He could possibly even swing getting her a cameo appearance on the show. The she-witch would lap that up and then rub it in his face, but it might be enough to get her to back off.

"We're not going to let Sunshine win this one," Hadley insisted.

"No, we're not," Hayes assured her with far more confidence than he felt.

Unfortunately, his plan and backup plan might not work, and if it didn't, then the ball would be in Sunshine's court. She could continue bargaining to get access to the wedding, or she could be the usual pisser that she was and release the emails. Right now, he didn't have a clue which way this would go.

He went to his sisters and grandmother, hugging them one by one. Or that's how it started, anyway. It turned into a group hug, with Em gathering Cait into the mix. It was sort of a sealing of the pact to defeat the evil force bearing down on them.

But Hayes could feel something else, too.

The overwhelming pressure to fix this. Not just for his family but for Ivy's folks, too. If he failed, there'd be a shitstorm in the press, and some of that crap could fly right at them.

Hayes headed out of the kitchen, hoping Em and his sisters would be able to get back to the wedding sewing and decorations so they'd have a much-needed distraction. Hoping, too, that he could shove away this dark cloud he felt descending on him. Damn Sunshine for poking at his unresolved feelings about Ivy. His grief. And for bringing all those dark memories straight to the surface again.

Cait followed him to the front door, and he figured she was about to try to give him words of encouragement. Or cheer him up with a joke. Or maybe she would volunteer to use her badge in some way to get Sunshine to back off. Instead, she took hold of his arm.

"Come on. I think you need to get out of here for a while," Cait said.

Hayes froze and mentally replayed that. He didn't believe it was his imagination or wishful thinking that her voice had had an enticing silky purr. He stared at her, studying her. No, not his imagination. That enticement was in her eyes, too.

"Are you taking me to Prego Trail?" he joked.

"No. Someplace better." Her voice was still purring. "I'm taking you home with me."

CAIT TRIED NOT to think of this as playing with a big ol' ball of fire. But that's exactly what she was doing by taking Hayes to her place. A place with privacy.

And a bed.

Of course, she'd had other men in her house, and she hadn't made it a habit of dropping into bed with them, but come on—this was Hayes. There was also the fact that both of them were riding massive waves of emotional crap right now. His because of his mother and hers because of Adam. Waves of emotion could lower barriers and screw around with all those other feelings.

Especially sex feelings, of which she had legions when it came to Hayes.

Still, she had seen his expression and knew that he needed something to keep from falling face-first into a deep well of grief. Grief that might lead to another bout of depression. Cait also knew she couldn't just pull him out of depression. No. That took meds and maybe even a good therapist. Hayes thankfully had those. But she thought maybe she could get his mind off his troubles for a little while and give him a short reprieve from the crud that his mother was tossing at him.

Hayes followed her out the door, but he put Em's keys in the ignition of her truck before he got in the SUV with her. She suspected he did that so that Em wouldn't be inconvenienced when it came time for her to leave.

"You're doing this because you feel sorry for me," Hayes said, buckling his seat belt.

"Absolutely." Here's where she could start helping with some attempted humor. "First, a pity kiss. Now a pity visit to my lair."

"Your lair? Do you have an S and M room like that *Fifty Shades of Grey* guy?"

"Duh. Of course. Doesn't everyone? Except mine is more of a closet than a room, but I'm sure there's enough junk in there to do bondage and stuff. I could tie you up with my gym socks and spank you with my old tennis racket."

He smiled, and mercy, it was good to see it. That didn't vanquish the dark mood, but it eased a little of the tension. For a couple of seconds, anyway. When Hayes stayed silent on the drive, Cait went ahead and broached the proverbial huge elephant squatting between them on the seat.

"You want to talk about Sunshine?" she asked.

"No," he quickly answered, but then he hesitated. "Maybe you could spank her with a tennis racket."

Now she smiled, but it was short-lived. "Or I could look into having her arrested. What she's trying to do is frowned upon and a crime that we folks in law enforcement like to call extortion. It'd be hard to prove, a he-said, she-said sort of deal, but if she calls you back, you should tell her you're recording the conversation. You could tell her you're doing that so your sisters can hear it, and then you could try to get her to say something incriminating."

Of course, that last part would be next to impossible. Sunshine had played these games many times before and knew, mostly, how to stay out of legal hot water. Still, people did screw up all the time.

Case in point—she was taking Hayes to her house.

"I can do that," he said, not sounding hopeful. "And I can tell Ivy's parents to do the same."

Now, that was a good idea. Cait didn't think Sunshine was accustomed to dealing with them, so it might make her slip and say the wrong thing.

Cait pulled to a stop in the driveway in front of her house. The place wasn't grand in looks or size like her family's ranch. It was a log cabin with the expected rustic exterior and porch. The red barn—which was double the size of the house—sat behind it and suited her four horses.

Ditto for the ten acres of pasture. It was no frills, low maintenance. Like her.

And there wasn't a white picket fence anywhere in sight.

"This used to be the Carson place," Hayes remarked, glancing around as he got out.

"It was. I bought it about eight years ago."

No need to mention that she hadn't changed much other than upgrading the barn, because he could see that for himself. Hayes had likely been out here many times because the Carsons' daughter had been a love interest for Hayes for a while. Then again, nearly every woman in town had fallen into that category for him.

Cait started for the porch and felt a bout of nerves sweep over her. Nope, this wasn't smart. She was going to end up another has-been love interest. A soon-to-be-discarded one. That reminder should have had her at least rethinking this visit, but apparently even nerves and sensible thoughts weren't a deterrent today.

The moment they were inside, she turned to Hayes to go ahead and kiss him. Something that she was certain would happen soon anyway. But he wasn't even looking at her. Instead, he opened the closet that was in the entry and smiled.

There was indeed a tennis racket inside. A gym bag, too, though she rarely used it. Cait preferred to get her exercise by tending to her horses. But she was betting if he dug through the bag, he'd find some old socks for the fantasy tying up that she'd joked about on the drive over.

"Belts," he said, perusing the contents, and his smile brightened when he spotted the item dangling from a coat hanger. "Handcuffs."

"Standard-issue," she muttered and realized that her closet was perhaps a mini red room after all. Though she wasn't sure the rarely used bowling ball and box of old paperbacks would qualify as kink.

He kept his attention on the handcuffs for several more moments, and when he finally turned to her, Cait figured he was about to suggest they use them. Or maybe make some other poorly veiled sexual remark. But he didn't.

"Thank you," he said, his tone as serious as a heart attack. "You brought me here to cheer me up, and I appreciate that."

Cait didn't think she deserved any thanks. Not when it was something that might help lift him out of this dark mood.

Might.

She didn't mind the "serious as a heart attack" tone, proving to her that her cheering attempts were failing, but she hated seeing that grim expression on his incredible face. It was like seeing a super-sexy, super-sad fallen angel who'd just realized he was screwed six ways to Sunday.

"Well, actually, I brought you here for the handcuffs," she told him, moving their conversation off the serious track to steer it back to a lighter one.

It didn't work. He still had the sad fallen-angel face. Of course, any expression on Hayes was still hot. She was certain she could adorn him with every oddball thing in that closet and he'd still manage to look incredible.

Hayes opened his mouth but then promptly closed it as if he'd changed his mind about what he'd been going to tell her. "I don't want to lead you on," he finally said. But he stopped again and shook his head. "Shit, that sounds way too confident. I'm not confident at all when it comes to you."

"Sure you are," she insisted to make him smile.

When he did, when the corner of that gorgeous mouth lifted just a little, Cait swooped in and kissed him. She didn't even try to reason with herself not to do this. Nope. She just went with it and was immediately glad she had. She

doubted that anything—including doing the right thing—
would taste better than Hayes's delicious mouth.

He made a sound of surprise and staggered back a little.
He would have landed in the closet/red room mess if she
hadn't hooked her arms around him to steady him. And
that's when she heard another sound. Not one of surprise,
either. She was dead certain it was a grunt of pain.

Crap.

She'd forgotten all about his cracked ribs. Lust could do
that, make you forget things you should remember. Like
broken bones and bad ideas.

"I'm sorry," she said, stepping back.

She saw the quick flash of pain on his face. Saw him try
to mask it just as fast. He reached for her, no doubt to pull
her right back against his aching ribs, but Cait stepped away.

"I'm sorry," she repeated. "Your angel face got the best
of me."

Of course, he didn't have a clue what that meant since
he hadn't been privy to the lustful thoughts she'd just had
about him. And she didn't want him to have that kind of
info, either.

"How about a beer or something to eat?" she asked.

His eyebrow came up, and he reached out, gently cuff-
ing her wrist in his hand. By teeny-tiny degrees, he brought
her back toward him. Until they were face-to-face. Body
to body. But still not actually touching. However, Hayes
only left a little bit of space between them. Close enough
that she could have sworn she felt the heat coming off him.

Or maybe it was coming off her.

The world was suddenly a very hot place, and her house
was definitely the center of all that boiling heat.

Hayes didn't swoop on her as she'd done. In fact, there
was no speed or urgency whatsoever. With the light grip

still on her wrist, he held her in place while he leaned in. Touched his mouth to hers.

And he caused the world to explode.

Massive fireworks went off in her head, and Cait was sure if a camera had been able to film it, it would have rivaled a top-notch Fourth of July celebration. Complete with a marching band. The band, though, was likely her heart that had taken off in a gallop, probably to keep pace with the rest of her body. Hayes and she might have been moving slow, but everything else was flashing, clanging and...amazing.

She hadn't wanted it to be amazing. Cait had wished the kiss would be pleasurable but forgettable. But sadly, it was the opposite of forgettable, and it got even more memorable when he increased the pressure. He angled his mouth, adjusted here and there, and sent her flying straight to the moon.

Mercy, he was good at this, and he'd barely gotten started.

He pushed past the starter stage, but he kept it slow and easy. Probably because of his ribs, but it was causing the heat, tension and anticipation to build inside her. By the time he finally used his tongue, she was hot, ready and aching.

She eased her wrist out of his grip so she could lift her hands, first one and then the other, and slide them around his neck. Cait desperately wanted some body-to-body contact, but his injured ribs were like a chastity belt. Which she might have considered a good thing, had parts of her not started to whine for more.

No way had she expected *more*, but Hayes managed it. He turned her, putting her back to the wall next to the closet, and he deepened the kiss even more. Their tongues met and fooled around, imitating what Cait wanted the rest of their bodies to be doing. But, no, she reminded herself. The "chastity belt" injury would keep this a PG-rated making out.

She soon learned that Hayes could do plenty with PG stuff. While she couldn't touch him, he touched her, and he did some hand sliding over the front of her shirt that had her moaning in pleasure. Since his mouth was still on her, the sound mingled with the kiss as his hand mingled with her breasts.

Just as he'd done at the start of the kiss, he kept his touch light. She was certain it was a clever ploy to make her want more. And it worked. Yep. Her breasts began to whine for more, specifically for skin-on-skin contact, and even though she wasn't what anyone would call busty, her girls felt ready to spill out of her bra in hopes of contact.

Hayes gave the girls what they wanted. That clever hand pushed its way beneath her shirt. Onto her stomach. Then higher. Her bra was obviously child's play for him because he flicked open the front clasp and brushed his fingers over her nipples.

Oh, the pleasure of it all. It was enough to make her melt into a puddle of something. More important, it was something that could make her beg.

"Chastity belt" ribs, she reminded herself.

Plus, it didn't seem right that she was the one on the receiving end of all of these pleasure spikes. Hayes should be getting his share, too. Cait would have told him that, too, but then he lowered his head, shoved up her top and replaced his fingers with his mouth.

She forgot all about the reminder. Forgot her own name, what planet she was on and possibly how to breathe. Hayes could do all of that with some tongue kisses to her nipples. Sucking, tugging tongue kisses.

"Phone," he said, lifting his head.

Cait nearly whimpered at the loss of contact, and it took

her several long moments to fight through the lust haze and realize what he was saying. And what she was hearing.

Her phone was ringing.

It took her even more long moments to remember what to do with a ringing phone. Good grief, Hayes's mouth had really done a number on her.

Cait dug her phone from her pocket, and once she was able to focus her eyes, she saw Shaw's name on the screen. "I should take this," she said, but mentally she was debating if that's what she was actually going to do.

Hayes solved her dilemma by stepping back. Then, giving her some privacy, he went into the living room. Still within sight, where she could see the snug fit of his well-worn jeans. The equally snug fit of his black tee. He made a picture standing there with his carelessly rumpled hair and "to die for" body. Seeing him like that meant her body revved up again.

"Shaw," she said when she finally managed to take the call.

Silence for a few seconds. "You sound out of breath."

Cait frowned because that seemed like a "nosy big brother" kind of comment. One with ESP undertones of, *Did I interrupt you doing something you shouldn't have been doing in the first place?*

The answer to that was yes, of course.

"Are you calling me because you know I'm with Hayes?" she came out and asked.

"No." Shaw's flat response told her that he'd had no idea Hayes was with her. All right, so maybe not brotherly ESP after all.

More silence, but she could practically feel him scowling. "I'm calling about Adam."

Oh. Him. She certainly hadn't forgotten about her nephew. Well, maybe she had a little. "Is he okay?"

"To be determined. His grandmother and I will be tied up with the paperwork for a while longer, and I'm hoping you can drive Adam to San Antonio to pick up some of his things. He also needs to run by his school and clear out his locker since he'll be taking his courses online. If you leave now, you'll be able to get to the school while the offices there are still open."

Cait groaned softly, and with the heat from the lust fading, she felt a punch of guilt. She should have already volunteered to help with the boy, especially since it was her day off.

"Adam's at the lawyer's office with us," Shaw added, obviously waiting for her answer.

"All right," she finally told him. "I'll be there to get him after I drop off Hayes."

"Good." Then Shaw paused. "Should you be with Hayes?" he pressed.

She glanced at the subject of Shaw's question. Hayes had his back to her, looking at the pictures on the mantel. He could manage to look rock-star hot even while doing something as mundane as that. And maybe it was all the hotness that made her answer easy.

"No," Cait said. She shouldn't be with Hayes.

But that for darn sure wasn't going to stop her.

CHAPTER TEN

Are we still on for our date tonight? Hayes texted Cait. *If so, I can pick you up in about thirty minutes.*

Normally, he would have put his phone away and waited for a reply, but he watched the screen. Waiting. And expecting her to tell him that something had come up and that she'd have to cancel.

Again.

Cait had had to bow out of their date that should have been the night before because she'd needed to take Kinsley to a parent/teacher deal at the school. The old saying of it taking a village to raise a child was true, but in this case the village was the Jameson clan. All her siblings and her mom had been busy, so Cait had stepped up to do it. And had therefore rescheduled their Friday date for tonight—Saturday.

Hayes didn't have to guess that Cait was having second and third thoughts about going out with him. The fact that she'd avoided him confirmed it. Now that she wasn't under the influence of their kissing session, she had probably come to her senses and remembered that he was bad news.

He was.

And he was especially bad news for Cait, but that didn't stop him from wanting her.

Still watching his phone screen for the little dots to indicate she was texting him back, he went downstairs to the kitchen to grab a Coke. From the sewing room just up the hall, he could hear the chatter. Em and his sisters. They were apparently putting the final touches on the wedding dresses. Of course, they'd supposedly done that two days ago, so he figured there'd be more "finals" to come.

Outside, there was a low rumble of thunder, and the thin drops of rain began to hit against the kitchen window. A storm was moving in. Maybe that wasn't some kind of bad omen of—

His hand jerked when his phone dinged with the text message. Yes, we're still having dinner, Cait texted. I'll be there with bells on.

He smiled and felt the relief release some of the tension that had settled in his chest. She wasn't going to ditch him. Well, maybe not. A lot of things could happen in a half hour.

Sipping his Coke, he looked at the magnetic calendar that Em had on the fridge. The wedding date was framed with a red heart, and Em had even done a countdown to the big date. Just two weeks away. Not long. Especially considering things still weren't resolved with Sunshine.

His mother had given them another week to agree to her terms before she claimed she would release Ivy's emails. What Sunshine hadn't done was spell any of this out in the phone conversations that Hayes and Ivy's parents had recorded. Sunshine had been sly, using phrases like *I'll have to do what we've already discussed.*

In other words, his bitch of a mother would drag Ivy's name through the tabloid mud. Hayes didn't need another reason to despise Sunshine, but that was one in spades. Of course, Ivy was in a place where she didn't have any worries about tabloids and Sunshine, but there'd be casualties in this particular Sunshine war. Her parents for sure. But also Hayes and anyone who'd cared for Ivy. It ate away to have someone you loved used this way.

He looked up when he heard the footsteps and saw Hadley walk in. She had her phone sandwiched between her shoulder and ear and was doing some stitches on…well, something that didn't look as if it had anything to do with a wedding. If he wasn't mistaken, it was a small hat in the shape of a duck's head. The yellow brim was the duck's bill.

"All right," she said to the person on the other end of the line. "I love you, too, Boo Boo."

"I'm guessing that wasn't Leyton," he remarked when she put her phone away. "He's not the Boo Boo type."

"Nope. He's the hot-sex type."

It was good to hear, and see, his sisters happy, but especially this one. Hadley had been through more hell and back than the others, and it had taken her a long time to find her way back to her former teenage love, Leyton.

"I was talking to Bailey," she explained. The child Hadley had carried as a surrogate. "And this is what she wants to wear as part of her flower-girl outfit for the wedding. She's gotten obsessed with the *Slackers* books."

That made sense since Sunny was the illustrator for those books. Ironically, Marty was the author of those books, something that he'd only recently spilled to the family. But a duck hat definitely wasn't traditional flower-girl attire. Still, this probably wouldn't be a traditional wedding, so it would probably fit in just fine.

Hayes hadn't actually seen the dresses, but he'd heard Em say something about them not being "cookie-cutter" and that they matched the personalities of each of the brides. Hayes had visions of McCall looking like a fairy princess, Sunny wearing something simple and sleek, and Hadley wearing black leather.

Hadley grabbed a Coke, too, and sat at the table to continue sewing the duck bill. "We're having pizza delivered from the diner," she said. "Should we order some for you, or is Cait going through with the date?"

Smiling in such a way that would have made a lovesick teen proud, he showed her Cait's confirmation text.

Hadley shrugged. "I guess she blew off the advice that her brothers gave her."

"What advice?" Hayes questioned.

"That she should treat you like a case of typhoid and run the other direction," Hadley answered without hesitation.

"Harsh," he grumbled.

She eyed him over the Coke she was sipping. "And what would you have told McCall, Sunny and me if we'd accepted a date with an actor with your shady reputation?"

"The same," he readily admitted. "But my reputation is more hype than shady. I haven't been with a woman in months." And he hated that the particular dry spell might be playing into this aching need he had for a smart-mouthed deputy. Of course, feelings might be playing into it, too.

Plenty of feelings.

Those were things he was going to have to sort out, and he'd tried to convince himself that the sorting out should happen before falling into bed with her. Unfortunately, he knew he would fail. If Cait offered him the fall, he wouldn't be able to stop himself.

His sister studied him for several moments and then said, "Ivy. You haven't been with a woman since her death," she concluded.

Bingo, and even he wasn't slick enough to convince himself that the two things weren't tied together. "FYI, it was the truth when I told you that Ivy and I were never lovers."

Hadley nodded. "I know." She paused again. "But I'm

guessing the emails that the she-bitch has access to will make it seem as if you were."

Oh, yeah. Then there would be the speculation that he'd been the father of the child she'd lost, and things would blow up all over again. Having a bad reputation played well with *Outlaw Rebels*, but Hayes didn't want that slung around on his real life.

"I still think I should pay a visit to the she-bitch," Hadley threw out there. "I might be able to convince her to back off."

He couldn't have possibly given her a flatter look. "You'll end up arrested and maybe in jail for your wedding. No, you're not risking that. I have one other ace up my sleeve that might work."

Might was a stretch, though. It had a thin chance of working.

"Care to tell me what you have?" Hadley asked.

Hayes shook his head. "Let's wait and see if it'll be necessary. Ivy's parents might be able to legally stop Sunshine."

Again, the injunction Ivy's folks were trying to get was a stretch, but Hayes was going with a glass half-full on this. He wasn't sure if he could credit his meds for helping him with that outlook or if he'd just grown weary over allowing Sunshine's crap to ruin his day.

He brushed a kiss on the top of Hadley's head. "Let Em know I'm heading out."

"Good luck tonight with Cait," she murmured, and then she slid her hand over his, gave it a gentle squeeze. Hadley's eyes met his. "You know, there's nothing wrong with you. You're not an asshole."

That was likely Hadley's version of a glass half-full. "Thanks."

She held on to his hand a moment longer. Kept the eye contact, too. "So, because you're not an asshole, I'm sure it's occurred to you that you can't just diddle around with Cait and walk away as if it doesn't matter. Because it will matter to her."

And there it was. Not a glass half-empty but the truth.

"Yeah," he agreed.

With that sobering thought giving him some gloom and doom, Hayes headed out to Cait's. Even though his motorcycle had finally been fixed and delivered to the ranch, he didn't use it. Not with the rain already starting and with his ribs still a little tender. Instead, he used Em's truck, but he hadn't even gotten it in gear when his phone dinged with a text.

Shit.

It was probably Cait canceling, and while that would be good in the long run, he really wanted to see her. In fact, it was a want that felt more like an aching need.

Worse, he wasn't sure that need was all below the belt.

He took out his phone and damn near jumped for joy when it wasn't Cait's name on the screen but rather his agent, Abe Simon. The joy went south, though, when he realized this wasn't one of Abe's emoji conversations. It contained real words.

OR might get ax, the text said.

OR was *Outlaw Rebels*, but unless the *ax* was a typo, the show might be canceled. Hayes hit the button to call Abe rather than text back.

"What the hell?" Hayes asked the moment Abe answered. "Is the show actually being canceled?"

"Might," Abe corrected. "There's chatter about it. Will let you know when I know." And with that minimal bit of info, Abe hung up.

Hayes considered calling him right back, but if Abe knew any more details he would have told him. Abe wasn't one to sugarcoat anything, either.

Well, hell.

With the rain pattering against the truck, he sat there a moment, trying to let the news sink in and process it. The show had been his life for nearly a decade, and, yeah, there was always talk about wrapping things up so that some of the cast could move on to other projects they wanted to tackle. Hayes didn't have another project. Didn't want one. In fact, he hadn't been sure he'd wanted to continue with *Outlaw Rebels*. Still, it would feel like a kick to the teeth to have it end with a cancellation.

Well, there went his "glass half-full" mood.

That didn't stop him from making the drive to Cait's, but Hayes thought this would put a damper on any notion of him making this more than a dinner date. In other words, no sex for dessert. Because Hadley was right when she said it would matter to Cait. It would. Ditto for Hadley being right about him not being an asshole. Which was exactly what he would be if he pushed things sexually with Cait.

With his resolve bolstered enough that he thought he could make it through this date, he parked in front of her house. Maybe it was another bad omen, but the sky opened up the moment he stepped from the truck. No more soft patter. These were mean kamikaze raindrops that felt like pellets of steel. He hurried to her porch, causing his ribs to start aching again, which in turn only added to his sour mood.

But his mood changed when Cait opened the door.

She was wearing bells. And lots of them.

Some were on a knit cap, while others jangled from the bracelets on her wrists and ankles. There were even dangling bell earrings and a matching necklace. Toe rings, too, which he could easily see because she was barefoot. Cait swiveled her hips, causing the bell-studded belt around her short blue dress to clang with the rest of her accessories.

"It's an outfit for feeding Slackers, the duck," she said, smiling and looking at her right foot that she was wiggling to make those bells join in with the others. It was like Santa's sleigh on steroids.

"Huh?" was the best he could do.

"The bells scare the crap out of Slackers, literally." She took his arm and led him inside. "I mean, he poops himself and runs and hides while I put the food in his pen. It's genius. And it was your grandmother's idea."

Of course it was. This had Em written all over it, and just like that, he felt a little less sour.

"When did you have to feed Slackers?" he asked. Normally, that was something Em asked him to do. And he had the peck marks on his legs to prove it.

"Earlier today while you were in San Antonio."

Oh, that. He'd been at his therapy appointment. He hadn't told his family exactly what kind of doctor he'd been seeing, but since none of them had pushed for info, they had likely figured it out. Soon, he'd need to sit down with them and explain what he was dealing with.

Cait was about to shut the door, but she looked out, scowling just as a bolt of lightning cracked through the already-dark sky.

"You should get inside," Hayes warned her. "With all that metal on you, you're an easy target for the next bolt."

Cait made a sound of agreement and did indeed step back so she could shut the door. She also began to peel off the bells. First the hat, which she dumped into a large wooden bowl that she was obviously using for keys.

"Say, what with this weather, we don't have to go out to eat," she said. "Besides, your ribs are hurting you."

He wasn't sure how she'd known that, but it was possible he'd grimaced when he'd run in from the rain. No grimace for her when she stripped off the necklace, though he could clearly see the scar left from her stitches. It was still in the pink-healing stage.

"Not hurting," he corrected. "Just some twinges."

That was close enough to the truth, anyway. In fact, the pain had already gone away, but that was possibly because he was distracted by the striptease Cait was doing. She wasn't removing any clothes, but his body was very interested in the way she was now sliding her hand down her ankle and over her foot to remove the bells there.

She didn't notice that he was noticing. Not at first, anyway. But when she finally lifted her head, she must have seen some heat in his eyes.

"Are you going to say something totally lame about me ringing your bell?" she asked.

He might have if his mouth hadn't gone dry.

She dropped the gob of bell adornments in the bowl with the hat and belt, but she continued to cast glances at him. Cait was no doubt wondering why he'd lost the capacity for human speech.

"Or were you figuring that polite chitchat was called for and wanted to ask me how things are going with Adam?" she added with plenty of tongue in cheek.

Ironically, he was thinking about her tongue, too. And about her taste. It was hard not to think about having sex with her now that he'd had his hands on her breasts. That was only a second-base kind of move, but touching her that way had made an impact.

"Adam," he finally managed to say. Hayes gave his head a shake to clear it. "How's he doing?"

It wasn't just chitchat, though. He did want to know since he'd been there at the start of this particular drama, and it felt like a personal investment for him.

Cait smiled and motioned for him to follow her into the kitchen. "He's settling into the ranch in a quiet but not too sulky kind of way. Kinsley's got some family duty this time since Adam and she are close to the same age. She's helping him adjust."

That made sense, and considering that it'd only been a couple of months since Kinsley had ended up at the ranch, she would know all about settling in and adjusting not only in the family but also in the town. Even though Adam might not live at the ranch for long, it was possible he'd want to come back for visits since the Jamesons were his family.

Cait opened the fridge and took out two beers. "But Kinsley says she doesn't want anyone knowing that she's an aunt because it makes her feel like an old fart. Of course, I rather quickly pointed out to her that using such an expression does indeed make her an old fart."

He smiled, had a sip of beer and wondered if he could forget all about logic and what was right and just haul Cait to him and kiss her. The thought had no sooner crossed his mind, though, than the world plunged into darkness. It took Hayes a moment to realize that he hadn't been struck by some kind of divine protest and that the electricity had simply gone out.

"Crap," Cait muttered, and he heard her fumbling around in one of the drawers. "There's no generator," she said, coming out with a flashlight. "I'll get some candles."

Cait fanned the flashlight right into his eyes, temporarily blinding him, and then brushed past him, her hip sliding against his. That caused him to go hard—which he also hoped was temporary. He really didn't want Cait to see the bulge and assume he couldn't control himself.

Which he clearly couldn't.

She cursed, using a creative mixture of words, when she banged into the corner of the countertop, but she did indeed come up with some candles and some matches that were in a cabinet next to the fridge. Hayes set his beer aside so he could help her light them. The trio of candles were in glass jars, and the one he lit smelled like vanilla. However, he frowned when he saw the labels on the two that Cait was lighting.

"'Besties before Testes,'" he read. "'Asshole Repellent'?"

"Oh, the asshole repellent isn't for you," she said, as if everyone had a candle by that name in their house. "Hadley gave them to me for my birthday."

Yeah, he could see Hadley doing that. He took a sniff of the repellent one. Lemon and vanilla. The other was peppery.

"There," Cait said when the wicks were all lit. "Dinner by candlelight. Of course, without power I can't cook anything, but there's some cold leftover pizza in the fridge."

She turned to get it before he could give in to that whole kissing impulse. It was just as well. Once his dick softened, maybe he'd be able to think of something other than stuff that would lead to sex.

"Any updates about Sunshine and the crap she's trying to pull?" Cait asked, her back to him. The candlelight gave him an amazing view when she leaned into the fridge and took out the pizza box.

"She's still being an asshole." Which pretty much described his mother not just for this situation but also for everything else she did in life.

Cait made a sound of agreement, got out napkins and sat on one of the bar stools at the counter. "Maybe you could try the candle on her," she joked. But her expression turned serious when he sank down beside her. "If there's anything I can do to help, just let me know. I've had some experience dealing with an asshole parent."

She had indeed, and Hayes thought Sunshine and Marty were neck and neck when it came to the "shitty parent" award.

"Thanks," he said, taking a slice of pepperoni pizza from the box. "I do have something I could maybe hold over her head. When I was a teenager, I set up one of those nanny cams in my room because I thought someone was messing with my stuff while I was at school. I ended up recording Sunshine going down on one of the cameramen."

He frowned. He hadn't told this to Hadley when they'd been talking about it earlier, but he'd just blurted it out to Cait. Why? The only reason he could come up with was that apparently dick stirrings made him chatty.

Cait stopped, her teeth clamped around the bite of pizza she'd just taken. "Holy shit."

That had been his reaction, too, along with a "hell no" or two. "I didn't actually watch it when I realized what it was. Definitely not something a teenage boy wants to see his mother doing. But I kept it, thinking it could come in handy down the road."

"And this situation could be *down the road*." She finished her bite of pizza, drank some beer. "You can threaten her with it?"

"Yeah, but Sunshine might not see it as a threat. She might think a sex tape will give her the publicity she craves. If she believes releasing it will benefit her, then she might want it bad enough to back off the wedding demand. If so, I might be able to use it as a last resort to bargain with her."

First, though, he was going to let Ivy's parents do their thing with the lawyers. If that didn't work, then he could step in and see how it played out with offering up the recording.

"No wonder you looked so down when you got here," Cait said. "A sex tape like that will blow up in the tabloids, and that in turn will put you and your sisters back in the spotlight."

It would indeed. Because fallout on Sunshine was family fallout. He didn't want to drag Em and his sisters through that, but his mother might not give him a choice. If something was indeed going to be dragged through the mud, he wanted the muddiest mess to get on Sunshine.

Since the candlelight and cold pizza had caused him to confess all, Hayes just kept going. Maybe the old adage of confession being good for the soul was true. "The bad mood was also because I talked to my agent on the way over. *Outlaw Rebels* might be canceled."

Cait froze again, but this time the shock had an even bigger side order of concern. She set her pizza back on the top lid of the box so she could slide her hand over his. "I'm so sorry."

He waited for her questions, asking him how he felt about that possibility, wondering what he would do if the cancellation did indeed happen, but she just sat there, her hand over his and with that look of sympathy in her eyes. Maybe that's why he kept on talking.

"The cast of *Outlaw Rebels* is like a family to me," he went on. "But it's more than that. The show made me believe I was somebody."

Shit, that sounded way too deep for cold pizza and Asshole Repellent candle glow. He eased his hand from hers so he could wave that off. "If it's canceled, there'll be other roles."

As if to make a cosmic challenge to that, there was a flash of lightning that lit up the whole kitchen, and it was followed by a loud crack of thunder.

"You were always somebody," Cait assured him. "But, hey, I get it. You were the odd man out, being the only boy and the oldest at that. For a long time, I was the only girl and the youngest. That plays with the way you feel about yourself."

Since she hadn't gone for a joke, Hayes tried one. "Maybe we can find a candle scent for that?"

She smiled, shrugged. "Or maybe we just find a new place when someone takes the old one away."

Wise words. Serious words. The thing he liked about Cait was that she didn't make him dig too deep. She could always cheer him up, keep things right at or just below the surface.

Maybe it's because he was the big brother, but Hayes didn't like admitting that he could be shaken. He had to stay strong for his sisters. For himself. He didn't like sliding back into the dark, where he had been shaken to the core.

Where he wasn't strong.

Where he grieved for a friend and a past that had left him broken. Over the last couple of weeks, he'd repaired some of those breaks, but they were still there. Maybe they always would be, which wasn't much of a comforting thought.

"When I was a kid," he continued, "I used to sit at my bedroom window and look out at the sky for airplanes. Then I'd imagine being on them. I didn't care where they were going. Anywhere but here was where I wanted to be, and I wanted to be doing anything else other than what I was doing." Hayes looked up and saw that she was staring at him. "Can't relate to that, huh?"

"Oh, I don't know. I get that need to escape." She drew in a deep breath. "But I'm Marty Jameson's daughter, and that DNA made me want to stay put because *here* was the one place I knew he wouldn't be."

And there it was again. Their common ground with both of them having to deal with a crappy parent.

"Breaks," he muttered. "You've got them, too."

"Oh, yeah. Marty saw to that."

He nodded. "But you chose to deal with those breaks here in Lone Star Ridge, where you have daily contact with memories of the old baggage."

Cait made a sound of agreement. "But daily contact, too, with the people who share the baggage and can help me. When it comes to siblings, 'misery loves company' applies, and the effects are like double."

Hayes smiled when she did, and he let the moment settle with silence between them. The problem with silence, though, was it meant he was looking at her again. Really looking at her. At that smile. At the way the candlelight was flickering on her face. Now it was time to move in for a kiss. But Cait stopped him by speaking before he could put a move on her.

"You've got two weeks before the wedding," she reminded him. "That's two weeks and one day before you leave."

"Who says I'm leaving?" he countered, only because he didn't like being reminded that his time here was indeed short.

She pointed out the window to the sky. "Those airplanes, the ones you used to watch. If you stayed, you'd be back to wishing you were on one of them. *Anywhere but here,*" she repeated.

He frowned. "I don't like having my own words foul up any chance I have of kissing you again."

"It isn't only a kiss you want, Hayes Dalton," she scolded, but she was smiling when she said it.

And it was a dazzling smile. One that only made him think of kissing her again. Of course, he only had a one-track mind around Cait. Okay, two tracks. Kisses and sex.

"Yes, I want more," he verified. He leaned in, but Cait pressed her hand on his chest.

Hell. She was stopping him.

Or not.

"I want more, too," she admitted. "Not that kind of more," she clarified when his eyes widened. "No white picket fences for us."

He couldn't have made a sound of agreement any faster, but Cait still kept her hand in place, which meant she kept him at bay.

She looked him straight in the eyes. "I've decided to see what all the hype is about."

Now he was back to being confused. "What hype?"

"Duh. About you. According to all those tabloid stories and the opinion of a teenage girl, you're straight fire. I think I'd like to live out a fantasy by having a one-night stand with Slade Axel McClendon."

She couldn't have cooled him down more if she'd doused him with a bucket of ice water. A fantasy? Shit. That's what his fans and the groupies said to him. Not Cait. She wasn't the sort to get sucked into the hype.

Was she?

Hell, he hoped not. He stared at her, trying to figure out if this was some kind of test. Like maybe if he tried to jump her right now, she could just say, *See, all you want is sex for the next fourteen days?*

Which he did.

But not sex like this.

"Well?" she prompted, finally taking her hand from his chest.

Even though she'd removed the barrier, Hayes stayed in place. "Two days," he threw out there. Though he didn't know why he'd chosen that random number. "Give this some thought for the next forty-eight hours. Be sure," Hayes advised her. "Then, if you still want the fantasy, we'll go for it."

Cait blinked, stared at him. He couldn't tell, though, if that was shock or disappointment in her eyes. Either way, she quickly recovered. She smiled again and had a long sip of her beer.

Just as the electricity came back on.

"Three days," Cait bargained. "Then you can decide if you want your own fantasy to come true."

"My fantasy?" He was about to add that, yeah, he'd been having some fantasies about her. Specifically about getting her naked and kissing every inch of her.

She stood and dropped a chaste kiss on the tip of his nose. "The fantasy of having sex with the only eligible woman in town you haven't already nailed."

With her mouth bent in a self-satisfied grin, she puckered her lips and blew out the Asshole Repellent candle.

CHAPTER ELEVEN

CAIT WAS SO tired that she thought she should maybe check and see if her butt was literally dragging on the ground. A twelve-hour shift could do that. A shift that'd started with a bad night's sleep could do it even faster.

A bad night's sleep was becoming the norm for her, though, and she knew exactly where to place the blame.

Hayes.

And, well, herself.

She had to share that blame because she'd been the one who'd thrown out that stupid sex challenge. Three days to think about doing what they'd both been thinking about doing since he'd come back to town. That meant tomorrow either he was going to show up at her place, expecting sex, or he could go in the other direction. Hayes could decide that she'd insulted him by the whole fantasy/Slade stuff, and it had jogged him to his senses.

Senses that would prevent him from following through and showing her what the fuss was all about.

Cait wanted to experience that fuss. Wanted Hayes naked and in her bed. Or anywhere else she could get him. But this particular fuss would come with a ding to the heart when he left. Maybe Hayes didn't want to leave her with a heart ding even if it was accompanied by what would no doubt be an amazing orgasm. Or three.

Cursing the fatigue and the unsettled feelings bubbling

inside her, Cait drove home with one thing in mind. Sleep. It was only five thirty and still plenty light outside, but she was exhausted. She needed a nap, bad, and then she could eat and crash for the rest of the night. Maybe tomorrow— which was decision day for Hayes—she'd have a better handle on her blasted hormones.

Her stomach lurched a little when she saw someone on her porch. For a split second, she thought it might be Hayes coming to collect early on the fantasy. But the stomach lurching took a nasty turn when she spotted someone else instead.

Her father.

Since she didn't have any chairs there, he was sitting on the porch, his back resting against her front door. She couldn't see his face because he'd pulled his Stetson low, but she recognized the snakeskin band. Ditto for his long, nearly shoulder-length hair that was now threaded with gray.

He put his thumb under the brim of his hat to push it back, and smiling, he stood. His lanky body and face were showing signs of age. Character lines, some people called them. As if her father needed any more character on that famous handsome face. Yep, handsome. Even her severe ire for him couldn't cause her to see him as butt ugly. Too bad that handsome face, and his fame, had gotten him into too many women's beds.

"Cait," he greeted her when she got out of her SUV.

His voice was lazy and unruffled, similar to the way he'd gotten up from his sitting position. He moved as if he had all the time and not a care in the world.

Well, she sure as heck had some *cares*, and over the years, he'd been the reason for plenty of them.

She glanced around, looking for how he'd gotten there, and she finally spotted the chestnut mare in her corral. It belonged to Shaw, which meant Marty had already paid a visit to the family ranch. She wondered why her brother hadn't texted or called to warn her, but it was possible that Shaw hadn't been home. Or that Marty hadn't told Shaw that he'd be riding over to her house.

"Where have you been?" she snapped, ignoring Marty's friendly greeting and his equally friendly smile. Both were BS that he could dole out on a whim. "Your grandson showed up nearly a week ago."

He nodded, and again, it was slow and easy. Friendly, still. As usual, he wasn't affected by her tone or scowl. And that only made the cut even deeper. It was bad enough that her father didn't care squat about his kids and now his grandkid, but he couldn't even muster up enough emotion to lash out at her.

"I had some things I needed to settle first," he said, the corner of his mouth lifting into a smile. "I went over to the ranch, but Shaw said McCall and Kinsley took the boy into San Antonio for some clothes. I decided to ride Missy over here and get your take on things. I asked him not to let you know I was coming 'cause I was a mite worried if you knew, that you wouldn't want to be here."

Nothing he could have said would have cooled her temper, but it especially riled her that he'd called the mare by name when he hadn't done the same for his own grandson. And, yeah, she might have skipped out on his visit if she'd gotten word of it first. Or at least that's what she would have wanted to do. But she wouldn't have. Not when she needed to get some things straight with Marty.

"Adam," Cait emphasized. "That's his name, and he needed you here last week."

"I'm here now," Marty drawled, as if that fixed everything.

It fixed nothing. But that was typical. She wasn't actually sure Marty was capable of fixing anything other than a broken guitar string or maybe a stuck zipper on his jeans. He had no trouble lowering said zipper, though, so he could knock someone up.

Cait took out some of her frustrations on the door by jamming the key into the lock with far more force than necessary. Marty moseyed in right behind her. There was no other word for it. The man walked like he drawled. A slow good ol' boy pace that she figured some people found charming. Cait was too tired and fed up enough for it to be the straw that broke the camel's back. She dumped her purse and keys on the foyer table and whirled on him.

"Shaw and Mom had to sign papers to keep Adam from being taken by Child Protective Services. He was scared, and you made him feel like shit when you didn't step up to help."

He nodded, tipped his head to her fridge. "Mind if I get me something cold to drink, and then my throat won't be so dry while we talk?"

Cait wanted to say *no way in hell*, just because she was pissed off, but she gave a go-ahead motion to help himself. That would give her a couple of moments to find some calm to go along with those *cares*.

She dropped down onto the sofa, closed her eyes and didn't open them until she felt the nudge on her shoulder. Marty was standing over her, drinking a Coke, and he handed her one. She took it but didn't open it. Cait just slid her fingers through the cold moisture on the can.

"I went by the lawyer's and set up a fund with some money for the boy. For Adam," Marty amended, no doubt because he saw the renewed anger flare in her eyes. Really bad mean anger. "He'll be taken care of financially."

She aimed a hard stare at him as he sank down into the chair next to her. "You know he needs more than just money."

Marty nodded. "But not for long. The lawyer said Debra would be out of jail in only a couple of months. Lenore said it was all right if Adam stayed at the ranch until then."

Cait waited to see if Marty had fully understood what he'd just said. Apparently not. "Adam will be at the ranch for *a couple of months*," she repeated. "He'll need family, and whether you want to be or not, you're his family."

He bobbed his head in agreement. "And I made him feel like shit when I didn't step up to help." Marty looked her straight in the eyes. "Do you really believe I could have made him feel less shitty had I been here?"

The answer to that was easy, and she felt another tsunami of anger wash over her. "No. But you should have been here anyway. For once in your life, you should have at least made an effort to do the right thing." Saying all of this was useless, but she couldn't make herself stop. "Not just for Adam but for Kinsley, too. She's still a kid, and she's not raising herself. We're raising her. Mom, Shaw, Austin, Leyton, Sunny and me. *We're. Raising. Her.*"

Her voice had gotten louder with each word so that by the time she finished, Cait was shouting so loud she was surprised she hadn't caused the walls and floor to vibrate. The anger coming off her felt like an earthquake.

Despite her earthquake shouting, Marty still didn't jump to respond. He had a couple of sips of Coke first and took his time getting out the words he finally offered her. "And you're doing a fine job of it. I had a phone chat with Kinsley just last month. She's a good kid."

Cait sighed. "A kid who doesn't have her father." No shout that time. It was low, hoarse, but still filled with way too much emotion.

She felt her eyes burn, and she cursed. She hadn't cried over her father in years, and she sure as heck wouldn't do it now.

Well, she probably wouldn't.

She hated, hated, hated that he could pluck at her this way. Like taking her apart one small piece at a time and flinging those pieces carelessly aside. Hated that it still mattered that he hadn't been around enough to be even a marginally good parent. It made her feel too many things that started with *un*. Unhappy. Unwanted.

Unloved.

That was the worst of the *un*s. Because even a famous, busy father with a demanding career could still make his children feel loved. Cait had never felt that, and it broke her heart to think that Kinsley and Adam might not, either. It could burn into them the same kind of hurt and anger she was dealing with now, and she didn't want that for them. For anyone.

"I know what you want from me when it comes to Adam," he said, his words cutting through the pounding pulse that was now in her ears. "I can do lip service and tell you I will, but you know how this plays out."

She did indeed know because it had happened way too many times already. "You'll be around for a little while. Maybe a day or two at the most. And then you'll leave because it's more important for you to be somewhere else than here."

Cait thought of what Hayes had said. *Anywhere but here was where I wanted to be.* Marty probably felt that, too, but the difference was that Hayes was still a brother, still a grandson, still a reliable presence in his family's lives. Marty was none of those things and never had been.

"I can't be here for long," Marty went on, and she fig-

ured this was the part where he would try to explain that
he felt like a failure in this small town. That he didn't fit
in. That the urge to leave was more than a mere urge. It
had been as necessary for him as breathing.

But no.

That was all he said. *I can't be here for long.* The sum-
mation of why Marty Jameson was a steaming pile of
bullshit when it came to his family.

"Did you know when I was a teenager, I bought tickets
to your concerts?" she asked.

He pulled back his shoulders, the surprise lighting in
his eyes. Something else was there, too. He was obviously
pleased, and he doled out one of his smiles.

"I didn't do that because I like your music or because I
actually wanted to see you," Cait quickly explained. Her
voice was back to snapping again. "I did it because you look
at your fans as if they're the greatest things in the world.
You love them. And for three hours, I wanted you to look
at me that way."

His smile faded, and she watched as the verbal blow
landed hard. Just as she'd wanted it to. He nodded, stood
and turned away from her. She expected him to walk out.
Marty was a pro at walking out. But much to her shock,
he stayed put.

"I love you, but I can't look at you with love," he said.

Again, he paused for a long time. So long that Cait finally snarled, "What kind of bull crap is that? You can't
look at me?"

She hurried in front of him so he'd have to do just that.
Oh, he looked, but there was plenty of gaze dodging along
with it.

"Does the sight of me disgust you?" she demanded. Then
she went for another verbal blow, but he'd already struck

just by not looking at her. "Is it because I resemble you too much?"

He sighed, and that was his only response for more of those long draggy moments. "You look like your mother, too, and she's a beautiful woman. You're beautiful," he added.

"Then why can't you look at me?" she shouted. Cait latched on to each side of his jaw, locking his head in place so that he had no choice but for his eyes to finally meet hers.

He sighed again. A sound that made her want to throttle him. Then again, she usually felt that way about Marty.

Making her own sigh, Cait let go of him and backed away. "That part about me being beautiful is malarkey," she grumbled, hating that she'd latched on to it for even a second. Mercy, she wouldn't take even crumbs from him.

"I can't look at you," he repeated. But he turned to her and did exactly that. Full eye contact. His eyes staring into hers. "Because when I see you, I remember just how much I didn't do right by you."

Another crumb. That's all this was, and Cait mentally repeated that to herself a lot in the silence that followed.

"I know I'm the one who screwed you up," her father admitted. "I'm the one who failed you," he added in a mumble. "And despite all the emotional baggage I gave you, you turned out to be amazing. You're a damn miracle, Cait."

She was glad he wasn't looking at her because she didn't want him to see her blinking back tears. Didn't want him to hear her swallowing hard to get rid of the lump in her throat.

Crumbs. But this crumb hit her right in the heart. Apparently, she wasn't the only one who could land some powerful verbal blows.

"You hurt me," she whispered.

The moment she said the words, Cait wished she could

cram them all back inside and give them a shove to bury them deep. Just as she'd always done. She hadn't wanted him to know he had that kind of power over her. She wanted no man to ever know that.

And there was the gist of her insecurities.

She didn't need years of therapy or elevated enlightenment to know that her insecurities had started with this "been there, done that" country-music singer who'd fathered her but had never been a father. When she hadn't felt loved, she hadn't felt complete. Maybe that was Marty's fault, but she put some of the blame on her shoulders. Because he shouldn't matter. After all the crap he'd pulled, Marty Jameson shouldn't matter.

But he did.

Damn it. He did.

"I'm real sorry about hurting you," Marty finally said, and she thought maybe his voice was a little bit choked up.

She wanted to believe the emotion was real, but then again, she'd heard him spill out plenty of genuine-sounding emotions in the songs he sang for his adoring fans. Those fans whom he loved when he looked at them.

Cait didn't acknowledge the possibility that his apology had been sincere, but she wanted to hang on to the chance that it might be. She also wanted to hang on to the sliver of hope that she might finally be getting her message through Marty's thick head.

"You need to fix things with Adam before it's too late," she tried again. "You need to show him that he matters. Ditto for Kinsley. For Avery and Gracie. Please don't give them the clichéd baggage you handed over to the rest of us." Especially since those four had already been through enough.

He nodded his thick head. Just a nod. No verbal acknowledgment whatsoever that she'd said something that had finally made him take a hard look at what he was doing. And at what he'd done. He repeated that "just a nod" when she continued to stare at him.

Cait waited. Cursed herself for waiting. Then cursed herself for holding on to the possibility that her father could mend his sorry ways.

Now she was the one who broke eye contact and looked away. She'd had more than enough of this. Enough of Marty and the crap storm of emotions he always brought with him. There'd be other crap storms, other times when he was able to grab on to her heart and give it a good twist.

She wasn't a miracle, not to Marty. Not to anyone.

Unbearably exhausted to the bone, she was about to demand he leave when she heard a vehicle pull up in front of her house. It was one of her brothers, no doubt, who'd come to check on her since Shaw would have told everyone that Marty had ridden over to see her, and the troops would be arriving to try to pull a Humpty Dumpty and put her back together again. If there was a miracle in this scenario, it was her family. Minus Marty, of course. Then again, he had family status in name only.

Cait quickly wiped her eyes, steeled herself up and went to the door. She threw it open, ready to deliver a snarky line that would assure whichever sibling was on the porch that she was all right whether she was or not. But it wasn't one of her brothers.

It was Hayes.

He moved fast for a man with cracked ribs. Too fast for her to tell him that they weren't alone. Hayes hooked his arm around her waist, pulled her to him and kissed her. This wasn't an "it's good to see you" kiss, either. This was long, slow, deep and thorough.

And incredibly effective.

It gave all the hurt a quick shove and replaced it with a scalding heat. She stopped it only because she was about to pass out from lack of oxygen.

Hayes's breath gusted like hers, and he looked her straight in the eyes. "I want to have sex with you right now."

Cait couldn't answer. She could blame that on the shock and not enough air to form a verbal response. But that didn't stop Marty from saying something.

Marty cleared his throat, causing Hayes's gaze to fly across the room and land on her father. "I'm guessing the words you're looking for right now are along the lines of *holy shit*," Marty drawled.

YEAH, THOSE WERE definitely the words Hayes had been thinking. He'd come to Cait's house with just one thing on his mind.

Sex.

He sure as hell hadn't expected for Marty to be there. And for Marty to hear the sex demand that'd been for Cait's ears only.

"Mr. Jameson," Hayes said, stepping inside.

He glanced at Marty, then at Cait before Hayes studied their body language. He didn't know what had gone on here, what'd been said, but he was pretty sure Cait had been crying, and there was some bone-deep sadness in her expression. He didn't have to guess why, either. Her SOB father was responsible. Hayes was deciding if he needed to kick Marty's ass when Cait took hold of his hand.

"Uh, Hayes and I need to talk," Cait insisted, barely sparing her father a glance.

She didn't give Marty a chance to respond. She led Hayes out of the living room and to the back of the house and into a small laundry room. A very messy one. There were two hampers piled high on the floor and a heap of what appeared to be clean unfolded towels on the dryer. Bras and panties of all colors dangled from a clothesline that had been strung from wall to wall. Hayes had to bat aside a skimpy white lace bra so they could get far enough into the room for Cait to shut the door.

"I'm sorry I blurted out that sex thing," Hayes told her right off, and then he added the most important thing. "Are you all right?"

Cait drew in a long breath through her mouth and pushed her hair from her face before exhaling. "It's just draining to deal with Marty."

Hayes didn't think *draining* was the right word for it. *Pain in the ass* was a better way to put it, but he was pretty sure this encounter had gone well beyond that. And that's why Hayes pulled her into his arms. He doubted it would help any of the old baggage and eternally raw wounds she had because of Marty, but he didn't know what else to do.

Cait didn't exactly slide into the hug. She sort of melted against him. Not in a heated, sexual kind of way. No, this felt like serious fatigue, and the weary sigh that left her mouth confirmed it.

"You worked a twelve-hour shift," he said.

She made a sound of agreement but didn't look up. Cait kept her head on his shoulder. "How'd you know that?"

"I heard Em tell Tony when they were trying to work out who would pick up Austin's twins from school."

Another sound of agreement. "McCall had to reschedule some appointments because I got tied up with the Crocketts."

He knew about that, too. The Crocketts were the couple responsible for Cait's thermometer injury/stitches, and if Em had gotten it right, Cait had needed to go with them before a judge today so they could be sentenced. If Hayes had listened longer to Em's conversation, he likely would have heard the results of that sentencing, along with parts he hadn't wanted to hear about varicose vein surgery that a woman named Martha Ellis was having.

Cait and he stood there another few moments before she finally eased away and looked up at him. "Let me finish dealing with Marty, and then we can talk about the romantic, cleverly worded *offer* you made when you first got here."

He winced. His "I want to have sex with you right now" had definitely been lacking in the romantic/clever wording department. But by the time he'd made it to her place, Hayes had already jumped on the crazy train. His body had been burning for her, and he hadn't been able to think of anything else but taking her then and there. He was still thinking about that, but it could wait. Cait was right—she did need to deal with Marty first.

So did he.

It was time he had a "come to Jesus" meeting with her father. It didn't matter that it wasn't really any of his business. He might be able to get through to the man and convince him to at least try to make an effort with his offspring and the next generation of Jamesons. While he was at it, Hayes could emphasize that the asshole better not put tears in Cait's eyes again.

Cait took another of those deep breaths, and she pulled back her shoulders, which she immediately had to readjust again because she had to duck and weave her way through the dangling underwear. Hayes got smacked in the face by a black lacy bra that probably would have been a big-time distraction for him had he not wanted to be focused when they faced her father. With Hayes right behind her, they went back into the living room.

Only to find it empty.

Muttering some profanity, Cait went to the side window and threw back the curtain. "He left," she snarled.

Hayes glanced out and saw that the horse that'd been in the corral was no longer there. Well, what a shithead. Not the horse but rather the man who'd used it to make his getaway.

Still muttering those curse words, Cait looked around until her attention landed on the piece of paper on the coffee table. As if dreading what she would see there, she slowly made her way to pick it up.

"'I need some thinking time,'" Cait read aloud. "'Will be in touch soon. Love, Dad.'"

Hayes felt the punch of anger and knew it had to be a tiny speck compared to what Cait was feeling. "You want me to go after him?" Hayes asked.

"No," she answered without hesitation. Her sigh was long and weary. "It wouldn't do any good. *Thinking time* is his way of saying he's tucking tail and running again. I really thought I'd gotten through to him about Adam," she added in a mumble. "I mean, he only nodded, but I thought maybe…" She waved off the rest of whatever she'd been about to say.

There was so much pain in that one comment that it had Hayes stepping in front of her. He took the letter and tossed it back on the coffee table. "What happened?" Hayes asked. "What'd Marty do to make you cry?"

She shook her head, but even as she was doing that, he saw the tears start to shimmer again. His first reaction was a slam of anger, all of it directed at Marty, but Hayes felt her pain, too. He knew plenty about the past coming back to bite you in the ass. There wasn't much he could do about that. Hell, about Marty, either. But he could try to soothe away all the frayed edges he was seeing on Cait's face.

"You asked Marty to step up and give Adam some time and attention," Hayes guessed. "Marty, being Marty, dodged and deflected."

"Yes," she muttered. Then she paused. "But he nodded. I know that doesn't sound like much, but it seemed to be, well, a good sign. I thought he was at least toying with the wacky notion of doing the right thing."

A nod definitely wasn't something to write home to mama about, but if it'd given Cait some hope, even temporary hope, then perhaps it had been somewhat of a big deal.

"You thought you'd gotten through to Marty," he paraphrased. "And maybe you did. He could be thinking about the way to handle this right now."

Of course, it was just as possible that Marty was making another contribution to his "genetic" legacy, but he didn't want that reminder to drag Cait down any more than she already was. Then again, Hayes wasn't sure it was possible for her mood to get any lower, and talking about her father didn't appear to be making anything better.

"Have you eaten?" he asked.

Obviously, he'd surprised her, because her gaze whipped up to his. She smiled, but it didn't quite reach her eyes. "You came over for sex," she reminded him.

"Sex can wait." And he hoped he didn't lose his membership in the man club for saying that. "Why don't you have a long soak in the tub, maybe a glass of wine, and I'll fix you something for dinner?"

She stared at him. "You're, uh, going to take care of me?"

He wished that she hadn't asked that in the same tone as *Slackers is now going to be lovable?* He could do stuff to take care of her, and to prove it, he took her by the hand and led her to the bathroom. No tub in there, only a shower, so he went in search of the master bedroom. No tub there, either.

"I'm a shower person," she muttered.

Well then, he'd have to go with other stuff to help her through this. "Okay, how about that glass of wine or a beer?"

She sighed, pushed her hair from her face and glanced at the bed. Not in a sexual "why don't you join me there" kind of way. Nope. It was the look of a woman who was exhausted. So Hayes led her there, had her sit, and he stooped down to take off her shoes.

"Thanks. But I just need a nap. I can eat in an hour or two."

"I can hang around and cook once you're awake." Or even head to the diner and bring her back something.

"You're taking care of me," she added, mumbling now, and this time it didn't sound like something out of the implausible realm. "Thanks. Who knew you had layers like this."

"Layers?" he questioned.

She gave him a lazy smile. "Hot badass actor with a kind heart."

Hayes thought the only true thing in that was the actor part. It certainly didn't mean he had a kind heart just because he hated seeing her like this. It was as if the long workday and the encounter with Marty had sapped every drop of her energy.

"You want me to find you a nightgown or some pj's?" he asked.

Cait shook her head and fought to keep her eyes open. "I always sleep in my underwear."

That was of definite interest to him, and he got some very vivid images of Cait on that bed wearing that black lace stuff he'd seen in the laundry room. "Some of your underwear is…interesting. Don't take this the wrong way, but a couple of bras were borderline eye porn."

"Layers," she muttered, her voice a little groggy. She curled up on her side. "I've got them, too."

Yes, she did. The devoted sister who would do anything for her family. The smart-mouthed cop who was soft enough beneath to be hurt by her father, a man she should have long steeled herself against.

Hayes took the side of the quilt and draped it over her.

"Layers," she repeated, her eyelids fluttering down. He brushed a kiss on her cheek and turned to leave, but her mutterings stopped him in his tracks. "If I'm not careful, I could fall in love with you."

CHAPTER TWELVE

CAIT WOKE WITH the lovely dream still floating around in her head. A dream of Hayes, his mouth gliding over her body. Kissing her in all the right places. Making her feel as if she could linger in that slippery slide of pleasure for hours before he finished her off with an equally lovely orgasm.

She opened her eyes, glanced around, disappointed that he wasn't there with those right-place kisses. Too bad. She was still in that slide and could have used him to finish her off—

If I'm not careful, I could fall in love with you.

Those were her words. Her voice. Had that been part of the dream?

She shook her head to clear it. And then Cait cursed a blue streak. Because, no, it hadn't been in the dream. She'd actually said that to him before she'd drifted off from exhaustion. Well, she wasn't exhausted now. She was wide-awake and thoroughly pissed off at herself for baring her heart to him like that.

Hayes wasn't the sort to take that confession and use it to get her in the sack, but it was embarrassing and had made her sound like a starstruck fan. He already had so many of those, and Cait didn't want to be on that particular bandwagon.

Still muttering some profanity, all aimed at herself, she glanced at the clock on her nightstand. It was a little past seven o'clock, and the red dot next to the time let her know that she hadn't napped the night away. Good, because she was starving. Once she ate, she'd then deal with Hayes, lying to him that what she'd said had been the mutterings of a woman spent by fatigue.

Well, she'd deal with him if he was still here, that is.

He wasn't in the bedroom, but she did hear voices. Soft murmurs that made her wonder if he was watching TV. Something also smelled amazing. Roasted chicken, maybe? So Hayes had perhaps kept his promise to fix her dinner after all.

She freshened up in the bathroom, and, yes, that included fiddling with her makeup. It was vain, of course, but if she was going to eat crow—and the chicken—then she wanted to look her best. Too bad her best was nowhere in the range of what Hayes was accustomed to.

Cait stared at herself in the mirror, her attention lingering on every flaw, of which there were legions. No one would ever call her beautiful.

Tucking that depressing thought aside, she went into the living room to face the music, aka Hayes. But he wasn't there. The TV wasn't on, either, and she realized the voices she'd heard were coming from the front porch. She thought maybe he was talking to someone on speaker on the phone, but she recognized one of the voices as Adam's.

That sent Cait hurrying out the door, and she practically tripped over someone when she raced onto the porch. Not Adam or Hayes but Hadley. All conversation stopped, all eyes went to her.

Hayes was on the top porch step, and Adam was seated just below him. Hadley was sitting by the door with her back against the wall in an almost identical position as

Marty when he'd made his impromptu visit a couple of hours earlier.

It wasn't fully dark yet, but the sun was low—not enough, though, to cool things down much. It was still too hot to be shooting the breeze on the porch. Alarmed, she hurried out to them.

"Uh, what's going on?" Cait asked.

No one jumped to answer, so Cait settled her gaze on Hayes. "Hadley drove Adam here," Hayes explained. "He wanted to see you."

Cait shifted her attention to her nephew and wished for better lighting so she could tell if he'd been crying. Everything about his body language—the lowered head, slumped shoulders, downturned mouth—indicated he was upset. And she didn't have to guess why.

"What'd Marty do now?" Cait asked on a huff.

Again, there was more silence, and it was Hadley who finally spoke up. "Marty took off without saying anything. He left Adam a note," Hadley added, and she didn't bother to hide her disgust about that.

Cait didn't hide hers, either. "Let me guess. The note said he needed some thinking time."

Adam gave the slightest of nods and swatted at a mosquito that was zinging around them while it made that high-pitched sound.

"Bingo," Hadley verified. "Lenore tried to call Marty, but of course, he didn't answer. I was there doing some wedding stuff and heard what was going on. So I volunteered to drive Adam around to look for Marty, thinking that maybe he'd be at the diner or somewhere in town. There was no sign of him."

"See my shocked face," Cait grumbled, her tone as dry as month-old toast.

But the dynamics of this were somewhat interesting. Hadley wasn't a Jameson—not yet, anyway—and yet she'd taken on one of the recurring family duties of mopping up after one of Marty's messes. Not that Adam was a mess. He wasn't. No, the mess king in this family picture was none other than Marty.

"I just wanted to ask you if my grandfather said anything about me," Adam muttered.

Cait picked through the conversation she'd had with her dad and couldn't come up with anything that was going to make Adam feel any better. Still, she had to give him something. Preferably something that wouldn't give him false hope that he'd ever be more than a passing thought to his asshole of a grandfather.

"Marty said he'd made arrangements to take care of you financially," Cait settled for saying.

That got the response she'd expected. Adam shrugged. There weren't any indications that Adam wasn't already being taken care of financially, and since Marty was rich, that wasn't exactly a grand gesture on his part. He certainly hadn't volunteered his time. Then again, he never had. Money, running and dodging conflict were his go-to responses.

"He's mad at me, isn't he?" Adam asked her. "That's why he left without seeing me."

On a heavy sigh, Cait went closer and stooped down so she'd be at his eye level. Unlike her father, she had no trouble *looking*. "If Marty's mad at anyone, it's me, not you. He and I had a few choice words before he sneaked out of here."

Sneaked was the right word for it. Cait wouldn't cut her father any slack on that, but she would try to soothe Adam.

"When Marty gets cornered, he leaves," Cait went on. "He was doing that before you were born. Heck, before I was born." She'd heard plenty of stories about her father's long road trips. Apparently, though, he'd come home often enough to knock up her mother with four kids.

"I tried to call him, too," Adam went on. "My grand-father, I mean. I used the number Miss Lenore had, but the call went straight to voice mail. I left him a message and told him not to be mad at me, that it wasn't like he actually owed me anything 'cause I'm only his grandson."

Oh, that did a number on Cait's heart. Because there shouldn't be an *only* when it came to being a grandson. And this boy shouldn't be crushed because Marty couldn't see that.

"There's nothing *only* about you," she tried to assure him. "You're going through a tough time, and from what I see, you're handling it well."

He stared at her as if she'd just dished out a heaping serving of BS.

"Really," Cait insisted. "Trust me on that. You're not yelling or crying. I did both," she confessed. "I probably called him a name or two. I tend to do that when he makes me mad. Which is pretty much every time I set eyes on him."

She glanced at Hayes. Saw the kindred-spirit sympathy. Welcomed it. Of course, that didn't mean they wouldn't have to talk about the love stuff she'd said. But for now, she wasn't finished with Adam.

"Look, we're not a normal family," Cait continued, brushing her hand over Adam's arm. "But you're more than welcome into it. Not just for these next few months, either. You're welcome here anytime for as long as you want."

Adam stayed quiet a few moments and then finally glanced at her, then at Hayes. His mouth twitched a little in what might have been the start of a smile. "Never thought I'd be in a family with Slade McClendon. I mean, I know he's not blood kin, but Hadley said he'll sort of be like my uncle-in-law when she marries Leyton."

Yep, Hayes would indeed be family, and Cait figured that once all of his sisters had married her brothers, then the eyes of the town would be on him and her to make it a finished "set." Well, those eyes would be on them if he stayed. After her "If I'm not careful, I could fall in love with you," Hayes might be in a hurry to get out of Dodge.

Adam stood and surprised Cait by giving her a hug. It was probably the fastest hug in the history of that particular gesture, but it felt like a warm fuzzy blanket. Hayes stood as well and gave his sister a hug. Not a fast one, though. Hadley held on awhile.

"You'll let me know if Sunshine calls you back tonight," Hadley said.

Cait heard the worry in Hadley's voice. Saw it, too, on Hayes's face. Well, crud. Apparently, he'd had another run-in with his mother while she'd been napping.

Hayes and she waited on the porch while Hadley and Adam went to Hadley's car. Cait waited until they'd driven away before she turned to him.

"Sunshine called you?" she asked.

He nodded, scrubbed his hand over his stubbled chin. "Right before Hadley and Adam arrived. In fact, I was out here on the porch talking to her when they drove up."

Considering the weariness in his eyes, she didn't have to guess that the conversation with his mom hadn't gone well. Then again, chats with Sunshine never went well.

"Oh, the irony of your mother's name," Cait muttered, motioning for him to follow her back inside after she had to swat a persistent whining mosquito. "I doubt Em had a clue how her daughter would turn out when she put that cheery name on the birth certificate."

Hayes made a sound of agreement, but that was his only response until they were back in the house with the door closed. "Sunshine told me if she didn't have permission to film the wedding by tomorrow, then she'd release Ivy's emails."

Cait thought about the timing of that. The wedding was still a week and a half away. Not much time to arrange for a camera crew, but this was Sunshine. The woman probably already had a crew on tap.

"If she goes ahead and releases the emails," Hayes went on, "Sunshine could have something else up her sleeve. Something to try to get my sisters to cave in and meet her demands. Because once the emails are out there, she loses her leverage. She'd need a backup plan."

Cait wished that weren't true, but it made sense in a twisted kind of way. "Or she could extend the deadline. Because even if she has something else, the emails are a big hammer for her right now."

"Yes," he agreed. There wasn't any anger in his voice, just the frustration and fatigue. "I'll call Ivy's parents in the morning and give them a heads-up."

She was betting that wouldn't be a fun call. Those people had already been through enough, but Sunshine didn't give a rat's ass about that. It was all about her, her, her.

Cait went to the kitchen, got them both a beer and peered into the oven. Yep, it was a chicken baking, all right, complete with little red potatoes and baby carrots. And it would apparently be ready soon since there was only twenty minutes left on the timer.

"You cooked," she commented. "And you shopped."

Cait had figured out that last one because there was a grocery bag on the counter. Hayes must have driven into town to get the fixings for the meal. Good thing, too, because if he'd relied on what was in her fridge or pantry, they'd be having peanut butter sandwiches and some grapes that were just a day or two from turning into raisins.

"And you dealt with Adam," she added, which was a much bigger deal than all the other things combined.

Hayes nodded, and he gave a short-lived smile. "I can do things."

Maybe it was because of that dream she'd had about him, but that sounded sexual. Of course, Hayes was the walking, talking definition of *sexual*.

"Hadley said we should trick Sunshine into signing a contract," Hayes went on, leaning against the counter while he sipped his beer. "She thought we could get Sunshine to agree to only film the wedding in certain spots, and then we'd all make sure none of us was in those spots."

"Clever," Cait concluded. "Hadley can be sneaky like that."

The plan probably wasn't something Sunshine would even consider, but Cait thought of the logistics of such an idea. Logistics that wouldn't be in their favor. The wedding was at Em's ranch in a tent that would be set up between the house and the barn. There'd be a lot of going back and forth, so an equally sneaky camera crew could figure out a way to get plenty of shots of the brides and grooms.

"Yeah, I'm worried about Hadley's sneakiness," he murmured, and Hayes stared down into his beer as if it might hold some solutions for all of this.

Cait wished she had a fix, but without proof to haul Sunshine into the station and charge her with extortion, she could only stand back and watch. And what she was watching was the face of an exhausted man.

"You should have been the one taking the nap," she

pointed out. "You can grab a quick one before dinner if you want." She winced. "A quick nap," Cait clarified.

Hayes lifted his eyes, slowly, and his gaze connected with hers. It was as if Pandora's box had just opened. A box filled with all the heat and emotions they'd been bottling up for days.

He moved toward her, setting his beer aside in the same motion. The moment the bottle landed on the countertop, he had his arm around her and pulled her against him. His mouth landed solidly on hers.

This kiss shouldn't have been this much of a shock, and it sure as heck shouldn't have been this hot. Five seconds ago, they'd been talking about naps. Now her mouth was being taken by someone who knew exactly how to do it.

Hayes didn't wait to deepen the kiss. Nope. He moved straight in, tongue to tongue. She tasted the beer, but beneath it, that was all Hayes. She certainly wasn't an expert at kissing him, but Cait was pretty sure she'd be able to pick that taste out of a kissing lineup.

His lips glided over hers, creating a delicious pressure. A pressure that he moved to other parts when he pulled her against him. Cait set down her own beer so she could hook her arms around his neck.

Their eyes met for just a split second, and she saw the heat in his. And the surprise. Maybe surprise because the kiss wasn't supposed to be like this.

Or maybe because Hayes hadn't thought *she* would be like this.

Oh, he'd wanted her, of course. The heat was proof of that. So was his erection that she brushed against. But in his "conqueror of all available women" mind, maybe he hadn't believed that she could be more than just a conquest. Maybe there was something else there.

Then again, her own need might be blinding her to reality.

That this was just sexual attraction and nothing more.

She couldn't let herself believe it was more because that way led her down a path where she'd repeat things like, *If I'm not careful, I could fall in love with you.* It could lead to a whole boatload of pain and regret. Or worse. No regret, just the pain, and if that happened, then Hayes would ruin her for any other man. Some people came back from things like that, but Cait knew she wouldn't.

Still, she didn't stop this.

She took the kiss Hayes was doling out, added some moves of her own until it wasn't enough. Until she needed more. That was the problem with making out. More was always right there, crooking its finger to invite you to the next level. Hayes went to the next level by sliding his hand between them and over her breasts.

Hayes had touched her like this before, and maybe that's why he only lingered a second before he lifted her top and unhooked her bra. He'd done this before, too, but that thought flew out of mind when he lowered his head and took her nipple into his mouth.

This, they hadn't done.

This, she hadn't believed could spin her from "next" to "now."

It was obvious, though, that Hayes didn't intend to give her "now." He lingered there, tongue kissing her nipples while his left hand went to her butt. He squeezed her, shifting and aligning them so that the front of his jeans was against the front of hers. Zipper to zipper.

She felt his erection again, felt the delicious flicks of fire when her center rubbed against the long, hard length of him. This was "next," a couple of notches up from what he'd already done to her, and he still didn't stop.

He moved his hand from her butt to her stomach. Then

lower. And lower. Until his hand was between his erection and her. Normally, she wouldn't have considered that a good replacement, but it turned out that Hayes was just as clever with his hand on her jeans as he was with his tongue in her mouth. Which he did again. Touching her and kissing.

This was like the dream. The slow, slippery slide of heat. The knife-edge of need that was already starting to urge her on to take this higher and higher until she got some release from the heat. She had one of the hottest guys on the planet against her, and she wanted to make the most of it.

Hayes definitely made the most of it. He unzipped her, sliding his hand down into her jeans and to the front of her panties. The pleasure shot through her. No more slow slide. This was a fast ride down a mountain, and it didn't seem to matter to her body that there was still a millimeter of fabric between his fingers and her. Nope. It didn't matter because Cait felt that need soar. Too hard, too fast. She couldn't tamp it down and had no choice but to give in to it.

To give in to Hayes.

The orgasm came, rippling through her with that blinding pleasure that a good orgasm could. And this was a *good* one. So good that it was many long moments—maybe even a month—before she realized that it would have been even better if Hayes had been inside her.

Intending to remedy that "inside her" part now, Cait pushed him back just enough so she could go after his zipper. Her body was still pulsing, her heartbeat throbbing, but she still managed to cut through that and hear the sound he made. Not pleasure.

Pain.

Her gaze flew to his face, and, yes, that was a grimace of pain. Which he quickly tried to hide. No way, though, for him to hide that he moved his hand from her panties and to his side. The one with the cracked ribs.

Crap. How could she have forgotten he was still on the mend? Apparently, amazing foreplay and an orgasm could do that. But Cait sure as heck remembered it now.

"I'm sorry," she said just as the timer on the oven went off. It wasn't a quick beep-beep reminder, either, but an impatient shrill pulse of noise.

Cait gently untangled herself from Hayes and crossed the kitchen to turn off both the timer and the oven itself. It didn't take long, but it was enough for her to catch her breath. And re-zip her jeans. While her back was still to him, she also fixed her bra and top.

"I'm okay," Hayes said when she turned around to face him.

Because he still had an erection, Cait stayed put, anchoring herself in place to keep some distance between them. Her body was urging her to give him a hand job or figure out a way to take care of that erection with her on top of him in bed. But sex, and orgasms, tensed a person's muscles, and it could turn a "hurts so bad" into an actual bad kind of hurting way.

"You will be okay," she assured him. "But I think you should take another week before we do any bed gymnastics."

The corner of his mouth lifted in one of those smiles to let her know he wouldn't mind some pain. It melted her resolve a little, but Cait quickly latched back on to it.

"Another week," she repeated.

That would be five days before the wedding, so Hayes would still be around. Of course, it wouldn't give them much time for a full-fledged fling, but they could squeeze in a few rounds of sex before he left. If he was healthy enough, they could get all those rounds done in one day.

He stared at her a long time, obviously debating this. She could have put a superfast end to the debate by poking at his ribs again, but Cait went another route. She motioned toward the oven.

"I'm starving," she lied. The orgasm had satiated multiple parts of her, including her stomach. Still, she was sure her appetite would likely return in spades once she started eating.

Hayes finally nodded. Cursed, too. The profanity was a low, husky grumble under his breath. Sexy as hell. Then again, just his breathing was sexy.

"Oh, and that whole thing about me saying I could fall in love with you," she tossed out there as she grabbed an oven mitt. Taking out the chicken gave her an excuse to have her back turned to him again. Best to finish this part of the conversation while he wasn't looking at her. "It was total BS."

Hayes stayed quiet for a moment. "Total," he repeated.

It wasn't a question. Nor was there any snark in his tone. But Cait heard what she hadn't wanted him to see on her face.

That the *total BS* was a big fat lie.

CHAPTER THIRTEEN

HAYES SAT AT the kitchen table and waited. His sisters had called a 9:00 a.m. family meeting, but it would be another fifteen minutes or so before they showed up. Maybe, just maybe, he'd be awake by then.

He was pretty sure he was now immune to the caffeine in his coffee because it sure as hell wasn't working. Even after two huge mugs of it, he was still fuzzy-headed, still feeling a couple of steps off.

It was too bad that he couldn't have a sleep transfusion, since apparently he wasn't going to get a good night's rest without something like that. There were just too many things on his mind. Sunshine's deadline, which was today. The possible cancellation of *Outlaw Rebels*. His still-healing ribs.

And Cait.

Yeah, she was definitely on his mind.

Their make-out session the night before had had an abrupt ending because of his pain, and while he'd gotten his fill of the chicken dinner, the rest of the evening had left him with an edgy need that felt like a throbbing pulse all over his body. Not pain. Nope. But an itch in desperate need of scratching.

Cait was probably feeling some of that throbbing, too. She'd gotten off, but a hand job was no substitute for the real thing, and he was betting that he was on her mind, as well. At least he hoped he was. Because it would suck if he was the only one of them who was dealing with raging hormones and doubt. That doubt was so strong that Hayes knew he should reconsider seeing her again.

If I'm not careful, I could fall in love with you.

Yeah, those weren't good words for her to say, or for him to hear. She'd tried to cover them, of course, but Hayes thought she'd blurted out the truth when she had said them. He also wasn't sure that Cait could be careful enough to guard her feelings. Not that she would automatically fall in love with him. Nope. But they were getting closer, no denying it, and with closeness came sex. Sex could lead to... well, all sorts of things other than just climaxes.

He had just about convinced himself to put some emotional distance between them when he heard the sound of jingling bells.

Cait.

She was here at the ranch and wearing the accessories to feed the duck. That brought Hayes to his feet. It cleared out some of the cobwebs, too, and gave him a full kick of heat. Heat that quickly cooled when Tony, not Cait, came jingling into the kitchen.

As usual, Em's fiancé was smiling, and he was moving as many parts of himself as a man his age could manage to move, no doubt to heighten the noise from the bells. Some of the bracelets obviously hadn't fit around his wrists and ankles, so he had them dangling from the belt and his fingers.

"You're feeding Slackers this morning?" Hayes asked him.

"I am. Cait and Em swear the bells keep him at bay."

Hayes figured that assortment of jangles would keep almost anything at bay. Probably not him, though, if Cait was wearing them. Considering his reaction when he'd thought

she had come over, not much of anything was going to put
him off her.

"You can tell me this is none of my beeswax," Tony said,
rinsing out his coffee cup and putting it in the dishwasher.
"But you've got the look of a troubled man."

That certainly wasn't a newsflash. Hayes figured he'd
been troubled, and looked it, at least three-fourths of his
time in Lone Star Ridge. But he immediately rethought
that. Yeah, Sunshine was being a pain in his ass, and he was
worried about the show, his own head and Sunny's pregnancy. But there'd been plenty of bright spots on this stay,
too. Cait was one of those bright spots and so was Em and
his sisters. Hayes was still deciding if Tony would land in
the bright-spot column or the trouble one.

"We're having a family meeting about Sunshine this
morning," Hayes answered. "And it is your beeswax since
you'll soon be marrying Em." Though he did scowl at having to use the word *beeswax*. "Em's been more of a mother
to me than Sunshine ever was, and I'm feeling more than
a bit protective of her."

Hayes paused, tried to give the man some hard-ass eye
to let Tony know he'd better not be just dicking around with
Em. But it was next to impossible to give hard-ass anything
to a man wearing a boyish grin and a thousand jingle bells.

"I do so love Em." Tony's voice took on a dreamy quality, and there was no mistaking what Hayes heard. It was
the voice of a besotted man. "You know that feeling you
get when there's no other woman for you? The glow? The
warmth? The feeling that all is right with the world?" He
didn't give Hayes a chance to answer. "Well, I got that the
first time I saw Em."

Hayes wasn't sure of that feeling at all. He'd loved Ivy,
but there had been no sexual attraction between them.

None. It was as if they'd been long-lost siblings, close ones, joined at both the heart and hip. Ivy had known him all the way to the marrow of his bones. Or rather all the way to his old baggage. And she'd loved him anyway. But he was glad that Tony felt that way about Em because after everything Sunshine had put her through, his grandmother deserved somebody special. If Tony wasn't it, or if the man wasn't good to her, Hayes would gladly make him pay. However, he didn't think he'd have to do that.

Tony patted him on the shoulder and sent the bells clattering. "I'm sure whatever's bothering you will work itself out. Don't overthink it. The heart makes better choices than the brain."

Hayes was reasonably sure that was the kind of bad advice that led to teenage pregnancies and head-splitting hangovers, but he mumbled a thanks and stood when he heard the vehicle pull up in front of the house.

"I'll get Em," Tony volunteered, and he headed out of the kitchen and toward the sewing room.

Topping off his coffee again, Hayes went to the front window and spotted Leyton and Hadley. Since Hadley had already told Hayes that Leyton had to work this morning, that meant Leyton was dropping her off. However, he didn't just let her out and drive away. Leyton stepped from his truck, went to Hadley and pulled her into his arms for a kiss. It certainly wasn't a "see you later" kind of lip-lock. This was the real deal. A full body-to-body embrace, complete with Leyton's hand on Hadley's left ass cheek. There was no doubt some tongue involved.

And it was so intimate, so all-consuming, that Hayes had to look away.

His own body reminded him of the hard-on he'd had the night before. The one that hadn't seen nearly as much action as Leyton and his sister were getting in their grand-mother's front yard.

Hayes looked up again when he heard another vehicle. Sunny and Shaw this time. They both got out, and seeing Hadley and Leyton must have spurred them to their own kiss. It was just as lusty, the kind of mouth to mouth of a couple in love. Hayes figured none of the four was thinking with their brains right now. Hearts, yes. But other parts, too.

Smiling, giggling and generally looking like the love-birds they were, Hadley, Sunny and Shaw finally started toward the house just as Austin and McCall pulled up. Driving away, Leyton gave them a wave.

"You had sex right before you came here, didn't you?" Hayes grumbled when Hadley came in first.

"Yes, I did," Hadley answered with all the glee of a well-satisfied woman. "Great sex with several peak moments." The wink she gave him was also plenty gleeful.

Sunny was looking satisfied, too, and Hayes thought that might have to do with sex, as well. Or the fact that she'd finally gotten the all clear from her doctor to go back to doing what she normally did. Which no doubt included sex.

As they made their way to the kitchen, Hayes could feel the giddiness and glee start to melt away, so by the time they joined Em and Tony, the reminder of the reason for this meeting was sinking in. It was D-Day, and Hayes wished he had a better solution for dealing with Sunshine. Correction—he wished he had a solution, period, because the one possibility he did have was well beyond a long shot.

Still jingling with every move, Tony set a basket of blue-berry muffins on the table. Hayes grabbed the coffeepot. Em had already put out the cups, and Hayes waited until everyone was seated and had served themselves before he said anything.

"Are we all in agreement that Sunshine and her crew won't be filming the weddings?" Hayes asked.

"Absolutely." Hadley was the first to answer, but the others all quickly followed suit.

However, McCall's agreement was a little thin, and there was worry in her eyes. Worry that Hayes figured was mostly for him. "Are you going to be able to deal with the fallout over Ivy?" she asked.

Hayes would deal. Maybe not well. But he wouldn't let this be about him. There'd have to be *dealings*, too, if his sisters' weddings became a tasty meal for Sunshine to serve up. If Sunshine got her way, she'd ruin the day for all of them.

"I'll be okay," Hayes told her, and he glanced at the others to try to give them the same reassurance. "It's time to talk to Sunshine."

Shaw nodded, took out a small recorder from his pocket. "Leyton and Cait said we should record this."

Hayes had already planned to do that, but he doubted Sunshine would allow her temper to get the best of her and blurt out something that could land her sorry butt in jail. Still, he might be able to rile her up enough. Especially since he had Hadley and Em, who could contribute to the riling pool. Em was a pro at pushing her daughter's hot buttons.

Hayes watched as Austin slipped his arm around McCall. Shaw took Sunny's hand, and Tony did the same with Em. Hadley and Hayes exchanged a long glance, and she finally punched him on the arm. All in all, it wasn't a bad show of support.

He took out his phone, scrolled through the contacts to Sunshine, but his finger hovered over the call button while he waited for any other input, any objections. There was none. Good. Because as far as Hayes was concerned, it was best to finish this. He made the call, put it on speaker and set his phone on the table.

There were four rings before a groggy-sounding Sunshine finally answered. "Do you know what time it is?" she grumbled.

It might have been petty, but Hayes was glad he'd woken her up, and he hoped she had a serious hangover so there was pain involved. "Time for us to tell you a big hell no on filming the wedding," he informed her. "You'll have to find another way to use your bloodsucking leeches to make more money off us."

There was some groaning and grunting, the sounds of someone trying to wake up, but it didn't take her long. It was only a couple of seconds before Sunshine snapped, "Did you forget about me releasing Ivy's emails?"

Hayes would have had an easier time forgetting that his mother was a cold, heartless bitch. "No. And FYI, I'm recording this."

There were the sounds of some fumbling around. "Well, so am I. There's no law against me releasing emails that I came across. I mean, it's not as if they're classified. Either my camera crew is at the weddings, or the world will know you didn't do diddly-squat to stop your friend's death."

The arrow hit the mark and it hit hard and fast, just as Sunshine had known it would. But Hayes took out his own weapon.

"Release them," Hayes said as casually as he could manage. "I've already told Ivy's parents to steel themselves up for the onslaught." He paused only a heartbeat. "You should steel yourself up, too."

Sunshine's pause was significantly longer than a heartbeat. "This will put her parents through an emotional nightmare."

"Yeah, it will." Hadley spoke up. "But you're good at creating emotional nightmares, aren't you, *Mother*? Along with being a big smelly sack of shit, you're the queen of shoveling said shit."

"Hadley," Sunshine snarled. "Are your sisters and grandmother there with you?"

"We are," everyone in the kitchen answered in unison.

"So are Austin, Shaw and my fiancé, Tony," Em clarified. "We actually have people who love us. Of course, you don't know what that feels like, do you, Sunshine?"

Sunshine muttered some profanity, probably because she hadn't thought they'd be a united front on this. She'd likely counted on the triplets trying to protect Hayes and vice versa.

"It's just film of your weddings," Sunshine finally said. "It can be just one cameraman, and he'll be discreet."

So she was bargaining now. Or rather trying to do that. Hayes had gone through things like this often enough that he recognized the change in her tone.

"No," Hadley snapped, and the others joined in the "no" chorus. Hadley contributed a "Fuck you."

There was more silence, but Hayes figured every square inch of Sunshine's face was shooting off sparks of rage. "Hayes," she said a couple of moments later. She was still bargaining despite her temper kicking in. "If you explain to your sisters how much this'll hurt you, then they'll go along with the filming. And it's not as if the cameraman or I would actually be part of the wedding. We could be discreet."

Sunshine was a lot of things. Discreet wasn't one of them.

"No," Hadley snapped again, and the others joined in once more. This time, Hadley contributed, "Screw you, bitch."

Sunshine didn't have a silent reaction now. The growl—yes, a growl—was a whip of her rising temper. She had to be seething now. Which was why it surprised Hayes that she kept on trying to bargain.

"Hayes," she said, obviously realizing that it wouldn't do squat to try to appeal to the triplets or Em. "Rethink this. Rethink the reaction Ivy's parents will have at reading what's in those emails. It'll break their hearts. And you'll be responsible for that. You have the power to put an end to their pain and suffering."

Hadley added a second "Screw you, bitch," along with some other choice curse words, before Hayes even had a chance to curse Sunshine himself.

"You're responsible, Sunshine," he told her. "You and you alone. You're the one who can put an end to their suffering and pain by just doing nothing."

He heard another growl, more rustling around. "You're an idiot," Sunshine snapped. Hayes actually felt some relief that they'd finally gotten past the bargaining stage. "So are your sisters and your grandmother. All idiots," she repeated. "All you have to do is one thing to save face and you won't."

Hadley went with "Screw you, bitch," again. The others settled for repeated murmurs of "No." Em apparently was going to have her say.

"It must be hard to sleep with that stick up your ass," Em tossed out there. "Probably isn't pleasant for the stick, either."

And that produced another growl. "Then Ivy's emails will be released this morning," Sunshine snarled. Her voice was seething with temper.

In contrast, Hayes kept his own tone ice-cold. "And when the emails are released, I'll give the press a sex tape of you giving a blow job to a cameraman. That'll pretty much over-shadow any tabloid news about Ivy and the emails."

Hayes sat back and waited for his bombshell to sink in. It didn't take long. Sunshine made a sound. Not a growl this time. It was more a sort of garbled gasp, followed by less garbled cursing. "You don't have a sex tape of me," she insisted.

"Oh, but I do." Hayes gave her the exact date and time, down to the very minute. "I set up a camera to see who'd been sneaking into my bedroom when I was at school. I caught someone sneaking, all right. *You.* And you went down on the guy right there by my nightstand where I had the camera set up. By the way, the recording doesn't put you in a good light."

"It makes you look fat and old," Sunny piped in, even though she hadn't seen the actual recording. None of them had.

That was a good swipe, one that Hayes wished he had come up with. Hadley kept up the swiping.

"The camera had a wide enough angle to film most of your ass," Hadley added, tacking on a snicker. *"Most."*

"And you hadn't touched up your roots," McCall commented. "There's a skunk stripe on the top of your head. But there are some good shots of your face, so your *fans* will know with absolute certainty that it's you."

"They'll also know if you spit or swallow," Em contributed, causing all of them to turn to her. There was a moment of stunned silence before laughter broke out.

No laughter from Sunshine, though. She'd gone back to growling. "If you have such a tape and actually release it, I'll sue you for every penny you have."

Hayes figured that threat was aimed specifically at him since he had deeper pockets than his sisters or Em. "Go ahead. I've got a lot of money to pay for a lot of lawyers.

In the meantime, you and your ass will be a laughing-stock. I'll make sure of it. Hell, I'll even give some interviews about it."

"You won't get away with this—" Sunshine started, but Hayes decided he'd had enough. Besides, he'd already made his point, and that point was that he would play as dirty as she did.

So he hung up on her.

Of course, Sunshine tried to call him right back, and he had to smile at the thought of her growling and seething in the anger that she often caused for so many others. He declined the call, silenced his phone and stood.

"If the emails hit the press, so does the sex tape," he said, and Hayes checked everyone's expressions to make sure they understood.

They did.

There'd be some god-awful publicity, and while most of it would be aimed at Sunshine, Ivy and him, it would also spill onto his sisters. *Little Cowgirls* might be a thing of the past, but the tabloids would squeeze it for every drop of juice they could get.

"The publicity will die down by the time of the weddings," Sunny remarked, sounding both guarded and hopeful.

Maybe it would. The weddings were still a week and a half away, so it was possible the stories would fizzle out by then.

"And Sunshine might decide not to do anything," Shaw said. "A stalemate of sorts."

"I wish we could send Slackers to crap all over Sunshine," Em muttered.

The image of that made Hayes smile.

"Not Slackers," Hadley joined in. "But a dozen stables of horses with serious intestinal issues."

"Good one." Austin gave Hadley's arm a friendly jab with his elbow.

Their smiles stayed in place for a couple more seconds before he saw the reality set in. Hayes hated to put a damper on this, but he needed to voice that *reality.*

"It's not over," Hayes reminded them. "Sunshine will regroup and think of another way to come at us. She can make a million or more off the wedding video, so she won't just give up."

He waited, letting that sink in as well, and he knew where this was going before Tony even spoke up. "I've got some money. Not a million dollars, but it might be enough to pay her off."

Hayes could tell that wasn't just lip service. The man would indeed pony up. And it would be like throwing good money at something many steps past just being bad. Apparently, his siblings, their partners and Em realized that, too, because not a one of them brightened with the thought that might be the way to go.

"Thanks," Hayes told the man, "but Sunshine would gladly take your money and come after more. This is blackmail, and she thinks she's got the ammunition with those emails to carry out her threat. But the thing is, she'll just hang on to those emails and try to use them some other time."

Tony sighed, nodded. "Maybe then Sunshine will grow a conscience."

"Been waiting for that for decades," Em grumbled. "Sometimes, sorry-assed folks just keep on getting sorrier and sorrier."

True words. And with that accurate assessment, Hayes

wanted to get out of there. "I need some fresh air. Can I use your truck?" he asked Em.

"Of course." She went to him, though, took his face in both her wrinkled hands and pulled him down for a kiss on the cheek. "Sometimes, good just keeps on getting better, too. You're a good man, Hayes."

He had some serious doubts about that, but he brushed a kiss on the top of her head, muttered a goodbye to the others and headed out. He would have liked to believe he didn't know exactly where he was going. But he did. He needed to go to the one person who might help his mood.

Cait.

And he didn't even want to analyze why seeing her would make him feel better. Right now, he'd take a dose of her snark, but he also just needed to be with her.

Hayes got in Em's truck, heading to the police station since he knew she had the morning shift. A shift that wasn't over for another two hours. That's the reason he stopped first at the diner and picked up a box of doughnuts and assorted pastries. It might be a cliché to bring such things to a cop, but this way it would look as if he had an actual purpose for visiting her.

Opposed to just needing to see her.

Main Street was crowded today. Well, crowded for Lone Star Ridge. There were at least a dozen people milling around outside or in the doorways of the various shops. Hayes was positive each and every one of them noticed him and the bright pink box he was carrying. This would notch up the gossip that he was seeing Cait. Or rather "courting" her.

Unlike the folks on Main Street, Hayes didn't seem to get much notice when he stepped into the police station. That's because the dispatcher's desk was empty, and the sign perched in front of the nameplate said, "Take a seat. Be back in a few."

Hayes didn't take a seat. He glanced around and quickly spotted Leyton and Cait. They were in Leyton's office with their backs to him, and they were hovering over two teenage boys who were occupying the seats on the side of Leyton's desk. Judging from the boys' sour expressions, they weren't there voluntarily.

"You want to explain to me what you were going to do with seventy-three packs of chewing gum?" Leyton asked, pointing to the Juicy Fruit, Trident, Bazooka, Dubble Bubble and Big Red that were in a tumbling heap on the center of his desk.

Hayes really wanted to hear the answer, but he cleared his throat so that Cait and Leyton would know he was there. They looked over their shoulders at him. Hayes couldn't tell if Cait's quick smile was because she was glad to see him or glad to see the bakery box he was holding.

"Uh, it was like a challenge," one of the boys said. His black hair was gelled up in spikes, and he had a defiant look in his eyes. Hayes figured the kid was thirteen or fourteen. "Noah and me wanted to see how many packs of gum we could get in our pockets."

"And in our underwear," the other boy—Noah, no doubt—added. "But that didn't work 'cause we both wear boxers. The packs slid out of them and went down the legs of our jeans. That's how Mr. Sidler caught us."

Yeah, that would have done it. Mr. Jay Sidler was in his seventies and owned the local grocery store. Unless the man had gone blind and deaf, he would have seen or heard a trail of gum packets falling out of the boys' pants.

"A challenge?" Leyton repeated, sounding so much like a cop that it gave Hayes a nervous twitch between his shoulder blades. He'd never been arrested for anything, but that was only because he hadn't gotten caught.

The boys bobbed their heads to answer. They didn't offer anything verbal, anything that might have explained why they'd do something that stupid.

"And you did this challenge while you were cutting school," Cait stated.

That brought shrugs from the boys, which was just as good as full confessions. They'd skipped, done something stupid and gotten caught.

Leyton gave a heavy sigh and handed them each a piece of paper. "Write down your parents' numbers, and I'll call to have them come in," he grumbled.

Now, that got a response from the pair. "Can't we just handle this without them knowing?" the first boy whined.

"No." Leyton didn't hesitate, either. He jabbed his finger at the paper. "Write down the numbers."

Cait sighed, too, shook her head and murmured something to Leyton before she came out to reception. "A bribe?" she asked, motioning to the box.

Hayes thought about that a second. "Will a bribe work?"

"Depends. With just the right amount of sugar and fat, I can be talked into many, many things."

"Talked into bed?" Hayes kept his voice low. And, yeah, he was flirting with her now.

"Depends," Cait repeated. Fluttering her eyelashes at him in a gesture that told him in no way was she taking him seriously, she lifted the box and peeked inside. "Score!" She gave a fist pump. "Hayes brought bear claws," she relayed in a louder voice to her brother.

Leyton acknowledged that with a little wave and continued his call. The boys continued to whine and protest.

"You're having an interesting day." Hayes tipped his

head to the boys while Cait helped herself to a bear claw, one dripping with thick sugary frosting.

The dripping obviously didn't bother her. She just licked it off her fingers. And sent his body into a heated spin. Hell. He shouldn't have a reaction like that to mere licking.

She nodded. "Shoplifters who are learning that crime doesn't pay. Of course, the crime doesn't make sense, so maybe they're too stupid to learn much of anything from it. I mean, if you're going to skip school, make it count. Watch dirty movies and pig out on junk food. That's what I did when I skipped."

That made him smile, and Hayes realized this was why he'd come here. The arousal he got from her icing licks was just a bonus. "How dirty?" he asked.

"Dirty," she verified with a wink.

Hell, now her winks were turning him on. Much more of this, and he'd have to limp out of there with a hard-on.

Trying to get himself back on track, Hayes handed her the box of sweets. "I thought there'd be more people around to help finish them off."

"Oh, there will be. After Leyton and I have had our fill, I'll leave the box out for the other deputies. They'll be gone faster than those packs of gum glided through a thirteen-year-old's boxer shorts."

"Good. Then my job here is done." He said it light enough, but she must have seen something not so light in his eyes.

Cait stared at him a long time and then poked the pastry against his lips. "Take a bite. The sugar high might help."

It wouldn't, but Hayes liked the idea of his mouth being on the spot where hers had just been. He bit in and watched her watch him. Oh, she was trying to figure out what was going on in his head, but Hayes thought he had enough of a poker face—

"Sunshine is still vying for Mother of the Year," she stated. "Did your threat of releasing the sex tape do anything to get her to back off?"

So not a poker face after all. Then again, Cait would have heard about the family meeting from Leyton, and she would have easily guessed the primary topic of conversation.

"To be determined," Hayes answered.

There was always a slim chance that Sunshine might do the right thing. Very slim. Of course, she wouldn't do it because it was right but because she didn't have other options. That was the way Sunshine worked.

Cait had another bite of the bear claw and gave him another one as well while she studied him. "So, did you come here to get your mind off Sunshine or to get your mind on me?"

"Both." It was an honest answer, and at the moment, his visit was accomplishing both. Score one for him. "The mention of dirty movies helped," he added, again aiming for light.

"Glad I could be of assistance." There wasn't much lightness in her tone. She was looking at him as if he were a bear claw ready to be gobbled up.

Or maybe that was dick-thinking.

Because he had to touch her—and that was definitely dick-thinking—Hayes reached up and ran his fingers over the tips of her hair. "I got some advice today," he went on, then quoted Tony: "'The heart makes better choices than the brain.'"

She frowned. "That's really crappy advice."

He laughed, and even though a cop shop was the last place he should kiss a cop, that's what Hayes did. He leaned in, brushed his mouth over hers and got a full punch of lust. And more.

Mostly more.

He hoped that was dick-thinking. Because he didn't like the alternative. It really was crappy advice about the heart making those better choices.

"I'm having trouble sleeping because I keep thinking about you," he confessed.

She lifted her hand in a "me, too" gesture. "I've been up since three this morning, and other than my coffee, you've been the main thought in my head. It's hard to compete with coffee, but you managed it."

Hayes hated that her confession pleased him. Still, it was something they were going to have to deal with. "I go back and forth between trying to resist you and hauling you off to bed," he admitted.

She didn't raise her hand again, but Cait did lift her eyebrow. "What did you decide?"

"The second one." He paused to study her reaction to that.

She smiled. And took another bite of the bear claw. "Come to my place after I'm done with my shift," she invited. "We'll watch dirty movies and eat junk food. But you won't be hauling me off to bed. Not with your sore ribs."

On a scale of one to ten, his disappointment was legion.

Cait paused a heartbeat, dropped a kiss on his mouth. "I'll haul you instead."

CHAPTER FOURTEEN

WITH HER SUGAR high long gone, Cait was thinking clearer now. Hayes had really known how to fuel her weak spots, and bear claws definitely landed in the weak-spot zone. The gooey goodness had given her a rush and had possibly made her issue that cocky offer to haul him off to bed.

Then again, bear claws weren't needed for her to want to do that.

Nope. Hayes was plenty fuel enough, and even though her hauling offer had been spur-of-the-moment, it was what she wanted. What she'd wanted for days now. And her clearer thinking made her realize that.

Since she hadn't given Hayes a specific time to come over, Cait didn't dawdle when her shift ended. She drove straight to her house so she could freshen up and put on some sexy underwear.

Or maybe no underwear at all.

That would speed things along, and while speed wasn't the goal when it came to sex with Hayes, her body was reminding her that it needed a fast fix that only he could give.

The moment she pulled into her driveway, though, she thought the fix might have to wait. Shaw's truck was parked in front of her house, and since he wasn't on the porch, that meant he was inside. Maybe for a chat or to go over some other family business. Speed would count in this matter, too, because Cait intended to hear what he wanted and then get rid of him without raising any of his suspicions as to why she was hurrying him along.

She walked into her house, automatically tossing her keys and purse on the foyer table, and she froze when she saw the men milling around in her kitchen. Not only Shaw but also Austin and Adam. Shaw had helped himself to some coffee, and Austin and Adam were drinking Cokes.

Crap.

This was some sort of family intervention. One no doubt spurred because of Hayes. The two shoplifting, school-skipping teens were apparently blabbermouths and had perhaps seen Hayes and her kiss. Word must have gotten back to this trio of her kin. Ironic, though, that it hadn't reached Leyton's ears despite him being only yards away from where the kiss had gone down. Because if Leyton had heard about it, he would have given her a lecture about public displays of affection in the workplace. Then he would have doled out another lecture about why she shouldn't be tangling with the likes of Hayes.

Frowning and without saying a word, she went into the kitchen, weaving through the sea of males, and grabbed a Coke for herself. She had a long sip, giving all of them a dose of her best stink eye.

"Traitor," she grumbled to Adam, but since he was still looking a little shy and withdrawn, she also gave him a pat on the arm. She intentionally made the gesture awkward enough, though, so he'd know he was only getting partial preferential treatment.

"So, this is about me kissing Hayes earlier in the police station," she threw out there. "And this is an intervention."

The stares they gave her were of the flat variety, and the lifted eyebrows and "Huh?" told her that she was way off base. Well, heck. She'd spilled when spilling hadn't even been necessary.

"You kissed Hayes in the police station?" Shaw grumbled.

His "big brother" tone set her teeth on edge. "Yes, and I plan on kissing him again as soon as he gets here." Best not to mention the sexy underwear or "hauling" because of Adam. "Which should be any minute now. So, if this is an intervention about something else, speed it up."

"Marty called, and he wants to meet tomorrow morning at nine," Shaw said, clearly going with her "speed it up" demand.

All right, that was unexpected. But maybe it was a good sign, too, that he was finally going to do something more than write a check when it came to Adam. "Where does he want to meet?" she asked.

It was an easy question. One that was met with silence and hesitation.

"Crap," she spit out. "What's wrong now?"

"Marty doesn't want Leyton or you there," Austin supplied, and he watched her reaction from over the top of his can of Coke.

Cait's reaction wasn't good. She pulled back her shoulders, narrowed her eyes and wanted to say something significantly worse than *crap*. "Why?"

Shaw lifted his shoulder. "Marty didn't say. In fact, he insisted I not mention the meeting to Leyton or you."

It eased the knot in her stomach that Shaw had ignored that request and told her anyway. He'd no doubt be informing Leyton, as well. If not, she would. Marty didn't deserve to cherry-pick which offspring attended a meeting. A meeting that none of said offspring actually wanted, but that was beside the point. Marty wouldn't exclude any of them for whatever twisted reason he had.

"Leyton and me," Cait said, giving that some thought. "It sounds as if Marty might be thinking about doing something illegal and he doesn't want cops around."

The nods and sounds of agreement confirmed they believed that, too. Though Cait had to admit that she'd never known Marty to intentionally break the law.

"It could be about me." Adam spoke up. "Marty might want to do something to get me off the ranch."

Austin sighed, gave Adam a brotherly pat—which was more of a brotherly poke to the arm. "It's not that."

Cait picked up the assurance. "Marty's probably pleased as punch that you're at the ranch and not insisting you stay with him." Or do anything that would cause Marty to have to spend time with the boy. "It's not you. It's me and this." She tapped the badge clipped to her belt. "He knows I'll arrest his sorry butt if he tries to bend the law. So will Leyton. Our tolerance meters are rock bottom when it comes to Marty."

Adam gave a slight nod, but Cait could tell she had in no way convinced him. Too bad the boy would have to wait until tomorrow to hear it from the horse's mouth. Marty would almost certainly confirm this wasn't about booting Adam off the ranch, because if it had indeed been about that, Marty would have insisted that Adam, too, be excluded.

"I'm coming to that meeting," Cait insisted. "I'm sure Leyton will, as well."

"Good," Shaw grumbled, as if that was the only answer he'd expected. "Park out of sight, though, because I don't want Marty driving off before we hear what he has to say."

She could do that, but it was possible that once Marty

realized there was the threat of an arrest, he'd just do an about-face and leave. If that happened, well, it would happen. There wasn't much they could do to make Marty attempt to be even a half-assed parent, much less a full-fledged one.

"I'm also suggesting we keep as much venom as possible out of the meeting," Austin added.

Cait knew this was the specific reason for their in-person visit. She did tend to strike first when it came to Marty, and if she did that, the about-face might happen right off. Still, it was hard to keep her cool around the man who'd broken her heart too many times to count.

"Minimal venom," Cait agreed. "That's provided Marty doesn't say something totally stupid that—"

She stopped because saying something totally stupid was par for the course for Marty, and she couldn't let that interfere with him actually doing something that might make a difference. After all, there was a slim chance that he might actually do something to help Adam.

"Minimal venom," she repeated, and this time there was no added *but*. She would do her best to keep her mouth closed. That was doable when the stakes were this high. Adam deserved better than he was getting.

Shaw downed the rest of his coffee. "We'll head out so you can get ready for Hayes." He rinsed out his cup, put it in the dishwasher, all while keeping his eyes on her. "Do you need advice about that?"

The answer to that was easy. "No. I already got advice today. 'The heart makes better choices than the brain,'" she quoted.

"Shitty advice," Austin grumbled as Shaw said, "That's a surefire recipe for getting knocked up. Don't take that advice," he added to Adam, who was already agreeing in a nonverbal way about the shitty part.

And with those opinions expressed, the three Jameson males left, got in Shaw's truck and drove away.

Just as Hayes pulled up in Em's truck.

She couldn't tell, but Cait was reasonably sure that her brothers, maybe even Adam, too, shot warning glares at Hayes. It wouldn't put Hayes off. At least she hoped it wouldn't, but she did regret that she hadn't had the chance to freshen up.

Hayes stepped from the truck and made his way to her house while she watched. He was wearing his usual jeans, black T-shirt and motorcycle boots and looked like the hot guy he was. All lean and lanky. His hair was rumpled as if he'd just climbed out of bed instead of a truck.

And then there was his mouth.

Oh, yeah. She took plenty notice of that since it was one of his best features and because she'd just had such recent contact with it. The man could do magic things with his mouth, but Cait thought the magic might not be limited to just that one part of him.

"Everything okay?" he asked, hiking his thumb in the direction of her brothers' and Adam's departure.

"Same ol', same ol'," she answered.

Her tone was small talk, but Cait sent Hayes some signals with her eyes. Signals that she hoped he wouldn't have any trouble interpreting. She wanted him. In case there was an interpretation problem, Cait looped her arm around his neck the moment he stepped on the porch, and she pulled him down to her for a kiss.

She doubted she was sparking any magic with her mouth, but there were sparks, all right. She could feel the heat trail down the front of her body and settle in a needy kind of way in her panty region.

He made a sound, a soft grunt that seemed to be part surprise, part pleasure. Maybe he'd expected her to change her mind about this. Or at least let him get in the house before she started up. But thinking and waiting time were over. She was about to have her first real taste of Hayes.

Apparently, he intended to get in on that tasting, too, and he deepened the kiss. He also latched on to her belt to pull her closer. Cait had every intention of getting extremely close, but she had to lay down the ground rules. Which she started as soon as she tore her mouth from his and regained her breath.

"You can't touch me," she insisted. "I don't want you moving around and hurting your ribs."

He leveled those scorching blue eyes at her. "Excuse me?"

"No touching," she repeated. "I'll do all the work."

"While I'm sure I'd enjoy that, very much, I want to… move around. I want to touch you." He used that tone she was certain had caused women's clothes to evaporate.

Cait tried not to let the tone and just the sheer looks of him make her mindless. "You can touch me with just one finger," she bargained.

His suddenly cocky grin let her know that he could do a lot with a single digit. She didn't doubt that one bit, but in case he planned to argue with her, Cait swooped in for another kiss. She kept her arm around his neck, and walking backward, she moved him into the house and shut the door with her foot.

So that he wouldn't argue with her about that one-finger deal, she just kept kissing him, just kept moving them toward her bedroom. She had a split second of regret that she hadn't done that "freshening up" since that would have included picking up her things that were scattered around. But only a split second. Because the heat from the kisses distracted her from any regret she had about her housekeeping skills.

When they'd kissed their way to the bed, she eased him down to a sitting position. He hooked his one designated finger behind her badge and pulled her down with him until she was straddling him. All in all, not a bad position for her. Hayes must have thought so, too, because he shifted his hips, pushing his erection right into the center of her spread legs.

Cait got a fire shower of pure undiluted lust.

It was so strong that it blurred her vision, robbed her of her breath. And nearly made her forget that she needed to take it easy with him.

Best not to strip off his clothes in a heated rush or she could hurt him. So, slowly, she went after the bottom of his T-shirt, easing it up, up, up until she had it over his head. She watched for wincing or any signs of pain, but that wasn't the look of pain in his eyes. Nope. Hayes had gotten a fire shower of lust, too.

He played dirty, though, skimming his finger over the front of her jeans, going lower. Then lower. So low that he was giving her a modified hand job—with just his finger. Since she wanted this to be mutual torture for both of them, she went after his zipper.

And she didn't use just a finger.

Cait slid her entire hand down into his boxers and gave him a dose of his own medicine. He was huge and hard, and touching him only made the ache spread inside her. An ache that demanded release now.

"We need to get naked," she insisted.

She climbed off him, hopping around while she yanked

off her boots so she could shimmy her jeans down her legs. Her top went next, and she sent it flying over her shoulder. Cait had reached to open the front hook of her bra when she realized Hayes was just sitting there watching her.

He grinned at her. "Keep going. You've got on your borderline-porn panties."

Cait glanced down at the red swatch of barely-there lace. She hadn't made a conscious decision to wear them. They'd literally been on the top of the heap in her laundry basket of clean clothes.

"I got dressed when I was still half-asleep," she muttered. That explained the non-matching peach bra.

Apparently, Hayes didn't mind the clashing color combination, because his smile had a definite "I'm going to take a greedy bite out of you" look to it. Cait would have been looking at him the same way if he'd stripped, too.

"Let me help you get naked," she insisted.

She went to him, dropping to her knees so she could take off his boots and socks. The jeans were trickier, but that's because he took hold of them when she tried to drag them off him. He stopped her and retrieved a condom from the pocket.

"Because the heart doesn't always make better choices than the brain," he drawled.

No, it didn't, and she was glad he'd remembered something as monumental as safe sex. She had some condoms in her bathroom, but they'd been in there so long that it was best not to risk using them.

Cait finished tugging off the jeans and reached for his boxers. Why they weren't ripping at the seams from his erection, she didn't know, but Hayes was definitely testing the limits of the fabric. She reached to pull them down, but he stopped her with that damn index finger. It landed against her stomach.

His gaze slid from her face all the way down to where he was touching. Then lower.

"You obviously like borderline-porn panties," she said, resisting the urge to fan herself. Or just jump him where he sat.

"I like a lot of things about you." There it was again. That sexy drawl with just the right amount of gravel and sin. Heavy on the sin.

While he held her in place with his finger, he leaned in and kissed that tiny red swatch of lace. Oh, and he used his tongue. And his breath. A lot of breath. It didn't seem to matter that there was fabric between her and his tongue and breath. Cait could feel it as well as if he were inside her.

She stood there, her legs turning to jelly and the rest of her turning to lava, and she slipped her fingers into his thick hair, anchoring him. Taking everything that he was dishing out. Thankfully, though, she remembered that this was not how she wanted things to end.

"I want to use that condom," she mumbled.

"Sorry, but I plan to use it." He chuckled at his lame joke, and the breath from his laugh nearly made her come.

Cait fisted her hand in his hair, and since it wasn't anywhere near his sore ribs, she gave it a hard tug. Hard enough to get his mouth away from the front of her panties. Before he could go back to finish her off, she distracted him by unhooking her bra.

His eyes went straight to her breasts as they spilled out, and he had her right nipple in his mouth before she could even work the bra off her. Damn, the man was superfast. Cait tried to be faster because there was no way she was going to last much longer if he continued to locate all the hot spots on her body. Her breasts were definitely hot spots.

She wiggled out of her panties. And, yeah, she noticed that it distracted him, too. He would have probably resumed the kisses there, but she took hold of his erection to get his attention.

It got his attention.

"I want these boxers off you," she said, "but let's take it easy so your ribs—"

Hayes shucked off his boxers in one fluid motion. He didn't stop there. He tore open the condom and got that sucker on. Still not stopping, he pulled her onto his lap. Cait wasn't sure how he got the positioning right so fast, but he pushed into her with one long, hard stroke.

That got *her* attention.

Time didn't stop, probably, but it felt as if everything inside her pinpointed to that exact spot where they were joined. Pinpointed and erupted into a need so bad that she wanted to beg him to give her more.

Hayes gave her more. And more. He hooked his arm around her hips, sliding her forward to match the movements of those strokes inside her.

Their gazes met. Held. And even with the maddening, rhythmic strokes, he lifted his free hand, extended his index finger, and he traced it, slowly, from her mouth. To her neck.

To her breasts.

His touch was so light, a complete contrast to the hard thrusts, and he followed an invisible line to her stomach. Below her navel. Then lower. That one finger touched her in just the right spot.

Until the pinpoint built, built, built. Until she gave in to that building.

Until she'd gotten exactly what she wanted from Hayes Dalton.

HAYES COULDN'T HELP but notice that Cait napped with snark. There was no other word for it.

She'd crashed shortly after they'd had sex, collapsing on the mattress next to him, but she quickly turned into a bed hog. She shifted, twisted and turned until she was not only out of his arms but sprawled out. Obviously, the sex had relaxed her, and she was getting the sleep that had eluded them since they'd started lusting after each other.

No sleep for Hayes, though.

He was wide-awake, and his thoughts were going a mile a minute. Thoughts that weren't compatible with taking a nap, even if he did desperately need one.

Having sex with Cait had been inevitable. And it'd damn sure felt like a necessity. However, that didn't ease the guilt he was already feeling. Guilt that he'd known he would have, but it hadn't stopped him from coming over to her house and letting her haul him off to bed. All in all, she'd done a damn fine job of hauling, too, but now he had to face the consequences that he'd known from the start would be there.

Because soon, he'd have to walk away from her.

Hayes had gone over and over this, too. The leaving. He couldn't stay here. Even if *Outlaw Rebels* was canceled, his life and his work were in California. Soon, he'd have to return to the set to finish out the scenes that had been put on hold when he'd been given the order to leave town and get his shit together. His shit still wasn't together, but this was probably as good as he was going to get.

With that dismal thought making him feel even lower than he already did, Hayes eased from the bed without waking Cait. It wasn't hard to do because she apparently slept like the dead. Gathering up his clothes, he made his way to her bathroom so he could take a quick shower. First, though, he looked back at her.

Bad idea.

Cait was sprawled out naked on the bed, the quilt only covering her stomach. That meant he had no trouble seeing the rest of her. Her breasts. The curve of her hips. Her long, lean legs. And the rest of her.

She wasn't surgically perfect as so many people in his profession were, but her body was still amazing, and looking at her made him ache for her all over again. That's why Hayes forced his attention away and had that shower. A cold one. It didn't help, but then he hadn't thought water had the power to shed him of his need. A need that should have been sated but wasn't.

Keeping as quiet as he could, he dressed and considered how to handle his exit. No way would he leave her a note. Cait deserved better than that. But he needed to get out of there so that he wouldn't be tempted to have another round of sex with her. While that would no doubt be as amazing as her body, he couldn't let this turn into a nonstop fling.

He went back in the bedroom to wake her, to give her a goodbye kiss, but waking wasn't required. Cait was sitting up in bed, and she'd adjusted the quilt so that it covered so many of her interesting parts. Not the most interesting of all, though—her face. She yawned and gave him a sleepy smile.

"Sorry that I zonked out on you," she muttered.

Her smile faded, though, when she saw his expression. Hayes had tried not to look horny, troubled or anything else. He'd wanted blank, but apparently Cait saw right through that.

"Uh-oh." She pushed her hair away from her face. "Regret's a cold hard bitch, isn't it?"

Hayes almost wished the conversation wasn't this honest. A good facade would have gotten him out of there faster and with less emotion. But this was Cait. She wasn't big on facades.

"I don't want to hurt you," he said.

She flashed him another smile. "That's my line. That's why I didn't want you doing any heavy lifting or hauling. How are your ribs, by the way?"

"They're fine." They were, not much pain at all, but he would have given her that answer even if he'd been in agony. Hayes didn't want to add to any regrets she might be feeling.

She sighed, and holding the quilt against her, she stood, and dragging it along, she went to him. Cait gave him a quick kiss. "Sometimes, the heart really does make better choices than the brain."

Thinking this was going to be the start of a list of reasons why they should give this relationship a chance to bloom, Hayes silently groaned, but he would hear her out. Then maybe he could counter those reasons with his brain.

"And I think your heart is telling you to leave," she went on, "so that you won't have to say something you think will hurt me."

Oh. So, not a "giving this a chance" remark.

Cait took a deep breath before she continued, "You'll be around for another week and a half. So, I say we just have sex—rely on the heart—and not get too bogged down in this."

He gave that some thought. Yeah, he was bogging down, all right. And a little confused. "Having sex isn't relying on the heart," he pointed out.

With a wicked smile, she lifted her index finger and ran it from his mouth. To his neck. To his heart. Then lower. She tapped the front of his jeans, using just that single finger. It was as effective as a BJ.

"The heart is closer to here than the brain," she argued, giving his quickly forming erection another tap.

Closer, definitely, and his brain was already moving to shut off. To jump right back into another round of sex. And that was exactly what he would have done had Cait not given him another one of those quick kisses.

"I need to grab a shower and something to eat," she said. "You can either hang, or I'll see you when I see you."

It was the perfect laid-back "off the hook" thing to say. And the worst thing, too. Because it made him think he'd overrated what he meant to her. Of course, she could be fudging her feelings. She might be crying inside. If so, she was doing a damn good job of hiding it. Not an especially good job, though, of covering her ass. When she walked toward the bathroom, turning her back to him, Hayes got a full view of her naked bottom.

That gave him a quick nudge of heat. But he resisted. Barely.

"I'll head out," he told her, and because he couldn't come up with anything that wasn't sexual, he repeated her. "I'll see you when I see you."

If his dick had its way, the seeing would happen sooner rather than later.

Hayes ignored what felt like an invitation to join Cait when he heard the shower come on, and he forced himself to get moving out of the house and back to Em's truck. However, he hadn't even started the engine when his phone rang.

Sunshine.

Now his groan wasn't silent, but it was a call he had been expecting. And one that he shouldn't put off. Bracing himself for whatever shit his mother was about to dole out, Hayes hit Answer.

"I need a meeting with you," she said, her voice an order, not a request. "Just with you," she added. "I don't want to deal with your grandmother and your sisters right now."

He scowled. "Is that because you think I'll be an easier sell? Because if so, you're sadly mistaken."

"No, it's because I want to have a conversation without all of the arguing and the attitude."

"You deserve the attitude and arguing," he pointed out.

"Maybe, but I think you and I both want to end this stalemate." Sunshine continued before Hayes could speak. "Meet me tomorrow at noon at the sign for Lone Star Ridge. Not in town limits but on the other side of the sign."

"High noon?" Hayes grumbled. "Have you been watching too many old Westerns?"

"No. But we're going to settle this stalemate once and for all."

CHAPTER FIFTEEN

CAIT STOOD IN her mother's living room and waited for Marty to arrive. Everyone else was in place. Shaw, Austin, Adam and Lenore were seated on the various chairs, sofa and love seat. Leyton, too, even though both Cait and he hadn't been invited.

As if a non-invitation would have kept them away.

Both of them wore badges. Leyton even had on his shoulder holster, complete with his gun that he'd never drawn in the line of duty. Cait had her tiny can of Mighty Hold hair spray that she'd stuffed in the back pocket of her jeans. She'd never drawn it, either, but there was a first time for everything. If anyone deserved a good dousing with hair spray, it was Marty. The fumes might finally knock some sense into him.

Kinsley had opted out of this particular family delight and was at school instead. The triplets had chosen to stay away, as well. Wise women, indeed. They'd already had enough of their own family drama without taking on a steaming heap of dung from the sperm donor of their soon-to-be husbands.

Cait was looking forward to the steaming heap of this confrontation but wished she were feeling at least a little mean so that she'd be ready for this family gathering with Marty. Mean always helped her get through facing her father, but she just wasn't in a mean state of mind today.

She could blame Hayes for that.

Or rather thank him for that.

She'd finally gotten to have sex with him, and despite the restrictions of his injury, Hayes had been everything she'd thought he would be. Not just before and during, either, but also after.

Cait had seen the worry practically oozing off him after he'd left her bed. He was a good man, and good men didn't like to dick around with women. Well, dick around with them in the sense of breaking hearts. Normal dicking was often their specialty. It sure had been in Hayes's case.

But a good man and good sex couldn't stop the inevitable.

A broken heart was already tapping her on the shoulder, but she was hoping Hayes would do some other tapping, as well. She might have to talk him into returning to her bed, though. Maybe that wouldn't be that hard to do once they'd both settled their family businesses. Hers with Marty and his with Sunshine.

"Say, maybe we could try to get Marty and Sunshine together," Cait remarked. "Then they can screw over each other as often as they want."

Her comment was met with blank stares and a muffled chuckle from Adam. Cait was liking the kid more each day and gave him a thumbs-up.

"Sunshine's welcome to him," Lenore grumbled, but she perked up, too. A fake kind of perking up, though, because she obviously remembered Adam was hearing every word spoken in the room.

Cait had to hand it to her mom. Lenore was no doormat, but she usually managed to keep the Marty bad-mouthing to a minimum. It was hard to understand why Lenore bothered to do that, though. Marty had messed her over by cheating on her and then walking out, leaving her to raise the kids he so easily fathered and now grandfathered. Maybe Lenore just didn't want to add more ill will or bad blood, and Cait wished she knew the secret of how to make that happen in her own life. Her father was always going to be a painful pimple on her ass.

And apparently the pimple had arrived, because Cait heard the sound of a vehicle approaching the ranch.

Showtime.

"Don't arrest him before he's had a chance to say what he's come here to say," Shaw advised her. Cait noted that Shaw hadn't given the same warning to the more level-headed Leyton. "And keep your cursing PG-rated. We don't need Adam learning any new words."

Cait rolled her eyes because she doubted there was a single curse word that a teenage boy didn't already know. Still, she'd rein in the cussing even if Marty managed to push her pissed-off buttons.

Shaw stood and went to the door, and he opened it just as Marty was stepping onto the porch. The stepping, however, froze when he spotted her.

Marty sighed. "I asked that Leyton and you not be here."

"Tough titty," Cait fired back, and she'd found her mean. All it'd taken was getting a good look at him. "We're here. Deal with it."

Her father sighed again, shook his head in a weary gesture and came in. He glanced at everyone in the room, but his attention settled on her. He didn't say anything else, but Cait could have sworn that a thousand things passed between them. Hers was mostly anger, but she thought maybe he was doing a Texas-sized nonverbal apology.

"FYI, I would have come to Leyton and you after I'd

talked this over with the others," Marty finally said. "I just didn't want to have to deal with any cops just yet."

"Then deal with me as your son," Leyton instructed, and he used his cop's voice. His cop's scowl, too.

It was possible that Leyton's feelings had been stomped on by Marty not wanting him at this family meeting. Because Leyton was one of Marty's kids born outside of wedlock, Cait knew he'd always felt a little like an outsider, and she wanted to lash out at Marty just for making Leyton get a fresh reminder of that outsider status again.

Marty's next sigh was even longer, and he nodded. "I'm not sure what I want to do is legal."

Bingo. Cait had nailed it, and it might improve her mood if she could arrest Marty's sorry butt. Of course, Leyton might beat her to it.

"When I left Cait's the other day, I went back to my tour bus, did a lot of thinking," Marty said.

So the note he'd left Adam and her hadn't been total BS. Well, it still likely was mostly BS because it'd been a ploy for Marty to escape, but if he had indeed squeezed in some thinking, then maybe a shred of what she'd said to him had gotten through.

"I've been trying to come up with a way for me to help take care of Adam while I still work," Marty went on. "I want to take him on tour with me, but that means taking him out of state as early as tomorrow."

Cait felt some of her anger drop down a notch. Actually, most of the anger dropped. Of all the things that she'd thought Marty might say, this definitely hadn't been one of them.

"You want to take me on tour?" Adam asked, sounding both shocked and hopeful.

Of course, everyone in the room except Marty was

shocked. No *hopeful* for Cait, though, because she knew the drill. This could all be lip service from Marty to stop them from being so pissed off at him.

"I do," Marty verified. "But I have to be on the tour bus first thing in the morning, and we're heading to Oklahoma and then Tennessee. We won't get back until the day of the weddings."

Adam slowly got to his feet, and with that hope still in his eyes, he glanced around the room as if looking for any objections. Clearly, he wanted to go, but he probably wasn't certain enough of his place in the family to jump to agree.

"I had my lawyer go over Adam's guardianship paperwork," Marty continued, "and it says he's to stay here at the ranch. It doesn't give me permission to take him with me, and there's probably not enough time to get the paperwork amended before I have to leave."

Cait glanced at Shaw to see if that was indeed what the guardianship papers had said, and he nodded. Well, heck. Maybe this was a first. Marty might have done his homework and had reasons for legal concerns. Any amendments to the paperwork would have to be approved by Adam's mother, and that would mean a trip to the prison where she was serving out her sentence. That could definitely take more than a day to get done, especially since the paperwork would likely then have to be refiled.

"I want to make sure this is done right," Marty said. "I know you have plenty of reasons to believe I'm not capable of doing right, but I am."

"The jury's still out on that," Cait muttered just as Adam gushed, "I want to go with him." Yeah, it was definitely a gush, and it was the first time Cait had actually seen the boy happy.

Happiness that she might have to dash to bits.

"Even if the paperwork could be amended in time, do you really think it's a good idea to take a thirteen-year-old boy on a tour bus, what with the crew and the groupies?" Cait asked.

Marty's expression told her that he'd expected objections to come from her. "I've talked to my crew and told them that they'd have to be on their best behavior and not invite anyone back to the bus. They're not idiots. Heck, most of them are grandparents now themselves."

That still wasn't a sterling endorsement. Except it'd been years since Cait had heard any gossip or tabloid stories about Marty's band and crew doing any acting out. No trashed hotel rooms. No wild parties. So maybe age had toned them down.

"I made it clear," Marty went on, "that they'd have to give Adam some quiet time so he can get his homework done. And he'd have a computer so he could get all his assignments."

The last part was actually the least of Cait's concerns. From what Shaw had said, Adam was a good student, and he was doing his online classes without any prodding.

Marty shifted his attention, looking directly at Adam. "I want you with me on this tour so we can get to know each other. I don't want you to have to chase me down or buy a ticket to one of my concerts just so you can see me."

Cait felt the sting of that last remark. The memories of it, too, but thankfully Marty didn't single her out with a "yeah, I'm talking about you" glance. She didn't want her siblings or mother to know she'd done such a stupid, pathetic thing.

"You really want to go with him?" Shaw asked Adam, and before he'd gotten out the last word of his question, the boy did more gushing.

"Yes. Definitely, yes," Adam said. "I really, really want this." He repeated it, adding *really* a couple more times.

Shaw paused, nodded, and then he stood. "All right. Let me see if I can get the paperwork amended and then walk it through so we can have it ASAP."

"I'll do it," Leyton volunteered, also getting to his feet. He turned to Adam. "But if there are any hitches with the tour—*any hitches*—" he emphasized "—call me, and I'll come and get you."

Any one of them would do that for Adam, and considering this tour was Marty's, there could be plenty of hitches. After a day or two, Marty might even decide he'd filled his grandfather quota for Adam's lifetime and send the boy back to the ranch. If so, that'd crush Adam, but it would be the norm for Marty. He was a first-class crusher.

"I can go with him?" Adam asked, and now the hope was spewing like a geyser off him.

"You can go as soon as I walk through this paperwork," Leyton verified.

That started a chain reaction of hugs. First, Adam hugging Leyton, and then the boy doling out more to everyone else in the room. Especially to Marty. That hug lasted a long time, and Cait hoped that it was genuine happiness she saw in her father's eyes. Just in case it wasn't, she gave him one final warning glance. She added a finger slice across the throat in case he hadn't picked up on her glare.

"Pack your things and make sure you have all your school assignments," Marty told Adam when the boy finally pulled back. "If Leyton pulls this off, we'll be heading out bright and early tomorrow. Our first stop is Tulsa."

Even though it would likely only take a couple of minutes for Adam to do the packing and such, the boy hurried toward the stairs to get started. Marty stayed put, and Cait didn't think it was her imagination that he was waiting for Adam to get out of earshot. And that put a knot in her stomach. If Marty was going to do something to dash Adam's hopes, she was pulling out the Mighty Hold hair spray.

"Why this change of heart?" Cait demanded. "Why'd you decide to finally spend some time with your grandson?"

Marty muttered something she didn't catch and shook his head. "Christ, Cait. I'm not made of stone." He paused, huffed. "Everything you said got to me."

It had? Well, color her surprised, too. "That's a first," she grumbled, but she regretted the jab when she saw what might be genuine emotions in his eyes. Exactly what emotions, she didn't know.

"Adam left me a voice-mail message," Marty added. "Did he tell you?"

"Yes. I'm surprised you listened to it."

"Well, I did," he snapped, but then his expression instantly softened. "Hell. Adam was giving me an out. He was putting the blame for this on his own shoulders. He's a kid, and he was blaming himself because he thought I was mad at him. I wasn't mad," Marty added, but then his explanation came to a grinding halt.

"You were just running," Cait provided.

Marty lifted his head, his gaze connecting with hers. "Yeah. It's my 'Honey, Darlin'.'"

Cait was sure she looked confused by that, but she did know that Marty had had a huge hit song with that title. "Running away is like a sappy country-music song?" And she left the snark in it.

Marty's half smile had no humor whatsoever in it. "'Honey, Darlin'' is what I sing when I'm having a bad night on stage. When my head is pounding and my throat is too raw and when I just need an easy way out. It's my go-to for putting an end to what's happening so I can move on."

Cait let that run through her mind. "So you can move on to another city, another stage."

Marty nodded. "I was doing a 'Honey, Darlin'' with Adam," he admitted. "Hell, with all of you. Going for an easy way out." He paused again. "But after listening to Adam's message, I knew at least this once I was going to have to take a stab at 'Honkytonk Darlin'.'"

Yet another of Marty's hits, but Cait thought she understood the point he was trying to make. "It's a long song with a lot of hard notes," she provided.

He pointed his finger at her in a "got it" gesture. "Exactly. I only sing it on nights when I got a lot of feel-good going on."

Cait frowned. "And you have a lot of feel-good going on with Adam?"

"Not really. I'm sort of scared spit-less. I mean, he's a kid, and…" Marty stopped, stared at her. "And I don't want to hurt him the way I hurt your siblings and you. Still, I knew from the message he left that I was going to hurt him no matter which way I went. So, I decided it was time to try to do something right even if it'll be hard."

Well, if there was going to be a time for Marty to come to his senses, this would be it. Before he left another generation of Jamesons with his usual baggage. Still, Cait had some reservations.

"If you screw this up with Adam," she warned him, "I'll do everything—and I mean *everything*—to make your life a living hell. Singing 'Honkytonk Darlin'' will be the least of your worries if you hurt him."

Marty stared at her a long time. Then nodded. "I'm gonna try to make it work," he said.

Not exactly an overly enthusiastic guarantee. But it was better than anything else he'd offered.

Maybe this change of heart was because Adam was his grandson? Grandparents gushed about their grandkids all the time and wore T-shirts and carried coffee mugs proudly proclaiming their grandparent status. Perhaps because the offspring of their offspring was a way of continuing the family line or getting a second chance to get it right?

Cait frowned, not sure either of those applied to Marty.

A lot of things didn't apply to Marty. He was definitely one of a kind. And while this gesture could turn out to be a good thing, she needed to come up with ways to help Adam if the *gesture* fell apart.

"I'm gonna try to make it work," Marty repeated. "Try to make it work with Avery and Gracie, too."

"You're not going to take toddlers on a tour bus," Cait objected.

"No. But I could probably do something. Don't know what." Marty looked at her. "Do you?"

The question was the real deal, asked by a man who didn't have a clue how to be a grandfather. "I'll have Austin give you some suggestions." Because it occurred to her that playing cops and bobbers with Marty might stray into realms where Austin wouldn't want his girls to stray. Best to let Austin come up with any ideas that Marty might be prone to trying out.

Marty mumbled a thanks and then cleared his throat before he continued, "And on a totally different subject—last night Sunny and I were talking about the new book we have coming out."

Cait had geared up to sling some venom, but that stopped her. Sunny did indeed do the illustrations for Marty's popular children's book series *Slackers Quackers*, but Cait couldn't imagine what this had to do with Adam. Or maybe it didn't.

"Sunny told me what Sunshine was trying to do," Marty went on. "Sunny wanted me to know in case Sunshine stirred up some bad publicity."

Which Sunshine would almost certainly do. Cait relaxed a little but only because this didn't apply to Adam. However, it did apply to Hayes, his sisters and Em, so it was still important.

"Sunshine wants to film the weddings," Shaw supplied. "That's not going to happen."

"No," Marty agreed. "Hayes told Sunny that Sunshine had called him and asked him to meet her today."

Cait hadn't known about that, but maybe Sunshine thought she could better bargain with Hayes face-to-face.

And then her father said something else that shocked Cait all the way to the soles of her feet. "I think I can do something about Sunshine," Marty told her. "In fact, I'm sure I can fix the mess she's trying to stir up."

HAYES FIGURED NOTHING good was about to come of this. He watched from the living room window as Cait and Leyton pulled to a stop in front of Em's house. They were in the cruiser, and this looked like an official visit. There was definitely no "hauling off for sex" gleam in Cait's eyes.

He sighed, ready to steel himself up, when his phone dinged with a text. It was from his agent, and Abe was his usual chatty self.

Need u back here ASAP.

Hayes frowned, sent back a ?
Abe immediately answered, BWs want big jaw.

BW was bigwigs from the studio and network, and *big jaw* was an important meeting. One they apparently wanted now. Hayes got confirmation of that when Abe texted again.

NOW, his agent emphasized. Asses on the line.

Hayes figured it was his own ass in that particular peril, but it could be someone else on the cast or crew. Apparently, he was going to be making a trip to LA. However, he wouldn't be doing that until he found out what his visitors wanted.

He opened the door to them, his gaze sliding over Leyton before it settled on Cait. She looked worried, and amazing. Which concerned him more than a little. Because it wasn't just a punch of lust he felt when he looked at her. He was glad to see her despite this obviously not being a social call.

"Trouble?" Hayes asked.

"Maybe a fix to some trouble," Cait answered. "Marty has a plan to stop Sunshine."

If Hayes had been given a multiple-choice test of what she'd been about to say, he would have failed big-time. "What does Marty have to do with Sunshine?" He motioned for them to come in, but they stayed put on the porch.

"Marty's worried about Sunny and wants to help," Leyton explained. He checked his watch. "If it works, Cait and I need to leave now so we can be there to arrest Sunshine. *If it works,*" Leyton restated. "Cait thought you'd want to be in on that."

An arrest? He would have failed that in a multiple choice, too. "I would indeed want to see that, but what the heck are you talking about?" Hayes pressed. "What's Marty's plan?"

"We'll go over that on the way there," Cait said. "We need to leave now."

After Cait also checked the time on her phone, Hayes didn't hesitate. He was all for anything that stopped Sunshine, even if it was a long shot with a side dish of *if it works*. He fired off a quick text to Em to let her know that he was leaving, and he headed out with Cait and Leyton.

"Marty's at the café at Rustler's Ridge," Leyton explained as they got into the cruiser. Leyton and Cait in the front and Hayes in the back. "He got Sunshine to agree to meet him there in about fifteen minutes. So, she'll see Marty before she's scheduled to meet with me."

Rustler's Ridge was a guest ranch just outside of Lone Star Ridge. Definitely not a five-star kind of place that his mother would usually haunt. But if Marty had asked her to go, she would have.

Hayes wasn't positive, but he believed the pair had landed in bed at least once. Then again, Hayes could say that about most women his mother's age who'd lived in or around the area. However, that was not why Sunshine would have agreed to meet him. Marty still had cachet in the entertainment business, and Sunshine would see this as an opportunity to use that cachet to get something for herself. Plus, she might believe Marty could get her into the weddings since he was, after all, the father of the grooms.

"Marty has a cameraman and reporter from San Antonio with him," Cait went on as Leyton drove to Rustler's Ridge. "He told Sunshine that he's being interviewed for one of the big gossip shows about the weddings, and that there'll be some money in it for her if she participates in the interview. She jumped at the chance."

"Of course she did," Hayes grumbled. Anything that would put her in the limelight. "But I still don't see how that could lead to an arrest."

Cait looked back at him before she answered. "Marty will get Sunshine to sign a consent to being recorded, and the reporter will ask some general questions about the weddings. He'll keep it short as Marty has instructed him to do. When they're finished, the cameraman will pretend to turn off the camera and will set it down near Marty and Sunshine. The reporter and cameraman will excuse themselves to get something out of their van. Marty will then try to get Sunshine to admit to extortion. Not skirt around it but full out admit it."

Hayes could see why Leyton had added that *if it works*. Sunshine wasn't an idiot, and there was no reason for her to admit something like that even if she thought she wasn't being recorded. Plus, there was the legal side of this.

"Wouldn't that be entrapment?" Hayes asked.

"Probably," Cait readily admitted. "But it'd take time and money for Sunshine to fight the charges. Which I'm sure she'll do."

"She will," Hayes verified.

"In the meantime, the film crew will release the recording and air anything criminal that Sunshine says. Even if she wiggles out of the charges, people will know what she's trying to pull. The arrest will be just the cherry on top."

Hayes enjoyed the idea of his mother being charged with something—actually, with anything. But he gave this iffy plan some thought, playing around with various scenarios. If this worked, Sunshine would retaliate and release Ivy's emails, but maybe that would backfire and the public would turn on her. People could see this as a vindictive act against a dead woman.

"Sunshine will probably make public Ivy's emails no matter what happens," Hayes concluded, and that still felt like a mean fist squeezing around his heart. He couldn't stop it. He couldn't make things right for Ivy and keep her privacy. "This way Sunshine would at least get a dose of her own medicine."

And just the possibility of that had Hayes brightening a little.

"That and her bad publicity would overshadow anything about Ivy," Cait agreed, and she paused, giving him another glance from over the seat. "You could even layer it on by releasing the sex tape of Sunshine if any of this first wave of bad publicity dies down."

True. That would keep the mudslinging on Sunshine. Of course, it would also net her any number of interviews, but even that would dry up once the public grew tired of her. Ivy's emails would maybe get lost in all that mud so that Ivy's parents wouldn't have to relive her death again through the media.

Nor would Hayes.

Well, except that he relived it in every other way. But this was a good baby step. Again, if it worked.

"Crap," Cait muttered when her phone dinged with a message. "It's from Marty. He said Sunshine's already there, and she's pressing him to get started because she has other things to do."

"She's got a meeting with me," Hayes explained. "At noon." Which was only about an hour from now. "She said she wanted to put an end to this stalemate."

Cait knew what he'd face in that meeting with Sunshine, and that's probably why she gave him another look. More sympathy. More concern. And even with all of that and the looming Sunshine issue, Hayes couldn't help but smile at her. God, he was glad she was here. If this worked, he wanted to be able to celebrate with her, and if it blew up in their faces, well, they could console each other.

They reached the main house on the guest ranch, but Leyton didn't turn into the parking lot. Instead, he pulled into a small dirt-and-gravel side road that led to some of the guest cabins.

"It's Marty," Cait relayed when her phone rang, and Hayes heard her father's voice when she put the call on speaker.

"I'm leaving my phone on," Marty said in a whisper. "It'll be in my pocket so Sunshine doesn't know, but you should be able to catch at least some of the conversation."

Good. Hayes silenced his own phone so that Sunshine wouldn't be able to hear it if he got a call or text. He also took off his seat belt and moved to the edge of his seat to listen better. There wasn't much to hear, though. Marty had obviously rejoined Sunshine and the crew, and they were going over the consent form. Apparently, there was nothing in it that raised a red flag for his mother because a few seconds later, Marty said they could get started.

As expected, the reporter introduced Sunshine and Marty, adding the accolade of "country-music legend" for Marty. Sunshine's intro merely called her the mother of the *Little Cowgirls* and the star of *Outlaw Rebels*. Sunshine wouldn't be offended that none of those "credentials" was about her own personal accomplishments. That's because she didn't have any accomplishments. She had made a living off her kids, and would continue to try to do it as long and as often as she could.

The reporter moved on to making a big deal out of Marty's sons marrying Sunshine's daughters and finished it off with a question for Sunshine. "How do you feel about the *Little Cowgirls* being all grown up and getting married?" he asked.

"I'm thrilled for them." Sunshine let her Texas drawl dribble through a bit, but Hayes knew she turned it on and off as easily as a water faucet. "It's going to be such an exciting day. I suspect I'll do what all mothers do and cry a bit. But I assure you they'll be happy tears. I've been watching my girls fall in love with the Jameson boys for as long as I can remember."

Hayes was surprised he didn't throw up in his mouth. If he had anything to say about it, Sunshine wouldn't get within miles of the ceremony. In fact, he made a mental note to hire some security to make sure that didn't happen.

"And Marty?" the reporter continued. "Can you tell us how you feel about your sons' marriages?"

"They're all good men," Marty answered. At least that's what Hayes thought he'd said, but it was hard to tell because of the loud gurgling sound. Marty laughed. "Sorry, that was my stomach growling. I missed breakfast."

That brought on a couple of chuckles and some chatter about editing it out.

"Sunshine, what about your son, Hayes Dalton," the reporter said. "We all know he's the bad-boy star of *Outlaw Rebels*…"

Again, Hayes tried to move closer, but Marty's stomach growled, and it sounded as if a volcano had erupted. Hayes caught the words *matching set* followed by *Marty's daughter*.

So the reporter was asking about Cait and him, and even if Marty and Sunshine denied a possible pairing, it was still a juicy enough bite that it would almost certainly make its way into any articles that got written about this. If the reporters found out that Cait and he had actually done the deed, she would get caught up in the media hassles. Hayes wanted to avoid that, too.

Sunshine laughed, pulling Hayes's attention back to the interview. "Who knows what could happen between Cait and Hayes. I think it'd be a wonderful match since I've always thought of Cait as my own daughter."

"Since when?" Cait snarled under her breath.

Hayes hoped Sunshine hadn't heard that, but there was no way for him to know; in addition to the growling, Marty was apparently guzzling some water or coffee, because there was that sound, too. If they ever did another covert op like this, they'd need to feed the man first.

"What are you wearing to the wedding?" the reporter asked, the question no doubt meant for Sunshine.

Sunshine began to describe her outfit, but Hayes tuned her out when his now-silent phone flashed with a text from Abe.

Your flight's in two hours. Get to the airport now.

Well, hell. It'd take him nearly an hour of that to get his things and drive into San Antonio.

Might not be able to make that flight, Hayes texted back.

Make it was Abe's response.

Shit. Something else must have happened with the BWs and their requested *jaw* or else Abe wouldn't have booked him a flight.

Hayes motioned to Cait that he had to make a call, and he eased from the cruiser. He didn't go far, and he stayed out of the café's line of sight so that Sunshine wouldn't be able to see him from the window. He punched in Abe's number and then cursed when it went to voice mail. Abe probably didn't want any discussion or argument about his order for Hayes to get back to LA, but Hayes just kept trying.

"What the hell's going on?" Hayes asked when Abe finally answered on Hayes's sixth attempt.

"Plenty, and you need to be here for it. The studio wants

to talk to you about the show, and you have to reshoot a scene first thing in the morning."

Hayes wasn't sure which of those had caused the urgency. "Is the show being canceled?"

"That depends on the answer you give during the meeting with the bigwigs later today. Just make sure you say the right thing, Hayes."

Hayes huffed. "And what would the right thing be?"

"That depends," Abe repeated. He huffed, too. "They're going to ask if you want *Outlaw Rebels* to keep going."

Hell. He didn't know the answer to that, and despite what was going on in the diner, Hayes put his full attention on this conversation with Abe. "I need to talk to the rest of the cast—"

"I've already done that. They want to continue for at least another season. This is all on your shoulders now. Say no, and the show will get the ax. Say yes, and you're committed. Now, get your butt on that plane. I want you here for that meeting. You can think about what you're going to do while you're on the flight," Abe added right before he ended the call.

Hayes frowned and stared at his phone. He trusted Abe and didn't believe the man would lie to him, but Hayes wanted to talk to the cast himself. While he was at it, he'd take some of Abe's advice and do some thinking. Maybe if he could talk Cait into driving him to the airport, he could even run this past her. But Hayes knew that wasn't likely to happen when Cait practically jumped out of the cruiser.

"We got her!" Cait announced, and she frantically motioned for Hayes to get back in. They both did.

Hayes checked the time. He'd been dealing with trying to reach Abe and talking with him for less than ten minutes. "What happened?" he asked as Leyton drove toward the main house and the café.

"You can listen for yourself once we're inside. We've got it all recorded. The moment the cameraman and reporter stepped away, Marty asked Sunshine point-blank if she was trying to wheedle her way into the wedding."

"Wheedle?" Hayes questioned. That seemed a little confrontational for a man of Marty's charm.

Cait rolled her eyes. "Yes, he used that particular word. Sunshine said she was going to do whatever it took to see her babies get married." Another eye roll. "And, yes, she said *her babies*. She then went on to tell Marty that it was your fault the girls were trying to stop her from going to the wedding and that she was trying to pressure you to get you to back off."

Hayes had to get his teeth unclenched. "Right, pressure me by releasing the private emails of a dead friend. Did Sunshine cop to that?"

Cait outstretched her arms in a ta-da gesture. "She did. Of course, she claimed you'd backed her into a corner, and it sounded as if she was working up some crocodile tears when she said it."

Yeah, like her drawl, Sunshine could also fake cry on command, but maybe there would be some real tears once she realized she was screwed. Hayes would have definitely celebrated that particular screwing if his conversation with Abe hadn't been like dead weight on his mind.

Leyton pulled to a stop in front of the café, right next to a news van for one of the San Antonio TV stations.

"Now that you can skip your meeting with Sunshine, you want to come to the police station and watch us book her?" Cait asked as they all got out of the cruiser. She was smiling. Really smiling. But Hayes figured that wasn't going to last when he answered her.

"I can't. In fact, I'm going to see if Marty can drop me at Em's so I can get to the airport." He rethought that plan when the cameraman and reporter came out. It was obvious they recognized him, and Hayes would use that to call in a favor. "Say, can I hitch a ride to San Antonio with you guys?"

They looked as if he'd just handed them a big bucket of gold. Probably because they thought they'd get an interview and photos out of this. Which they would. But Hayes knew that Cait wasn't looking at this as any bucket of gold.

"Sure," the reporter told him. He checked his watch. "But we got to head out now."

"Now works for me," Hayes assured them, and he turned back to Cait.

Her smile had definitely faded, and her eyes were no longer sparkling with celebration over Sunshine's arrest. "You're leaving?" she asked.

Leyton must not have heard what they were saying, because he headed inside. "Let's get this done, Cait."

She kept her attention nailed to Hayes, and he did the same to her. "The studio wants me at a meeting they've scheduled for later today, and I can't get out of it. Go ahead," he added. "Finish up what you need to do with my mother. I'll give you a call later and explain everything, and you can tell me how the arrest went."

Maybe there'd be enough humiliation on Sunshine's part to soothe over some of the anger he felt for her. Then again, there wasn't enough humiliation in the universe for that. He could say the same for the sickening dread he felt over what he was doing to Cait.

She didn't cover her disappointment and surprise with

maybe even some hurt thrown in. And this was the problem with them being lovers. There were expectations, always were when it came to sex, and one of those expectations was that he wouldn't just bolt like this.

"I'll call you," Hayes repeated. "And I'm not leaving for good. I'll be back for the wedding."

"Of course. You gotta do what you gotta do." Her chin came up, and she adjusted her expression, taking out the disappointment. "Break a leg," she added with some of her usual snark.

He didn't think she was putting a silent curse on him or anything, but the hurt was definitely still there. Nothing he could do about it, though. Judging from the way the interview crew was shoving their gear into their van, they were more than ready to get out of there.

Because he needed it, he brushed a quick kiss on Cait's mouth, and he hoped what he told her wasn't a lie. He wouldn't be able to explain anything unless he worked it out first in his own mind. The bottom line was he had to decide what the hell he wanted.

His life in California. The show.

Or Cait.

He just didn't know. In fact, the only thing that was certain for Hayes was that he couldn't have both. He was going to have to give up one of them.

CHAPTER SIXTEEN

"Uh, you weren't really abducted by aliens, right?" Em asked.

Cait sighed and forced her attention away from the tabloid headline "*Little Cowgirls'* BFF, Cait Jameson, Alien Abduction Nightmare."

"No," she assured Em. "But I think my dad once was. That's why he's such a pain. They must have implanted some kind of probe in his butt."

Em hooted with laughter, which was exactly what Cait had wanted. This shopping trip was already going to be tough enough without adding Em's alien concerns to it. Or any other concerns, for that matter, because it was obvious that Em was worried about her.

Cait had considered putting on blinders for this trip to the grocery store to pick up the wine and snacks they needed for a bachelorette party. That's because she would have to walk past the rack that held tabloids. Tabloids with headlines that sometimes included her—like this one with the alien bombshell. However, she wasn't the primary focus of most of the magazines. Hayes and Sunshine held that honor. Possibly the aliens, too.

The store owner, Jay Sidler, obviously loved to keep up with all the Hollywood gossip, because he stocked seemingly every one of the tabloids. He had been especially diligent about stocking the ones that chronicled what Cait was calling the SSS.

The Sunshine Shit Show.

It had pretty much started a week ago, a couple of hours after Sunshine's arrest, when the San Antonio station had "leaked" the woman admitting to extortion. Sunshine had not taken that lying down.

Nope.

As soon as she'd gotten out of jail on bail, the SSS had snowballed with Sunshine releasing Ivy's emails. That'd happened within minutes, so Sunshine had likely had someone on tap to do the computer keystrokes necessary to put the SSS wheels into action. Shortly thereafter, probably about the time Hayes would have gotten to LA, Sunshine's sex tape hit the internet and the tabloids. As predicted, that had overshadowed any jabber about Ivy, and stories about her emails hadn't stayed headlines for more than a day.

The SSS had gotten real then with Sunshine whining to anyone in the press who'd listen that Hayes was trying to ruin her and that she was going to sue him for every penny he was worth. That was probably true. The woman might try to sue. But some of the tabloids had taken stories like that and spun them into outlandish tales and outright lies.

Some of those lies had included Cait. Or more accurately, the stories had been a tawdry mix of truth and lies meant to sell copies of the tabloids. The truth that Hayes and she had been seen "together" while he'd been back in his hometown. The truth that they were lovers, though Cait wasn't sure having sex only once qualified them as that. And besides, there wasn't proof of their screwing around that one time.

Some of the lies, like the alien abduction, had really been out there, but there'd been others. One stating there was proof that Cait had given birth to Hayes's "love child" and was passing her off as a half sister. There was another one that it'd been Cait who'd stirred up trouble between Sunshine and Hayes because she was jealous that Hayes wasn't making it a "complete set" by marrying her. Some of the stories claimed that Cait had been the one to release Ivy's emails—again, that one was blamed on jealousy.

Those stories and more had made tabloid front pages, accompanied by grainy photos that made Cait look like a frumpy serial killer. Well, except for the picture that one of the tabloids had gotten from her high school yearbook. That one had made her look like a candidate for *What Not to Wear* or a visual example on why colored hair extensions should have been outlawed.

She had already been contacted by two TV shows about giving her a makeover. Contacted as well by multiple tabloids and internet sites about doing interviews and photo shoots. Cait had declined all of them, though the makeover ones had been a little tempting.

Hayes was no doubt getting bombarded with such publicity and requests for interviews, though it was hard to know for sure since Hayes hadn't been exactly chatty. Yes, he'd called her as promised to tell her that he had a meeting with the top executives of *Outlaw Rebels* and that he'd be tied up for a couple of days shooting a scene and some promos for the show.

Apparently, "tied up" meant that he didn't have time to call her again to let her know what was going on. Then again, he was working and was caught up in this SSS, too, so maybe that's why he'd only texted to let her know he was okay, that there'd been no final decision from the studio as to the fate of *Outlaw Rebels* and that he'd be in touch soon.

Soon was dragging on into what felt like forever.

"How many of these do you think we'll need?" Em asked.

That question drew Cait's attention back to the woman, and Cait saw Em had put a dozen bottles of sparkling wine into the shopping cart that was already loaded down with other wine bottles and soft drinks.

"I think that's enough," Cait assured her.

After all, it wasn't going to be a big to-do since the triplets were hiding out from tabloid cameras and crews, too. That meant not having the party anywhere in a bar or other public place where a reporter could sneak in. Instead, they were having it at Em's, and it'd be more of a gossipy, winey snack fest with some dirty movies thrown in just to keep in the spirit of a bachelorette party. But not too dirty since Kinsley would be there. No need to give the fifteen-year-old any ideas, though Cait suspected Kinsley already had plenty of those.

There'd been some debate about the guest list. Or rather the lack of one. The triplets had friends in town. Friends out of town, too. But with each person they considered inviting, there was the potential that something that was supposed to be a celebration would instead turn into tabloid stories. Friends wouldn't necessarily spill gossip, but even idle chatter could become headlines. It could blossom from there into more "alien abduction" and "secret baby" hype.

"Let me get another shopping buggy for the snacks," Cait suggested just in case Em went overboard with that, too.

The diner was preparing the actual food and some cupcakes that they would deliver and set up, but they'd need something if the munchies struck them during the night.

Cait pushed the drinks-filled cart to the front of the

store, intending to leave it near the checkout. And that's
when she saw it. The tabloid cover in the rack by the cash
register. This one had no mention of her. Nor was it out-
dated or grainy.

It was Hayes with his arm around a busty blonde.

Busty, though, was a serious understatement. She qualified for thunder-tit status.

Cait knew the curvy woman whose image screamed "I'm
soooo hot" was Athena Marlow, the actress who played
Hayes's on-again, off-again love interest on *Outlaw Rebels*.
Over the years of the show's run, Hayes and the actress had
been purported to have a real-life on-again, off-again relationship, too. The photo made them look very much "on."
So did the headline, which claimed "Athena Climbed On,
Again." It was obviously a play on words of Slade's catchphrase. *Climb on, bitch, and kiss me.*

"Oh," someone said.

Cait glanced back to see that Em was watching her stare
at the tabloid. So was the store owner, the cashier and two
other customers. No reporters, thank goodness. Jay had
been good at keeping them out of the grocery, but all activity had stopped, apparently to see how she was going
to deal with this.

"I think we should get some Cheez Doodles for the
party," Cait remarked to Em. "And some of these." She
traded her full cart, and she raked the entire display of
malted milk balls into the empty cart that she grabbed.

Cait figured it was never a good idea to try to eat your
way out of a pissy mood, but she was going to give it a try.
While Em trailed along behind her, Cait went for those
Cheez Doodles, some chips and salsa, more candy and the
makings for chocolate-covered strawberries. By the time

she was done, Cait had blown her entire food budget for the next two years, and Jay had helped her load twenty bags, plus the wine and sodas, into the back of Em's truck.

With the tabloid photo of Athena and Hayes branded in her mind, Cait followed Em to her ranch, and with Tony's help, they unloaded all the stuff. The drinks got crammed into the fridge, where there wasn't an inch of space left, and she assembled the nonperishable goodies on the kitchen table. By the time she was done, Cait was sweaty, exhausted and in need of some sulking time, which she would get since she didn't have to be back at Em's for another two hours.

To fuel her trip home, Cait snagged one of the boxes of malted milk balls. One bag of the Cheez Doodles, as well. And because she didn't want to risk choking, she also took a bottle of water. She managed to down a sizable portion of all three on the drive to boost her blood sugar, hydrate and coat her fingers with orange-goo dust. Still, it was a start to a sulky two hours.

However, she knew her alone time would have to wait a little longer for her pity party when she pulled up in front of her house and spotted the burly silver SUV. A reporter, no doubt. It wasn't the first time they'd come looking for a story at her place, and while Cait had given the others a more or less polite *get lost*, she wouldn't bother with polite today.

Gathering up her food stash and her purse, Cait got out of her SUV, and she immediately called out, "Leave or I'll arrest your ass."

The driver didn't leave, though. He turned off the engine and stepped from the SUV.

Hayes.

Any sulking and fatigue vanished, and she could have

sworn that her heart skipped a couple of beats. But it was a good kind of skipping.

Mercy, she was glad to see him.

She forgot all about the picture of him with his costar. Forgot that the picture had hurt her in places she hadn't thought could hurt. Hayes was here, and that seemingly fixed everything.

Cait didn't move. In part because she was afraid he'd disappear, that maybe this was some lovely dream. If it was, she wanted to hang on to it as long as possible, even if standing out in the blazing sun might lead to heatstroke.

"I figured it was time for me to rent a vehicle instead of bumming rides," Hayes said.

Hearing his voice made him real. No heartbeat skipping this time, but she thought maybe there were some extra beats. Fast ones that made her breath a little thin and her head more than a little light.

He didn't move toward her. He just stood there, looking better than any man had the right to look. Actually, he looked sort of Hollywood. He'd had his hair trimmed, and there wasn't a trace of any of the bruises left on his face.

It hit her then. Maybe he'd come to tell her goodbye. Maybe her heart was acting up and skipping beats for no good reason. And that's why Cait stayed put, too. She needed her feet anchored in case he was there to tell her that it was over, that he was going back to LA for good.

"You willing to share those Cheez Doodles?" he asked.

He flashed her a smile that could have melted every glacier on the planet, and Cait felt the tightness in her chest ease. She felt other things, too. Hot, dreamy sex things when Hayes finally got moving. He went to her, hooked his arm around her neck and kissed her.

HAYES WOULD HAVE breathed a sigh of relief had his mouth not been on Cait's. He'd thought that maybe she would tell him to get lost, that she was done with him, and he couldn't have blamed her. After all, he'd barely been in touch with her over the past week.

But he'd missed her every minute, every second of that week.

It was as if she'd taken something from him. Exactly what that something was, he didn't know. Contentment? Peace of mind?

His heart?

The last seemed way too poetic for him, but during his entire time in LA, he'd felt as if something was off, something was missing. At the moment, he felt as if he'd found it.

And he would probably lose it just as quickly.

He tried not to get too caught up in the kiss. Hard to do, though, when Cait really got into it. Despite the fact she still had hold of her purse, the bag of Cheez Doodles and the candy, she pulled him closer, kicking the kiss up a heated notch and letting him know that she'd missed him, too. That she wanted him. Hayes sure as hell wanted her, too, but he wasn't about to play dirty and get her into bed. She had to know what was going on.

Cait finally broke the kiss and eased back. She looked up at him and smiled. God, that smile was good to see, and he hated to see it vanish. Hated as well that in just a couple of minutes, he might not see that hot invitation in her eyes. Everything about her was welcoming him to her bed.

"How are your ribs?" she asked, still smiling. Yeah, that was also an invitation.

"Good." And for the first time in weeks, that wasn't a lie.

Despite all the moving around he'd had to do on the set and filming location, the pain had finally decided to take a hike.

Hayes wanted to stand there a while longer, holding her, along with holding on to this moment. But he couldn't. He owed Cait the truth. So he took a mental snapshot of her amazing face and adjusted their positions, sliding his arm around her waist until they were next to each other so he could get her moving inside.

"How much time do you have before the bachelorette party?" he asked.

"About two hours. When do you have to be at my brothers' stag party?"

"The same." And it wouldn't take him long to get there since it was at the Jameson ranch. Like the brides, the grooms had opted for a private venue so they wouldn't be hounded by the press.

"Plenty of time," Cait concluded.

It was indeed long enough for them to fool around, recover and fool around again. But unfortunately, Hayes had to use that time for something other than fun.

"You're staying at the Jameson ranch tonight?" she asked before he could say anything.

He shook his head. "I'll risk going back to Em's." Where Cait would no doubt still be. That's why it was a risk. She would likely be tipsy, maybe even drunk, and her defenses would be down. That's why he had to handle this now. "We have to talk," he insisted.

She groaned, and he felt her muscles tense. However, she didn't say anything as they went into the house. Cait just turned and faced him.

"You're dumping me," she concluded. The invitation in her eyes was already gone, and he could see her steeling herself up. "Except it's not really dumping because you told me from the get-go that you'd be leaving after the wedding. I knew anything we had would be temporary."

All of that was true. But it still stung. Still hurt because Hayes knew he'd done exactly what he'd sworn he wouldn't do. He'd hurt her. That kiss sure as hell hadn't helped, either, because it'd given her a couple of seconds of false hope.

"Well," she continued, taking a deep breath. Cait repeated that one word, went to the kitchen and took out a bottle of water. She downed it as if it were medicine and faced him again. "So this is goodbye."

That stung, too. No. It was more than that. It hurt. Hayes thought he would have felt less pain had she just slugged him.

"I'll be leaving after the wedding," he confirmed. He didn't go closer to her. Best not to be tempted to pull her back into his arms. "The show wasn't canceled. The studio wants to sign everyone in the cast to another season."

That had taken some doing, though. Or as Abe had put it—Hayes had had to say the right thing. And the right thing was that he was committed to *Outlaw Rebels*. It hadn't been an easy decision to make, not until he'd actually stepped on the set. Then he'd remembered just how much he loved what he did. It wasn't just a show or a way of life—it was also who he was. Better yet, it was who he wanted to be.

But it would come with a huge price tag.

It would cost him Cait.

She tried to work up a smile. Failed. But there was plenty of concern on her face now. "Are you good with *Outlaw Rebels* continuing?"

He nodded, and again it was true. "The show and the cast have been my life for a long time now. We're like family.

We know we can't do it forever, but we thought we should give it at least one more year and go from there."

"The cast," she repeated, and her concern morphed into something with an edge. And Hayes thought he knew why.

"You saw the picture of Athena and me?" he asked.

"I caught a glimpse of it," she admitted. Yeah, definitely an edge along with some anger.

Now he did go to her. Hayes went into the kitchen and risked touching her. Not a big embrace. He probably couldn't have managed that anyway because she still had the food tucked in the crook of her arm. So he just ran his fingers over the sleeve of her shirt.

"Some of the cast went out to eat, and the paparazzi got some shots just as Athena and I were walking in. Not to-gether," he emphasized. "She's living with a pro wrestler." And the guy hadn't been pleased, either, about the photo. "I'm sorry it upset you."

She stepped away from his rubbing fingers and shrugged, obviously dismissing the hurt. Well, at first she tried to do that, but then she groaned. "I ate at least three thousand calories because of that picture."

Hayes couldn't help himself. He smiled. Not many women would have admitted that, but then Cait wasn't the sort to play games. That's why this was even harder.

She tried to make that easier for him, though. Her ex-pression turned light, but that light didn't quite make it to her eyes.

"Another season of *climb on, bitch, and kiss me*," she muttered. Still holding on to the food, she opened the fridge again, got out another bottle of water and handed it to him. "Your fans are going to be thrilled. And FYI, I'm one of them. I've watched every single episode, and I can tell you exactly how many times you bared your incredible ass for the camera."

He looked to see if that was a joke. It wasn't. "How many times?" Hayes challenged.

"Eighteen," she readily answered. "Nineteen if you count the shower scene where you're behind the rippled glass. I count that one," Cait added with a wink. "Hey, an ass glimpse is still a glimpse, even if it's somewhat obscured."

He wanted to latch on to that wink, to the moment she was trying to give him. A moment where she was trying to convince him that he hadn't been a dick to start up with her.

She finally set what was left of the Cheez Doodles and the candy on the counter. "Help yourself," she offered. "Then you can tell me all about the scene you had to re-shoot and what your schedule will be like now that you've agreed to do another season."

Cait must have believed this would be a long chat session, because she made herself comfortable on the bar stool. She didn't eat any more of the junk food, though, probably because she hadn't wanted to add to her already-high calorie count.

"The reshoot took most of the week," he said, figuring she didn't really want the details. The final product of the filming might look exciting, but a lot of rehearsals, takes and retakes went into it. "As for my schedule, there'll be twenty-two episodes in the new season, and each one will take about ten days to film. I'll need to be on set for about seven of those ten days." He stopped. "You really don't want to hear this."

"But I do," she argued. "I'd like to get a feel for how busy you'll be in case I decide to make a trip to LA. I get two weeks' vacation every year. I could spend a few days of it to go see you."

Hayes did a mental double take on that. It hadn't occurred to him that Cait would actually want to see him after he left. In fact, he'd thought she would want to completely wash her hands of him.

"You'd do that?" he asked, wishing that he didn't sound as stunned as he probably looked.

"Of course." She lifted her shoulder in what she probably thought was a careless shrug. "Well, unless I'll cramp your style—"

Hayes kissed her to stop the rest of that. He made sure he applied some finesse to it, too, and he let the taste of her slide right through him. There was just a hint of Cheez Doodles and chocolate, but it was still a taste that kicked his need for her into overdrive. Not good. He was trying to do the right thing here, and dragging her to the bed or the floor wouldn't be good in the long run.

It'd feel damn amazing, though. He was certain of that.

He forced himself away from her mouth and met her eyes with his. "I'd really like it if you came to visit me."

Her lips twitched a little. "But?"

Hayes hoped she didn't smile, because that would be giving him an out. He didn't deserve an out. "But we still wouldn't be together except for those couple of days." He cursed, scrubbed his hand over his face. "I can't give you what you want, Cait."

More lip twitching, and she smiled, and man, it had some snark to it. "What is it you think I want?" She didn't wait for him to answer. "And so help me, if you say a white picket fence, I'm going to throw a big handful of these malted milk balls at your crotch."

He was pretty sure a white picket fence equaled the futures that his sisters were about to get. With variations, of course. But they'd have lives that included marriage and kids.

In other words, normal.

His life was as far from normal as it could get, and it certainly wasn't here in Lone Star Ridge, where Cait was grounded. However, since he didn't want hard balls of candy thrown at his crotch, he gave some thought to his answer.

"You want me to love you," he muttered.

There. He'd said it. He'd spelled out what he feared most because it was what he couldn't give her.

"Why the heck would you think that?" She came right back at him, and again she didn't wait for an answer. "I've already got enough love, thank you very much. Love for my family, my job, for what I have here."

She motioned to her house and the grounds, specifically pointing to one of the horses in the corral. Then Cait glanced around as if looking for something else and finally plucked up one of the candies.

"This is what I already have," she explained. "A delicious crunchy center coated with yummy chocolate. Now, it would be even yummier with a thicker chocolate coating, and that's what you are, Hayes."

He frowned. "I'm a thicker chocolate coating?"

She nodded so fast that her neck popped. "Yes. A yummy nummy high-caloric treat that shouldn't be sampled too often."

Well, hell. He frowned and mentally repeated that *well, hell* a couple more times. He wasn't sure he liked that comparison. But at least she wasn't crying or looking especially sad. In fact, zero sadness.

With a sly smile, she sauntered toward him. There was

no other word for it. She sauntered and gave him a heavily-lidded look that made him think of sex. Then again, just looking at Cait made him think of sex.

"Let me get this straight," she purred. She touched the malted milk ball to his lips and then slid it down over his chin and to his throat. Then lower to his chest. "Whether we fool around or not, you'll still have to leave town after the wedding?"

"Yes," he managed. That was an accurate summary.

Cait skimmed the hard ball of candy over his stomach. It was like a slow, torturous tease. "So we can either take cold showers for the next three days or we can have multiple rounds of really good sex?"

"Yes," he repeated.

Again, an accurate summary. However, Hayes forced himself to admit that he probably would have said yes to anything when the candy, and her hand, slid over his erection.

He wanted to remind her that there might be cold showers after those three days. Or a broken heart. But she began to make very interesting circles with that candy. And she leaned in and nipped his bottom lip with her teeth.

"I don't want to hurt you," he said, biting off a groan.

Her gaze stayed locked with his while she kept up the odd hand job, pushing and pressing against that part of him that was already too hard. She kept her hand in place, slowly brought the candy to her mouth.

And licked it.

That was it, his breaking point, and Hayes figured he was going to hell for what he was about to do, but he took hold of Cait and dragged her against him. He heard the candy ball drop to the floor, but he didn't care where it bounced and landed. The only thing he cared about right now was making her mouth pay for the dirty little tease it'd just done.

He gave her a punishing kiss. Teeth and tongue. But she put up no resistance whatsoever. Just the opposite. She gave a naughty chuckle, cupped his balls and kissed him right back while managing to rub her body all over his.

Hayes snapped, and any remaining willpower vanished in a blink. Pushing her against the counter, he managed to do his own body rubbing. His chest to her breasts. Groin to groin. And with his hand squeezing her ass.

Apparently, she was all for that, too, but the chuckling stopped, and she got down to business, as well. Her kiss got hungrier. Her touching became an urgent demand for more. Since Hayes's body was doing some urging as well, he didn't hold back. He yanked off her top and went after her breasts.

What followed next wasn't pretty. They were off-balanced, and Cait's mouth and hands were battling with his to touch and kiss whatever parts they could reach. Hayes's arm swiped across the counter, knocking the Cheez Doodles and the malted milk balls to the floor. They pinged and bounced, the sound barely audible because of the throbbing in Hayes's ears.

His ears weren't the only part of him throbbing, though. No, that award went to his dick, which was now calling the shots. Obviously, Cait was okay with that, because she just kept kissing and groping while Hayes pulled her to the floor.

It was a bad idea because the tile was cold, hard and covered with the hard candy balls, but location wasn't a consideration now. Speed, however, was.

Cait nearly bloodied his nose when she went after his shirt, but he just let her have at it while he rid her of her jeans and shoes. Every movement they made crushed the Cheez Doodles, leaving them coated in orangey dust. He also suspected they'd have bruises all over their bodies because the candy didn't crush. The balls must have had extra coatings of chocolate, because they stayed like marbles beneath them.

"You'd better have a condom with you," Cait said, her breath gusting against his face.

"I do." He snagged the condom from his pocket as she tugged off his jeans.

Her eyes were wild now, and her hair tumbled around her face like a sultry siren. Hayes thought he'd never seen someone so beautiful. Or desperate. He totally got the desperate thing because he was feeling it, too.

Proving that his ribs were indeed healed, he flipped her on her back and levered himself up enough on his forearm to slide on the condom. He'd barely managed to get that done when Cait took hold of his butt and shoved him down inside her.

The sounds they made were pure relief.

Just being inside her sated the gnawing hunger. For a few seconds, anyway. For that short snap of time, there was the pleasure. The quiet sensation that this was exactly what they both needed. Her body clamping on to his erection. Him, buried deep inside all that wet, tight heat.

He started moving because he had no choice. Again, his dick was calling the shots. Hayes thrust into her, watching her react. And what a reaction it was. A silky moan left her mouth that was slightly swollen from their rough kisses. Her eyes narrowed with heat, and her body moved with one singular purpose. To pinpoint the pleasure until they finished.

Hayes wanted this to last a long, long time. Maybe the entire two hours before she had to go to the party. But her muscles began to squeeze his erection again. This was the ripple that turned into a full orgasm.

He watched her come, kissed her so that he'd have the taste of her in his mouth. And Hayes let her rippling finish him off.

CHAPTER SEVENTEEN

CAIT SCREECHED HER SUV to a halt in front of Em's place, grabbed her overnight bag and ran toward the house. Crap, she was late. It'd been for a good reason—a second round of sex in the shower with Hayes—but she didn't like having to explain why she was arriving a half hour late to a party she was cohosting. Maybe everyone was already having so much fun that they hadn't noticed her absence.

They noticed, all right.

The moment Cait hurried into the kitchen she became well aware of that noticing. The triplets and Em were there, chatting and munching, but both of those activities stopped, and Cait got their full attention.

"Sorry I'm late," Cait blurted out, setting her overnight bag on the floor. Her voice was way too breathy, but hopefully they wouldn't think that she'd been with—

"You were with Hayes," Sunny concluded.

What, was she wearing a sign? Did she have bits of Cheez Doodles in her hair? The second was actually a strong possibility since she had been distracted in the shower, mainly because of Hayes's clever mouth, and Cait wasn't sure she'd managed to wash out all the crushed bits.

"Hayes texted when he landed at the airport," McCall provided. "He said he was going to see you before he went to the ranch for the stag party."

So, no sign, sisterly ESP or Cheez Doodles residue.

Hayes had told them. But he wouldn't have told them that he'd gone to see her for sex—

"You tapped him, didn't you," Hadley piped in, and it wasn't a question. She sighed in disapproval. "He's going to trounce all over your heart when he leaves in a couple of days."

There was no doubt about that, but it wasn't a subject Cait wanted to discuss.

"*If* he leaves," Em interjected.

"He's leaving," Cait verified, and again this subject wasn't up for discussion. It would just put her in a sour mood, so she changed the topic of conversation. "The diner did a good job with the party food." She made a mental note to thank the owner, Hildie Stoddermeyer.

Clearly, though, party food wasn't what they wanted to discuss, but Cait just continued to peruse the offerings. Cocktail meatballs, stuffed mushrooms, finger sandwiches. She froze, though, when she got to the cupcakes. They were supposed to be topped with replicas of Chippendale strippers, which would have been PG-13-rated risqué, but instead there were some with candy boobs, huge ones, and others with skimpy sugar panties.

"Hildie called and said the stripper toppers didn't get there in time, so she had to substitute," Em explained. "It makes me wonder, though, if these were supposed to go to the stag party."

Cait was wondering the same thing. Wondering, too, what Hayes and her brothers got. She made another mental note to nix the thanks she had planned for Hildie.

"Where's Kinsley?" Cait asked, glancing around.

No one jumped to answer, and they probably thought they could wear her down with their probing, intense stares so she'd blab all about Hayes. Cait didn't give in to it. She poured herself a glass of the sparkling wine and popped a tiny sausage meatball in her mouth. Everyone was clearly waiting until she chewed and swallowed so that she could continue, but Cait just ate more food, a finger sandwich this time.

Hadley sighed again. "Kinsley's in the family room. She wanted to get a head start on the entertainment portion of this evening. She's watching porn."

Cait stopped in midbite of another sandwich. She'd taken care of the food and drinks for this shindig, but she had left the movie selection to Em. Sweet baby Moses in a basket. She hoped the woman hadn't chosen something totally inappropriate. Hoped, too, that if Em had indeed gone the inappropriate route, then one of the triplets would have stopped it. Maybe not Hadley but McCall or Sunny for sure.

"I'd better check on her," Cait insisted.

"We'll hold all conversation about Hayes and you until you get back," Hadley called out. "And FYI, you've got a chunk of what appears to be a malted milk ball in your hair."

Cait stopped long enough to feel around her head, and she did indeed come up with a chunk of candy clinging to the back of her hair. She three-pointed it into the sink, shot Hadley a scowl and practically ran to the family room.

Her sister was there, all right, sitting on the sofa, and the coffee table in front of her was littered with food, including a bowl of the Cheez Doodles. Good call on her part for choosing that particular party cuisine.

"You call this porn?" Kinsley grumbled the moment Cait got into the room.

Cait felt a big wash of relief when she saw the movie *Love, Actually* was playing on Em's big-screen TV.

"There's nudity and adult language," Cait reminded her,

"and if you imagine all the cast naked, then it'll be porn suitable for a teenager."

Kinsley rolled her eyes. "Which means it isn't porn at all."

True, but it was all the girl was going to get. Cait hoped. She made a mental note to check the other movies that Em had chosen.

"You should have at least hired a stripper," Kinsley added in a grumble. "A real one, not the ones on the cupcakes."

"Yes, because I want to corrupt my kid sister and set her on a path to gratuitous nudity and debauchery." Cait sank down beside her. She wouldn't be able to avoid Em and the triplets all night, but this was a start.

"You could have hired Hayes," Kinsley remarked. "I'll bet he'd be up for some gratuitous nudity."

So even here he would be the topic of conversation. "He only takes off his pants for *Outlaw Rebels*."

And for her, of course. Cait smiled thinking about just how he'd looked when his jeans had come off. The man did indeed have a fine ass even covered in food particles.

Kinsley snorted out a laugh. "Yeah, right. I'm betting many people have seen his butt in the flesh and not just on-screen."

Cait knew that was a bet her sister could easily win. Hayes did indeed have a rep for sleeping around, and that wouldn't have bothered her if she weren't now part of that sleeping-around flavor of the week. She consoled herself with the belief that he had feelings for her. Feelings that she could see on his face and feel in his touch. But those feelings wouldn't do squat to keep him here.

"How'd your *date* go with Hayes?" Kinsley asked.

That jolted Cait out of her thoughts and back to reality.

The look she gave Kinsley was more jaundiced than actual jaundice. "Who says we had a date?"

"I'm not deaf. I hear things." This was said after a "duh" and through the loud crunching sounds as they both ate some Cheez Doodles. "His sisters and Granny Em were talking about it when they were waiting for you."

Clearly, the volume on the movie wasn't up loud enough if Kinsley had heard that. Then again, maybe that particular conversation had happened when Kinsley had been in the kitchen loading up her snack stash.

"The date went fine," Cait settled for saying, and since Hayes was obviously on everyone's minds, she filled Kinsley in on some things that would soon become public knowledge anyway. "He finished the scenes he had to shoot in LA, did some publicity stuff and got the thumbs-up for another season of *Outlaw Rebels*."

"Publicity stuff," Kinsley repeated. "You mean like getting his picture taken with Athena."

Apparently, Kinsley was a sponge for info on all things Hayes. "Yes, that," she verified.

Kinsley munched more Cheez Doodles and watched Hugh Grant dance through Number 10 Downing Street. "Are you in love with him?" she asked.

Cait didn't think the girl was talking about the movie. "Who? Hayes?"

"No, the Gingerbread Man." She rolled her eyes. "Yes, Hayes. He's really hot, and I was thinking if you hooked up with him because you're in love with him that I'd get to see him more often."

The thought had occurred to Cait, too, and that was in both a good and bad way. If Hayes stayed, she would almost certainly be able to have more shower sex with him.

She'd be able to kiss him more often. They could have more than a fling that lasted only a few weeks.

Or not.

He could be miserable here. There was certainly the possibility of that since misery had been plentiful when he'd lived here as a boy. Maybe that's why he had immersed himself so deeply in his life in California. It was a long, long way from Lone Star Ridge. It could be that was his fix for keeping the memory storms at bay.

"I'm sorry," Kinsley murmured.

Cait felt the girl's hand slide over hers. Felt, too, Kinsley wipe off some of the Cheez Doodles dust onto the back of Cait's hand. Kinsley grinned. It was such a kid-sister thing to do, so Cait grinned back and squished a Cheez Doodle on Kinsley's nose. That escalated into a few more jabs with the snack food before they settled down to watch the movie.

This was good. Not exactly clean fun. But good. It almost made Cait forget that in three days, she'd be a miserable puddle of a mess. As opposed to just the sad puddle that she was now.

"I really am sorry about Hayes and you," Kinsley whispered just as the others came into the family room.

Cait managed a smile and gave Kinsley's hand a squeeze. One not to wipe off orange dust but to let her sister know that she appreciated the support. Then Cait put that all aside and got to work enjoying herself.

THE CUPCAKES HAD candy pink dicks and balls on them. At least Hayes thought that's what they were. The heat had obviously gotten to them when the diner had delivered them, so the dicks were limp and the balls were melting down the sides of the wrappers. Not very appetizing, but that probably wasn't the only reason they hadn't been eaten. Simply put, any kind of cupcakes, dick or otherwise, didn't go well with a keg of beer.

The evening had been better suited for pizza. And questions. And questioning looks. Hayes had gotten plenty of them, and most had been about Cait. Not a surprise since she was the sister of the grooms, and her brothers were concerned that she was in over her head with Hayes.

She was.

But Hayes hadn't done a damn thing to remedy that. In fact, he'd made things worse by having sex with her not once but twice today.

He didn't like lying to himself and had to admit that it probably would have been a threefer kind of day and night if it hadn't been for the parties. That had given Cait and him a needed break from each other, though it hadn't been much of a distraction. She'd been on his mind nine out of every ten minutes, and the only reason he hadn't thought of her the other sixty seconds was because it was when one of the grooms or a ranch hand had asked him something about the show.

Yes, *Outlaw Rebels* would be continuing.

Yes, he was going back to California.

Yes, he was a dick.

He hadn't actually given that last response out loud, but it had been implied many times throughout the night. A night that thankfully ended early because all the grooms had work the next day. So, at barely 10:00 p.m., Hayes said his goodbyes, well-wishes for the big day and headed out. He'd barely made it to his rental, though, when his phone rang, and he saw Athena's name on the screen.

Hell. What now?

The contract negotiations were all done, but maybe there'd been some kind of glitch. He really didn't want to make a trip back before the wedding. That way, he'd have to say goodbye to Cait twice. Once was going to be bad enough.

"Everything okay?" Hayes greeted her when he answered the call.

"Don't hang up," the woman said.

Not Athena but Shayla. Shit. His groan was so loud that Hayes was surprised that someone in the Jameson houses didn't come out to check on him.

"I'm sorry," another woman said. This time it was Athena. "Shayla convinced me that she had to talk to you. I think you'll want to hear what she has to say."

Hayes seriously doubted that, and when he did get back to LA, he would change his number and then have a sit-down with his friends and insist they not share his contact info with Shayla.

"I wanted you to know I've moved on with my life," Shayla said, speaking fast. She probably knew he was within a breath of hanging up on her. "I've found someone else, and I won't be contacting you again. This is the last time you'll ever hear from me, Hayes. I just wanted to wish you the best and say how sorry I am for following you around the way I did."

That took some of the frustration out of him, but he was still skeptical. After all, this was Shayla, who'd made stalking an art form.

"I'm sorry about Ivy's emails, too," Shayla went on. "It must have hurt to see them printed like that."

"It did," he admitted. Always would.

"You weren't to blame for anything that happened to Ivy, you know," Shayla added.

It sure felt like that.

"You weren't to blame," Shayla repeated, as if she'd

heard his thoughts. "I would needlepoint that on a pillow for you, but I don't think you'll want to have anything to do with me."

This was boggy ground. Shayla might sound "reformed," but anything he said to her could give her hope to continue trying to be with him. "Tell me about your new guy," Hayes settled for saying.

She sighed, a dreamy "in love" sound. "Marlon is wonderful. Perfect in every way." She seemed happy and not in an "I'm overly medicated" kind of way.

"Then I wish you the best with him." He paused. "But if things don't work out between you two, back off. Don't stalk him."

She laughed as if that were a fine joke. "I can't stalk him. Not at the moment, anyway. He's actually on his way to jail. A problem with his taxes, but it's all a big misunderstanding that he plans on fixing."

Hayes groaned again. "Shayla, you need to keep up with your therapy."

"Oh, I will. And I'll visit Marlon any chance I get. When you love someone, you always figure out a way to be with them."

Or else you didn't fall in love. That was the simplest solution.

And the hardest.

Until now, it hadn't really been a problem for him. He'd just kept his emotional distance and put up a shitload of barriers between him and anyone he might fall for. He hadn't quite managed that distance or barriers with Cait.

"Goodbye, Hayes," Shayla told him. "Have a good life."

That sounded like one of those bad clichés that you said when you were closing a door in your life. He hoped that's exactly what it would be.

"Same to you," Hayes answered, and he ended the call.

He stared at the phone a few more seconds, and he hoped this was one particular door that stayed shut forever.

Hayes made the drive back to Em's, and since the party would probably still be going on, he intended to slip in and go straight to his room. If he saw Cait, there'd be no way he could keep his emotions off his face, and his sisters would also see. Then he'd get another round of twenty questions. He wanted to skip another sibling interrogation tonight.

He parked next to Cait's SUV, and he quietly went in through a side door that led to the little-used living room. It was empty, but he could hear the sound of a TV and some chatter in the family room. There was talk of boob cupcakes and honeymoons.

Hayes pulled off his boots, and when he started up the stairs, he made sure he didn't step on any of the boards that squeaked. He had to do the same in the hall when he went to his room, eased open the door. And froze.

Because Cait was in his bed.

She was on her stomach, fully dressed, and appeared to be asleep. However, she lifted her head, her eyes meeting his, and she smiled.

"Em told me to use one of the guest rooms," she muttered, her voice both sleepy and sexy at the same time. She yawned. "But I thought I'd rather be in here. We saved you a tit cupcake," she added.

In her mind, she'd probably added an explanation or some kind of context to that cupcake comment, but then he saw the plate on his nightstand. There was indeed a cupcake with a tit on it.

"We had dick cupcakes," he said. "I didn't bring you one."

She sat up, stretched. "Oh, well. Maybe next time."

Yes, because there were so many opportunities in life when dick cupcakes would be available.

Cait moved to the edge of the bed, put her palms on the mattress, but she didn't get up. "Do you want me to leave or stay?"

Stay. That was the answer that nearly flew out of his mouth, and it would have been 100 percent true. He wanted her to stay, but the real question was—should she stay? If she did, they'd have sex. There was 100 percent certainty of that, too. And even though it was a certainty that Hayes knew he should fight, he didn't. He stepped in, shut the door and locked it.

He went rock hard in anticipation.

"This time," he drawled as he went to her, leaning down and kissing her, "I'm using more than just one hand."

CHAPTER EIGHTEEN

A PIANO VERSION of The Judds' "Love Can Build a Bridge" flowed through the wedding tent. So did the sounds of dozens or so of whirling fans that kept the air cool.

There was also the sound of quacking ducks.

The first was a contribution from the pianist Em had hired. The latter was because the flower girls had decided to add sound effects to go with the duck-bill tiara hats they were wearing.

This day was a testament to how something that shouldn't work managed to do just that.

The girls—Austin's twins, Avery and Gracie, along with Bailey, the child Hadley had carried as a surrogate—had wanted full fowl face paint. Bailey, however, had turned out to have an allergy to the paint, so they'd settled on the duck hats, which Hadley had glammed up with sparkles and more of those seed pearls. The girls wore flowing yellow chiffon dresses trimmed at the bottom with white feathers.

As the triple maid of honor, Cait walked behind the black-eyed Susan petals that the girls were dropping, or in Avery's case, flinging on the floor. Because the girls had gotten the yellow chiffon, so had Cait, though her dress wasn't billowing out like a duck's tail. At least she hoped it wasn't. From what she'd been able to tell from looking at it and herself in the mirror, it worked.

The "it works" applied to Hayes, too. He stood at the

front of the tent as the triple best man, and he was as mouth-watering as usual. He'd opted for a Texas tuxedo like the grooms. Jeans, cowboy boots, a black jacket and yellow ties. They looked like a lineup for hot guys.

Soon, her temporary hot guy would be leaving. Maybe as soon as immediately after the reception. Cait hated for that miserable thought to even enter her head, especially at a happy time like this, when she was about to see her three brothers married to the women they loved. But still the thought came, and Cait knew she would soon be paying the piper for the fun times she'd had with Hayes.

Kinsley flashed Cait a wink and a smile. Her sister was serving as the triple bridesmaid, just as Adam was doing that particular duty for the grooms. Cait was glad he'd been included because heaven knew how long it'd be before there was another Jameson wedding. This would hopefully make him understand that he truly was part of the family.

For better or worse, just like the wedding vows.

Adam would almost certainly provide better, and if past behavior indicated future behavior, then the worse would come from Marty.

Cait kept walking down the makeshift aisle, avoiding the clumps of flowers that the girls had dropped so that she wouldn't trip over them. There were the appropriate amounts of oohs and aahs from the one hundred or so guests. Some giggles as well at the quacking girls.

She spotted Marty, who was in the front row with her mother, Em and Tony. No Sunshine, of course. Nor had the triplets' father shown up. Even though they hadn't heard from him in years, Cait had been afraid that he might arrive just to stir up some trouble. Then again, he hadn't taken that particular trouble-stirring path like his ex-wife, Sunshine.

As everyone else in the family and wedding party were

doing, Cait checked for any signs of reporters. None. She recognized every face in the crowd. That didn't mean, though, that one of them wouldn't snap a picture and sell it to the tabloids. A whole lot of temptation there. But at least it wouldn't be a photo that would put a dime in Sunshine's greedy hands.

Cait's eyes met Hayes's just for a second, and she tried to give him some ocular reassurance that all was well with her, that the smile she was giving him was the real deal. And it was. He made her happy, and she was glad she'd had a taste of that particular happiness.

She silently cursed.

She had become that stupid cliché of it being better to have loved and lost, blah, blah, blah. But it was true. She wouldn't want to undo what'd gone on between Hayes and her even if she would have to pay for it for the rest of her life. She loved him, and she knew in her heart that it was a done deal. Every man who crossed her path from now on would have to measure up to Hayes, and those other men would fall flat on their faces.

The sounds of people clearing their throats got her attention, and when Cait glanced around, she realized she had stopped. And along with the stopping, she was also staring at Hayes. Good grief. Not only was it embarrassing, it would give people something to gossip about for years.

Poor pitiful, lovestruck Cait.

It probably wouldn't look very believable, but she reached down and fiddled with the bottom of her dress to make it look as if she were un-snagging it. Then she finished her walk to the front of the tent and stood on the opposite side of her brothers and across from Hayes. The moment she was in place, the wedding march started.

The aisle hadn't been wide enough for all of the triplets to walk side by side, so they'd chosen to go in order of their births. Sunny came first in her sleek silk strapless gown that sported a flash of yellow on the beaded belt. Instead of a veil, she had some sprigs of baby's breath and a single black-eyed Susan in her hair. She smiled and didn't take her eyes off Shaw as she made her way to the front.

McCall was next, and she was wearing a fairy-tale gown that had been Avery and Gracie's choice. The girls had also helped with the bouquet, which had little glittery magic wands sticking out of it. A small yellow rubber duck, too, to go with the rest of the theme.

Hadley was last in her white leather dress. Yes, leather. Nothing traditional for her. Well, except for that look of total love that was on her face when she spotted Leyton. Cait was surprised their eyes didn't send out little throbbing cartoon hearts.

Unlike her sisters, Hadley had worn her hair down. The black curls and waves cascading down her back were adorned with several dozen tiny duck barrettes. Her bouquet was sunflowers and duck feathers. On paper, that hadn't sounded like a good mix, but Hadley made it look like a work of art.

Behind Hadley waddled the real duck, Slackers. Having the mean-tempered critter there had spurred many long debates and conversations, but the twins and Bailey had matched that with pleas and promises to clean up any poop. Which, of course, no one would have let them do. In the end, the wedding party had decided for Slackers to wear a disposable diaper and a little sign warning visitors not to touch him.

Slackers wandered over to a food dish that Em had set up by the piano, and the ceremony started. Cait thought it was probably a good idea that she couldn't actually see Hayes because it allowed her to focus on the vows. Again, all were as unique as the brides. Sunny and Shaw wrote their own. McCall and Austin went traditional. And Hadley and Leyton went with a version of Hayes's catchphrase "climb on, bitch, and kiss me."

There were indeed some kisses after the minister pronounced them married, and then the shuffling began almost immediately. Em had laid out this part the way a general would diagram a battle plan. While a crew moved in to take down the wedding stuff and set up the tent for the reception, the wedding party would wait in the house. The guests would go to the backyard, hopefully not for long or there'd be risk of heatstroke.

With the chatter about how beautiful the ceremony had been, the wedding party brought that happiness and invisible cartoon hearts into the kitchen, where Em had set out food and drinks for them while they waited. The flower girls had opted to stay outside, which was probably a good thing, considering that a kissing fest immediately started with the newlyweds. That left Kinsley, Adam, Hayes and Cait to pretend they were blind and deaf and couldn't hear or see what was going on.

There was an awkward silence where Cait was trying not to notice Hayes and he was trying not to notice her, but thankfully Adam gave them a reprieve.

"I had a good time on tour with Granddad," the boy blurted out, and then he stuffed a canapé into his mouth.

Cait felt ashamed that she hadn't quizzed the boy on how that'd gone, but Marty and his tour bus had only cruised in that morning. Still, she should have made sure Adam was okay.

And he apparently was.

Even if Cait hadn't picked up on his tone—which practically qualified as gleeful, by Adam's normally somber standards—she couldn't have missed the *Granddad*. It had rolled off the boy's tongue, letting her know that he was comfortable with it. That likely meant Marty was, too, because she doubted Adam would have just started calling him that on his own.

"You didn't see anything you shouldn't have seen?" Cait pressed.

Adam glanced at Hadley and Leyton, who were French-kissing. "No naked women or anything. The band is all right. Friendly," he added. "I guess Marty talked to them and told them not to cuss or anything in front of me."

Well, that was a first for Marty to follow through on that kind of concern for one of his kin. So maybe past behavior didn't have to keep on into the present. Then again, this was Marty, and it was just one short road trip. It didn't qualify the man for The World's Greatest Granddad coffee mug.

Kinsley pulled out her phone from a side pocket when it dinged with a text, and the girl flushed and smiled when she looked at the screen. "Uh, I want to go outside and wait."

Cait had her own look at the girl's phone and wasn't surprised to see Jason Crawford's name there. Jason was sixteen, the star quarterback of the high school team and had started to show some interest in Kinsley.

Which meant he was someone Cait would keep her eye on.

He seemed like a good enough kid, but she had a "big sister" duty to make sure Jason understood that she would do him grievous bodily harm if he did anything to hurt Kinsley. She'd also let Jason know that anything of the grievous nature she did to him would be a teeny-tiny drop in the bucket compared to what Leyton, Shaw and Austin would dole out. After all, they had "big brother" duties, too.

It occurred to her that her brothers might feel the same

way about Hayes. But their relationship was different. Yes, there'd be hurt, but Cait was old enough to know exactly what she'd be facing.

Kinsley grabbed one of the plates of party food and hurried out. Adam lasted another minute, tops, before he muttered an excuse about needing to check on his granddad before he headed out, as well. That left Hayes and her surrounded by billowing clouds of newlywed lust. Then again, Hayes and she didn't have any trouble creating their own lust clouds, billowing or otherwise.

"Thank you for making me the happiest woman in Texas," she heard Sunny murmur to Shaw.

Hadley must have heard it and taken it as a challenge. "Thank you for making me the happiest woman in the entire universe, black holes included."

McCall just chuckled, dismissed that with the wave of her hand and gave Austin a very hot kiss.

"I would tell them to get a room," Hayes commented, tipping his head to the newlyweds, "but they might just do that and miss the reception."

Yes, they did seem eager to get the honeymoon started. Their new lives, too. The kissing turned to sweet talk and promises before the gushing finally started about how beautiful the ceremony was. The consensus was that it'd been perfect, that they were happy their friends and family had been there to share it, that there'd been no interference from Sunshine or the press. And there was also talk they should somehow coax Slackers back into his pen before he pecked any of the guests or crapped through his diaper.

"I can help with that," Cait offered. Not that she was especially eager for the chore, but she thought some fresh air might clear her head, even if that air was hotter than Hades and smothering with humidity.

Cait dumped some of the snacks into a napkin so she could use it to lure Slackers and wasn't especially surprised when Hayes followed her out. She doubted it was just so he could give the couples some alone time.

"If you're going to say goodbye," she started the moment they were outside, "then you should just do it." And so they'd have some privacy for that, Cait went to the side porch, away from the crowd that was milling around under the shade trees in the backyard.

Hayes didn't say anything until they'd stopped. "I am going to say goodbye."

Here it was. What she'd dreaded. But Cait refused to let the tears come. She wanted Hayes to have no visual and no indication whatsoever that this was indeed crushing her.

"I'll be leaving tomorrow," he added while he stared at her. Watching her. And probably feeling like crap that he was doing exactly what he'd warned her he would do all along.

"Tomorrow," she repeated. She stared down at the napkin full of snacks. Thinking about why she shouldn't try to eke out some last few hours with him. Debating with herself about cutting her losses now.

She lost that debate.

Cait tossed the food onto one of the chairs, pulled Hayes to her and kissed him. She made it count and let her taste seep into him. There was some tongue play involved, of course. And heat. Lots and lots of heat. She was pleased that he seemed a little out of breath when she finally pulled back.

He opened his mouth and then closed it as if he'd changed his mind about what to say. "Would it be easier on you if I left now?"

The answer to this was so simple, now that she'd lost that debate. "No. The time for easy has passed." She kissed him again and wanted to smile when she heard his groan of pleasure.

Hayes looked as if he intended to keep groaning when he stared down at her. "I just want—"

She kissed him again to stop him. Because she already knew that he wanted to fix this so she wouldn't be hurt. But that ship had sailed, too.

"Come to my place tonight for a real farewell," she invited with her mouth still against his. "This time, I'll let you use both of your hands."

CAIT WAS GLAD she woke up first because it gave her a chance to watch Hayes sleep. She supposed that was a little creepy, but she just wanted to take him all in. Not in a sexual way.

Not at the moment, anyway.

They'd done plenty of "taking in sexually" the night before, and while she wanted him again more than she wanted her heart to stop aching, she needed this time with him. She could keep this image of him in her head and conjure it up whenever she was feeling lower than dirt.

And what an image he was.

He was on his stomach, the left half of his face buried in a white pillow. Rock-star handsome, no question about it. He had certainly won the DNA lottery to give him all those incredible features.

One of the better features was his naked body, and now that the sun was starting to peek through the windows, she could see plenty of it. That's because he'd kicked off most of the covers. His back and legs were bare, and even though he had a sheet over his midsection, she could see the outline of his butt. A butt she'd probably see again if she watched the new season of *Outlaw Rebels*. Then she would remember

what it was like to have gripped on to it, her hands squeezing those famous cheeks while he drove into her.

Yes, she would remember that.

She glanced at the clock. Then frowned. It was already
past six o'clock, and she would need to be at work at eight
o'clock. A necessity since Leyton was on his honeymoon,
and she'd have to fill in for him. There'd be a lot of people
filling in for Shaw and Austin, too. The ranch work didn't
just go away because the ranchers weren't there.

All the newlyweds had already left on their honeymoons
by now. Sunny and Shaw to the Virgin Islands. Austin
and McCall to the Outer Banks of North Carolina. Hadley and Leyton to Vegas. Austin's twins would be staying
with their maternal grandparents while Austin and McCall
were gone, and Kinsley had said she would be with Lenore.
Cait suspected that had been the girl's preference because
Kinsley thought Lenore might not be as vigilant if the girl
wanted to see her football hottie, but Kinsley was in for a
surprise. Lenore had raised a houseful of kids and knew
all the tricks they could pull.

Sighing, Cait was about to put an end to her Hayes
watching and grab a shower, but he stirred. Moaned. When
his eyes opened, they zoomed right in on her. He gave her
a lazy smile, one that didn't match the level of emotion she
was feeling, but a moment later, she forgot all about that
emotion. Hayes reached out, pulled her down to him, and
in a blink, he rolled on top of her.

He was hard as steel and had clearly awakened with her
on his mind. Or maybe with just sex on his mind. But this
was her fantasy right now, and she was going to pretend
that this was all just for her. While she was at it, she'd pretend there was no goodbye.

That this wouldn't be the last time they'd be together.

It was fairly easy to push all that aside when he kissed her. Like that smile, it was lazy and slow, as if they had all the time in the world. He nipped her bottom lip with his teeth and then did the same to her neck. By the time he worked his way down to her breasts, she was totally mindless except for one thing.

Hayes.

Fortunately, Hayes was in the mindless mode, too, with one single purpose. To drive her insane and then hopefully cure that insanity by giving her an amazing orgasm.

He continued the trail of kisses, lowering to her stomach, where he used his tongue and his breath to awaken every nerve in that general vicinity. Other nerves, the ones lower than the current position of his tongue, definitely wanted that same kind of attention, so she didn't stop him or his mouth when it cruised lower. Then lower.

Until he used his tongue and breath in the center of those nerves.

Just like that, one flick of his tongue, and he sent her flying. Cait didn't even try to hold on, to make it last. She gave in to wave after wave of pleasure that racked her body.

She was still waving and racking and nowhere near recovering when Hayes kissed his way back up. He also snagged the condom he'd left on her nightstand. There'd once been three, but this was the last one. That did register in her still-muddled brain, but not for long. Hayes brought back the mindlessness by getting the condom on fast and slipping right into her while she was still quaking from the orgasm.

Watching her, he started to move inside her, and she wondered if he was gathering memories of her, the way she was of him. But that was a very fleeting thought because Cait experienced something of a miracle. The tension inside her started to rebuild. The need came clawing back with a vengeance. And just like that, she was ready for another slam of pleasure.

Hayes gave her just that.

He pushed into her until all that pleasure spiraled, coiled and released. It took away what little breath she'd managed to regain and left her feeling sated, wonderful. And it would have worked its way to sad if she hadn't pushed it away. There'd be plenty of time for that later.

For now, she held him and skimmed her hands over as much of his naked body as she could reach. He seemed content to let her do just that, and the minutes slipped away. Cait might have even fallen back asleep, but the jarring sound of her alarm cut through the room.

"Work," she grumbled, slapping off the alarm with far more force than necessary.

Hayes cursed and rolled off her, landing on his back. Not for long, though. He took only a few seconds to catch his breath and got up.

"I won't be long in the bathroom," he said, gathering up his clothes from the floor. "Then I'll get out of your hair."

She got up as well, located a T-shirt. Panties, too. The clothing wasn't exactly armor, but she didn't want to be naked when she faced him. Apparently, Hayes was of a like mind, because a couple of minutes later, he walked out of the bathroom fully dressed.

He stopped, looked at her, and she saw the sadness. No way could she handle that now, so Cait took hold of his arm and led him out of the bedroom and toward the front of the house.

When they reached the front door, she reached in and took out a letter. "I wrote this yesterday and thought it would be easier than a long goodbye. Read this after you've left Lone Star Ridge," she instructed, putting it in his hands.

He volleyed glances between her and the letter. "You said you'd come to visit me."

"And I will."

That was perhaps the truth. However, it was just as possible that she wouldn't be able to face him once she'd started to mend this crack in her heart. Plus, even if she did go to him, it would be just that—a visit.

"Don't read the letter before you're back in California," she emphasized, "or a spell will be released that'll feel like a serious kick to the nuts."

He winced but smiled. "I wanted to hear one of your wiseass remarks before I left."

"Glad I could accommodate you." Cait kissed him, but this time she kept the passion out of it. Closed mouth and quick.

She opened the front door, and he gave her a chaste kiss. Or rather it would have been, had it come from anyone other than Hayes. She wasn't sure that mouth could produce chaste.

As he made his way to his SUV, he looked back at her and smiled.

Goal accomplished. She had wanted him to walk away happy. She'd wanted him to leave, knowing that their fling might be over, but as flings went, it surely qualified for some big-assed award.

She watched him leave and then she sat down on the floor to get started with what she'd known she would have to do.

Cait broke down and cried like there was no tomorrow.

CHAPTER NINETEEN

HAYES STEPPED INSIDE the quiet house. The chaos of the wedding planning and the wedding itself was gone. So were the steady streams of people who'd been coming and going over the past couple of weeks.

Normally, he would have liked the quiet, but now it meant there were no distractions, and he sure as hell could have used one. Then again, it was probably best this way. He wasn't fit to be around people, not with him feeling like the dick that he was.

Despite all the lectures and glares from Cait's brothers, he'd still done the very thing that could hurt her.

Maybe.

She'd looked pretty calm and content when he'd left her, so maybe she would indeed come out of this without getting hurt.

He frowned.

Then he cursed himself. That "calm and content" should have made him feel like less of a dick, but it didn't. It just made him feel…hurt. Which only proved his dickhood. He should be glad and relieved that Cait hadn't handed herself to him on a silver platter. So, why wasn't he happy about either of those things? He did a gut check and verified that. No gladness. No relief.

He looked at the letter she'd given him and considered opening it despite her smart-ass curse warning. But he didn't. Hayes hoped he didn't have to explain it to anyone, but as long as the letter stayed sealed and unread, it was as if there was unfinished business between Cait and him. He still didn't get any gladness or relief over that, but reading it would give him something to look forward to.

Hayes glanced up and saw Em standing in the living room doorway. Watching him from over a mug of coffee. He wasn't sure how long she'd been there, but Em was no fool. She knew he was deep into that bag of mixed emotions right now.

"You're ready to get back to filming your show?" she asked, but Hayes got the feeling it wasn't such a simple question. It seemed to be some kind of lead-in for him to spill his guts.

He nodded and put Cait's letter in the back pocket of his jeans. "It's what I do," he settled for saying.

That was true, but it was also true that he wanted to do what was right. He had a contractual obligation and one not grounded in duty. The cast was like his family, too, and he would give the show 100 percent because that's what they wanted.

But 100 percent sure as hell felt like way too much at the moment.

Em went closer, patted his arm and smiled in that "sweet little old granny" way that was as effective as a truth serum. She wanted something—a reassurance or some soul-baring— so Hayes gave her some.

"I'm on depression meds," he explained. "And I'll probably be on them for the rest of my life. If things get bad, if I start sinking again, I'll see my shrink. I'll ask for help."

His grandmother's next smile and arm pat let him know that hearing that pleased her. It pleased him, too, because it was the truth. He couldn't swear to her that he wouldn't lapse into another state of depression, but he had a game plan to deal with it as best he could.

"I've got some good news that might cheer you up," Em said. "Sunshine got arrested for smacking a reporter with one of those big-assed handbags she carries. The bag had a serpent's head on it. Fitting," she concluded in a mutter. "Anyway, the serpent also had fangs, and one of them cut the guy."

That was indeed good news. Well, not the cut reporter, but Sunshine's arrest.

"The reporter said something about the sex tape not being very flattering," Em went on, "and that he was betting Sunshine wished she'd shown a better side of her ass, *if she had a better side, that is*. I'm guessing it was a 'straw that broke the camel's back' kind of comment, because she knocked him in the head with the snake and then broke his camera. Turns out he's got gobs of money, and along with the criminal charges, he's suing her."

Hayes smiled even though it wasn't really a smiling matter. His sisters would undoubtedly be pulled into the publicity from this. Still, it might tie up Sunshine for a while, and that would give her less time to think of ways to screw over her family.

Em's next arm pat stayed in place, and she looked up at him. "You'll be leaving this morning, then?" she asked.

He nodded. "I'm heading up to pack now. The goodbyes are done." He'd given those to his sisters before they'd left on their honeymoons. Given one to Tony, too, shortly after the reception. Hayes gave Em a goodbye kiss now on the cheek. "I'll miss you."

"I'll miss you, too. And just because you gotta leave doesn't mean you have to stay gone. I mean, you could come back soon."

He didn't want to give her any false hopes. "I spend weeks filming the show."

"Which means you spend weeks when you aren't filming the show," Em pointed out just as quickly.

Hayes huffed. He knew they weren't talking about work schedules now. "Look, I'm a bad bet when it comes to Cait. She's had enough bad bets with her father."

"That's true about her dad." Em shrugged. "But you're nothing like Marty Jameson."

In some ways that was true. However, Hayes knew there was one point they had in common. Marty and he had both hurt Cait. But again, that thought gave him a mental poke. Maybe she wasn't hurt after all. And if so, he was back to this having been just a fling while he'd been killing time before his sisters' weddings.

He gave his grandmother another cheek kiss and headed up the stairs to pack. He'd have plenty of time to get to San Antonio, grab something to eat and turn in the rental car before his flight. However, when he went to his room, he stood there frozen while he glanced around.

So many memories here. During the *Little Cowgirls* days, it'd become his hideout, and later it'd been the place where he'd sneaked in girls. Of course, it was also the site of Sunshine's now-infamous sex tape. With all those memories, the one that was the clearest was of him finding Cait in his bed. A bed where they'd had some damn good sex.

He smiled, realized he was smiling and immediately tried to somber up. It didn't feel right to remember the sex. Because it shouldn't have happened. Still, Hayes figured it would be a while before those images weren't so clear, and they would almost certainly stay with him forever.

Curing that dismal thought, he whipped out the letter. Thankfully, there wasn't any real chance it would lead to a kick in the nuts, but it might feel like a kick to the teeth. Still, he wanted to know what Cait was thinking and find out if he'd left as big of a mark on her as she had on him.

He opened the envelope and sat on the bed, figuring it would take a while for him to get through whatever she'd written. However, he quickly realized that wouldn't be the case. It was just one paragraph. A very short one. So short it could have fit on a Post-it note instead of a piece of stationery paper.

Hayes, best of luck with the new season of Outlaw Rebels, he read. *I'll be tuning in to see if your bare butt will make appearance number twenty. (Remember, I count the shower scene where you're behind the rippled glass. A naked ass is still a naked ass even with visual obstructions.) Have a good life. Cait.*

He stared at it a moment, reread it and then read it again. *Well, hell.*

MAKEUP AND VISINE couldn't completely hide her tear-reddened eyes and slightly puffy face, but Cait thought she'd spackled on enough concealer to disguise the worst of it. If anyone asked why she looked as if she'd been on a crying jag, she would blame her condition on allergies.

She needed to work on her attitude, though, too. She had to make it seem as if it were no big deal that Hayes was gone, and people would be looking for any sign that she had that broken heart they were all sure she'd get. Her heart was broken, all right, and there'd no doubt be more tears. However, she wasn't going to bare those tears and broken heart for the town to use to serve her up as tasty gossip. Nope. When folks looked at her, they were going to see her usual wiseass self.

With allergies.

She still had nearly a half hour before she had to be at work, but Cait grabbed her things to leave early so she could stop by the diner and get a second cup of coffee and a bear claw. Since that was something she often did, she could get a jump on convincing everyone that she was A-okay, hunky-dory and any other stupid descriptor she could think of. But she had just opened the door when the massive tour bus lumbered to a stop in front of her house.

Marty.

Cait was ready to groan, which was her automatic response to her father, but she had to put that on hold when she saw Adam step from the bus. Marty was right behind him, and there was no way she could groan after seeing Adam's smiling face. The boy was obviously A-okay, hunky-dory and plenty of other happy descriptors.

Marty took his time coming to the house, but the boy hurried toward her. As if he'd been doing such things all his life, Adam pulled her into his arms for a hug.

"Granddad and I wanted to stop and say goodbye before we head back out on tour," Adam said.

Cait hugged him right back, and it, too, felt as if they'd had a lifetime of this. There'd be other hugs, other times when she got to see him. She would make sure of it. Make sure to contact Adam's mother, too, once she was out of jail. After all, the woman was Cait's half sister, and she shouldn't miss out on being part of this wacky mess that was the Jameson clan.

She pulled back but kept her palm on his cheek for a long moment. "You're sure you're okay with being with your granddad for a couple of months?"

Adam's smile widened. "Better than okay. It's fun, and Granddad's teaching me to play the guitar."

Cait was happy for him, she truly was, but there was

that little pang to remind her that Marty had never given that kind of attention to his kids. It was good, though, that he was doing it for the next generation.

"You'll have to write me a song," Cait said. "And keep up with your homework," she added.

"I will." Adam was still beaming when he hugged her again. "Granddad wants to say goodbye to you, too."

It'd be her third one of the day, and it wasn't even mid-morning yet. These last two were a piece of cake, though, compared to the first one, so Cait didn't have too much trouble mustering up a "bon voyage" smile for her nephew. Adam waved at her and headed back to the bus as Marty stepped forward.

"I don't want you to worry about him," Marty offered. He didn't even attempt to hug her and crammed his hands in the pockets of his jeans. "I'll keep a close eye on him."

"And teach him to play the guitar," she muttered.

Marty smiled, nodded. "The boy's a natural." And that was pride she heard in his voice. "Once he's had a little more practice, he'll be ready to make an appearance with me on stage. He said he'd like that."

The shy boy had come a long way in a short time, and whether Cait wanted to give credit or not, Marty was responsible for that.

"Don't forget about Kinsley," she reminded him.

"Oh, I won't. I've talked to her about joining me on tour for her Christmas break. Adam should be back with his grandmother by then, but she might let him come with us. I've figured out something to do for Avery and Gracie," Marty added before she could speak. "I'm writing a *Slackers Quackers* book just for them. They'll be characters in it. I thought they'd get a kick out of that."

They would. The twins loved the *Slackers Quackers*

stories. But all of this gushing Marty was doing—and it was gushing—felt as though he were speaking in a foreign tongue.

While Cait knew she should hold her own tongue, she couldn't. "Why the sudden interest in members of your gene pool?"

He didn't wince or flinch, but he did lower his head for a moment. When Marty looked at her again, she saw what she thought might be a lifetime of guilt.

"I want to do the best I can do," he said, and there was some weariness in his voice. "I'm trying to work my kids and my grandkids into my life." Marty paused, met her eyes. "But I can't do it here. Too many memories. This is where I failed, over and over again, and being here would make me feel like that pen y'all built for the ornery duck."

She knew that, but she hadn't understood it until this morning when Hayes had left. Now she had memories, too, that would haunt her. She'd see him in all the places they'd been together, and it would hurt. Still, she wouldn't give up her home. She would just learn, somehow, to live with it.

"This place was never your home," she muttered. "That is." Cait tipped her head to the tour bus. "And what you're doing for Adam, Kinsley, Avery and Gracie is a good thing."

Some surprise flashed through his eyes, and he smiled. "It's like compromise parenting and grandparenting."

That should have riled her, made her remember what a crappy father he'd been to her brothers and her. But any compromise for Marty was huge. Including Kinsley and his grandchildren in his life was somewhat of a miracle. And that was enough.

It had to be enough.

"By the way," Cait added, "I wanted to thank you for helping with Sunshine."

"Glad I could do it. The woman was making a lot of people's lives miserable." He glanced away again. "So did I. Maybe that's why I thought I could do something. Atonement, I guess."

She didn't like that they had worked their way back to the conversation about him and his shitty parenting skills, and it was time to put an end to this. "I need to get to work. I hope Adam and you have a good time on the tour."

He nodded but stayed put, and he took a small envelope from his pocket. "It's a VIP pass," Marty explained. "If you're ever so inclined, it'll get you backstage or front row to any of my gigs. I don't want you to have to buy a ticket to see me."

Cait pulled out the pass, looked at him but couldn't speak. That's because of the sudden lump in her throat.

"Oh, and if you ever want to go on tour with me," he added, "just let me know. I'd be plenty happy to have you along."

She had to swallow hard. "Thank you," she finally managed to say.

"I know this doesn't undo what I've done to you," Marty went on. "I can never undo that. Not enough atonement in six worlds to fix that. Just don't keep on hating me, Cait. Hate eats up too much of you."

"So does love," she mumbled before she could stop herself.

When she looked up at Marty, he was blurry, and she realized she had tears in her eyes to go along with that lump in her throat. She had a debate with herself as to what to do. She could send Marty on his way with a snarky comment or with a heartfelt daughterly goodbye.

Cait went with a hug instead.

Because she was tired of hating. Tired of carrying this weight of believing the man who'd fathered her could ever be anything more than the man who'd shredded her heart too many times to count.

She felt Marty's muscles tense. But only for a second. Then she felt the relief, too. His arms came around, holding her as if he were trying to make up for some of those sins.

And he did.

Who knew that a hug could perform such miracles?

They stood there, holding on to each other, before Cait finally pulled back. She didn't even mind that he saw the tears in her eyes because he had some tears, too.

"Gotta go," Marty said, brushing his fingers over her cheek. "Got a gig in Dallas tonight. See you soon, Cait."

Not a goodbye. In some ways, it was more like a hello, something that regular fathers said to regular daughters. They hadn't had much of *regular* in their lives, but maybe this was a start. She'd make sure it was a start.

She waved and watched as her father made his way back to the bus. Then Cait cursed the fresh tears that would require another makeup repair. There was no time for that, though, because her phone rang, and she saw the dispatcher's number on the screen.

"Cait," the dispatcher, Thelma Waters, said the moment Cait answered. "We just got a call about the Crocketts. They're at it again."

Cait groaned. She so didn't want to deal with the ornery couple this morning, but she had no choice since she was the one on call. Besides, after the emotional upheaval of the morning, being around yelling, fighting senior citizens might help her level out.

She went to her SUV, unlocked the glove compartment and eased aside the standard-issue weapon she kept secured there. Her pepper spray had expired, so she took out the small can of Mighty Hold hair spray and shoved it into her pocket. If one of the Crocketts tried to stab her again, they were getting an eye full of maximum-hold goo.

The drive didn't take long, thank goodness, because Cait didn't want any thinking time. She just wanted to let everything settle inside her, and maybe then she could figure out where the heck to go from here.

She pulled to a stop in front of the Crocketts' and had no trouble spotting the couple. That's because they were in their front yard, and Wilma was hurling pine cones at Harvey, the man she'd once promised to love until death do they part.

Harvey, who was still in his pj's, had wisely taken cover behind an oak tree, and he was hurling acorns at his beloved. They probably wouldn't hurt each other with such puny weapons, but there were little pointy ends on pine cones, and Cait didn't want Wilma inflicting scratches. If the woman did, then this would move from a domestic abuse situation to assault.

Cait didn't especially want to do all the paperwork that'd go along with charges for an assault with a pine cone, and besides, it wouldn't do any good. The couple would just start up again in a couple of weeks.

"Stop it!" Cait snarled when she stepped from her SUV. It wasn't hard to do her cop's voice with these two because she'd had plenty enough practice. What she hadn't had a lot of was them actually doing as she said.

Unlike now.

The couple actually quit, and while they didn't come out from the cover of the trees, they both did turn to her.

"I figured you'd be crying," Wilma said. "A broken heart, huh?"

Cait hoped that crying part was all speculation and that Wilma couldn't actually see her red eyes from this distance. Of course, with all the gossip no doubt floating around, speculation was going to happen. That's why Cait didn't bother addressing it or pretending that it was her allergies.

"Drop any acorns or pine cones you're holding," Cait warned them. She whipped out the can of Mighty Hold hair spray. "And this time I'd better not get hurt if you two go at each other again."

The sympathetic look Wilma was giving her lasted another nanosecond before Harvey called out, "She started it. She always starts some kind of mess before I've even had a chance to have my coffee."

"That's because you farted in the kitchen when I was trying to have my coffee," Wilma countered. "It stank so bad I nearly puked."

Cait was reasonably sure that there'd been other such incidents like that, but it was a first for her.

"It stank because of that slop you cooked for dinner," Harvey countered. "It tore up my stomach like it usually does." He shifted his attention to Cait. "I think Wilma's trying to poison me."

Of course, Wilma didn't take that insult well. "I should poison you, you old goat, and then I wouldn't get farted on in my own kitchen."

Harvey didn't take that well, either. "You're the old goat, and it's my kitchen, too. You smell it up with all that slop you cook."

And that started up another round of hurling.

Wilma had missed her calling. She probably could have played outfield for the Yankees with the speed and accuracy of the next pine cone she aimed like a missile at her husband. Thankfully, Harvey ducked in time, and it went sailing past him, but Wilma geared up to send another one his way.

"I said stop it!" Cait yelled, going closer. She positioned

her finger over the dispenser button on the hair spray. "That's it. I'm taking you both in for disturbing the peace and being a general pain in my ass."

Again, she didn't expect them to actually stop, but they did. Not because of her order, though, but because the approaching vehicle drew their attention. It drew Cait's, too, because it was Hayes's rental SUV.

"Oh, no," Wilma muttered. "Is he gonna make you cry again?"

Cait sure hoped not, but she hadn't steeled herself up nearly enough to see Hayes this soon.

Hayes got out of his SUV not in a "laid-back rock star" kind of way. It was more of a "man on a mission," and he practically stalked toward her.

"How'd you know I was here?" Cait asked, and she tried not to take a step back. He looked supremely pissed.

"I called the police station, and the dispatcher said you were here." He stopped only a few inches away from her and didn't even spare the Crocketts a glance. However, he did look at the mini can of Mighty Hold hair spray. *"Have a good life?"* he snapped. *"Have a good life!"*

It took Cait a moment to realize he wasn't talking about her choice of weapon. She remembered that she'd written those very words to him in her goodbye letter. A letter he whipped out of his back pocket as if it were proof of some vile crime she'd committed.

"What kind of stupid-assed thing is that to say to a man?" Hayes snarled.

Cait was truly confused. "Uh, a nice thing?" Though judging from his expression, that was not the correct answer.

Hayes's teeth actually clenched, and he went silent as if trying to rein in his temper. Wilma and Harvey must have thought they were about to witness something more interesting than their squabble, because with their hands still filled with the pine cones and acorns, they ambled closer.

"You told him to have a good life?" Harvey asked, but he didn't wait for an answer. He snorted as if that was the dumbest thing in the history of dumb things.

"You were just trying to spare his feelings," Wilma concluded. "You didn't want him to leave while he was worried about making you cry."

"No," Cait snapped. "I was telling him to have a good life."

"Bullshit," Hayes insisted, though he didn't justify why he thought that. He just took hold of her shoulders, anchoring her in front of him. "Are you in love with me, Cait?"

He couldn't have stunned her more if he'd Tasered her. She couldn't waffle on this. Even a couple of seconds' delay in responding might make him think that she did indeed have a broken heart and that she'd been crying her eyes out over him.

The delay happened anyway, though.

Cait felt a sharp jab on her arm, followed by an equally sharp jab of pain. She whirled to see the pine cone that Wilma had poked into her. It gave Cait a bad jolt of memories of getting a very painful shot. It was that jolt that caused her finger to react, too.

And she hit the dispenser tab on the hair spray.

The aerosol came spewing out in a thick cloud, and Cait wasn't sure what came next: Hayes's cursing, or her own cursing as the Mighty Hold hair spray went straight into her eyes.

CHAPTER TWENTY

"I DON'T WANT to go to the ER," Cait snarled.

Since she'd said at least a dozen variations of that, Hayes wasn't surprised by her comment, and like the other variations, he ignored this one, too. Cait's eyes were red and slightly swollen, and she was blinking fast enough to cause a breeze with her eyelashes. She was clearly in pain, and while he wouldn't have liked the idea of a visit to the hospital, either, she needed to be checked out.

He pulled his SUV to a stop by the ER doors and saw that the Crocketts were right behind him. Thankfully, Cait probably couldn't see them, because the couple certainly wouldn't have improved her mood since it was their fault she'd gotten hair spray in her eyes. While the nurse was checking out her eyes, Hayes would suggest looking at her arm, too. It had a bit of pine cone sticking out of it, and there was a trickle of blood making its way to her elbow.

"Just take me home and I can try flushing my eyes with water," Cait grumbled.

She'd also said variations of that as well, along with having Hayes actually try the water flushing at the Crocketts'. It hadn't worked. Her eyes were still stinging, and she had tiny drops of what appeared to be clear glue stuck to her eyelashes.

Hayes ignored her protest and helped her out of the SUV.

He considered leading her into the ER by taking hold of her arm, but scooping her up was faster.

"I can walk," Cait snapped. She added a groan and token protest by poking him with her elbow. "Do you have any idea the paperwork this is going to cause?"

He didn't, but he was guessing it'd be considerable. Maybe charges would even be filed against Wilma since her pine cone was what started the hair-spray injury. For reasons that Hayes didn't want to know, Wilma still had hold of that pine cone, and instead of running from Cait's inevitable wrath, the couple continued to follow them into the ER.

"What happened?" the nurse on duty immediately asked.

Hayes knew her. She was Bev Dennison, one of his old girlfriends. Thankfully, though, Bev didn't spare more than a glance at him and scrambled to get a wheelchair for Cait.

"Hair spray," Hayes explained. "Cait took a full spray in the face at point-blank range. The blood on her arm is from a pine cone."

He had to hand it to Bev. She didn't so much as raise an eyebrow at his description of Cait's injuries, which made him wonder how often weird things like that happened. With the Crocketts around, probably way more than they should. A small-town deputy, and apparently a nurse, encountered some weird shit.

"I don't want a wheelchair," Cait protested when Hayes sat her in it.

Bev blew off that protest and started pushing Cait toward an examination room. Now she did more than glance at Hayes, and he was pretty sure he saw condemnation in the nurse's eyes.

"I thought you'd left town," Bev remarked, her voice cool

and clipped. "Is part of the redness in Cait's eyes because she was crying, or is it all from the hair spray?"

"The hair spray," Cait insisted.

But since Cait couldn't see him, Hayes gave Bev a look to inform her that, yes, there'd likely been some crying involved. In fact, when he'd gone over to the Crocketts' to confront Cait, that's what he'd first noticed.

Those tear-reddened eyes.

And that's when he'd known that her *have a good life* in the letter was pure bullshit. She didn't want him to have a good life. Well, not in the overall sense of it being a polite goodbye. Cait was hurting because he'd left.

Bev shot Hayes a chilly look to let him know she didn't approve of his hurting Cait. Well, he sure as hell didn't approve of it, either, but Cait had led him to believe that the hurt was far less than he'd thought. And now he somehow had to fix it. First, though, Cait had to be fixed.

"You can wait out there," Bev said to the Crocketts when they tried to come into the examining room. "You, too," she added to Hayes when he stayed put.

Hayes realized he should have expected this. Bev clearly wasn't going to cut him any breaks since he was the man who'd jacked Cait around.

"I'd like to stay and make sure Cait's okay," Hayes insisted. But he knew Cait had to be okay with him staying, and to up his chances of that happening, he took her hand and added, "You'll get out of here soon, and I can drive you home."

Cait might have been waylaid by her injuries, but she was still sharp as a tack. She looked up at him, and even though Hayes wasn't sure how much of him she could see exactly, she sighed. "It's okay. I don't want you to miss your flight."

Missing the flight was a given. He should have already

left for the airport, and he had no intention of doing that until he made sure Cait was all right. And until he heard the answer to the question he'd asked her at the Crocketts'.

Are you in love with me, Cait?

Thanks to the pine cone and the Mighty Hold, she hadn't given him a yes or no. He wanted that. But not in front of Bev. He didn't want to dish up any more gossip fodder.

"I can get another flight," Hayes settled for saying. "I don't have to be on set until the day after tomorrow."

He'd planned on using those forty-eight hours to make sure everything was running as it should at his house. He knew he would also want some time for his brain to settle. Hayes felt as if he'd been caught in a whirlwind for the past month.

Cait stayed quiet a long time, and he figured she was dealing with her own whirlwind along with the pain. "He can stay," she finally said to the nurse.

Bev scowled at him, a warning to let him know not to do anything to make things worse. Hayes wasn't sure it could get worse. He'd really screwed up with Cait, and in the process screwed up himself. No way could he just jet off to LA and not try to mend what he'd broken.

"I'll get something to flush out your eyes," Bev explained. "I'll check that arm, too, to see if it needs any stitches." She cast Hayes another warning before she walked away.

"You're not giving me a shot," Cait called out to Bev. "Don't let her give me a shot," she added in a mumble to Hayes. "Last time, you did a shitty job of stopping that."

"True. I weighed your options for you. The shot or lockjaw. The shot won out."

Even though it was next to impossible for Cait to narrow her swollen eyes, she managed it.

Since Hayes figured the judgmental nurse wouldn't be gone long, he got busy laying some groundwork. First things first. "Are you okay? Are you hurting?" he asked.

"Yes," she snapped, but then she groaned and shook her head. "No," Cait amended. "My eyes and arm are stinging, that's all. And I feel stupid." Another groan. "My brothers will have something to rib me for the rest of my life."

Yeah, they would. No way around that. Ribbing was a sibling right.

"I'm sorry," he told her, and that was an apology for many things.

For hurting her. For distracting her at the Crocketts' so that she hadn't seen the pine cone coming. But what Hayes couldn't be sorry about was getting involved with her in the first place.

Though he should be.

"I'm sorry," he repeated in a mumble. "You deserve better."

Her forehead bunched up. "Better than what?"

"Me." Hayes mumbled that, too.

Again, she looked at him, and she blinked hard, obviously trying to focus. "Better than you?" Her mouth tightened in disgust. "Yeah, because the world is just filled with guys who are kind, hot and caring. Every hour, I have to beat off hordes of them with sticks."

Since the "hot" was all DNA, Hayes hadn't had any part in that. And he was kind, most of the time. *Some of the time*, he silently amended. But he'd fallen on his ass on the caring stuff, because a caring man wouldn't have hurt Cait.

"I'm tied up with *Outlaw Rebels* two out of every three days," he reminded her. "I live in LA. I have a life there. I also need to stay in therapy. Need to keep healing." Though he had made plenty of progress in that area. He'd always miss Ivy, but he could forgive himself for what had happened to her.

Cait smiled in a way to let him know she accepted all of that, and she eased her hand out of his so she could pat his arm. She didn't miss with the patting, which meant some of the blurriness was fading.

She opened her mouth, maybe to finally answer that question he'd asked her at the Crocketts', but Bev came in, carrying a tray of supplies. The nurse's timing sure sucked.

He stood back and watched as Bev did the eye flush, which looked very similar to what Hayes had tried. When she was done, Hayes saw that the redness was still there, but Cait's eyes looked marginally better.

"I'll give you some drops to take home with you," Bev explained, and she examined Cait's other injury. Using a pair of tweezers, she plucked out the bit of pine cone stuck in Cait's arm and cleaned it. "You don't need any stitches. Or a shot. No need to see the doctor, either, unless you just want to."

Cait's breath of relief was audible, and she watched as Bev put a bandage on the wound. "No, I don't want to see him."

"Okay, then wait here while I get the drops and the paperwork."

Again, Hayes figured the woman wouldn't be gone long, so he jumped right into the thick of it.

"I asked you if you were in love with me," he reminded Cait. "Are you?"

"He did ask that," he heard Wilma say, and that's when Hayes realized Bev had left the examining room door open. He scowled at the Crocketts, closed it and sat on the examination table so he could meet her eye to eye.

"Are you?" he pressed.

She studied him a long moment, and he didn't think that it was because she was trying to bring him into focus. "Yes," she said. "But I don't want you to do anything about it," she quickly added.

She loved him. Cait loved him.

Hayes felt the tightness ease in his chest. His stomach unclenched. He wasn't sure if what he was about to say would make this better or worse, but he wouldn't walk out of this room until he said his piece. As pieces went, it probably sucked.

"I can only offer you part-time," Hayes told her, repeating what had been going through his head. "I can come back in between shoots and you could maybe come out to see me. I'll totally understand, though, if that's not enough."

He'd understand. But it would crush him if she wanted more than what he could give her.

Cait stood, faced him. "Let me get this straight. You're offering me *you*? Or rather you in short increments? You could split your life between here and there? You could give me one out of three days?"

Hell. That made him sound and feel like the dick that he was. "Like I said, you deserve better."

"You bet I do. I deserve a man who loves me." Cait managed a flat look. "If I had that—a man who loves me—then one-third sounds like, well, a whole hell of a lot."

She stepped closer, fitting her body to his, and she slid her arm around his waist. Then she smiled and touched her mouth to his. Not quite a kiss, but it seemed to hold a promise of much more. That *more* was a risk. Because it could change everything.

"What if I did love you?" he asked. "I could end up hurting you."

Cait shrugged. "Or you could end up making me stupid

and giddy with happiness. Maybe making yourself stupid and giddy, too, though you're on your own there. I won't be able to help you with that." She was smiling when her lips came back to his. More than a touch this time.

So much more.

The woman had a mouth on her. A mouth that Hayes took as he pulled her closer. She went into his arms as if she belonged there. And she did. Hayes knew that was exactly where Cait belonged.

"You really think we can make this work?" he asked, though he already knew the answer.

They would.

They would make it work because they were in love with each other.

"Oh, yes," she assured him with complete confidence. "I just want to hear you say one thing first."

Hayes smiled. "I love you."

She shook her head. "I want to hear you say something else. I want to hear what you're famous for saying."

He studied the borderline-porn glint in her eyes, and Hayes gave it to her. "Climb on, babe, and kiss me."

Bingo. And Cait did exactly that.

* * * * *

Turn the page for Whatever Happens in Texas, *a special bonus story from* USA TODAY *bestselling author Delores Fossen!*

WHATEVER HAPPENS
IN TEXAS

CHAPTER ONE

"A TEN-SECOND French kiss can spread eighty million germs," Lila Novak heard her eleven-year-old niece, Sophia, mutter.

The girl angled her eyes toward the bride and groom and had spoken behind the fluffy bridesmaid bouquet that she'd lifted in front of her face. "And that kiss is definitely French and is lasting way over ten seconds," Sophia added.

Lila couldn't exactly argue with the duration or the type of kiss, but using her "maid of honor" bouquet to hide it, she shot the girl a disapproving frown. Now wasn't the time for such a discussion. They were literally standing at the altar where Sophia's mom and Lila's sister, Crystal, had just exchanged vows with her brand-spanking-new husband, Jeremy Kendall.

Crystal and Jeremy finally finished the "you may kiss the bride" lip-lock, but they kept their hands linked and their gazes fastened on each other. Lila could practically see little cartoon hearts flashing from their eyes.

No one in the room could doubt these two were crazy in love, and Lila was reasonably sure the pair didn't care diddly-squat about sharing germs. Besides, the amount of kissing Jeremy and Crystal had done over the past six months since they'd gotten engaged, they had to be immune to each other's germs by now.

"Well, it's done," Sophia declared on a sigh, and Lila

used the cheers and applause of the onlookers to cover her whispered reassurance to the girl.

"It'll be fine," Lila told her. "Jeremy will be a great stepdad."

Sophia made a noncommittal sound, practically mandatory for a preteen who seemed to be in a constant Debbie Downer mood. Still, Lila knew the girl got along with Jeremy just fine. Ditto for getting along with her new stepbrother, Noah Kendall, the fourteen-year-old groomsman who was standing across from Sophia and her. Next to Noah was Cooper Kendall, the best man and the groom's brother.

"I'm betting you wouldn't kiss Cooper like that," Sophia added when the bride and groom finally turned to face the guests seated in the small country church.

Lila frowned again and glanced at the girl to see why she'd made such an out-of-the-blue comment. When she followed Sophia's gaze, Lila saw that it was now on Cooper. He wasn't paying attention to Sophia, though. Nope.

He was looking at Lila.

Since she'd arrived back in their hometown of Lone Star Ridge three days ago for wedding preparations, Lila had done her level best to avoid prolonged eye contact with Cooper, but she certainly failed at it now. She was looking, all right, matching him lingering gaze for lingering gaze, and she had to wonder if he was thinking about her previous trip home two years ago.

When Cooper and she had landed in bed.

That had happened after the wedding of their mutual friends. She couldn't even blame it on too much alcohol. Not on her part, anyway. Maybe it'd played into it for Cooper. For Lila, it'd been her getting caught up in the romance of the wedding and the prospect of a happily-ever-after.

Even though the friends' marriage hadn't lasted past the first year, the memories of that night with Cooper lived on.

The corner of his mouth lifted in a lazy underwear-melting smile. Yes, he was remembering it. And she was trying very hard to convince her body that it didn't want another round with the hot cowboy.

Emphasis on *hot*.

Cooper had the body of a Viking warrior. Lean and muscled. The looks, too, with his rumpled blond hair and scorching blue eyes. He'd never had a problem getting women into the sack, but nary a one, including her, had had any staying power. However, Lila hadn't exactly *stayed* around so he could give her the boot. She'd left the next day, sneaking out of his bed and leaving him a goodbye note to say that it had been fun. And she hadn't looked back.

Well, mostly she hadn't.

Lila had thought of him more often than she'd ever admit. Thought about their one perfect night together. The nerd and the star quarterback turned cowboy—who would have thought it? But she couldn't repeat what had happened between them. Nope. Her heart wouldn't be able to handle being rejected by the one and only guy she'd ever wanted. Because star quarterbacks and nerds didn't have any lasting power beyond a "brief opposites attract" kind of thing. It was best for her to keep the memories of their one encounter and move on.

Except she couldn't.

As proof that she'd lost her mind, Lila had agreed to "babysit" Sophia and Noah while Jeremy and Crystal went away for a long honeymoon weekend in Vegas. As proof that Cooper had also lost his mind, he was going to share those duties with her. In the same house. Under the same roof. With sex memories that suddenly seemed as fresh and hot as if it'd happened five minutes ago.

The bride and groom stepped down from the altar, and Crystal gave Noah a hug as Jeremy did the same to Sophia. Then the couple reversed the gesture. It was a nice show of love for their new blended family.

"Eighty million germs," Sophia muttered to her mom when Crystal leaned in to hug her.

Crystal only chuckled. "Jeremy and I will aim for the trillion mark."

Sophia grumbled something about that being gross, but she wasn't fooling her mom or Lila. The girl adored Jeremy. A good thing since Sophia's own father had never married Crystal and skipped out on them when Sophia had been just a baby. And while Sophia might not approve of all the smooching going on, Lila knew that would change.

In a couple of years, if not sooner, her niece would meet some boy she didn't mind sharing germs with. Sophia would meet her own Achilles' heel, just as Lila had with Cooper. Maybe the guy wouldn't be a hot cowboy or star quarterback who would trounce on Sophia's heart.

Like Cooper was about to do to Lila's.

She saw that heart-trouncing look in his eyes when they fell in step together to walk out of the church. Of course, he'd think of it as an "I want you in my bed again" look, but Lila knew the score. The next three days, and nights, would be long and filled with potential sexual potholes. The saving grace was the kids would be around. Probably not around enough to stop Cooper from making a move on her, but Lila would somehow have to make it work.

They stepped outside into the sweltering June temp, which was the norm for central Texas. Crystal and Jeremy didn't seem to notice the sauna level of heat, and the moment they were inside the church's reception hall, they were on the dance floor—wrapped in each other's arms.

Crystal's petal-pink dress fluttered as Jeremy spun her around to the George Strait song the DJ was playing. Noah, Sophia and Cooper scattered, too, and the guests began to trickle in behind them.

Lila glanced around the large room, making sure everything had been set up according to the plan Crystal and she had come up with. It was. The tables with the party food and the bar were against the walls, leaving the center space for the dance floor and some tables and chairs. There was no head table for the wedding party, and there'd be no formal toasts. Actually, nothing would be formal, which was why Jeremy, Noah and Cooper and most of the male guests were all wearing Texas tuxedos—jeans, boots and black jackets.

"Did you know that a ten-second French kiss can spread eighty million germs?" Cooper asked, handing her a glass of sparkling wine. He'd snagged a longneck bottle of beer for himself.

Lila frowned but accepted the wine. "You've been talking to Sophia."

"Yeah. I told her in a few years she wouldn't mind such things."

Since Lila had already thought the same thing, she couldn't dispute that, but Cooper's choice of conversation seemed to be foreplay. So was the look he gave her. And he chuckled all manly and low when her frown turned to a scowl.

"Don't worry, Lila," he drawled. "I won't do anything with you that you don't want me to do."

That was the problem. She wanted him to do many, many things to her and vice versa. A repeat performance of their one-nighter. But that couldn't happen, and even though there were plenty of guests milling around, it was probably time for her to lay down some ground rules.

"I'm here in Lone Star Ridge to babysit my niece and your nephew," she reminded him.

Crystal hadn't had a choice about tapping her for that duty, either, because none of the grandparents had been able to fill in. Noah's maternal grandparents had health problems, and Cooper's folks had passed away years ago. It was the same for Lila and Crystal's mom. Their dad was on wife number whatever and hadn't seen fit to visit his only grandchild in years, so he hadn't been a babysitting candidate, either.

"I'll leave in three days and go back to San Antonio," Lila added a moment later since Cooper appeared to be waiting for her to say something else.

"Which is less than an hour away," he pointed out.

True. Some people in town, including teachers like her, commuted there for work each day. But not her. She liked her job well enough, teaching history at a San Antonio high school. Added to that, Lila couldn't risk seeing Cooper on a daily basis, or she'd become another notch on his already-seriously-notched bedpost.

"I don't want anything temporary," she insisted. "And you're the walking, talking definition of *temporary*."

Something went through his eyes. Not the cocky lust she'd seen earlier. Hurt, maybe. A surprise since she'd always believed that he enjoyed his "love 'em and leave 'em" lifestyle.

"What if I told you I was looking for something more?" he asked.

Lila had a quick answer for that. "I'd say it sounds like a lame come-on."

She thought she saw the hurt deepen in his eyes. He turned away from her, having a long sip of his beer, and he tipped his head to the bride and groom, who were slow dancing and gazing at each other as if they were the cure for all ills.

"What if I told you I wanted that? What they have. They're damn happy," Cooper muttered. That wasn't a cocky drawl, either. It sounded genuine and coated with relief.

Lila totally got the relief part. Her sister had been a single mom for over a decade now and deserved some happiness. So did Jeremy, who'd lost his wife three years ago in a car accident. It was a second chance and a fresh start, and Lila couldn't be happier for both of them. What she wasn't so happy about was the three-day honeymoon.

"I don't want to have sex with you again," Lila spelled out.

She would have been proud of her determined tone if it'd been for Cooper's ears only. It wasn't. The DJ had paused the music at the exact moment she'd spoken, and without George Strait's crooning to cover her voice, there were people close enough to have heard every word she'd said. People who included the mayor and Sheriff Leyton Jameson. But the person Lila especially hadn't wanted to hear that was the tall, attractive brunette, Evelyn Darnell, who owned the town's flower shop and the antiques store.

She was also Cooper's ex-girlfriend.

Of course, he had plenty of exes, but Evelyn was the woman who had the honor of having had the longest relationship with him. Nearly a year. Their breakup had happened months ago, and judging from the smile Evelyn aimed at Cooper, she wanted him back. Evelyn had no such smile for Lila, and even narrowed her eyes a bit when she finally spared Lila a glance.

"Lila. Cooper," Evelyn greeted them. "It's good to see you."

"Good to see you, too," he mumbled back. Cooper nodded greetings to the mayor and sheriff, who stepped away to go to the bride and groom. Evelyn stayed put.

"The flowers look amazing," Evelyn purred. Yes, her voice was a purr. Smoke, silk and sex, and she was aiming all that purring at Cooper. Evelyn definitely didn't mention the comment she must have heard Lila make about no more sex. "I know you're happy for your brother."

It wasn't an unusual remark coming from a wedding guest, but Lila read a lot into it. *I know you're happy for your brother, and figured you'd want a dose of that marital happiness, too. Well, you can have it—with me.*

It probably wouldn't have bothered Lila so much to believe that's what Evelyn was thinking had it not been for what Cooper had said to her just a minute or two ago.

What if I told you I was looking for something more?

Lila had blown that off, but she wasn't doing any dismissing now. Maybe Cooper was ready to settle down, and Evelyn was rich, attractive and likely in love with him. The woman definitely wasn't a nerd and was more of a match for a hot cowboy star quarterback than Lila ever would be.

And that cut Lila to the core.

Lila cursed that feeling. Cursed herself for even wanting Cooper to be hers.

"If you need any help with Noah or Sophia," Evelyn went on, speaking to Cooper, "all you have to do is ask."

"Thanks, but I think we can handle it," he answered before he slid his arm around Lila.

Because she hadn't been expecting the contact, Lila went stiff, and it took her a moment to realize this was an act. It was Cooper's way of getting Evelyn to back off. That pleased Lila. Sort of. She didn't want his ex using the kids to try to make a play for him. Still, Lila didn't like being used, either. Especially since Cooper's mere touch sent her body into a heated tizzy.

"All right," Evelyn said. Her voice was a little less purry now. "But the offer still stands." She patted his arm, letting her fingers trail down his sleeve before she finally stepped away.

Cooper did no such stepping away from Lila, though. He kept his arm around her, probably because Evelyn didn't go far. The woman went over to the bride and groom to offer her well-wishes and congrats.

"Eighty million germs," Sophia muttered to Lila as she walked behind Cooper and her.

Obviously, her niece had noticed the embrace. Thankfully, though, no one else seemed to be gawking at them. The mayor was partly responsible for that. He bumped into one of the chairs and sent it crashing to the floor. The noise caught everyone's attention. Everyone but Evelyn. Aiming another smile at Cooper, she walked out of the reception hall.

Lila released the breath she'd been holding and looked up at Cooper. "Evelyn's gone now, so you can cut the act."

Cooper still didn't move, and he stared down at her. Not good, because those amazing eyes could do amazing things to her already-needy body. So could other parts of him.

And Lila soon remembered that when Cooper lowered his mouth and kissed her.

CHAPTER TWO

COOPER DIDN'T HAVE to guess if what he was doing was stupid. Nope. It was stupid with a capital *S* to kiss Lila in a place where half the town would see them. Where it would stir up enough gossip to get back to every ear in the county.

However, the actual kiss wasn't a mistake.

Cooper was certain of that. This was just a case of the wrong time, wrong place, but that didn't make it wrong. Not totally, anyway. He'd wanted to let Lila know that he hadn't been using her to try to distance Evelyn. Also, he'd thought it best to clarify that he hadn't been BS-ing when he'd asked her—*What if I told you I was looking for something more?*

More was exactly what he wanted, and he thought he might have a chance of getting that with Lila.

Or not.

Lila didn't exactly look aroused or pleased when he pulled back from the kiss. Her cat green eyes were wide with shock, and color had pinked up her cheeks. Her mouth was slightly open, too, making him wish that he'd just gone ahead and tried for French. He'd do that later. If he got the chance. For now, though, Cooper stood there in case Lila was about to give him a piece of her mind.

"You," she managed to say.

So, definitely not an eloquent bashing of why he shouldn't have done that. She attempted to say something else, but when that failed, Lila took hold of his arm. Weaving them through the other guests, she led him outside. She had to keep leading him, though, because there were people at every turn.

Cooper wanted to tell her that the quest to find a secret place for them to talk would only fuel the gossips, but he wanted to hear what she had to say. And there were some things he wanted to say to her. For now, though, he just watched her move, the silky bluebonnet-colored dress slipping and sliding with each step she took.

The woman had curves. Curves that she hadn't had in high school, that's for sure, and the dress was doing them justice.

Lila finally stopped under a massive oak that would hopefully prevent them from getting heatstroke, and she whirled around to face him. Her cheeks were even pinker now, and she shifted her long brown hair to get it off her neck, probably as a way to cut down on the sweating. But Cooper figured sweat was a given, which hopefully meant Lila wouldn't want to waste too much time fussing at him.

"You kissed me," she said, clearly going with the obvious.

He nodded, readily admitting that. "You left me a note." Judging from her blank stare, Cooper should have given her a bit more info. "When you sneaked out of my bed, you left me a note."

Huffing, she threw up her hands. Since she was still holding the bouquet, it went in the air, too, and tiny white flowers came fluttering down on both of them. "That was two years ago. The kiss just happened."

Cooper saw the point she was trying to make, but damn it, that note had hurt. He'd thought Lila and he had made a real connection that night. One that'd gone beyond just sex, and she'd left him a "son of a bitching" note.

"I kissed you because I wanted you to know I wasn't using you," he stated. "Notice that I didn't kiss you while Evelyn was standing there. I waited until she'd left so you'd know it was about us and not her."

"You shouldn't have kissed me at all," she snapped. Lila made a shuddering sound of frustration.

Welcome to the club.

Lila had been frustrating him for months now. He hadn't been able to get her off his mind, and Cooper had planned on using this time together to… Well, he wasn't exactly sure yet. However, he was either going to have to get her out of his system or… He wasn't sure about that, either, but he didn't intend for her to leave him with only a note this time.

"We just need to focus on the kids," Lila insisted several sweat-popping moments later.

"For three days, we will," Cooper assured her. "For three days, we'll be the best babysitters in the history of baby-sitting while I also take care of my brother's livestock. But after that, there's no reason why we can't give this heat between us another try."

She stared at him as if he'd grown another nose. "Nerd," she said, tapping her ample chest. "Not a nerd," she added, pointing to him.

Now he frowned. "You're bringing up high school stuff? Good grief, Lila, we're thirty-four. We're past all of that."

Her stare continued, and it became more than a little flat. "We're never past all of that. And the only reason you're interested in me is because I left you before you had a chance to leave me. You've got a reputation, Cooper, and I didn't want to be another flavor of the week."

That stung, bad, but he deserved it. He hadn't exactly

aimed for celibacy. Not until recently, anyway, but a man could change.

He could change.

"Maybe I could take nerd lessons," he said.

It had the exact effect Cooper had wanted. Lila's lips twitched with a ghost of a smile. A smile that didn't last or grow.

"I stand more of a chance of being a hot Viking princess than you do of being a nerd," she grumbled.

Cooper slid another long glance down her body. "You could be a hot Viking princess."

Though he didn't know why she'd want that. She looked great as Lila, the high school history teacher. And seeing her that way was proof that he had indeed changed. The trick would be to convince Lila of that. The second trick would be to get her in bed to test out his notion that there could actually be something more than just heat between them.

He frowned.

Cooper had to see the flip side of this, too. Because it could mean the "test" would fail. What he felt for her could be attraction and nothing else. But Cooper didn't think so. Still, it would be a risk since he could end up hurting her.

When he glanced back up, he realized Lila was studying him, and she was also frowning. "We're not having sex again," she repeated. She brushed past him, her arm skirting against his before she headed back into the reception hall.

Cooper turned to watch her leave—and to give himself another cheap thrill at seeing her butt in that dress. Several other people were watching her, as well. Or rather they'd been watching Lila and him, no doubt wondering what they were talking about. One of those people was his brother, and Jeremy walked toward him.

Hell. This wouldn't be good. Jeremy had far better things to do at his own reception than to come outside and speak to him. Obviously, though, that's what his brother had in mind.

Jeremy joined him under the shade tree, and he turned, watching and waiting until Lila was inside and therefore out of earshot.

"You want to talk about this?" Jeremy asked.

The answer to this was simple enough. "No."

Talking wouldn't do any good, and it sure as heck wouldn't convince his body to change directions toward any woman other than the very one who didn't seem to want him.

Except she did.

Cooper had felt the hunger in that kiss. Had seen it in her eyes. He wasn't mistaken about that. Lila wanted him, all right, but she was going to fight it tooth and nail.

Jeremy sighed. "Do you know what the hell you're doing?"

Again, the answer was simple enough. "Nope. Not a clue."

But Cooper was pretty sure the next three days were going to be plenty interesting.

LILA DRANK HER iced tea and frowned at her lunch companions. Sophia and Noah both had their attention fixed to their phones.

This was not what she'd had in mind when she'd agreed to babysit. She'd envisioned watching movies, playing board games or even going horseback riding with them.

So far, none of that was happening.

Both Sophia and Noah had slept until nearly lunchtime and then had told Lila they'd be hanging with their friends all afternoon. Friends who would be arriving to pick them up right after lunch. Lila had cleared the "hanging out" part with Jeremy and Crystal, but she hadn't expected the kids to want to do that on their first day with Cooper and her.

Of course, Cooper wasn't actually around, either.

All four of them had headed straight for bed after the reception that hadn't ended until well after midnight. They'd been too tired to do any hanging out then. Too tired for any more kisses or sex talk between Cooper and her.

Lila had been thankful there was none of that sex talk/kissing. She'd been exhausted and hadn't wanted to tangle with Cooper while her defenses were down. But not only had he not tried anything before they'd gone to their separate guest bedrooms, he'd been up and out of the house before dawn. He'd left her a note to say he needed to take care of some chores on his own ranch before coming back to do the ones at Jeremy's. Noah had pitched in, too, and had done an hour or more in the barn and stable before coming in to shower and have lunch.

Cooper's crammed work schedule was for the best, Lila assured herself. If the next two days were the same, then she wouldn't see him all morning. Maybe not in the afternoons, either. But that left the evenings. Three of them, to be exact. And while her willpower told her she could hold out long enough to resist him, her body was urging her to take him up on his offer.

There's no reason why we can't give this heat between us another try.

There was a reason. A huge one. Lila didn't want to spend the next decade of her life trying to forget a man who was basically unforgettable. And that was something she would have to live with, because despite the other things

Cooper had said, he wasn't the sort to settle with just one woman. Especially someone like her.

"Forty percent of teenagers fail the test for their learner's permit on their first try," Sophia said.

Lila glanced up from her "yet to be eaten" sandwich to see what'd prompted her niece to volunteer that tidbit. The girl had stopped peering at her own phone screen long enough to look at Noah's.

"He's already studying for his learner's permit," Sophia told Lila.

This wasn't the first Lila had heard about that. Noah had mentioned it to his father, Crystal and Cooper.

"I can't even take the test for another six months and four days," Noah grumbled. He looked up at Lila, and there was some hope in his eyes. "But I can get a waiver if there's like some hardship in the family. You know, if I really need to be able to drive because everybody else is too sick or something to do it. I could really help out more around here if I had a license," he added.

Lila wasn't sure what he expected her to do about that. "Six months isn't that long to wait," she settled for saying, which was similar to what he'd already heard from Crystal.

"It's forever," he complained, but then he immediately jumped to his feet. "Gotta go," Noah said, stuffing the rest of his sandwich into his mouth before he hurried to the door.

She hadn't heard the vehicle approaching the house, but she saw the minivan as it pulled into the driveway. Sandy Kellerman gave Lila a wave, and Noah piled into the back seat with Sandy's son, Jace, and another boy whom Lila didn't recognize. Jace's older brother, Beckett, was in the front, riding shotgun.

Lila nearly went out to the minivan just to find out what the boys had planned—probably some of the same "hang-

DELORES FOSSEN

ing out" ideas as she'd had. But if she did that, Noah would probably consider it hovering. So instead, she waved good-bye to him, called out a reminder that he had to be home by nine o'clock, and she turned to Sophia to see if she could manage any quality time with her before she, too, headed out.

Nope.

Lila heard another vehicle, an SUV this time, and Sophia scooped up her backpack that she'd already positioned by the front door. "I'll be at Ella's," the girl said, hurrying out to the SUV.

She repeated the goodbye wave, this time with Ella Benton and her dad, Taylor, who was apparently doing chauffeur duty for his daughter. Then Lila stood there on the front porch, wondering what to do with this un-expected free time. However, it wasn't a decision she had to make, because another vehicle pulled into the driveway. A candy apple–red vintage Mustang this time. And the woman who stepped from it wasn't there for the kids.

Evelyn.

Cooper's ex was dressed in a snug red top that matched her car and skinny jeans. Emphasis on the *skinny*. She'd scooped up her long blond hair into a ponytail and was wearing designer sunglasses that probably cost more than Lila made in a month.

Evelyn reached into her Mustang and brought out a cov-ered casserole dish. She aimed a cool smile at Lila. "I'm here to see Cooper."

The woman's tone was polite enough, but Lila heard the subtext that went along with it. Evelyn was letting her know that she didn't even consider Lila to be a rival for Cooper's affections. No doubt because Evelyn just didn't see Lila as any kind of real competition.

"Cooper's not here," Lila informed her.

That stopped Evelyn in her tracks, and she glanced around as if she thought that might be a lie. "Where is he?" Evelyn asked.

It was petty of Lila to answer "I'm not sure," but it was possibly true. *Possibly.* If Cooper had finished his chores at his ranch, he could be in town on some other errand.

"Oh." Evelyn stood in the yard a moment longer before she started for the porch. "Well, I wanted to give this to him. Lasagna, his favorite. Cooper's not much of a cook, and I didn't want him to starve while he's helping out his brother."

With the hopes of hurrying the woman along, Lila reached for the dish, but Evelyn shifted it, hanging on tight. She used her other hand to take off her sunglasses, and her eyes went straight to Lila's.

"I'll just bring it by later," Evelyn insisted. "I'm guessing you'll be around all afternoon, keeping an eye on things?"

Again, there was subtext, and Lila thought the woman was implying she was there only to be close to Cooper. "Yes, I'll be around," Lila assured her, and she added a sly smile that she figured would give Evelyn some subtext, as well.

Lying subtext, that is.

The smile might make Evelyn believe that something was indeed going on between Cooper and her. Something that Lila could be discouraging instead of taking a poke at Evelyn, but darn it, the woman was riling her. It didn't help that Evelyn was turning up her nose as if she'd caught a whiff of something bad. Apparently, nerd air wasn't very pleasant.

"And then you'll go back to San Antonio," Evelyn supplied, her eyes slightly narrowed.

Lila shrugged. "We'll see." She added another of those smug smiles. One that quickly faded when Cooper's truck turned into the driveway.

No more narrowed eyes for Evelyn. She turned, posing for Cooper by angling her long, lean body and flashing him a smile that was bright enough to be seen from Jupiter.

"I'm glad I caught you," Evelyn said, stepping to the side, which meant she moved in front of Lila.

Still feeling plenty riled, Lila nudged the woman aside with her elbow and matched her fake smile with one of her own. Clearly, this confused Cooper, because he stopped midstep and eyed them.

"Is, uh, everything okay?" he asked.

"Fine," Evelyn rushed to say. She lifted the dish. "I made you some of my famous lasagna."

"Thanks," he muttered with his forehead still bunched up. "Is everything okay?" he repeated, this time aiming it specifically at Lila. "Where are the kids?"

"They're with friends." Lila widened her smile and went to him. And as if she had a perfect right to do it, she came up on her toes and kissed him.

Cooper stiffened for only a second before he made a grunt of pleasure and kissed her right back.

CHAPTER THREE

COOPER HAD NO trouble figuring out what was going on here. Evelyn had gotten under Lila's skin—something that Evelyn was a pro at doing—and this was Lila's way of striking back.

The kiss was just a pretense.

However, when Lila's mouth moved over his, Cooper forgot all about Evelyn, her lasagna lure and why Lila was doing this. Hell, he forgot how to think or breathe. The only thing he was doing was reacting. And it wasn't an especially smart reaction, either. Because he moved right into the kiss and took Lila's mouth as if it were his new favorite thing to have for lunch.

Lila was having a reaction, too, and he didn't think it was all part of the pretense. She made a sound of pleasure. A silky moan that rumbled deep in her throat, and her palm flattened on his chest. It didn't stay still, either. Her fingers moved, stroking him. That gave him another reaction. One that started stirring below his belt. And that's when Cooper knew he had to stop this and regroup.

Or at least move to a private place.

Making out in front of his ex—or anybody else, for that matter—just wasn't right. It might get Evelyn to finally back off, but this was also something Lila would regret once she regained her senses. Which would happen within a split second after he pulled back from her.

It did.

He watched as the shock flared through Lila's eyes, and then reality sank in. They'd just kissed the living daylights out of each other, and the heat beneath the pretense was real. This was a situation of opening a Texas-sized Pandora's box, and that kind of heat just wasn't going to cool without, well, sex.

Cooper hadn't needed the kiss to urge him in the direction of sex. Lila had been on his mind all day. Heck, for months now. And now he'd gotten a really good sample of how things could be between them. Well, once they had some privacy, that is.

Evelyn cleared her throat, no doubt to get their attention, and Cooper finally took his gaze off Lila so he could deal with the woman. But Evelyn apparently wanted to deal with Lila first. She practically thrust the lasagna into her hands.

"You can reheat it in the oven, three hundred degrees for about fifteen minutes," Evelyn said. There was no venom in her voice, no worry whatsoever in her cool eyes when she shifted her attention to Cooper. "Call me when you're…"

Evelyn smiled but didn't verbally fill in the blank. Cooper didn't have to hear the words to know what she meant. *Call me when you're done with Lila.*

Cooper wished he could scald her with a denial, but he couldn't, not with his track record. Evelyn wouldn't buy his "changed man" deal any more than Lila had, and words were cheap. It was going to take some action, and time, to convince Lila and everybody else that there was no longer a revolving door on his love life.

"See you soon," Evelyn added, again to Cooper.

His ex didn't even spare Lila another glance before Evelyn sauntered back to her car and drove away.

Cooper turned to Lila to see if she wanted to start the

conversation they needed to have about that kiss. Or maybe he should just give her some time to vent. But she stayed quiet, sliding glances between him and the dish.

"You're going to burn that lasagna, aren't you?" Cooper asked.

"Perhaps." She paused. "Yes."

"Good. It's not even my favorite," he confessed. "I had it once at Evelyn's and said it was good, and she's been making it for me ever since."

Lila's shoulders seemed to relax a bit, and she took the foil off the top of the dish and upended it. The lasagna thudded onto the ground in one giant blob and splattered bits of sauce and cheese everywhere.

The air was suddenly filled with the scent of tomato and Italian spices. It didn't make him hungry. Cooper hadn't lied about it not being his favorite. But seeing the satisfied smile on Lila's mouth made him want to kiss her again.

"I'm sorry I came on to you like that," Lila said, stomping on the lasagna and grinding it into the grass and dirt. The meaty sauce oozed around her flip-flops, but she didn't stop.

He shrugged. "Seemed like a good way to get your point across to Evelyn. And FYI, I'm not sorry. I don't regret what happened one bit."

Or at least he wouldn't regret it once his body started to soften. Apparently, that brainless part of him behind his zipper hadn't realized why Lila had started that lip-lock, and it thought it was about to get lucky.

Her head whipped up, and her gaze flew to his. "Well, you should regret it. It shouldn't have happened. I used you to get back at a woman who—"

She stopped, gathered her breath, and it appeared she was trying to steady herself. "When Evelyn and I were in third grade, she flicked gum in my hair. In middle school, she called me The Zipper because I was skinny and had no boobs. At the prom, she smeared French onion dip on my chair so I'd sit on it and ruin my dress."

Cooper cursed under his breath. He knew that Evelyn wasn't especially sweet, but he hadn't known about the bullying. Hell. If he hadn't already ended things with Evelyn, that would have done it. Instead, he assisted Lila in doing some lasagna squishing. Surprisingly, it helped tamp down his anger.

"Well, you've got boobs now," he assured her. "And you're a better kisser than she is."

Lila gave him what could only be interpreted as a skeptical look. "You're just saying that so I'll kiss you again."

"Nope." He paused, pretended to think about it. "But maybe I should have another sample to see if I got that right."

She laughed, just as he'd intended. He savored the moment, almost as much as he'd savored the kiss she'd just laid on him. *Almost.* The laughter stopped, though, when she glanced down at her gooey flip-flops. Except it wasn't just on her shoes. The sauce had gotten on her toes, as well.

"Next time I have to stomp on lasagna, I'll wear boots," she muttered. The lightness was gone when she lifted her gaze to him again. "Being with you really would be a bad idea."

He wanted to reassure her that it wouldn't be. But instead he found himself leaning in to kiss her again so he could prove just what a good idea it would be.

She didn't make a silky sound of pleasure this time. It was more of a protesting groan, but Lila didn't pull back from him. Just the opposite. She melted against him, giving him her mouth.

Cooper took it.

He went for long and deep, just the way he liked his kisses. Clearly, Lila did, too, because the protest was gone from her next groan. Only the pleasure remained. Not just for her but for him, as well. They stood out in the scalding sun and kissed each other as if their lives depended on it.

Because of that sun and because someone might come driving up, Cooper began to back her toward the house. No need for anyone to see them and start gossip about them not doing their babysitting duties. Of course, since the kids weren't around, the only thing that actually needed tending was this unfinished business between Lila and him.

It wasn't easy to walk through the yard, but that was because neither of them stopped kissing long enough to see where they were going. He felt some flowers crush beneath his boots and figured he was going to need to fix whatever damage he was doing before Jeremy and Crystal got back. But it was damage that would be worth it since every step took them closer to having some privacy.

They stumbled going up the porch steps. There'd be bruises, but Lila didn't seem to care about that. Neither did he, but they finally had to break from the scorcher of a kiss just so they could each take a breath. They did that, dragging in some much-needed air, but went right back for more as they finally made it through the door—which Cooper kicked shut. He decided not to go much farther, though, because he didn't want them to crash into any furniture or get lasagna all over the floor. Instead, he pressed Lila against the wall so he could put them body to body.

All in all, that was a very good place to be.

Her breasts pressed to his chest, and the rest of them had a nice fit, too. One that allowed him to touch and kiss her at the same time.

Cooper wasn't done with her mouth, but he took a quick detour to drop some kisses on her neck. Apparently, that was the right move on his part, because she gripped fistfuls of his shirt and dragged him even closer. That kicked up the heat even more.

Using the grip she had on him, she shifted, switching their positions and putting him against the wall. Somehow she managed all of that without breaking the intimate contact. In fact, she upped that by unbuttoning his shirt so that her hand could move against his bare chest. Cooper very much intended to do the same to her, but he had more kissing to do first. He went lower, kissing her breasts through the front of her dress.

Cooper thought the sound he heard was his ears ringing, and it took him a couple of moments to realize it was his phone. He cursed and considered just ignoring it, but it could be important. Hell, it could be his brother checking on the kids.

Cursing some more because he had to stop kissing Lila and untangle himself from her, Cooper got enough wiggle room to take his phone from his pocket. He frowned when he saw Noah's name on the screen. He loved his nephew a whole lot, but he sure as hell didn't want to talk to him right now.

"Yeah?" Cooper answered, and he kept his tone clipped and tight. Easy to do because that's exactly how he felt.

There was a long silence, and it put Cooper on full alert. "Noah?" he snapped. "Are you okay?"

That got Lila's attention, and she stepped back, tuning in to that silence, as well.

"Uh, Uncle Cooper," the boy finally said, but Cooper didn't feel much relief at hearing his nephew's somber voice.

"What's wrong?" Cooper snapped. "What happened?" And just like that, his mind started spinning a dozen worst-case scenarios.

"Uh, I'm in trouble. Don't get mad," Noah quickly added. "Please don't get mad."

Cooper wasn't mad, not yet, but he got the feeling he soon would be. After all, he'd once been a teenage boy, so he knew what kind of trouble one could get into. "What happened?" he repeated.

"I need you to come and get me," Noah finally said after more of that snail-crawling silence. "I'm at the police station. I've been arrested."

Cooper heard each word, but it took a few seconds for them to sink in. It obviously sank in a little faster for Lila, because she gasped and took the phone from him. She hit the speaker button.

"Arrested?" Lila repeated. "You only left the house a half hour ago. Why were you arrested?" she demanded.

Noah didn't answer, but there was a shuffling sound, and several moments later, Cooper heard another voice.

"I arrested him because he was driving without a license," Sheriff Leyton Jameson said. "Noah ran Sandy Kellerman's van into the Crocketts' mailbox and then their fence. At the time, he had both of Sandy's boys in the vehicle with him."

Like those worst-case scenarios, plenty of emotions and thoughts flooded Cooper's mind, but he quickly picked through them and came up with his biggest concern.

"Are Noah or the other boys hurt?" Cooper asked.

"No," Leyton quickly answered. "Thankfully, they were wearing their seat belts, but there's damage to both the van and the Crocketts' property. They're pissed and are filing charges."

Of course they were. The Crocketts were a crotchety couple in their eighties who didn't get along with anyone—including each other.

"Sandy's on her way here," Leyton continued, "but I need you to come in and deal with Noah." He paused. "Noah asked me not to call his dad, and we'll discuss that when you get here."

Cooper waited for Leyton to end the call before he cursed a blue streak and yanked his truck keys from his pocket.

"I'm going with you," Lila insisted, grabbing her purse.

There was no trace of the heat between them now. No, that phone call had managed to chill them down fast.

Hell's bells.

What was the boy thinking? And what the devil was Jeremy going to say about this, especially if he had to be called back from his honeymoon?

After they cleaned up and Lila changed her shoes, they hurried to his truck. As he drove toward town, Cooper forced himself to settle down. It wouldn't do anyone any good if he lost his temper and yelled at Noah. Even if yelling was exactly what he wanted to do.

Thankfully, it didn't take long to get to the police station. That was the advantage of living in a small town. Everything was close. The disadvantage was that soon, very soon, everyone would know what'd happened. Word might have already gotten back to Jeremy.

Cooper parked next to Sandy's minivan, and he had no trouble seeing the damage to the front end. The bumper was crumpled, and one of the headlights had been broken. It wasn't much more than a fender bender, but that wasn't the big issue here. Noah had been the one behind the wheel, and he damn well shouldn't have been.

Lila and he practically ran from the parking lot and into the police station, and Cooper immediately spotted Noah. He was sitting in a chair in Leyton's office. Standing next to him was Sandy Kellerman and her two sons, Jace and Beckett. No one was shouting. In fact, no one was saying anything, but Noah groaned and lowered his head when he saw Cooper.

It was a tight fit when Lila and he went into Leyton's office, and the sheriff shut the door even though there were no other deputies around. However, there was a dispatcher/receptionist, and Leyton probably wanted to try to keep this as private as he could.

"They're okay," Sandy assured Lila and him. The woman didn't seem angry, just worried.

Cooper knew how she felt. He was worried as well, and it relieved his mind a little when he didn't see a mark on any of the boys.

"Please don't call Dad," Noah said, still looking at anything but Cooper.

"He'll have to know," Cooper fired back.

"Yeah, but wait until he's home. Then I can tell him face-to-face." Since Noah had a "firing squad" tone, it was obvious that the boy knew that wasn't going to be a pleasant conversation.

"I've got insurance, so that'll pay for most of the repairs." Sandy spoke up. "But the bigger issue here is my sons allowed a friend to drive when they didn't have my permission and when the friend didn't even have a license."

"Noah's the one who wrecked," one of the boys protested.

Sandy stopped him with a withering stare. "My sons will be punished," she said. "I'm thinking they'll be grounded all summer." That caused loud groans and grumbled protests from the boys. "I'm sure whatever punishment Jeremy doles out to Noah will be just fine."

The woman was certainly making this easier. Well, for Cooper, anyway. He was betting Sandy would stick to the grounding punishment.

"I'll pay for whatever your insurance doesn't cover," Cooper volunteered.

Sandy nodded, brushed a reassuring hand on both Lila's and his arms before the woman turned back to Leyton. "Can I take these two home now, or will you be filing charges against them?"

"No charges against them," Leyton answered, but he, too, gave the boys a glare. It was a formidable one, and it even silenced the boys' grumbles as Sandy led them out of the office.

All attention turned to Noah.

"We can work this two ways," Leyton started. "I can arrest you, which will give you a juvie record. It could mean time in detention or community service. It could pretty much screw up your summer and maybe the rest of your life."

The color drained from Noah's face.

Good. Cooper wanted the boy scared spit-less, because what he'd done was a thousand gallons of wrong. He could have been hurt. Or worse. Along with hurting his friends or, hell, even the Crocketts.

"Or since it's your one and only brush with the law, I can appease the Crocketts by convincing them you've learned your lesson and that you'll make sure their damaged property gets fixed. Then I can give you a warning and agree to let your dad and Cooper handle this," Leyton went on after he let Noah suffer a little longer.

Noah's suddenly hopeful gaze flew to Cooper. "Please handle this."

Of course, Cooper had already decided to do just that, but like Leyton, he paused as well so that Noah could stew a few more seconds.

"This is serious crap," Cooper told the boy. "Swear to me you'll never do anything like this again."

Noah answered fast. "I swear."

Cooper nodded but continued to glare at the boy. "You're grounded until your dad gets back, and then he can dole out whatever he wants to add to it." He suspected it would be more grounding and that the sentence would be for the rest of the summer like Sandy's boys.

Noah nodded. "Do you have to call Dad right now?" he asked Cooper.

Cooper looked at Leyton for guidance on that, and the sheriff sighed. "Sandy will have to give a copy of this police report to her insurance company, and it's possible they'll contact Jeremy."

He definitely didn't want Jeremy learning about this fiasco from someone at the insurance company. Or even from someone in town who might text him about it.

Hell.

As soon as he got Noah home, Cooper knew he would have to call his brother.

CHAPTER FOUR

LILA SHARED THE "crap" duty with Cooper. After they'd arrived back at the house with Noah, Cooper had immediately gone into the guest room to have a chat with Jeremy. Lila went into her room to call Crystal. Noah had fled to his room, too, to wait for what would almost certainly be a follow-up conversation with his father.

"What's wrong?" Crystal said the moment she answered Lila's call.

Lila tried not to hesitate because she knew any kind of pause would only make her sister's fears skyrocket. "The kids are fine," she quickly assured her. "But Noah got in some trouble."

"What kind of trouble? Is that why Cooper's talking to Jeremy right now?" Crystal asked, her worried words running together.

"Trouble with a very minor car accident. And, yes, that's why Cooper and Jeremy are talking. Noah's fine, really," Lila emphasized. "But he was driving without a license and damaged Sandy's minivan when he hit the Crocketts' fence and mailbox."

Crystal didn't groan. She sighed, probably because she knew how much grief this was going to cause her husband. "Jeremy and I will be home as soon as we can get there."

"Don't rush. Cooper and I have it under control." She hoped that was true, anyway. "I'm so sorry," Lila added.

"Sophia's okay?" Crystal went on. "She wasn't in the van with Noah, was she?"

"No. She's fine. In fact, I just texted her before I called you to let her know there was a problem with Noah. I'll call her back and give her details, unless that's something you'd rather do."

"No, you go ahead and tell her. I need to get on my laptop and reschedule our flights back home. I'll call Sophia later and make sure she's okay." Her sister finally paused. "It sounds as if Jeremy is talking to Noah now. I'll keep you posted as to when we'll be in."

Now it was Lila who sighed when her sister ended the call. She hadn't done a good job with her "crap" duty, because Crystal was obviously worried and upset. Maybe, though, there'd been no way to prevent that. Verbal reassurance just wasn't going to cut it in a situation like this.

Lila called Sophia next, and considering the girl answered on the first ring, she must have been waiting. However, Lila didn't get a word out before Sophia spoke.

"It's all over about Noah wrecking Miss Sandy's van," Sophia blurted out. "Is he okay?"

Lila frowned at the lightning-fast gossip mill but nearly smiled over the girl's concern. She'd been afraid that Sophia would be upset like Crystal. Or maybe quote stats about teenage drivers.

"Noah's fine but grounded," Lila told her. "Jeremy and your mom will probably come back early from their honeymoon."

Sophia groaned. "But I was supposed to get to stay with Ella tomorrow night. You said it was okay, and it might not happen if Mom and Jeremy are in a bad mood when they get home."

Lila doubted either Jeremy or her sister would take their

anger and disapproval out on the girl, but it might be better if Sophia was out of the house to give them time to deal with Noah.

"If it's all right with Ella's parents, you can stay there tonight," Lila told her.

"Sweet, it's okay. Ella's mom was going to call you to let you know the sleepover was still on," Sophia gushed, and then she must have remembered that her new stepbrother wouldn't be in such a gushy state. "I hope Noah's okay."

"He will be," Lila assured her before they ended the call.

She slid her phone into the back pocket of her cotton dress and went up the hall. Noah's bedroom door was closed, and he had Keep Out scrawled on a chalkboard mounted to the door. Lila couldn't hear him, so maybe he was no longer on the phone with his dad. Or it could be that Jeremy was the one doing all the talking.

Lila kept walking and stopped outside the guest room Cooper was using. She didn't hear him, either, and pressed her ear to the door.

Just as Cooper opened it.

He didn't seem amused that she'd been trying to eavesdrop, but he did look as beleaguered as she felt.

"As babysitters, we suck large," he grumbled.

She nodded. It had all gotten away from them so fast, and hindsight wouldn't make them feel better. Jeremy had given Noah permission to spend the afternoon with his friends, so it wasn't something that Lila or Cooper would have nixed. Well, they wouldn't have unless they'd developed ESP to know that the boy was going to screw up.

"How mad is Jeremy?" she asked.

He shrugged. "Not as mad as he would have been had he not had a padding of being damn happy and on his honeymoon. Of course, once it sinks in that he's having to cut the honeymoon short because of Noah, then I figure he'll arrive home as one unhappy camper."

Yeah, that was Lila's take on things, too. Noah deserved punishment, no doubt about that, but it was going to be a miserable start to the summer with the inevitable grounding that the boy would get.

Cooper scrubbed his hand over his face, and it occurred to her that she rarely saw him tired. No, not just tired—weary.

"I have to check on Jeremy's horses," he grumbled.

She nearly mentioned that Noah had already done that before he'd left to go do stupid things like driving without a license, but Cooper looked as if he could use some fresh air. So could she, and that's why Lila went with him when he motioned for her to follow him.

"How'd your sister take the news of cutting her honeymoon short?" Cooper asked as they went out the back door and started across the yard toward the barn.

"Well enough. She's a mom, so she knows things don't always work out as planned." She shook her head. "I wish this hadn't happened."

Cooper stepped in the barn just ahead of her. "Feeling guilty, huh? So am I."

Lila made a sound of agreement and glanced around. There were no horses, but she spotted several in the pasture that was behind the barn. She hoped that was where they were supposed to be, and she looked at Cooper to verify that. He had his hands on his hips, his gaze fixed on the horses, and his expression was one of weary frustration.

Something she totally understood.

Lila went closer and pulled him into her arms for a hug. Except she knew it wouldn't just be a simple hug. Not between Cooper and her. They had this lightning-fast heat between them, and just as she'd expected, it hit fast. Still, she forced herself to step away. This wasn't the time to bring sexual attraction into the mix.

Or maybe it was.

Lila amended that notion when Cooper took hold of her arms, yanked her back to him and kissed her. It wasn't a "nice" kiss. Like his expression, it was filled with all the emotions of what they'd just gone through with Noah. Maybe some frustration, too, over the fact that she'd been fighting this.

Well, she didn't fight it now.

Maybe it was because her own defenses were down, but Lila thought it had a whole lot more to do with the fact that she was tired of wanting Cooper and not having him. This had nothing to do with Noah, Evelyn or even the fact that she could become another notch on his bedpost. It had to do with the aching need that she was certain he could fill. Even if that "fill" was only temporary.

Cooper kissed her as if she were the cure for what ailed him, too. So maybe this was a right kind of wrong. Yes, she'd have to pay for it, but for now he would soothe and pleasure.

Emphasis on the *pleasure*.

The man could kiss, no doubt about that. And touch. Yes, he was really good at that, too.

"This is a really bad place for this," he muttered when he trailed his mouth down to her neck.

It was. There was nothing especially romantic about a barn, and it lacked a bed, but the house—where there were beds—suddenly seemed miles away. Plus, Noah was in there. He was shut in his room, where he'd no doubt stay, but it didn't seem right for hanky or panky to go on with him just up the hall.

"Tack room," Cooper insisted.

While he continued to torture her neck, he backed her into the small room and shut the rickety wooden door. The place smelled of saddle leather, hay and liniment. Not exactly sensual smells, and it was way too warm, but Lila figured after a few more moments of Cooper's kisses she wouldn't even notice the heat.

She didn't.

Lila pretty much lost her mind when Cooper shoved up her loose dress, pulling it off over her head. He sent it flying over his shoulder, and in the same motion, he took his clever mouth to the tops of her breasts. Her breath vanished. The heat soared. And Lila could only hang on and let him do whatever he wanted.

Thankfully, she wanted it, too, and she didn't put up even a token protest when he rid her of her bra, which basically left her nearly naked. However, she wanted to hide herself when he stepped back and had a long look at her body.

She squeezed her eyes shut, knowing she wasn't his usual sort. Nope. Evelyn's body was his norm. And that's why it surprised her when he gave her a very naughty smile.

"Lila, you're my fantasy," he said.

She blinked and would have asked if he was joking, but he came at her with another assault from his mouth. He kissed her breasts. Then went lower. Kissed her stomach. Then went lower. Until he shimmied down her panties and kissed her in a spot that had her cursing him and fisting her hands in his hair to anchor herself.

Now, this pleasure. Soaring, hot, needy pleasure. It flooded her from head to toe and was especially strong in the area he was kissing. He lingered there awhile until she was ready to beg for surrender.

But Cooper didn't finish her off. No. He took her right

to the brink of release and then snapped away from her, making his way back up her naked body.

He wasn't naked, though.

And Lila tried to do something about that. Hard to go after his shirt, though, when he was giving her more neck kisses. After she cursed, he stopped to help her, and she finally got her hands on his naked chest. It was toned and perfect, covered with a fine mat of hair that she ran her fingers through.

Despite the rising ache inside her, she took the time to look at him. She did more looking when she unzipped him and shoved his jeans and boxers down over his hips.

The man took her breath away.

"Cooper, you're my fantasy," she managed to say. Unlike his comment, there was no chance hers had a trace of BS in it. "Except you're better than a fantasy because you're real."

The corner of his mouth hitched in a grin that made her even hotter. But she frowned when he didn't dive back in to finish this. Instead, he fished around in his back pocket to take a condom from his wallet. Thank goodness one of them had thought of safe sex, because Lila had only been able to manage the "sex" part.

Once he had on the condom, Cooper managed the "sex," too. He lifted her, pressing her back to the door, and Lila hooked her legs around his waist. He pushed into her with one hard thrust.

A thrust that nearly pushed her right over the edge. But she forced herself to hang on. She wanted to savor this. Wanted to keep him close to her like this just a little longer.

Cooper paused, too, clearly regrouping, and he met her eye to eye when he started the strokes inside her. All the heat and need poured out in those strokes. Harder and deeper.

Faster.

Lila lost her breath again and didn't care. The only thing that mattered now was Cooper. She needed him to sate this searing heat, to release the powder keg of need. And he did. While watching her, he took her.

And Cooper finished her.

CHAPTER FIVE

COOPER STOOD IN his brother's kitchen, sipping a beer and waiting. Across from him, Lila was doing the same, except she'd opted for a glass of wine. A big one. If there'd been a picture in the dictionary of *waiting for the other shoe to drop*, it would have been of them.

The mood in the house was definitely in suck mode.

He was reasonably sure he now knew what it was like to be a human yo-yo. Up and down, at times spinning. All accompanied by the realization that he didn't have control over squat right now.

Especially anything involving Lila.

The sex with her had been great, as he'd known it would be, but it'd been more than just sex for him. Much more. But he sure as heck couldn't say it was the same for Lila.

She hadn't given him any signals that she intended to have sex with him again or that she'd reconsider having an actual relationship with him. Then again, maybe she was doing her own yo-yoing, since only minutes after they'd gotten their clothes back on, Lila had gotten a call from her sister. Crystal and Jeremy had managed to get a flight out and had immediately headed to the Vegas airport. It wasn't easy to think about relationships, sex and such when a parental shitstorm was heading their way.

Well, maybe the sex part.

It was always easy to think about sex when it came to Lila.

Since Jeremy had left his truck in the parking lot at the airport, Cooper hadn't gone to pick them up, but his brother had texted well over a half hour ago to say they'd landed and would start the drive home. That meant they'd be arriving any minute now to deal with Noah.

Yeah, a parental shitstorm, all right.

The boy was still in his room, where he'd been ever since they'd gotten back from the police station, but Cooper had checked on him a couple of times. So had Lila. Cooper might feel like a yo-yo, but Noah probably felt as if he were about to face a firing squad.

"According to Sophia," Lila said, reading from her phone, "digital grounding is thirty percent more effective than actual grounding. Digital grounding is limiting phone privileges and the internet."

Cooper glanced at her from over the top of his beer, but he didn't respond verbally. That's because for the past four hours Sophia had been sending one text of advice after the other. Obviously, the girl was concerned about her stepbrother and had even offered to come home, but Crystal had talked her into staying put at her friend's.

"Wonder what the stats are on hickeys?" Lila muttered.

That got his attention. "Hickeys?"

"Love bites," she said, as if he'd asked for a clarification. And in a way, he supposed he had.

"Do you want me to give you one?" he asked, hoping to make her smile.

She didn't. She frowned instead and motioned toward the general vicinity of his neck. "I gave you one. I'm sorry about that. I guess I got a little carried away."

Now Cooper frowned. He set his beer aside and went

into the powder room just off the kitchen so he could take a look in the mirror. Yeah, that was a hickey, all right, on the left side of his neck. It was his first in, well, at least a decade and a half.

"I'm really sorry," Lila repeated, coming up behind him.

Cooper shrugged, glad to have her this close to him again. She'd showered after their romp in the tack room, and she smelled delicious. "No one will even notice a hickey," he assured her.

She made a sound that made him think she wasn't quite buying that, and her gaze met his. Finally, they were about to have the talk, the one they needed to have.

"It wasn't just sex," he blurted out before she could say anything. "And you really are my damn fantasy."

In hindsight, he wished that last part hadn't been coated with some anger and hurt, but damn it all to hell, he'd told her the truth. And he wanted to keep telling her the truth until she believed him.

Lila opened her mouth, closed it and repeated doing so as if she kept changing her mind about what to say. But she didn't get a chance to say anything at all because he heard the vehicle pull into the driveway.

"This discussion isn't over," he snarled, knowing full well that it hadn't even gotten started.

They went to the front door, opening it just as Crystal and Jeremy stepped onto the porch. It was just after 7:00 p.m. and still light out, so Cooper didn't have any trouble seeing their faces or expressions. They looked exhausted…and Jeremy was sporting a hickey on his neck. Apparently, Lila and her sister had a knack for such displays of affection.

"Is that some kind of pasta dish in the front yard?" Crystal asked, motioning behind her.

Cooper had forgotten all about cleaning up the lasagna. "Long story," he muttered. "So are the trampled flowers, but I'll replace them."

Jeremy stepped into the house, met his gaze, and then that gaze lowered to Cooper's neck. Right to the hickey. Apparently, someone had noticed it after all.

"Noah's in his room," Cooper volunteered to shift his brother's attention to something other than his love bite. "Leyton said if you've got any questions, you can call him. Sandy, too. She's not mad but figured you'd want to speak to her."

Jeremy nodded, gave a weary shake of his head. "Thanks. I appreciate everything Lila and you did."

Cooper didn't feel as if he deserved any thanks or appreciation, and considering the way Lila's head dipped, neither did she. "I'm sorry about this," Lila and he said at the same time.

Jeremy gave another nod and doled out some pats on their backs. It had a definite "you can leave now" vibe to it. Which was fine with Cooper. But that left Lila with a bit of a dilemma since she didn't have her own place to go to in Lone Star Ridge.

But she did have his place.

"Give me a second," Cooper told his brother, and he led Lila out onto the porch, where they'd have some privacy. "I'm ready to hear your apology for the hickey you gave me," he said. "I think we should go to my house and discuss it."

Her eyes narrowed a little, but there was no anger in them. "If we go to your house, we'll have sex."

"You say it like there's a downside to that." But he waved that off because he didn't want to go down that path just yet. "Jeremy, Crystal and Noah need to talk. We need to talk. Better for us to do that in the air-conditioning. The heat might make my hickey itch."

This time, she rolled her eyes. Then sighed. "Crystal, I'll be at Cooper's if you need me," Lila called out to her sister.

Cooper didn't dare smile or look even a little smug at getting his way. After all, Lila had chosen him over possible heatstroke or staying on the fringes of that family shitstorm. He'd won out pretty much by default.

Lila followed him home in her car, probably so she'd have a way to leave if things took a bad turn between them. Cooper very much wanted to make sure he took all the right turns with her. However, the moment he turned into his driveway, he knew that "right turns" were going to have to wait.

Hell.

Evelyn's Mustang was parked in front of his house, and she got out the moment he pulled to a stop behind her. She flashed him a welcoming smile that dimmed considerably when she spotted Lila.

"Oh," Evelyn muttered. "Word is that your brother and Crystal got back, so I figured you'd be coming home *alone*."

Cooper dragged in a long breath since he figured he needed to clarify to Evelyn, again, that they weren't getting back together. "I want Lila to stay the night with me. I'm not sure she will, but it's what I want. Do you understand that, Evelyn? Lila's what I want."

He hadn't been sure Lila had heard what he said until she made a little sound. Maybe of surprise. Heck, maybe it was just a hiccup.

"I see," Evelyn said. Her gaze zoomed to Lila, who stepped up to Cooper's side. "Can we talk, woman to woman?"

"No," Cooper answered for her. "You're not going to get the chance to bully her again."

Evelyn flinched as if he'd slapped her, and then she squared her shoulders, steeling herself up. "I know I was mean to you, and I'm sorry," she told Lila. "But don't do this. Don't punish me by using Cooper."

This time the sound Lila made was definitely surprise. Cooper recognized it because a similar sound came from his mouth, followed by a "huh?"

Evelyn turned back to him and folded her arms over her chest. "Lila doesn't want you. She wants the idea of you."

"The idea of me?" he repeated.

"You know, hot and popular. You're this unattainable—"

"He's my fantasy," Lila interrupted.

Cooper looked at her to make sure she wasn't about to cave to Evelyn's BS. She wasn't. Lila pointed to Cooper's neck. "I gave him that, and there are others."

He wasn't sure how that fit with what Evelyn was spewing out, but it made him smile. "Lila's my fantasy, too," he said, not even sparing Evelyn a glance.

Evelyn huffed. "Opposites might attract, but birds of a feather flock together. Cooper, you and I are of the same flock."

"I'm betting you don't have any stats to back that up," Lila argued.

Because there was a little smile on Lila's mouth, Cooper didn't want to take his eyes off her. So he didn't. He leaned in and kissed that smiling mouth, and while it didn't mean everything was hunky-dory between them, it was a good start.

"Goodbye, Evelyn," he said, and hooking his arm around Lila, he led her into his house.

"Screw you, Cooper," Evelyn shouted, and a moment later, he heard her peel out of his drive.

Good riddance. Maybe the woman would move on to someone else she could flock and feather.

He kissed Lila again when they stepped inside, and he led her to the sofa. "Wait here while I do something."

Cooper hurried to take out his phone so he could look up some things. Too bad he didn't have Sophia here to help him with this, but he finally worked his way through what he needed to find.

"The average person has six relationships before they find the one," Cooper said, sitting down next to her.

Her smile faded. "I've only had three."

"I've had enough to make the averages work in our favor." Not to be deterred, he continued, "The average couple has three dates before sex and a dozen dates before considering themselves a couple." He looked up from his phone. "I clearly owe you a dozen dates."

Her mouth quivered a little. Then it quivered a lot in a different kind of way when he leaned in and kissed her again. He kept it soft and sweet.

"The average couple has over twenty dates before falling in love," he went on. "I owe you twenty dates."

The next kiss he gave her wasn't soft or sweet. He knew how to make it dirty enough to heat her up, and the hitch in her breath told him he'd succeeded in doing just that.

"You want to fall in love with me?" she asked, her voice and face all dreamy. And hot. Mercy, she had his number.

"Already done that. The trick will be to get you to fall in love with me. Think that'll happen after twenty dates?"

She shook her head, causing his heart to stop until she said, "Much sooner than that."

That was damn good news, and it brought on another kiss. Lila could do dirty, too, and when he eased back after a half hour or so, he was the one with a hitch in his breath.

"How many dates before deciding we don't want to live without each other?" she asked.

Cooper smiled and went for even dirtier with his next kiss. "Let's find out."

* * * * *

*Vanessa Whitman thought coming to her family's castle in the
Colorado mountains would be the escape she needed. Before
long, though, a guest turns up dead and it might be connected to a
twelve-year-old cold case. Thankfully she has local sheriff
Ty Coleman to help learn the truth. If they survive that long...*

Keep reading for a sneak peek at
Cold Case Colorado,
An Unsolved Mystery Book, from
USA TODAY *bestselling author Cassie Miles.*

When Vanessa slipped through the sliding glass doors, he felt
profound relief. She was still wearing her white shirt with the
rolled-up sleeves and her jeans. He noticed her oversize silver belt
buckle that appeared to be some kind of award for barrel racing.

He commented on the buckle. "I thought you were only a kid
when you left the mountains, but it looks like you were old enough
for rodeo."

"Little Britches Rodeo," she said. "I was nine, and the junior
barrel race wasn't even a sanctioned event. I've seen what the adult
racers can do, and they're amazing. I wouldn't dream of putting
myself in the same class with them."

"Did you win?"

"Damn right I did." She flashed a cocky grin. "Why did you
want to see me?"

"I'm getting bounced out of here. Morris made it clear that he doesn't need my help. He told me to send the deputies home, and I should leave, too. But he wants us back after dark to keep an eye on the castle and make sure nobody else gets hurt."

"That's not right." Her voice was firm. "He can't come in here and start ordering people around. Who does he think he is?"

"An agent for the Colorado Bureau of Investigation. And I gave him jurisdiction." Ty had been impressed with the work done by the CBI, including deep research on the witnesses. The woman on the computer turned up clue after clue. "After last night, I'm concerned about your safety. If anything weird turns up, give me a call. Later tonight, we should sneak into Aunt Dorothy's sewing room for a look around. I'll check back with you after dinner."

"Is that a date?"

"Not unless your idea of a good time is breaking crime scene tape and poking around in a room that's been unoccupied for twelve years."

"Actually," she said, "that sounds better than a lot of dates I've had."

Don't miss
Cold Case Colorado *by Cassie Miles,*
available February 2021 wherever
Harlequin Intrigue books and ebooks are sold.

Harlequin.com

Get 4 FREE REWARDS!

We'll send you 2 FREE Books plus 2 FREE Mystery Gifts.

FREE
Value Over
$20

Both the **Romance** and **Suspense** collections feature compelling novels written by many of today's bestselling authors.

YES! Please send me 2 FREE novels from the Essential Romance or Essential Suspense Collection and my 2 FREE gifts (gifts are worth about $10 retail). After receiving them, if I don't wish to receive any more books, I can return the shipping statement marked "cancel." If I don't cancel, I will receive 4 brand-new novels every month and be billed just $7.24 each in the U.S. or $7.49 each in Canada. That's a savings of up to 28% off the cover price. It's quite a bargain! Shipping and handling is just 50¢ per book in the U.S. and $1.25 per book in Canada.* I understand that accepting the 2 free books and gifts places me under no obligation to buy anything. I can always return a shipment and cancel at any time. The free books and gifts are mine to keep no matter what I decide.

Choose one: ☐ **Essential Romance**
(194/394 MDN GQ6M)

☐ **Essential Suspense**
(191/391 MDN GQ6M)

Name (please print)

Address   Apt. #

City   State/Province   Zip/Postal Code

Email: Please check this box ☐ if you would like to receive newsletters and promotional emails from Harlequin Enterprises ULC and its affiliates. You can unsubscribe anytime.

Mail to the **Reader Service:**
IN U.S.A.: P.O. Box 1341, Buffalo, NY 14240-8531
IN CANADA: P.O. Box 603, Fort Erie, Ontario L2A 5X3

Want to try 2 free books from another series? Call 1-800-873-8635 or visit www.ReaderService.com.

---

*Terms and prices subject to change without notice. Prices do not include sales taxes, which will be charged (if applicable) based on your state or country of residence. Canadian residents will be charged applicable taxes. Offer not valid in Quebec. This offer is limited to one order per household. Books received may not be as shown. Not valid for current subscribers to the Essential Romance or Essential Suspense Collection. All orders subject to approval. Credit or debit balances in a customer's account(s) may be offset by any other outstanding balance owed by or to the customer. Please allow 4 to 6 weeks for delivery. Offer available while quantities last.

Your Privacy—Your information is being collected by Harlequin Enterprises ULC, operating as Reader Service. For a complete summary of the information we collect, how we use this information and to whom it is disclosed, please visit our privacy notice located at corporate.harlequin.com/privacy-notice. From time to time we may also exchange your personal information with reputable third parties. If you wish to opt out of this sharing of your personal information, please visit readerservice.com/consumerchoice or call 1-800-873-8635. **Notice to California Residents**—Under California law, you have specific rights to control and access your data. For more information on these rights and how to exercise them, visit corporate.harlequin.com/california-privacy.

STRS20MAX